EARLY BLACK WRITERS

General Editor
DAVID DABYDEEN

The Letters of Ignatius Sancho

edited by
PAUL EDWARDS
and
POLLY REWT

EDINBURGH UNIVERSITY PRESS

© Edinburgh University Press Ltd, 1994

Edinburgh University Press Ltd
22 George Square, Edinburgh

Typeset in Linotron Garamond Stempel
by Nene Phototypsetters Ltd, Northampton, and
printed and bound in Great Britain by
The Alden Press, Oxford

A CIP record for this book is available from
the British Library

ISBN 0 7486 0453 7

Contents

List of Letters

Portrait of Ignatius Sancho, 1768, Thomas Gainsborough, reproduced by kind permission of The National Gallery of Canada, Ottawa.

Preface

The Letters of Ignatius Sancho was originally intended to be edited solely by Paul Edwards, who completed much of the work before his death in May 1992. Prior to this, he asked me to finish the edition, which I agreed to do. Paul had completed the Introduction, Appendices I–III and VI and was working on the notes to the letters, having finished about half of them. I finished incomplete notes, wrote notes to the remaining sixty or so letters and prepared Appendices IV, V and VII. In consultation with David Dabydeen, editor of the Early Black Writers Series, it was decided that the amount of work required to complete the *Letters* warranted acknowledgement of co-editorship.

Some material in this edition has only recently come to light. Through an extraordinary series of events, I was contacted by John Gurnett who has researched Sancho's letters and family for over a decade. He made available to me invaluable information and sources to complete and develop the notes to the letters, and his research is the basis of Appendix VII. Paul would have welcomed this important information and I am delighted to be able to incorporate it into the new edition of Sancho's *Letters*. John's knowledge, enthusiasm and friendship were as unexpected as they are appreciated.

It has been a special privilege to undertake Paul's request and complete this work, and I could not have done so without the help and encouragement of Angus Calder and David Dabydeen. It is also a pleasure to thank David Carroll for solving more than one mystery in Sancho's letters, and to acknowledge Ken Parker's support and good advice. The guidance of Moreen Prior and Penny Clarke at Edinburgh University Press hastened the research process; I am grateful for their enthusiasm about and commitment to this project. I relied on the Reference Room staff at Edinburgh University library, particularly Lorna Cheyne and Jill Evans, who took a special interest in the 'detective work' and were generous with their time.

It has been a somewhat daunting privilege to complete Paul Edwards' work. His expertise and standards of academic excellence could only guide my work. The distance between Paul's scholarship and my own abilities is measured by shortcomings in the text, all of which are my responsibility.

POLLY REWT
10 May 1933

Foreword

DAVID DABYDEEN

Paul Edwards came to visit me at Warwick University in 1988. Over curry, a cask of wine and countless beers (against doctor's orders) he outlined plans for a series of books on early black writers. He was excited at the prospect of the republication of these texts and I immediately agreed to be his co-editor, even though I was up to my neck in other work. Paul had a way of persuading people on to his side out of the sheer enthusiasm of his character. To say no to him would be like committing a grievous error, something one would regret forever. In any case he had such a roaring humour and irreverent erudition that I wanted to be associated with him. Academic life can be mostly wearisome and administrative; Paul offered, in his own character and ideas, the prospect of a delightful partnership.

Over the years he suffered heart-attacks, strokes and associated ailments, but his letters were bursting with life and sprinkled with unrepeatedly unholy and vulgar remarks. I was always late in handing in work. But he always covered for me. He did most of the paperwork involved in setting up the series, negotiating contracts with the publisher and writing to potential authors. I came to respect the energy of the man and his total commitment to work. I believe it was partly the work on this series, and the vision that he had of popularising black texts, which kept him alive in his final years. A few months after the first book in the series appeared (*Early Black Writers in Britain*), he died.

Paul's last book was this edition of Sancho's *Letters*. He was working frantically on the man up to his final hospitalisation. His dearest wish was to complete the job before he died. I believe Paul had a peculiar relationship with Sancho. He found in Sancho's life correspondences with his own. Sancho was a man of style. He was talented. He was something of a rogue. He acquired rakish habits – like losing his clothes at a card game. He was above all a survivor.

The WISH

1801

Sancho's trade card, reproduced by kind permission of the
Department of Print and Drawings (Janus Collection),
British Museum.

The underdog, 'anancy' figure who survived by his wits was the character that most appealed to Paul. In West Africa, where he lived and taught for a while, Paul encountered many living Sanchos. His relationship with eighteenth-century black texts was inseparable from his relationships with living Africans.

We (and by 'we' I refer to African and Caribbean peoples) owe Paul Edwards a great debt. He pioneered the study of Black British writing, working diligently on neglected texts with no personal profit to his academic career. I am sure that in the 1960s, 'mainstream' scholars in English Literature would have considered his interests to be eccentric. Paul persevered, and the fruits of his labour are that the works of Equiano, Sancho, Mary Prince and others are receiving increasing attention in the academies. It is no longer considered odd, in the 1990s, to speak of 'British Slave Narratives'. Equally important is the fact that Paul's work inspired a generation of new researchers – people like Ron Ramdin, Peter Fryer, Ziggy Alexander and Clem Seecharan, to name but a few writers who have subsequently published on the African and Caribbean diaspora. His influence spread across the Atlantic, so that scholars like Henry Gates, Keith Sandiford and Angelo Costanzo have, in their writings on Black Literature, acknowledged Paul's original research. He kept up a correspondence with African writers like Chinua Achebe and scholars like S. E. Ogude, and his 1960s' editions of Sancho and Equiano's books were circulated in African libraries, finding their way on to the Literature curriculum of many African universities.

What is finally memorable about Paul is the irrepressible humour with which he conducted his research. He delighted in the books, speaking of Equiano and Sancho as if they were close friends. On occasions he *gossiped* about them in a lowered conspiratorial voice, as if they were still alive and within earshot. I used to joke in turn with Paul that he looked remarkably like Sancho (as in the Gainsborough portrait), and he was flattered by the comparison and mused on the illicit processes of miscegenation whereby he had become a descendant of the black African. His playful attitude to the writing is of considerable relevance. Various ideologues of the 1970s and 1980s used the black slave narratives as battering rams against the white academic establishment in Britain and America. Using Equiano *et al.* as weapons against academic conservatism was a necessary process. It succeeded to the degree that the curriculum was opened up to new voices and new perspectives. The danger, however, was that these ideologues developed a solemn political reverence for the text, robbing them of their comic content. Paul's project, up to the very end of his life, was to retrieve the humanity of the early Black Writers, showing them to be serious, erudite, contradictory, stylish, mischievous, playful, and always remarkable in their fragile triumph over plantation brutalities.

June 1993

Introduction

Of the number of books in English published by Africans in Britain during the latter half of the eighteenth century,[1] two are generally agreed to be exceptional: the *Letters* of Ignatius Sancho (1782) and the autobiography *The Interesting Narrative of Olaudah Equiano* (1789).[2] These two books form something of a contrast, in that radical elements, veiled or less aggressively delivered in Sancho, are more overt in Equiano, perhaps suggesting the growing confidence of the Afro-British voice of the movement for the abolition of slavery in the later years of the century. There may be other reasons for the differences of tone. Sancho had no memories of Africa: he had been born aboard a slave ship and employed as an English household servant virtually from childhood. Meanly treated by his first 'owners', he was taken up as a protégé of the 2nd Duke of Montagu in his teens and was in due course largely assimilated into the polite English society of his day as an amateur of literature, music and painting, a friend of the novelist Sterne and the actor Garrick, and a respected senior servant in a noble household, cushioned in his declining years by a pension and a comfortable living as a fashionable Westminster shopkeeper.

Though fortune eventually led him to a fair degree of social prosperity, Equiano, on the other hand, spent the first eleven years of his life in a village in the interior of what is now Nigeria, the son of an Igbo elder and titled man. Kidnapped into slavery at the age of eleven, Equiano stresses in his autobiography the importance of those early years, and records his experience of the chances, sufferings and adventures of his life as a slave, seaman, world traveller, successful author and man of business:

> for whether the love of one's country be real or imaginary, or a lesson of reason, or an instinct of nature, I still look back with pleasure on the first scenes of my life, though that pleasure has been for the most part mingled with sorrow. (Equiano, I. 46)

Inevitably, the differences in the lives of these two men are reflected in their written works. In the year of Sancho's birth, 1729, the English Attorney General, Yorke, and the Solicitor General, Talbot, had declared that slaves settled in Britain were not legally entitled to their liberty, despite the common belief that setting foot in Britain automatically conferred freedom. Twenty years later it was reasserted by Yorke, by then Lord Hardwicke, that the status of a slave was that of property or trade goods – 'They are like stock on a farm.'[3] But Sancho was a man in his late thirties and starting his correspondence with Sterne when the teenage Equiano bought back his hard-earned freedom in the 1760s. These years saw the beginnings of effective legislation against slavery in England with Granville Sharp's successful lawsuits on behalf of various runaway slaves, to be uneasily reinforced by Lord Justice Mansfield's decision in 1772 that slaves who had managed to settle in England could no longer legally be recaptured and returned to slavery in the Americas.[4] However, their exact legal status remained unclear. Slavery was unambiguously rejected by Scots Law in 1778, but in England the sale of slaves continued to be advertised in the press for twenty years after Mansfield. During the two decades after Sancho's death in 1780,[5] Equiano was to establish himself as principal black British spokesman, acting with Granville Sharp, Thomas Clarkson and other leaders of the movement for the abolition of slavery.

Out of the meagre opportunities granted by the painful circumstances of his birth and early employment, Ignatius Sancho was to fashion himself into the most patently literary of the black authors of the late eighteenth century – the only black British writer of his time to achieve an entry in the *Dictionary of National Biography*. Sancho's biographer, Jekyll, whose *Life of Sancho* prefaced his letters of 1782 and is reproduced in this edition, tells how the infant Sancho was sold to three hardhearted London sisters who treated him as their household slave, and denied him an education on the grounds that it might lead him to expect freedom and independence. The 2nd Duke of Montagu, a liberal humanitarian, met him by chance and, recognising his potential, encouraged him with the loan of books. After the Duke's death in 1749, the Duchess took him into service in her household, but she too died in 1751, leaving Sancho a small annuity. But, Jekyll tells us, he rapidly dissipated his assets on cards and women, and it is during this period that he may briefly have taken up employment as an actor in Garrick's theatrical company. It was also during this period that the Montagus' daughter Mary, who was heiress to the estate, married George Brudenell, 4th Earl of Cardigan, in 1730, and he had adopted the title of Duke of Montagu which became defunct on the death of the 2nd Duke. He therefore became the 1st Duke of Montagu of the new creation. Soon Sancho was taken back into service with the family, so continuing until 1773, when ill-health led to his retirement – on a pension – to the shop in Westminster. Indeed,on 2 May 1767, Elizabeth, one of the Duke's daughters, married the 3rd Duke of Buccleuch – a connection which led Sancho to Scotland for a short period, letters being written from Dalkeith in the summer and autumn of 1770.

In his letters, Sancho gives the impression of being almost wholly assimilated into the lifestyle and values of polite eighteenth-century English society, while displaying tensions and contradictions on matters of race, which have more recently been seen as conscious strategies of protest.[6] While I raise questions below about this view of his ironic manner, there is no doubt that, though he never suffered from the more extreme prejudices and cruelties of the society in which he settled, the very fact of the colour of his skin and the attitudes towards race adopted by many members of that society would have made him acutely conscious of his racial origins, despite his having no direct memories of Africa. The sense of race emerges in his letters in a more muted fashion, however, than is the case with authors writing marginally later than himself, such as Equiano and Ottobah Cugoano,[7] whose early youth was spent in Africa.

As Jekyll tells us, 'towards the close of 1773, repeated attacks of the gout, and a constitutional corpulence, rendered him incapable of further attendance on the Duke's family' and Sancho settled down in London's fashionable Mayfair with his West Indian wife Anne, to run a grocery business in Charles Street, Westminster. His customers included the London literati, and we have occasional sketches of him from visitors. On 17 September 1779, George Cumberland wrote:

> I must tell you (because it pleases my vanity so to do) that a Black Man, Ignatius Sancho, has lately put me into an unbounded conceit with myself – he is said to be a great judge of literary performances (God send it may be true!) and has praised my Tale of Cambambo and Journal wh. I read to him, so highly, that I shall like him as long as I live – nothing less

than publishing I fear will satisfy him – but what would not one do to satisfy so good a kind of man? – In the mean time as he is a grocer I think it would be proper to buy all my Tea and Sugar of him ...[8]

Jekyll's introduction bears witness to the respect in which Sancho was held for his literary and artistic judgement:

Garrick and Sterne were well acquainted with Ignatius Sancho.

A commerce with the Muses was supported amid the trivial and momentary interruptions of a shop: the Poets were studied, and even imitated with some success; – two pieces were constructed for the stage; – the Theory of Music was discussed and dedicated to the Princess Royal[9]; – and Painting was so much within the circle of Ignatius Sancho's judgment, that Mortimer[10] came often to consult him. (see p. 24)

Sancho was probably also acquainted with Dr Johnson, who, according to a handwritten note by Jekyll in his own copy of Sancho's *Letters* 'had promised to write the Life of Ignatius Sancho, which afterwards he neglected to do'.[11] Since Dr Johnson was nearing the end of his own life when Sancho died, his failure to write Sancho's life is understandable.

Another of Sancho's contemporaries, John Thomas Smith, biographer of the sculptor Nollekens, offers a brief description of Sancho's domestic life, a recurrent topic of the *Letters*:

In June 1780, Mr. Nollekens took me to the house of Ignatius Sancho, who kept a grocer's, or rather chandler's shop, at No. 20 Charles-street, Westminster ... Mr. Nollekens having recollected that he had promised him a cast of his friend Sterne's bust, I had the honour of carrying it; and as we pushed the wicket-door, a little tinkling bell, the usual appendage of such shops, announced its opening: we drank tea with Sancho and his black lady, who was seated, when we entered, chopping sugar, surrounded by her little 'Sanchonets'. Sancho, knowing Mr. Nollekens to be a loyal man, said to him: 'I am sure you will be pleased to hear that Lord George Gordon is taken, and that a party of guards is now escorting him to the Tower.' Nollekens said not a word and poor Sancho either did not know, or did not recollect, that he was addressing a Papist. I can also remember Sancho's visiting Mr. Nollekens at his studio, he spake well of art ... [12]

The 'Sanchonets' or 'Sanchonettas' as Sancho himself called his children, appear again and again in his letters. One of them, William (Billy) – who was later to work as assistant librarian to the great botanist, Sir Joseph Banks – continued to run the shop after his father's death, but as a bookshop. William was responsible for the publication of the 1803 edition of the *Letters*, and in a copy, formerly owned by the historian, Christopher Fyfe, is inserted a manuscript letter from William Sancho to Jekyll,[13] to whom the volume appears to have been sent by William as a gift. Sancho gives a pleasant picture of William as a child, and of the family, which in its very ordinariness brings out engaging aspects of Sancho's Sterne-like sentimentality:

> You cannot imagine what hold little Billy gets of me – he grows – prattles – every day learns something new – and by his good-will would be ever in the shop with me – The monkey! he clings round my legs – and if I chide him or look sour, he holds up his little mouth to kiss me. – I know I am the fool – for parents' weakness is child's strength: – truth orthodox – which will hold good between lover and lovee ... Mrs. Sancho is so-so – The virgins are as well as youth and innocence – souls void of care and consciences [consciousness?] of offence can be. – Dame Sancho would be better if she cared less. – I am her barometer – If a sigh escapes me, it is answered by a tear in her eye. – I oft assume a gaiety to illume her dear sensibility with a smile – which twenty years ago almost bewitched me: – and *mark*! – after twenty years enjoyment constitutes my highest pleasure! (Letter 54)

Five letters from one of Sancho's daughters, Elizabeth (Betsy), have also survived, one sent with the gift of Gainsborough's portrait of Sancho, painted in Bath in 1768, to his friend William Stevenson (the Mr S——, or 'dear Stee' to whom several letters are addressed).[14]

Sancho's reputation as a writer initially came about largely as a consequence of his correspondence with Sterne, during the years 1766–7, which was published, after Sterne's death in 1772, in the 1775 edition of Sterne's letters.[15] The most famous and influential of Sancho's letters – though not, I think, the best – was that of 21 July 1766 on the subject of the slave trade prompted by his reading Sterne's *Tristram Shandy* (Letter 36):

> Reverend Sir,
> It would be an insult on your humanity (or perhaps look like it) to apologize for the liberty I am taking. – I am one of those

people whom the vulgar and illiberal call '*Negurs*'. – The first part of my life was rather unlucky, as I was placed in a family who judged ignorance the best and only security for obedience. – A little reading and writing I got by unwearied application. – The latter part of my life has been – thro' God's blessing, truly fortunate, having spent it in the service of one of the best families in the kingdom. – My chief pleasure has been books. – Philanthropy I adore. – How very much, good Sir, am I (amongst millions) indebted to you for the character of your amiable uncle Toby! – I declare I would walk ten miles in the dog days, to shake hands with the honest corporal. – Your Sermons have touch'd me to the heart and I hope have amended it, which brings me to the point. – In your tenth discourse, page seventy-eight, in the second volume – is this very affecting passage – 'Consider how great a part of our species – in all ages down to this – have been trod under the feet of cruel and capricious tyrants, who would neither hear their cries nor pity their distresses. – Consider slavery – what it is – how bitter a draught – and how many have been made to drink it!' – Of all my favourite authors, not one has drawn a tear in favour of my miserable black brethren – excepting yourself, and the humane author of Sir George Ellison – I think you will forgive me; – I am sure you will applaud me for beseeching you to give one half-hour's attention to slavery, as it is at this time practiced in our West Indies. – That subject, handled in your striking manner, would ease the yoke (perhaps) of many – but if only of one – Gracious God! – what a feast for a benevolent heart! – and sure I am, you are an epicurean in acts of charity. – You, who are so universally read, and as universally admired – you could not fail – Dear Sir, think in me you behold the uplifted hands of thousands of my brother Moors. – Grief (you pathetically observe) is eloquent; – figure to yourself their attitudes; – hear their supplicating addresses! – alas! – you cannot refuse. – Humanity must comply – in which I hope I beg permission to subscribe myself,

Reverend Sir &c.
IGN. SANCHO.

That Sancho's heart is in the right place is apparent, perhaps too apparent. Sentiment lapsing into sentimentality of expression has been recognised as one of the weaknesses even of his literary master, Sterne, and this was a period in which not only the sentimental writings of Sterne, but such novels as Henry Mackenzie's emotionally extravagant *The Man of Feeling* were best-sellers. I am not suggesting that strong feelings on the subject of the slave trade were in themselves in any way questionable: quite the contrary. But the way those feelings are expressed in this letter seems to me to display something spurious and self-indulgent. Sancho's social position placed him under less immediate pressure than poorer and less articulate fellow blacks. Consequently, the voice of his protest is closer to the popular sentimental manner of his age than to the impassioned voice of angry and outraged feeling. His plea on behalf of slaves in this letter is eloquent: but when Sancho asks Sterne to 'think in me you behold the uplifted hands of thousands of my brother Moors ... figure to yourself their attitudes; – hear their supplicating cries', the gestures might seem more than a little theatrical, their manner closer to those of liberal cliché. And when he calls Sterne 'an epicurean in acts of charity', enjoying his generous impulses as 'a feast to a benevolent heart' at the release 'if only of one – Gracious God!', we might detect behind the generosity of heart something of a self-indulgent benevolism as much concerned with enjoying the virtue of its own conduct as with the cruelties it sought to alleviate. The letter achieved great popularity in its day, and it is not hard to see why: it invites a comfortable moral glow and a generous tear, while keeping the bare brutalities of slave-ownership and the trade at a 'civilised' distance.

My point might be reinforced by reference to the case of William Ansah Sessarakoo, who (like the 'fortunate slave', Job ben Solomon, lionised by polite English society after being discovered to be literate in Arabic),[16] was indebted for his good fortune to English commercial interests in West African trade. William Ansah's father, Chief John Corrente of Annamaboe, was being wooed commercially by both the English and the French. When his son, later known by the nickname Cupid, who had set sail for London by way of Barbados with a 'friendly' English captain, was cynically sold as a slave in the West Indies, it was clear that, in the interest of English trade negotiations with his father, he should be freed, and well looked after. On his release he was brought to London, and fêted. While attending a performance of Aphra Behn's *Oroonoko*, he was seen to be moved to tears by the similarity of its hero's case to his own. The incident was seized on enthusiastically by the press and popular literature,[17] as was his subsequent baptism. Though it is clear that the initial concern for his well-being stemmed as much from commercial interest as from any active desire to see justice done to a victim of the slave trade, it also reflected the popular sentimental appeal of the proto-romantic literature of the age, not necessarily specifically connected with the appalling realities of the slave trade, but rather with the fictional appeal of exotic romances; and possibly, even, as a palliative to the nagging guilt felt by many about slavery, upon which they were unable or unready to take more positive action. Tears were easier and certainly fashionable, and such individual rescues as those of Job or Cupid may have been attractive to the public because they were theatrical.

Some of Sancho's wry, at times jocular references to common-place daily racial hurts seem more painfully pointed, for all their self-defensiveness, than this consciously emotive letter. The comparison with a dog in the following might appear on the surface to be self-abasement, but at a subtler level it conceals layers of satirical anger that such an analogy should be possible. It is applicable, as the last clause shows, even to himself, who has had the good fortune to rise above the 'state of ignorance and bondage' which has been unjustly imposed upon his 'brethren'. It is less ingratiating than at first might appear, and not designed to give his white audience comfort, but rather to remind it of the inhumanity of the master/slave relationship and the limitations of paternalistic condescension:

> I thank you for your kindness to my poor black brethren – I flatter myself you will find them not ungrateful – they act commonly from their feelings: – I have observed a dog will love those who use him kindly – and surely, if so, negroes in their state of ignorance and bondage will not act less generously, if I may judge them by myself. (Letter 13)

Sancho writes to a friendly acquaintance:

> Tell me more about yourself – and more about your honoured parents, whom I hope you found as well as you wished – your kindred at Lancaster, to whom my hearty wishes – and to all who have charity enough to admit dark faces into the fellowship of Christians. – say much for me of your good father and mother – Excepting conjugal, there are no attentions so heart-soothing as the parental ... (Letter 66)

In such a passage as this, the bitter touch of ironic wormwood at the core brings out all the more sensitively Sancho's awareness of being a stranger in need of family and community affections which the circumstances of his life had threatened to deny him. Again we might feel the knife turning in Sancho's own wound when we read: '... our best respects to Miss A-s and to every one who delighteth in Blackamoor greetings ...' (Letter 70).

From time to time Sancho makes direct reference to the experience of racial hostility. On a family outing, 'we went by water – had a couch home – were gazed at etc. etc. but not much abused' (Letter 49). But the casualness here is deceptive, for writing to a fellow African, Julius Soubise, a favourite of the Duchess of Queensberry[18] the pain is nearer the surface: 'Happy, happy lad, what a fortune is thine,' he writes of Soubise's pampered life. 'Look round upon the miserable fate of almost all of our unfortunate colour – superadded to ignorance – see slavery, and the contempt of those very wretches who roll in affluence from our labours. Superadded to this woeful catalogue – hear the ill-bred and heart racking abuse of the foolish vulgar – You, S[oubise] tread as cautiously as the strictest rectitude can guide ye – yet must you suffer from this ...' (Letter 14).

Sometimes, then, Sancho will afford us a glimpse of the face of the stranger in a strange land, almost simultaneously with his assimilated face, that of a conservative patriotic Englishman troubled by the seeming decline of English power, as for instance in the last sentence of the following quotation. Sancho has heard a report from the West Indies of a French naval success: 'We fought like Englishmen' he declares patriotically, then goes on:

> Lord S[andwich] has gone to Portsmouth to be a witness of England's disgrace – and his own shame. – In faith, my friend, the present time is rather comique – Ireland almost in as true a state of rebellion as America – Admirals quarrelling in the West-Indies – and at home Admirals that do not chuse to fight – The British Empire mouldering away in the West, annihilated in the North – Gibraltar going – and England fast asleep. What says Mr. B– to all this? – he is a ministerialist: for my part, it's nothing to me, as I am only a lodger, and hardly that. (Letter 105)

Of the black American poet, Phillis Wheatley – whose poems, published in 1773, were required to be prefaced by letters written by white gentlemen confirming the poems' authenticity, and testifying to Phillis's virtues and talents – Sancho writes:

It reflects nothing to the glory or generosity of her master – if she is still his slave – except he glories in the low vanity of having in his wanton power a mind animated by Heaven – a genius superior to himself. The list of splendid, titled, learned names in confirmation of her being the real authoress, alas! shows how very poor the acquisition of wealth and knowledge are – without generosity – feeling – and humanity. These good, great folks all knew – and perhaps admired – nay, praised Genius in bondage – and then, like the Priests and the Levites in sacred writ, passed by, not one good Samaritan amongst them. (Letter 58)

The reference to his 'wanton power' may not be entirely fair to Phillis's owner, John Wheatley, who appears to have treated her more as a poor but deserving relative than as a slave, but Sancho is right in principle in recognising the potential cruelty and injustice of such patronage and condescension. His awareness of the racism lurking in the hearts even of some of his English friends is brought out by his letter to Jack, the son of one of his correspondents, Mr Wingrave, a London bookseller. Young Jack had gone out to India and had written to his father from Bombay, 'I am now thoroughly convinced, that the account which Mr. G– gave me of the natives of this country is just and true, that they are a set of deceitful people, and have not such a word as Gratitude in their language, neither do they know what it is – and as to their dealings in trade, they are like unto Jews' (Letter 68). Sancho was shown this, and wrote a reply:

I am sorry to observe the practice of your country (which as a resident I love – for its freedom, and for the many blessings I enjoy in it, shall ever have my warmest wishes – prayers – and blessings); I say, it is with reluctance that I must observe your country's conduct has been uniformly wicked in the East – West Indies – and even on the coast of Guinea. – The grand object of English navigators – indeed of all Christian navigators – is money – money – money – for which I do not pretend to blame them. – Commerce was meant by the goodness of the Deity to diffuse the various goods of the earth into every part – to unite mankind in the blessed chains of brotherly love – society – and mutual dependence: – and the enlightened Christian should diffuse the Gospel of peace – with the commodities of his respective land. – Commerce, attended with strict honesty – and with Religion for its companion, would be a blessing to every shore it touched at. (Letter 68)

Sancho goes on to blame not only the unchristian avarice of the white slave-traders but African savagery too for the sufferings of the slaves:

> In Africa, the poor wretched natives – blessed with the most fertile and luxurious soil – are rendered so much the more miserable for what providence meant as a blessing: – the Christians' abominable Traffic for slaves – and the horrid cruelty and treachery of the petty Kings – encouraged by their Christian customers – who carry them strong drink to encourage their national madness – and powder and bad fire arms, to furnish them with the hellish means of killing and kidnapping. But enough – it is a subject that sours my blood – and I am sure will not please the friendly bent of your social affections. (Letter 68)

This letter requires to be discussed in more detail, in connection with late-eighteenth-century economic ideas. It is important to recognise that such arguments for the virtues of 'Christian Commerce' were common enough at this time among abolitionists, who not only had to argue the immorality of the slave trade, but soothe widespread fears, canvassed by the West India planters and their friends in anti-abolitionist writings, of the damage that might be done to the English economy should slavery be abolished.

Equiano, who might be said to have suffered rather more from 'Christian Commerce' than Sancho, shows a certain ambivalence about slavery, condemning the cruelty of its practices more explicitly than the institution itself.[19] But in his final chapter, he proposes to ensure the economic stability of Britain by means of a shift from trade in slaves to trade in goods. I believe there are two voices of Sancho recognisable in the letter just quoted. Sancho the African, and ex-slave, is revealed in his indignation, and bitter overtly ironic reference to 'Christian navigators', with its outraged conclusion that their aim has been nothing but 'money – money – money': but as the argument develops, Sancho the business man takes over to praise Commerce under the benevolent guidance of religion. The argument, used at the time against those who feared the abolition of slavery as a threat to property, seems to me to express the unease of a divided self, rather than one of the 'basic strategies of the eighteenth-century satirist' seen by Lloyd W. Brown. In Brown's review of an earlier edition of Sancho's *Letters*, he writes that:

> after deploring the depredations of Christian traders, [Sancho] ironically echoes the mercantilist's usual apology for Commerce in general and the slave trade in particular.

Brown sees Sancho's attitude as an ironic strategy, and goes on:

> it is clear that 'the blessed chains of brotherly love' are not the only kinds of bond with which Sancho is preoccupied here. He is not being the unquestioning disciple of mercantilism which Paul Edwards supposes him to be in this letter. Indeed, Sancho's ironic insinuations are so effective because his knowledge of his society enables him to subvert its prejudices and ambiguous values from within. The personality of the assimilated African has incarnated one of the basic strategies of the eighteenth-century satirist.[20]

Brown raises a question, which invites close attention. But to begin with, I did not argue in the earlier edition that there is no irony here, but think the irony to be explicit rather than concealed and strategic; and though I agree that Sancho's words echo the usual mercantilist arguments, I do not think he is being ironic in his defence of these, but subscribing to commercial values broadly acceptable to him as an eighteenth-century 'commercial man'. In his references to 'Christian navigators', and his bitter repetition, 'money – money – money' Sancho's anger is open and outraged, hardly 'ironic insinuation', and too explicit to be called 'strategic'. His anger is directed at the abuse of an otherwise enthusiastically endorsed spirit of virtuous Christian trade, in which the modern reader, possessing hindsight on matters of Empire, might discover ironies not present in the mind of the eighteenth-century author. Brown sees Sancho's mercantilism as an ironic parody of that of apologists for the slave trade, whereas I would understand it as acceptable doctrine to Sancho, as it was to Equiano in his argument in his *Narrative* for 'a system of commerce' in which 'the native inhabitants [of Africa] will insensibly adopt the British fashions, manners, customs &c. In proportion to the civilisation, so will be the consumption of British manufactures'. (Equiano, II. 249–50)

Such economic ideas were in fact commonplaces of abolitionist argument at this time when the abolitionist cause was under attack by the West India planters and their narrowly mercantilist parliamentary supporters as likely to result in serious economic damage to the nation ('which as a resident I love for the many blessings I enjoy in it' declares Sancho in the letter, not apparently ironically). Further, what are we to make of his earnest request that his young friend 'guard against being too hasty in condemning the knavery of a people who – bad as they may be – possibly – were made worse by their Christian visitors', where the 'knavery' of both camps is blamed, hardly ironically? Indeed, if one reads on to the end of the paragraph under discussion in Sancho's letter, the absence of the kind of irony against mercantilism which is seen by Lloyd Brown becomes increasingly apparent, I think, as Sancho shifts at least part of the responsibility for the cruelties of the slave trade on to the African 'national madness', the 'hellish' purchase of arms, the barbarism of local 'petty Kings' and an African population who 'bad as they may be', are made worse by contact with Europe. Such arguments hover uncomfortably on the fringe of those proposed by some supporters of the slave trade, that enslavement was a means of saving the Africans from their own devilish culture. The abolitionist reply to such views was that responsible trade in goods and civilising amenities conducted on Christian principles would offer precisely this salvation, while making 'clean' money in the process, and this appears to conform to Sancho's view.

In fact, such 'mercantilism' as Brown sees as ironic in Sancho was found by Equiano in unimpeachable abolitionist sources acknowledged by him in the *Narrative*, such as Benezet,[21] or the pamphlets of the distinguished Scots abolitionist James Ramsay, whose war of words with the planter and slave-owner James Tobin, Equiano was to review in a letter to *The Public Advertiser*.[22] Indeed, Jekyll's *Life of Sancho* draws attention to the efforts of benevolent political economists, specifying Benezet, to defend Africa against racist exploitation, by way of trade on virtuous commercial principles:

> To the harsh definition of the naturalist, oppressions political and legislative have been added; and such are hourly aggravated towards this unhappy race of men by vulgar prejudice and popular insult. To combat these on commercial principles, has been the labour of Labat, Ferman, and Bennezet ... (see p. 24)

As an illustration of the abolitionists' need for benevolist economic arguments, in 1772, a few years before Sancho wrote the letter under discussion, the pro-slavery lobby was arguing against the abolition of slavery in terms of jingoist mercantilism:

> All our pretended reformers of the age ... under a cloak of furious zeal in the cause of religion and liberty do all they can to throw down those essential pillars, commerce, trade and navigation, upon which alone must depend their own enjoyment of any freedom, civil or religious.[23]

These words were quoted in parliament in 1789 by Wilberforce, as an example of the cruel and narrow self-interest of those involved in the exploitation of Africa through the slave trade. But their reception in the House of Commons is an indicator of the state of British economic thought. Far from arousing general reproach, the words, not of Wilberforce, but of the pamphlet, were cheered. 'A cry of assent was heard in several parts of the house.'[24] In such a climate of economic opinion, it was necessary for members of the abolitionist movement, even those laying claim to the purest humanitarian motives, to demonstrate that virtue might go hand-in-hand with commercial and political interest. Wilberforce himself was to express such a view early in the following century in defence of Christian commerce:

> At such an enlightened period as this, when commerce herself adopts the principles of true morality, and becomes liberal and benevolent, will it be believed that the Almighty has rendered the depression and misery of the cultivators of the soil in our West Indian Colonies necessary, or even conducive, to their prosperity and safety? No, surely the oppression of these injured fellow creatures, however it may be profitable in a few instances, can never be generally politic; and in the main, and ultimately, the comfort of the labourer and the well-being of those who have to enjoy the fruits of his labour will be found to be co-incident.[25]

Whatever strategies might be at work in Sancho's letter of 1778, to call the references to Christian commerce ironic is, I believe, to avoid the issue of Sancho's assimilation of the values of his day, and misinterpret the nature of the contrary impulses being displayed.

The interest of such letters as this lies, I think, more in their revelation of Sancho's effort to come to terms with his assimilated experience, than in any calculated, ironic or subversive strategy.

Generous, good-natured, domestic, sometimes pained or perplexed, often sentimental, Sancho's characteristic voice expresses a kind of conventional decency: 'Make human nature thy study wherever thou residest – whatever the religion or the complexion, study their hearts.' We might contrast this, not simply with the gross, strident and often viciously racist assertiveness of the voices ranged against him and his fellow Africans, but with a comparatively 'polite' view of London Africans from the pen of Dr Johnson's friend Hester Thrale, Mrs Piozzi:

> Well! I am really haunted by *black shadows*. Men of colour in the rank of gentlemen; a black lady covered with finery, in the Pit at the Opera, and tawny children playing in the Squares, – in the gardens of the Squares I mean, – with their Nurses, afford ample proofs of Hannah More and Mr. Wilberforce's success in breaking down the *wall of separation*. Oh! how it falls on every side! and spreads its tumbling ruins on the world! leaving all ranks, all custom, all colours, all religions, *jumbled together*.[26]

Sancho, however, a member of the small new, black middle class which made Hester Thrale and others[27] so nervous, has a dream of a raceless Heaven both less apocalyptic and more humane. We should bear in mind that it was Sancho's words to which the public most responded by buying his highly popular, heavily subscribed and widely praised collected letters, even though we still have a long way to go to realise the enthusiastic vision of his innocent, benevolent eye:

> We will mix, my boy, with all countries, colours, faiths – see the countless multitudes of the first world – the myriads descended from the Ark – the Patriarchs – Sages – Prophets – and Heroes! My head turns round at the vast idea! – We will mingle with them and untwist the vast chain of blessed Providence – which puzzles and baffles human understanding. Adieu. (Letter 44)

Once again, as in the letter Brown finds ironic, it is the great chain of being to which Sancho refers. To read this as an ironic reference to the chains of slavery is, I believe, to strain towards a significance the letter does not carry. Nevertheless, such disturbances as the Gordon Riots of 1780 evoke in Sancho a descriptive ironic gusto, reminiscent of Keats's observation, 'Though a quarrel in the streets is a thing to be hated, the energies displayed in it are fine.'[28]

Sancho's energies are roused to a fine pitch by the riots, though perhaps a fact uppermost in the mercantile part of his mind was that his shop windows were under threat (Letters 134 and 135).

The first letter on the riots displays Sancho's sense of absurdity as much as of outrage, and its few shafts are hardly meant to draw blood. 'The worse than Negro barbarity of the populace' and 'I am not sorry I was born in Afric' are, in the essentially tolerant and urbane context, more like ironic nudges than barbs. The quarrel was between the anti-Catholic rabble in the streets, and the gentlemen in parliament who wished to bring in legislation to relieve British Roman Catholics of some of the burdens that the profession of their faith placed upon them in public and private life. Lord George Gordon, the leader of the riots, is seen by Sancho as a manipulative rabble-rouser: 'Lord George Gordon has this moment announced to my Lords the mob …' suggests in its sarcastic use of the title for both Gordon and the mob, that Gordon had, in Sancho's eyes, disgraced the privileged role of traditional authority to which he had been born, and that the riots, far from demonstrating a democratic involvement of the people – in fact at that time 'the people' had little electoral say in matters of government – were an assault on the respectable values Sancho held dear:

> This – this – is liberty! genuine British liberty! This instant about two thousand liberty boys are swearing and swaggering by with large sticks – thus armed, in hopes of meeting with the Irish chairmen [i.e. carriers of sedan chairs] and labourers. (Letter 134)

Sancho sees the uprising as an anarchic intrusion upon the civilised business of parliamentary legislation. 'I am forced to own that I am for universal toleration. Let us convert by our example and conquer by our meekness and brotherly love.' Consequently, he does not denounce the mob so much as mock their disorderliness and their assumption of an authority he sees them as, absurdly, making claim to. They are ironically, 'my Lords the mob', and 'the gentry' who tell the Sardinian ambassador that 'they would burn him if they could get at him' and proceed to destroy 'a painting of our saviour' and 'an exceptionally fine organ', grossly offensive to Sancho the Christian, and amateur of painting and music. It is clear that he stands conventionally with sober authority, but his sympathies go in all directions. On one hand, even the mob is seen with avuncular concern in terms of its amiable domestic potential:

'Thank heaven it rains; may it increase so as to send these deluded wretches safe to their homes, their families, and wives!', while the military powers, far from being presented as aggressive imposers of law and order by force, are part of suffering mankind: 'the poor fellows are just worn out for want of rest ...' In the end, Sancho leaves his correspondent with an image of the cheerful energies of the mob, rather than its destructiveness: 'Upon this, they gave a hundred cheers – took the horses from [Gordon's] hackney-coach – and rolled him full jollily away. They are huzzaing now ready to crack their throats. *Huzzah.*'

Sancho's next letter on the riots leaves no doubt about his conservative stance: it begins,

> Government is sunk in lethargic stupor – anarchy reigns – When I look back to the glorious time of a George II and a Pitt's administration, my heart sinks at the bitter contrast. We may now say of England, as was heretofore said of Great Babylon – 'The beauty of the excellence of the Chaldees is no more.' (Letter 135)[29]

The identification of England with Babylon might be seen as ironic, but in the end, I believe the benevolent, reconciling spirit of Sancho's letters largely subverts the ironic elements, usually too open to be strategic. He represents essentially the assimilated African in eighteenth-century English society.

Notes

1. For examples of Afro-British writing of the period, see Paul Edwards and David Dabydeen (eds), *Black Writers in Britain, 1760–1890* (Edinburgh University Press, Edinburgh, 1991).

2. *The Letters of the Late Ignatius Sancho, an African* (London, 1782); the same, in the fifth edition of 1802–3, with a new introduction by Paul Edwards (London, Dawsons of Pall Mall Colonial History Series, 1968); *The Interesting Narrative of the Life of Olaudah Equiano, or Gustavus Vassa the African* (London, 1789); the same, with a new introduction and notes by Paul Edwards (London, Dawsons of Pall Mall Colonial History Series, 1969).

3. H.T. Catterall, *Judicial Cases Concerning American Slavery and the Negro* (Washington DC, 1926) vol. I, pp. 9–12.

4. For the Mansfield Decision and the cases leading up to it, see Peter Fryer, *Staying Power: The History of Black People in Britain* (Pluto Press, London, 1984) pp. 115–26.

5. Sancho died 14 December 1780 after a long illness aggravated by the gout and corpulence from which he had suffered for many years. His death is noted in *The Gentleman's Magazine*:

    > In Charles-str. Westminster, Mr. Ignatius Sancho, grocer and oilman; a character immortalized by the epistolary correspon-dence of Sterne.

    He was buried at Westminster Broadway.

6. Keith A. Sandiford, *Measuring the Moment: Strategies of Protest in Eighteenth-Century Afro-English Writing* (Associated University Presses, London and Toronto, 1988) pp. 73–92.

7. Ottobah Cugoano, *Thoughts and Sentiments on the Evil and Wicked Traffic of the Slavery and Commerce of the Human Species* (London, 1787); the same, with an introduction and notes by Paul Edwards (London, Dawsons of Pall Mall Colonial History Series, 1969).

8. George Cumberland, British Library Add. MS. 36491 p. 204 recto, p. 204 verso. I must thank Dr Michael Phillips of Edinburgh University, who came across this reference to Sancho in the course of his research on the Cumberland Papers, for bringing it to my attention.

9. Neither Sancho's poetic imitations nor his pieces for the stage appear to have survived, nor has any trace been found so far of his Theory of Music. However, several of his musical pieces are in the British Library, listed in Edwards's introduction to the 1802–3 facsimile edition of the *Letters*, p. viii, n. 9. Some pieces received their first broadcast performance in a BBC talk by Edward Scobie, 'African Composers in Eighteenth-Century London', 8 August 1958. Sancho's music has been edited and discussed by Josephine Wright, whose 'Research has yielded a harvest of sixty-two compositions that were published by Sancho from *c.* 1767 to 1779', in *Ignatius Sancho (1729–1780): an Early African Composer in England: the Collected Editions of his Music in Facsimile* (Garland, New York and London, 1981).

10. John Hamilton Mortimer (1741–1779), a respected minor painter, studied under Reynolds, was Vice-President of the Incorporated Society of Arts in 1773, had a house near Covent Garden, fairly close to Sancho and, like Sancho, lived extravagantly for a period of his life, and damaged his health. Sancho knew him well, and often praises him, for example Letter 88.

11. See Appendix III.

12. John Thomas Smith, *Nollekins and his Times*, (ed.) G. W. Stonier, (London, 1949) pp. 14–15. The Gordon Riots were anti-Roman Catholic, so it is not clear why Nollekins, as a Catholic, should have been embarrassed by Sancho's en-

thusiasm for Lord George Gordon's imprisonment. Perhaps Sancho should have tactfully stayed away from the subject. But as we can tell from the first of his letters on the Riots (Letters 134–37), his spirits were almost as much excited as offended by them, and bubbled up at the chance of talking about them to Nollekins.

13. The letter is given in Appendix III of this edition, and also in Edwards's 1968 introduction to Sancho's *Letters*, p. vi. William was wrongly identified by the Abbe Gregoire as a son of Equiano in his *De la Litterature des Negres* (Paris, 1808), p. 252: 'Son fils, verse dans la bibliographie, est devenu sous-bibliotecaire du Chevalier Banks.' The sentence occurs in a short separate paragraph at the close of Gregoire's account of Equiano, and is clearly misplaced. That William Sancho worked as Librarian for Banks is known from Jekyll's handwritten note in his copy of the 1803 edition of Sancho's *Letters*, details of which can also be found in Appendix III. After Sancho's death, William continued to run the Charles Street store, but as a bookshop. Josephine Wright (*Ignatius Sancho*, p. xxxiv, n. 12) records that he 'later moved to Mews Gate in London and succeeded Thomas Paine as the proprietor of a bookstore there *c.* 1808'. See *The Farrington Diary*, (ed.) James Grieg, 3rd edn (George H. Doran Co., New York, 1923), vol. I p. 27. Miss Wright's claim now seems doubtful since recent research shows Thomas Paine, known as 'honest Thomas Paine', ran the bookshop until his death and was succeeded by his son who continued in the bookshop until well after William Sancho's death. According to Ian Maxted's *The London Book Trades 1775–1800*, William was for a short time a bookseller in Thomas Paine's shop, but later had a bookshop of his own, also in Mews Gate, Castle Street, Leicester Fields. It was from this shop that the fifth edition of his father's *Letters* was published in 1803. William Sancho died some time before 1814; also see Appendix VII.

14. J. R. W. (J. R. Willis), 'New light on the life of Ignatius Sancho – some unpublished letters', *Slavery and Abolition*, (1).3, (1980) pp. 345–58. The papers in Professor Willis's possession include fourteen autograph letters; a list of the names of many of Sancho's correspondents given only as initials in the edition of the *Letters*; and 'a little known undated pamphlet which explains the circumstances surrounding the portrait of Sancho rendered by Gainsborough'. The pamphlet also gives some information on Stevenson himself. He was an artist who had studied under Sir Joshua Reynolds and was by profession a painter of miniatures.

15. *Letters of the Late Rev. Mr. Laurence Sterne To his most intimate friends etc., and Published by his Daughter, Mrs.*

Medalle, 3 vols (London, 1775). For Sancho's letter, vol. 3, pp 22–6; for Sterne's reply, vol. 3, pp. 27–30. See also Percy Fitzgerald, *The Life of Laurence Sterne*, 2 vols, (London, 1864), pp. 370–3; and Appendix IV.

16. Douglas Grant, *The Fortunate Slave*, (London, 1968); Thomas Bluett, *Some Memoirs of the Life of Job, Son of Solomon the High Priest of Boonda in Africa* (London, 1734).

17. Grant, *The Fortunate Slave*, pp. 145–7; Anon., *The Royal African: or, the Memoirs of the Young Prince of Annamaboe* (London, 1749); *The London Magazine*, February 1749, p. 94; and for extracts from Bluett's *Life*, Paul Edwards and James Walvin (eds), *Black Personalities in the Era of the Slave Trade* (Macmillan, London, 1983) pp. 211–17.

18. More details of Soubise can be found in Appendix III, esp. n. 3.

19. For some discussion of Equiano's ambivalence towards slave ownership, see Paul Edwards, '"Master" and "father" in Equiano's interesting narrative', *Slavery and Abolition*, (11).3, pp. 217–27.

20. *Eighteenth Century Studies*, 3 (Spring 1970), pp. 415–19.

21. For a discussion of this aspect of Anthony Benezet's *Some Historical Account of Guinea* in the edition of 1788, Appendix X, see Edwards's introduction to the facsimile of the 1789 edition of Equiano's *Narrative*, vol. I, pp. xlix–l.

22. For Equiano and Ramsay, see the introduction to the Equiano facsimile edition, vol. I, pp. li–lii; also Folarin Shyllon, *Black People in Britain 1555–1833* (Oxford University Press, London, 1977) pp. 231–4.

23. Anon., *Reflections ... on what is commonly called The Negroe-Cause, by a Planter* (London, 1772).

24. Roger Anstey, *The Atlantic Slave Trade and British Abolition* (London, 1965) pp. 313–14.

25. *An Appeal to the Religion, Justice, and Humanity of the inhabitants of the British Empire in behalf of the Negroe Slaves in the West Indies*, by W. Wilberforce, Esq., M.P. (London, 1823) p. 71.

26. Oswald G. Knapp (ed.), *The Intimate Letters of Hester Piozzi and Penelope Pennington 1788–1822* (London, 1914) p. 243.

27. In 1710, Philip Thicknesse had noted a 'little race of Mulattoes' in London, and later in the century, Edward Long was to fear that as a result of such racial mixing 'the whole nation [might] resemble the Portuguese and Moriscos in complexion of skin and baseness of mind. This is a venomous and dangerous ulcer, that threatens to disperse its malignancy far and wide, until every family catches infection

from it.' (Quoted in Edwards and Walvin, *Black Personalities*, p. 21.)

28. Robert Gittings (ed.) *Letters of John Keats: a new selection* (Oxford University Press, London and New York, 1970) p. 230.

29. 'And Babylon, the glory of kingdoms, the beauty of the Chaldees excellency, shall be as when God overthrew Sodom and Gomorrah.' Isaiah, 13: 19, predicting the fall of Babylon and the triumph of Israel.

Jekyll's *Life of Ignatius Sancho*

'Quamvis ille niger, quamvis tu candidus esses.'

VIRGIL

The extraordinary Negro, whose Life I am about to write, was born A. D. 1729, on board a ship in the Slave-trade, a few days after it had quitted the coast of Guinea for the Spanish West-Indies; and at Carthagena he received from the hand of the Bishop, Baptism, and the name of Ignatius.

A disease of the new climate put an early period to his mother's existence; and his father defeated the miseries of slavery by an act of suicide.

At little more than two years old, his master brought him to England, and gave him to three maiden sisters, resident at Greenwich; whose prejudices had unhappily taught them, that African ignorance was the only security for his obedience, and that to enlarge the mind of their slave would go near to emancipate his person. The petulance of their disposition surnamed him Sancho, from a fancied resemblance to the 'Squire of Don Quixote.

But a patron was at hand, whom Ignatius Sancho had merit enough to conciliate at a very early age.

The late Duke of Montagu lived on Blackheath: he accidentally saw the little Negro, and admired in him a native frankness of manner as yet unbroken by servitude, and unrefined by education – He brought him frequently home to the Duchess, indulged his turn for reading with presents of books, and strongly recommended to his mistresses the duty of cultivating a genius of such apparent fertility.

His mistresses, however, were inflexible, and even threatened on angry occasions to return Ignatius Sancho to his African slavery. The love of freedom had increased with years, and began to beat high in his bosom. – Indignation, and the dread of constant reproach arising from the detection of an amour, infinitely criminal in the eyes of three maiden ladies, finally determined him to abandon the family.

His noble patron was recently dead. – Ignatius flew to the
Duchess for protection, who dismissed him with reproof. – He
retired from her presence in a state of despondency and stupe-
faction.

Enamoured still of that liberty, the scope of whose enjoyment
was now limited to his last five shillings, and resolute to maintain it
with life, he procured an old pistol for purposes which his father's
example had suggested as familiar, and had sanctified as hereditary.

In this frame of mind the futility of remonstrance was obvious.
The Duchess secretly admired his character; and at length consented
to admit him into her household, where he remained as butler till
her death, when he found himself, by her Grace's bequest and his
own economy, possessed of seventy pounds in money, and an
annuity of thirty.

Freedom, riches, and leisure, naturally led a disposition of
African texture into indulgences; and that which dissipated the
mind of Ignatius completely drained the purse. In his attachment to
women, he displayed a profuseness which not unusually character-
izes the excess of the passion. – Cards had formerly seduced him;
but an unsuccessful contest at cribbage with a Jew, who won his
clothes, had determined him to abjure the propensity, which appears
to be innate among his countrymen. – A French writer relates, that
in the kingdoms of Ardrah, Whydah, and Benin, a Negro will stake
at play his fortune, his children, and his liberty. Ignatius loved the
theatre to such a point of enthusiasm, that his last shilling went to
Drury-Lane, on Mr. Garrick's representation of Richard. – He had
been even induced to consider the stage as a resource in the hour of
adversity, and his complexion suggested an offer to the manager of
attempting Othello and Oroonoko; but a defective and incorrigible
articulation rendered it abortive.

He turned his mind once more to service, and was retained a few
months by the Chaplain at Montagu-house. That roof had been ever
auspicious to him; and the present Duke soon placed him about his
person, where habitual regularity of life led him to think of a
matrimonial connexion, and he formed one accordingly with a very
deserving young woman of West-Indian origin.

Towards the close of the year 1773, repeated attacks of the gout,
and a constitutional corpulence, rendered him incapable of further
attendance in the Duke's family.

At this crisis, the munificence which had protected him through various vicissitudes did not fail to exert itself; with the result of his own frugality, it enabled him and his wife to settle themselves in a shop of grocery, where mutual and rigid industry decently maintained a numerous family of children, and where a life of domestic virtue engaged private patronage and merited public imitation.

In December 1780, a series of complicated disorders destroyed him.

Of a Negro, a Butler, and a Grocer, there are but slender anecdotes to animate the page of the biographer; but it has been held necessary to give some sketch of the very singular man, whose letters, with all their imperfections on their head, are now offered to the public.

The display those writings exhibit of epistolary talent, of rapid and just conception, of wild patriotism, and of universal philanthropy, may well apologize for the protection of the Great, and the friendship of the Literary.

The late Duchesses of Queensberry and Northumberland pressed forward to serve the author of them. The former intrusted to his reformation a very unworthy favourite of his own complexion. – Garrick and Sterne were well acquainted with Ignatius Sancho.

A commerce with the Muses was supported amid the trivial and momentary interruptions of a shop; the Poets were studied, and even imitated with some success; – two pieces were constructed for the stage; – the Theory of Music was discussed, published, and dedicated to the Princess Royal; – and Painting was so much within the circle of Ignatius Sancho's judgment and criticism, that Mortimer came often to consult him.

Such was the man whose species philosophers and anatomists have endeavoured to degrade as a deterioration of the human; and such was the man whom Fuller, with a benevolence and quaintness of phrase peculiarly his own, accounted

'God's Image, though cut in Ebony.'

To the harsh definition of the naturalist, oppressions political and legislative have been added; and such are hourly aggravated towards this unhappy race of men by vulgar prejudice and popular insult. To combat these on commercial principles, has been the labour of Labat, Ferman, and Bennezet – such an effort here would be an impertinent digression.

Of those who have speculatively visited and described the

slave-coast, there are not wanting some who extol the mental abilities of the natives. D'Elbee, Moore, and Bosman, speak highly of their mechanical powers and indefatigable industry. Desmarchais does not scruple to affirm, that their ingenuity rivals the Chinese.

He who could penetrate the interior of Africa, might not improbably discover negro arts and polity, which could bear little analogy to the ignorance and grossness of slaves in the sugar-islands, expatriated in infancy, and brutalized under the whip and the task-master.

And he who surveys the extent of intellect to which Ignatius Sancho had attained by self-education, will perhaps conclude, that the perfection of the reasoning faculties does not depend on a peculiar conformation of the skull or the colour of a common integument,* in defiance of that wild opinion, 'which,' says a learned writer of these times, 'restrains the operations of the mind to 'particular regions, and supposes that a luckless mortal may be born 'in a degree of latitude too high or too low for wisdom or for wit.'

* In farther illustration of this passage the Editor has thought it not irrelevant to the general tenor of this publication to subjoin the following observations from the celebrated work of professor Blumenbach intitled – 'Observations on the bodily Conformation and mental Capacity of the 'Negroes. From *Magazin fur das neueste aus der Physik*,' Vol. IV.

'During a tour which I made through Swisserland, I saw in the picture-gallery at Pommersfeld four negro heads by Vandyk, two of which in particular had the lines of the face so regular that the features seemed very little different from the European. At that time, as I had never had an opportunity of acquiring a proper knowledge respecting the form of the negro head and cranium, by studying nature, and as I remembered that Mr. Camper, in a dissertation read in the Academy of Painting at Amsterdam, had mentioned that the greater part of the most eminent painters, and especially Rubens, Vandyk and Jordaens, when they painted Moors, copied from Europeans whose faces had been blackened for that purpose, I ascribed the European look of the above negro heads to this common fault. Some months after, however, I had an opportunity of convincing myself that there are real negroes whose features correspond very nearly with those of the Europeans, and that the above heads in the gallery of Pommersfeld might be a true representation of nature.

'Going to pay a visit at Yverdun to the two brothers Treytorrens, one of whom, the chevalier, had been thirty-five years in the French service, particularly at St. Domingo; and the other, by means of the opportunities which his brother enjoyed, had a collection of natural curiosities that contained many rare articles, when I entered the court of their elegant habitation, which is situated on the road to Goumoens, I saw no person to show me into the house, except a woman of an agreeable figure, who was standing with her back towards me. When she turned round to give me an answer, I was much surprised to find that she was a female negro, whose face perfectly corresponded with her figure, and fully justified the fidelity of likeness in Vandyk's negro heads, which I had seen at Pommersfeld. All the features of her face, even the nose and lips, the latter of which were a little thick, though not so as to be disagreeable, had they been covered with a white skin, must have excited universal admiration. At the same time she was not only exceedingly lively, and possessed a sound understanding; but, as I afterwards learned, was extremely well informed and expert in the obstetric art. The handsome pretty negress of Yverdun is celebrated far and near as the best midwife in the Italian part of Swisserland. I was informed by her master, the chevalier, who has in his service also a negro man as elegantly formed as a statue, that she was a creole from St. Domingo; that both her parents were natives of Congo, but not so black as the negroes of Senegal.

'Since that period I have had an opportunity of seeing and conversing with many negroes, and have procured for my collection a great many anatomical preparations from negro bodies, which, together with what I have read in different voyages, tend more and more to convince me of the truth of the two following propositions:

'1. That between one negro and another there is as much (if not more) difference in the colour, and particularly in the lineaments of the face, as between many real negroes and other varieties of the human species.

'2. That the negroes, in regard to their mental faculties and capacity, are not inferior to the rest of the human race.

The three negro skulls, which I have now before me, afford, by the very striking gradation with which the lineaments pass from the one to the other, a very evident proof of the first proposition. One of them, which Mr. Michaelis was so good as to bring me from New-York, and of which I have given an accurate description in another place†, is distinguished by such a projecting upper jaw-bone, that, if the same peculiarity belonged to all negroes, one might be tempted to suppose that they had another first parent than Adam. On the other hand, the lineaments of the third have so little of the exotic form, and are so different from the first, that, if I had not dissected the whole head perfectly entire, and just as it was when cut from the body, I should be in doubt whether I ought to consider it as having actually belonged to a real negro. The second holds a mean rank between both, and in its whole form has a great likeness to the head of the Abyssinian Abbas Gregorius, a good engraving of which by Heifz, in 1691, from a painting by Von Sand, I have now before me, and which not only proves in general the close affinity of the Abyssinians with the negroes, but approaches much nearer to the ugly negroes, to speak according to the European ideas of beauty, than the well-formed negress of Yverdun, or the handsome

† In my Osteology, p. 87.

young negro whose head I dissected as before mentioned, or than a thousand others whose features are little different from those of the Europeans. What I have here said is indeed nothing else than a confirmation of a truth long known, which has been already remarked by unprejudiced travellers, as will appear by the following quotations. Le Maire, in his Voyage to Cape Verd, Senegal, and Gambia†, says: 'Blackness excepted, there are female negroes as well made as our ladies in Europe.' Leguat, in his well-known Voyages‡, tells us, that he found at Batavia several very pretty negresses, whose faces had the perfect European form. Adanson, in his Account of Senegal§, speaking of the female negroes there, has the following passage: 'The women are almost as tall as the men, and equally well made. Their skin is remarkably fine and soft: their eyes are black and open; the mouth and lips small, and the features are well proportioned. Some of them are perfect beauties. They are exceedingly lively, and have an easy, free air, that is highly agreeable.' Ulloa, in his *Noticias Americanas*§§, observes, that some of the negroes have thick projecting lips, a flat nose, eyes deeply sunk in the sockets, which in general are called *geiudos* and wool instead of hair. He then adds: 'Others, whose colour is equally black, have features perfectly like those of the whites, particularly in regard to the nose and the eyes, and smooth but thick hair¶.'

'The testimonies and examples which serve to prove the truth of the second proposition, respecting the mental faculties, natural talents and ingenuity of the negroes, are equally numerous and incontrovertible. Their astonishing memories, their great activity, and their acuteness in trade, particularly with gold dust, against which the most experienced European merchant cannot be too much on his guard, are all circum-

---

† Voyages aux Cap Verd, Senegal et Gambie, p. 101.

‡ Vol. ii. p. 136.

§ Page 23.

§§ Page 92.

¶ The following observations of an intelligent Danish traveller may serve still further to confirm the truth of Professor Blumenbach's proposition: 'Almost all the negroes are of a good stature, and the Akra negroes have remarkably fine features. The contour of the face, indeed, among the generality of these people, is different from that of the Europeans; but at the same time faces are found among them which, excepting the black colour, would in Europe be considered as beautiful. In common, however, they have something apish. The cheek-bones and chin project very much; and the bones of the nose are smaller than among the Europeans. This last circumstance has probably given rise to the assertion, that the negro women flatten the noses of their children as soon as they are born. But noses may be seen among some of them as much elevated and as regular as those of the Europeans. Their hair is woolly, curled and black, but sometimes red. When continually combed, it may be brought to the length of half a yard; but it never can be kept smooth.' See P. E. Isert Reis ha Guinea. Dordrecht 1790, p. 175. EDIT.

stances so well known, that it is not necessary to enlarge on them†. The great aptitude of the slaves for learning every kind of nice handicraft is equally well known; and the case is the same in regard to their musical talents, as we have instances of negroes playing the violin in so masterly a manner, that they gained so much money as enabled them to purchase their liberty‡.

'Of the poetical genius of the negroes instances are known among both sexes. A female negro, who was a poetess, is mentioned by Haller; and a specimen of the Latin poetry of Francis Williams, a negro, may be found in the History of Jamaica. The interesting Letters of Ignatius Sancho, a negro, are well known; and the two following instances will serve as a further proof of the capacity and talents of our black brethren, in regard to literature and science. The protestant clergyman J. J. Eliza Capitein was a negro; a man of considerable learning, and a great orator. I have in my possession an excellent print of him engraved by Tanje, after P. Vandyck. Our worthy professor Hollman, when he was at Wittenberg, conferred the degree of Doctor of Philosophy on a negro who had shown himself to advantage, not only as a writer but as a teacher, and who afterwards came to Berlin as a counsellor of state to his Prussian majesty. I have now before me two treatises written by him§, one of which, in particular, displays extensive and well digested reading of the best physiological works of the time. Of the uncommon knowledge which many negroes have had in the practice of medicine, very favourable testimony has been given by Boerhaave and De Haen, who were certainly competent judges; and the sound skill and delicate expertness of the Yverdun accoucheufe are, as already said, celebrated throughout the whole neighbourhood.

'To conclude, the Academy of Sciences at Paris had among the number of its correspondents M. Liflet, a negro, in the Isle of France, who excelled in making accurate meteorological observations. On the other hand, whole provinces of Europe might, in my opinion, be named, from which it would be difficult to produce at present virtuosos, poets, philosophers, and correspondents of a learned academy.

---

† Barbot, in his Description of the Coasts of North and South Guinea, to be found in the fifth volume of Churchill's Collections, relates many interesting things on this subject. Thus he says, p. 235. 'The blacks are for the most part men of sense and wit enough, of a sharp ready apprehension, and an excellent memory beyond what is easy to imagine; for, though they can neither read nor write, they are always regular in the greatest hurry of business and trade, and seldom in confusion.'

‡ See Urlsperger's Americanisch Ackerwerk Gottes, p. 311.

§ One of them is entitled: *Dissert. inaug, philosophica de humanæ mentis αποθεια, sire sensionis ac facultatis in mente humane absentia, et carcen in corpore nostro organica ac vivo prasentia, quam* Praes. D. MART. GOTTH. LOESCHFRO *publied defendit auctor* ANT. GUIL. AMO, Guinea-Afer, Phil. et A. A. L. L, Mag. et J. V. C. *Witterbergæ 1784, m. Apr.* The title of the other is: *Disp. philosophica, continens ideas: distinctam eorum que competunt tel menti vel corpori nostro vivo et organico, quam Præside M.* ANT. GUIL. AMO, Guinea-Afro, *d.* 29 *Maii* 1734, *defendit* JO. TREODOS, Meiner Rochliz-Misnie. Philos. et J. V. Cultor. In an account of Amo's life, printed on this occasion in name of the Academic Council, it is said, among other things respecting his talents: 'Honorem, meritis ingenii partum, insigni probitatis, industriæ, eruditionis, quam publicis privatisque exercitationibus declaravit, laude auxit – Compluribus philosophiam domi tradidit excussis tam veterum, quam novorum, placitis, optima quæque selegit, selecta enucleatè ac dilucidè interpretatus est.' And the president, in defending the first-mentioned treatise, says expressly, in the annexed congratulation to Aino, 'Tuum potissimum eminet ingenium felicissimum – utpote qui istius felicitatem ac præstantiam, eruditionis ac doctrinae soliditatem ac elegantiain, multis speciminibus hactenus in nostra etiam academia magno cum applausu omnibus bonis, et in præsenti dissertatione egregiè comprobasti. Reddo tibi illam proprio marte eleganter ac eruditè elaboratam, integram adhuc et planè immutatam, ut vis ingenii tui eo magis exinde elucescat.

The Letters

Note to the Reader

Sancho's correspondents, and many of the people mentioned in the *Letters*, are not named in previous editions, being designated only by a first initial. Here, when an individual can be identified (see Appendix VI), their name is filled in in italics. Miss Crewe's editorial notes to the *Letters* are designated by an asterisk (*), as in previous editions. Arabic numerals replace Roman in the numbering of the *Letters* and the long 'f' has been normalised to 's' throughout.

1

Charles Street, Feb. 14, 1768.[1]

MY WORTHY AND MUCH RESPECTED FRIEND,

Pope observes,

> 'Men change with fortune, manners change with climes;
> 'Tenets with books, and principles with times.'[2]

Your friendly letter convinced me that you are still the same – and gave in that conviction a ten-fold pleasure: – you carried out (through God's grace) an honest friendly heart, a clear discerning head, and a soul impressed with every humane feeling. – That you are still the same – I repeat it – gives me more joy – than the certainty would of your being worth ten jaghires: – I dare say you will ever remember that the truest worth is that of the mind – the blest rectitude of the heart – the conscience unsullied with guilt – the undaunted noble eye, enriched with innocence, and shining with social glee – peace dancing in the heart – and health smiling in the face. – May these be ever thy companions! – and for riches, you will ever be more than vulgarly rich – while you thankfully enjoy – and gratefully assist the wants (as far as you are able) of your fellow creatures. But I think (and so will you) that I am preaching. I only meant in truth to thank you, which I most sincerely do, for your kind letter: – believe me, it gratifies a better principle than vanity – to know that you remember your dark-faced friend at such a distance: but what would have been your feelings – could you have beheld your worthy, thrice worthy father – joy sitting triumphant in his honest face – speeding from house to house amongst his numerous friends, with the pleasing testimonials of his son's love and duty in his hands – every one congratulating him, and joining in good wishes – while the starting tear plainly proved that over-joy and grief give the same livery?

You met with an old acquaintance of mine, Mr. G——. I am glad to hear he is well, but when I knew him he was young, and not so *wise* as *knowing:* I hope he will take example by what he sees in you – and you, young man, remember, if ever you should unhappily fall into bad company, that example is only the fool's plea, and the rogue's excuse, for doing *wrong* things: – you have a turn for reflection and a steadiness, which, aided by the best of social dispositions, must make your company much coveted, and your person loved. – Forgive me for presuming to dictate, when I well know you have many friends much more able from knowledge and better sense – though I deny – a better will.

You will of course make Men and Things your study – their different genius, aims, and passions: – you will also note climes, buildings, soils, and products, which will be neither tedious nor unpleasant. – If you adopt the rule of writing every evening your remarks on the past day, it will be a kind of friendly *tête-à-tête* between you and yourself, wherein you may sometimes happily become your own Monitor; – and hereafter those little notes will afford you a rich fund, whenever you shall be inclined to re-trace past times and places. – I say nothing upon the score of Religion – for, I am clear, every good affection, every sweet sensibility, every heart-felt joy – humanity, politeness, charity – all, all, are streams from that sacred spring; – so that to say you are good-tempered, honest, social, &c. &c. is only in fact saying you live according to your DIVINE MASTER's rules, and are a christian.

Your B*ury* friends are all well, excepting the good Mrs. C*ocksedge*, who is at this time but so, so. Miss C*rewe* still as agreeable as when you knew her, if not more so. Mr. Rush,[3] as usual, never so happy, never so gay, nor so much in true pleasure, as when he is doing good – he enjoys the hope of your well-doing as much as any of your family. His brother John has been lucky – his abilites, address, good nature, and good sense, have got him a surgeoncy in the battalion of guards, which is reckoned a very good thing.

As to news, what we have is so incumbered with falsehoods, I think it, as Bobadil[4] says, 'a service of danger' to meddle with: this I know for truth, that the late great Dagon of the people has totally lost all his worshippers, and walks the streets as unregarded as Ignatius Sancho, and I believe almost as poor – such is the stability of popular greatness:

'One self-approving hour whole years outweighs
'Of idle starers, or of loud huzzas,' &c.[5]

Your brother and sister C——d sometimes look in upon us: her boys are fine, well, and thriving; and my honest cousin Joe increases in sense and stature; he promises to be as good, as clever. He brought me your first letter, which, though first wrote, had the fate to come last: the little man came from Red Lion Court to Charles Street by himself, and seemed the taller for what he had done; he is indeed a sweet boy, but I fear every body will be telling him so. I know the folly of so doing, and yet am as guilty as any one.

There is sent out in the Besborough, along with fresh governors, and other strange commodities, a little Blacky, whom you must either have seen or heard of; his name is *Soubise*.[6] He goes out upon a rational well-digested plan, to settle either at Madras or Benegal, to teach fencing and riding – he is expert at both. If he should chance to fall in your way, do not fail to give the rattlepate what wholesome advice you can; but remember, I do strictly caution you against lending him money upon any account, for he has every thing but – principle; he will never pay you; I am sorry to say so much of one whom I have have had a friendship for, but it is needful; serve him if you can – but do not trust him. – There is in the same ship, belonging to the Captain's band of music, one Charles Lincoln,[7] whom I think you have seen in Privy Gardens[8]: he is honest, trusty, good-natured, and civil; if you see him, take notice of him, and I will regard it as a kindness to me. – I have nothing more to say. Continue in right thinking, you will of course act well; in well doing, you will insure the favor of GOD, and the love of your friends, amongst whom pray reckon

Yours faithfully,
IGNATIUS SANCHO.

1. Wrongly dated: the year should almost certainly be 1778 (see Letter 44 n. 1, and Appendix I for reasons). Nor did Sancho live in Charles Street until 1773 (see Letter 2, n. 1 below).
2. Quotation: Alexander Pope, *Moral Essays: Epistle I, To Cobham*, ll. 172–3. Sancho quotes inaccurately. Pope's words are: 'Manners with Fortunes, Humours turn with Climes / Tenets with Books, and Principles with Times.'
3. Mr Rush: John Rush of Bury is the 'Mr. R——' who is the correspondent of many of Sancho's letters. His brother George, a medical man, is also referred to in several letters. However, John Rush's profession is given in Stevenson's index of Sancho's correspondents (Appendix VI) as 'Valet to Sr. Chas. Bunbury'. If it is borne in mind that the barber and

the surgeon were often the same profession at this time, there need be no anomaly. John Rush had also sufficient social standing to be Clerk of the Course at Newmarket, no doubt reflecting Sir Charles Bunbury's influence as a Steward of the Jockey Club and first winner of the Derby – a race of which he was one of the founders (see Fiske, *Oakes Diaries*, vol. II, p. 332; Sir Henry Bunbury, *Correspondence of Sir Thomas Hanmer*, p. 398). Rush's surgeoncy in the Guards would place him on the reserve and not involve him in full-time service.

4. Bobadil: a pretentious blusterer in Ben Jonson's first published play, *Everyman in his Humour* (1598), given as Captain Bobadill in the play's list of characters.

5. Quotation: Alexander Pope, *An Essay on Man*, Ep. IV, ll. 255–6.

6. Soubise, see Appendix I, n. 3. Julius Soubise, a favourite of the Duchess of Queensberry, whom she had educated in fashionable skills, including horsemanship and fencing, but who disgraced himself by sexually assaulting one of her maids, for which he was packed off to Madras. There is a short account of his relationship with Sancho and other London residents in Edwards and Walvin, *Black Personalities*, pp. 223–37; Shyllon, *Black People in Britain*, pp. 41–3.

7. Charles Lincoln, an Afro-Caribbean musician, see Appendix VI. For fuller detail, also Letter 22, n. 2.

8. Privy Gardens: a wealthy residential part of London, in which stood the London house of the Duke and Duchess of Montagu and its grounds (see Letter 26, n. 2).

2

TO MR. M'[EHEUX]'.

August 7, 1768.

Lord! what is man? – and what business have such lazy, lousy, paltry beings of a day to form friendships, or to make connexions? Man is an absurd animal – yea, I will ever maintain it – in his vices, dreadful – in his few virtues, silly – religious without devotion – philosophy without wisdom – the divine passion (as it is called) love too oft without affection – and anger without cause – friendship without reason – hate without reflection – knowledge (like Ashley's punch in small quantities) without judgment – and wit without discretion. – Look into old age, you will see avarice joined to poverty – lechery, gout, impotency, like three monkeys, or

London bucks, in a one-horse whisky, driving to the Devil. – Deep politicians with palsied heads and relaxed nerves – zealous in the great cause of national welfare and public virtue – but touch not – oh! touch not the pocket – Friendship – religion – love of country – excellent topics for declamation! – but most ridiculous chimera to suffer either in money or ease – for, trust me, my *Meheux*, I am resolved upon a reform. – Truth, fair Truth, I give thee to the wind! – Affection, get thee hence! Friendship, be it the idol of such silly chaps, with aching heads, strong passions, warm hearts, and happy talents, as of old used to visit Charles Street,[1] and now abide in fair G——h House.[2]

I give it under my hand and mark, that the best recipe for your aching head (if not the only thing which will relieve you) is cutting off your hair – I know it is not the *ton*; but when ease and health stand on the right – ornament and fashion on the left – it is by no means the Ass between two loads of hay – why not ask counsel about it? Even the young part of the faculty were formerly obliged to submit to amputation, in order to look wise. – What they sacrificed to appearances, do thou to necessity. – Absalom had saved his life, but for his hair. You will reply, 'Caesar would have been drowned, but his length of hair afforded hold to the friendly hand that drew him to shore.' Art, at this happy time, imitates nature so well in both sexes, that in truth our own growth is but of little consequence. Therefore, my dear *Meheux*, part with you hair and headachs together; – and let us see you spruce, well shorn, easy, gay, debonnair – as of old.

I have made inquiry after L——'s letter. My friend *Rush* went to demand the reason for omitting to publish it, and to reclaim the copy. The publisher smiled at him, and bid him examine the M. C. of J. 13,[3] where he would find L. and the same paper of the 20th instant, where he would also find P—— B——'s very angry answer. – Indeed the poor fellow foams again, and appears as indecently dull as malice could with him. I went to the coffee-house to examine the file, and was greatly pleased upon the second reading of your work, in which is blended the Gentleman and the Scholar. Now, observe, if you dare to say I flatter, or mean to flatter, you either impeach my judgment or honesty – at your peril then be it – For your letter of yesterday, I could find in my conscience not to thank you for it – it gave a melancholy tint to every thing about me. Pope had the head-ach vilely – Spenser, I have heard, suffered much from it – in short, it is the ail of true geniuses. – They applied a thick wreath of laurel round their brows – do you the same – and, putting the best foot foremost – duly considering the mansion – what it has suffered through chance, time, and hard use – be thankfully resigned, humble, and say, 'It is well it is no worse!'

I do not wish you to be any other than nice in what new acquaintance you make – As to friendship – it is a mistake – real friendships are not hastily made – friendship is a plant of slow growth, and, like our English oak, spreads, is more majestically beautiful, and increases in shade, strength, and riches, as it increases in years. I pity your poor head, for this confounded scrawl of mine is enough to give the head-ach to the strongest brain in the kingdom – so remember I quit the pen unwillingly, having not said half what I meant; but impelled by conscience, and a due consideration of your ease, I conclude, just wishing you as well as I do my dear self.

Yours,

I. SANCHO.

Your cure in four words, is

CUT—OFF—YOUR—HAIR!

1. Charles Street: Sancho did not move to his shop in the basement of the house at 20 Charles Street until 1773, so the date given this letter by Miss Crewe, 1768, must again be wrong (for further evidence, see Appendix I below). The house on three floors, built *c.* 1750, still stands, though extensively altered in the mid-to-late nineteenth century. The basement is probably still much as it was, structurally, when Sancho lived and kept shop in it. A wall-plaque states that the house was later the home of the 5th Earl of Rosebery (1847–1929). The phrase 'as of old used to visit Charles Street' would indicate a date for the letter much closer to 1780. I suggest below that Sancho might be referring here to former naval seamen wounded in the war and regularly accommodated in Greenwich House, a naval hospital.

2. G——h House: Sancho probably refers here to Greenwich Hospital, one of the royal palaces. After the Restoration of 1660, the main building, Greenwich Palace, was used as a royal residence by Charles II and William III, but in 1694 it was converted into a naval hospital, which was its function in Sancho's day. Many of its residents would have been black sailors, who made up a considerable number of the seamen on naval vessels. Briton Hammon, author of one of the early

black autobiographies (1760) spent a period there after being
wounded in battle. The Sanchos were hospitable people who
entertained a number of black friends, for instance the
musician Charles Lincoln, and Mrs Sancho's brother John
Osborne. There are several references to gatherings of
London Africans in houses where African servants were
employed, for instance the households of the painters
Gainsborough and Cosway, and that of Dr Johnson. No
doubt similar gatherings took place at Charles Street, and
might well have included a number of the naval seamen, in
whose welfare Sancho is known to have been much concerned (see Letter 42a to *The General Advertiser*).

3. 'M. C. of J 13 ... angry answer': Sancho probably refers to
the *Morning Chronicle*; the month signified by 'J' is most
likely June or July. Unfortunately it has proved impossible
to trace relevant copies of the *Morning Chronicle*, so the
subject of L——'s letter, and P——B——'s answer, remain
a mystery. 'The publisher' to whom Sancho refers is
probably William Woodfall (1746–1803), newspaper reporter
and drama critic who edited the *Morning Chronicle* from
1774 to 1789. Woodfall was renowned for his amazing feats
of memory, and perhaps Sancho's letter records just such
a feat: when confronted by Rush, who demanded reasons
why L——'s letter had not been published, 'the publisher
smiled' (smugly, perhaps?), apparently quite certain not only
that the letter in question, and a response to it, had been
published, but also certain of the names and dates involved.
Woodfall's DNB entry records that he could listen to
a speech and then accurately transcribe it. His acts of
memory became so well-known that during a trip to Dublin
crowds followed him in the streets because he was supposed
to be 'endowed with supernatural powers'. Near the end of
his life Woodfall was an unsuccessful candidate for the office
of city remembrancer.

3

TO MR. M'[EHEUX]'.

Sept. 17, 1768.

I am uneasy about your health – I do not like your silence – let some
good body or other give me a line, just to say how you are – I will, if
I can, see you on Sunday; – it is a folly to like people and call them
friends, except they are blest with health and riches. – A very
miserable undone poor wretch, who has no portion in this world's

goods but honesty and good-nature, has a child to maintain, and is very nearly in a state of nature in the article of covering, has applied to me. – I do know something of her – No greater crime than poverty and nakedness. – Now, my dear Meheux, I know you have a persuasive eloquence among the women – try your oratorical powers. – You have many women – and I am sure there must be a great deal of charity amongst them – Mind, we ask no money – only rags – mere literal rags – patience is a ragged virtue – therefore strip the girls, dear Meheux, strip them of what they can spare – a few superfluous worn-out garments – but leave them pity – benevolence – the charities – goodness of heart – love – and the blessings of yours truly with affection, or something very like it,

I. SANCHO.

4

TO MR. M'[EHEUX]'.

Sept. 20, 1768.

Oh! my Meheux, what a feast! to a mind fashioned as thine is to gentle deeds! – could'st thou have beheld the woe-worn object of thy charitable care receive the noble donation of thy blest house! – the lip quivering, and the tongue refusing its office, thro' joyful surprize – the heart gratefully throbbing – overswelled with thankful sensations – I could behold a field of battle, and survey the devastations of the Devil, without a tear – but a heart o'ercharged with gratitude, or a deed begotten by sacred pity – as thine of this day – would melt me, altho' 'unused to the melting mood.'[1] As to thy noble, truly noble, Miss ——, I say nothing – she serves a master – who can and will reward her as amply – as her worth exceeds the common nonsensical dolls of the age; – but for thy compeers, may they never taste any thing less in this world – than the satisfaction resulting from heaven-born Charity! and in the next may they and you receive that blest greeting —— 'Well done, thou good and faithful,'[2] &c. &c. Tell your girls that I will kiss them twice in the same place – troth, a poor reward; – but more than that – I will respect them in my heart, amidst the casual foibles of worldly prejudice and common usage. – I shall look to their charitable hearts, and that shall spread a crown of glory over every transient defect – The poor woman brings this in her hand; – she means to thank you – your noble L——, your good girls – her benefactors – her saviours. I too would thank – but that I know the opportunity I have afforded you of doing what you best love, makes you the obliged party – the obliger,

Your faithful friend,
I. SANCHO.

1. *Othello*: Act 5, Sc. 2, l. 345.
2. Matthew: xxv: 21.

5

TO MR. K'[ISBY]'.

Richmond, Oct. 20, 1769.

What, my honest friend K*isby*,[1] I am heartily glad to see you, quoth I – long look'd for, come at last. – Well, we will have done with that; – you have made ample amends for your silence – have approved yourself, what I ever esteemed you – an honest hearty good lad. – As to your apologizing about your abilities for writing – 'tis all hum[2] – you write sense; – and verily, my good friend, he that wishes to do better must be a coxcomb. – You say you was thrown from your horse but once – in my conscience I think once full oft enough – I am glad, however, you escaped so well. – The description of your journey I return you thanks for – it pleased me much – and proved that you looked rather farther than your horse's head. – A young man should turn travel – home – leisure – or employment – all to the one grand end of improving himself: – from your account of Dalkeith, I now view it 'in my mind's eye,' (as Hamlet says) and think it a delightful spot. – I was wrong, I find, in my notions of the Edinburghers – for I judged them the grand patterns for – cleanliness – politeness – and generosity. Your birth-day entertainments[3] made a blaze in our papers, which said, amongst other things, that the puncheons of rum stood as thick in your park as the trees – Oh! how I licked my lips, and wished the distance (400 miles) less between us – You do not say a word about coming back again. – Poor Pat has paid his last debt – peace and bliss to his spirit! rest to his bones! – his wife and daughter (both with child) and his youngest child all came down;[4] – what a scene had I to be spectator of! – Trust me, James, I cry'd like a whipt school-boy – But then my noble master – Great God! reward him! – Tell me not of ninety covers – splendour – and feasting – to wipe away the tears of distress, to make the heart of the widow to sing for joy. – May such actions ever (as they have long been) be the characteristic of the good Duke of Montagu![5] Dr. James, thy favourite, twice came here; – at his first visit he gave no hope – the next day he came, and poor Pat had resigned up his spirit two hours before he got here. – His Grace paid him the tribute, the rich tribute, of many tears – and ordered me to get a lodging for his widow and children. – In the evening he ordered me to go to them from him – and acquaint Mrs. W—— how very sensible he was of her great loss, as well as his own – that he would ever be a friend to her – and as to the boy – though he was perfectly well satisfied with his conduct in his place – yet, if he would like any trade better than continuing his servant – he would put him out, and support him through his apprenticeship; – and he would give him a year to consider it. – Pat has chose to stay, and his Grace promises whoever uses him ill shall be no servant here. – On the night of his interment, after all was over, the Duke wrote to the widow himself, and enclosed a twenty-pound bill – and repeated his promises. – Your own heart, my dear James, will make the best comment – which is grandest – one such action – or ten birth-days – though in truth the latter has its merit; – it creates business, and helps the poor. – I suppose you will expect me to say something of our family. Her Grace, I am truly sorry to say it, has been but poorly for some time – and indeed is but indifferent now – God of his mercy grant her better health! and every good that can contribute to her happiness. – The good Marquis[6] is with us, and has been ever since you left us. – Are not your tired? This is a deuced long letter. – Well, one word more, and then farewell. Mrs. M—— is grown generous – has left off swearing and modelling. S—— is turned Jew,[7] and is to be circumcised next passover. W—— is turned fine gentleman – and left off work – and I your humble friend, I am for my sins turned Methodist.[8] – Thank God! we are all pretty hobbling as to health. Dame Sancho[9] will be much obliged to you for your kind mention of her – she and the brats are very well, thank Heaven! Abraham gives up the stockings – and monkey Tom his box – They both, with all the rest, join in love and best wishes to your worship. – I, for my own share, own myself obliged to you, and think myself honoured in your acknowledging yourself my pupil. – Were I an ambitious man, I should never forgive you, – for in truth you by far excel your master. – Go on, and prosper, 'Render unto Cæsar the things which are Cæsar's' – laugh at all the tall boys in the kingdom. – I rest, dear Jemmy, thy true friend and obliged fellow servant,

I. SANCHO.

1. James Kisby, Sancho's friend and 'fellow servant' at Richmond, the residence of the Duke and Duchess of Montagu, having travelled north to Dalkeith, does not 'say a word about coming back again'. He appears to be temporarily employed at Dalkeith House, the family home of Henry, 3rd Duke of Buccleuch, and his wife Elizabeth, one of the Montagu daughters, who had given birth, in London, on 21 May 1769 to a child, Lady Mary, mentioned in Letter 9 (for details see James Balfour Paul, *The Scots Peerage*, vol. II, pp. 242–3). Kisby had probably been sent by the Montagus to accompany their daughter the Duchess and her baby on their journey from London to Dalkeith House. This took place a year before Sancho's own visit to Dalkeith, described in Letters 9 and 11, so he views Dalkeith 'in my mind's eye' as Hamlet says, (*Hamlet*, Act 1, Sc. 2, ll. 184–5): that is, in his imagination. Sancho is writing to tell Kisby news of his fellow-servants in the Montagu household at Richmond. The letter and its sense may not be wholly clear to the reader, as it is personal, about friends of Sancho and Kisby who served in the Montagu household. A servant, Pat W——, had died and the Duke of Montagu is concerned to ensure the welfare of the bereaved family. He has offered the dead man's son, also called Pat, the chance of an apprenticeship to a skilled trade, though the Duke is 'perfectly well satisfied with his conduct in his place' i.e. as a household servant. However, young Pat, 'the boy', has decided to stay on in service at Richmond. Apart from Mrs Sancho, others named in the letter, such as monkey Tom and Abraham, cannot be identified and appear to be fellow-servants.
2. 'A hum': a humbug, nonsense.
3. 'Birth-day entertainments': celebrations at Dalkeith House of the birth of Lady Mary to the Duke and Duchess of Buccleuch.
4. 'All came down': all fell sick.
5. This is oddly expressed, but it appears to mean that the Duke of Montagu has been equally generous in his arrangement of a funeral feast, to cheer the widow, after the death of 'poor Pat', as the ninety covers (i.e. the provision of ninety places for guests) at the Dalkeith birthday party which Kisby

mentioned in his letter to Sancho. Elsewhere, Sancho
suggests that mourning is inconsistent with the Christian
message, and that a celebration ought to be part of the
human response to a death – see his own response to that of
his daughter Kitty; though deeply distressed by Kitty's death
in a letter of 9 March, by 11 March he writes, 'Poor Kitty!
happy Kitty I should say, drew her rich prize early – with
her joy!' and adds that 'tomorrow night' he has invited Mrs
Sancho's brother John Osborne to Charles Street, with a few
friends, 'We intend to be merry' (Letters 87 and 88).

6. The good Marquis: Lord Monthermer, son of the Duchess of
   Montagu. See Letter 7 for his death.

7. Like the names Abraham and Tom, the names given as initial
   letters I have not been able to identify. They refer to friends
   or fellow servants.

8. Sancho had begun to attend Methodist worship and became
   a regular member of the congregation at the fashionable
   Charlotte Chapel of Dr Dodd at Pimlico (Letter 16, n. 3.) In
   Letter 11 he declares himself 'half a Methodist', and confes-
   ses to having been influenced by the preaching of Erasmus
   Middleton, then in Dalkeith, one of the 'St Edmund
   Martyrs' expelled from Oxford for over-zealous evangelical
   preaching. See Letter 11, n. 2.

9. Dame Sancho: Sancho married Ann Osborne, a West Indian
   woman, in the Church of St Margaret's, Westminster, the
   parish church of the House of Commons, on 17 December
   1758. The marriage certificate shows Sancho's full name as
   Charles Ignatius Sancho. We know that near the end of her
   life Ann was living at Great Audley Street. She died aged 84,
   and was buried on 25 November 1817, probably laid to rest
   by her husband's side in Westminster Broadway.

6

TO MRS. F——.

Richmond, Oct. 20, 1769.

I sent you a note in Mrs. Sancho's name this day fortnight
– importing that she would hope for the pleasure of seeing you at
Richmond before the fine weather takes its leave of us. – Neither
hearing from nor seeing you – though expecting you every day – we
fear that you are not well – or that Mr. F—— is unhappily ill. – In
either case we shall be very sorry – but I will hope you are all well
– and that you will return an answer by the bearer of this that you
are so – and also when we may expect to have the pleasure of seeing

you; – there is half a bed at your service. – My dear Mrs. Sancho, thank God! is greatly mended. Come, do come, and see what a different face she wears now – to what she did when you kindly proved yourself her tender, her assisting tender friend. – Come and scamper in the meadows with three rugged wild girls. Come and pour the balm of friendly converse into the ear of my sometimes low-spirited love! Come, do come, and come soon, if you mean to see autumn in its last livery. – Tell your coachman to drive under the hill to Mr. B——'s on the common, where you will be gladly received by the best half of your much and greatly obliged friend,

IGN. SANCHO.

7

TO EDWARD YOUNG, ESQ.
On the Death of Lord Monthermer, Son to the Duke of Montagu.
Richmond, April 21, 1770.

HONORED SIR,
I bless God, their Graces continue in good health, though as yet they have not seen any body – I have duly acquainted his Grace with the anxious and kind enquiries of yourself and other of his noble friends. – Time will, I hope, bring them comforts. Their loss is great indeed; and not to them only. The public have a loss – Goodness – Wisdom – Knowledge – and Greatness – were united in him. Heaven has gained an Angel; but earth has lost a treasure. Hoping you are as well as you wish your friends, I am, honored Sir,

Your most obedient and grateful
humble servant to command,
I. SANCHO.

8

March 21, 1770.

'He, who cannot stem his anger's tide,
'Doth a wild horse without a bridle ride.'[1]

It is, my dear M*eheux*, the same with the rest of our passions; – we have Reason given us for our rudder – Religion is our sheet-anchor – our fixed star Hope – Conscience our faithful monitor – and Happiness the grand reward; – we all in this manner can preach up trite maxims: – ask any jackass the way to happiness – and like me they will give vent to picked-up common-place sayings – but mark how they act – why just as you and I do – content with acknowledging a slight acquaintance with Wisdom, but ashamed of appearing to act under her sacred guidance. – You do me much more honor than I deserve, in wishing to correspond with me – the balance is entirely in your favor – but I fancy you were under the malady of your country, hypp'd[2] for want of fresh air and exercise – so sitting in a pensive attitude, with lack-lustre eye, and vacant countenance – the thought obtruded on your fancy to give Sancho a letter – and after a hard conflict 'twixt laziness and inclination – the deed was done. – I verily believe you commit errors – only for the sake of handsomely apologizing for them, as tumblers oft make slips to surprise beholders with their agility in recovering themselves. – I saw Mr. B—— last night – who by the way I like much – the Man I mean – and not the Genius (tho' of the first rate) – he chatted and laughed like a soul ignorant of evil. He asked about a motley creature at ——. I told him with more truth than wit – that you was hypp'd. – I enclose you a proof print: – and how does Mad. M——, &c. &c.? Is Miss S—— better? – is Mrs. H——, Mrs. T——, Mrs. H——.[3] Lord preserve me! what in the name of mischief have I to do with all this combustible matter? Is it not enough for me that I am fast sliding down the vale of years? Have not I a gout? six brats, and a wife? – Oh! Reason, where art thou? You see by this how much easier it is to preach than to do – But stop – we know good from evil; and, in serious truth, we have powers sufficient to withstand vice, if we will choose to exert ourselves. In the field, if we know the strength and situation of the enemy, we place out-posts and sentinels – and take every prudent method to avoid surprise. In common life we must do the same; – and trust me, my honest friend, a victory gained over passion, immortality, and pride, deserve *To Deums*, better than those gained in the fields of ambition and blood. – Here's letter for letter, and so farewell.

Yours – as you behave,

I. SANCHO.

1. Quotation: Colley Cibber, in *Love's Last Shift*, Act 2, Sc. 7. Equiano quotes almost identically, *Interesting Narrative* (1789) vol. II, p. 210, and may have found it in Sancho, though the expression was proverbial, and a commonplace.
2. Hypped: melancholy.
3. I have not been able to identify the people designated by these initials, like many others in these letters. Of the two called Mrs. H——, one, a regular correspondent of Sancho, appears to be a servant in the Montagu household, and possibly mother of the Miss H—— ('Kate' in Letter 12) with whom Kisby is in love in Letter 9.

9

TO MR. K'[ISBY]'.

Dalkeith, July 16, 1770.

Sunday.

Alive! alive ho! – my dear boy, I am glad to see you. – Well, and how goes it? – Badly, sayest thou – no conversation, no joy, no felicity! – Cruel absence, thou lover's hell! what pangs, what soulfelt pangs, dost thou inflict! – Cheer up, my child of discretion – and comfort yourself that every day will bring the endearing moment of meeting, so much nearer – chew the cud upon rapture in reversion – and indulge your fancy with the sweet food of intellectual endearments; paint in your imagination the thousand graces of your H——,[1] and believe this absence a lucky trial of her constancy. – I don't wonder the cricket match yielded no amusement all sport is dull, books unentertaining – Wisdom's self but folly – to a mind under Cupidical influence. – I think I behold you with supple-jack[2] in hand – your two faithful happy companions by your side – complimenting like courtiers every puppy they meet – yourself with eyes fixed in lover-like rumination – and arms folded in sorrow's knot – pace slowly thro' the meadows. – I have done – for too much truth seldom pleases folks in love. – We came home from our Highland excursion last Monday night, safe and well – after escaping manifold dangers. – Mesdames H——, D——, and self, went in the post-coach, and were honor'd with the freedom of Dumbarton. By an overset the ladies shewed their – delicacy – and I my activity* – Mr. B—— his humanity; – all was soon to rights – nothing broke – and no one hurt – and laughter had its fill. – Inverary is a charming place – the beauties various – and the whole plan majestic; – there are some worthy souls on the spot, which I admire more than the buildings and prospects. – We had herrings in perfection – and would have had mackarel; but the scoundrels were too sharp for us – and would not be caught. The Loch-Loman – Ben-loman – Domiquith – and Arsenhoe – with Hamilton and Douglas houses – are by much too long for description by letter. – We paraded to Edinburgh last Friday in a post-coach and four; – H—— D——, Mrs. M——, house-keeper, and self, were the party; – we saw the usual seeings, and dined at Lord Chief Baron's, but – dare I tell you? – H——'s figure attracted universal admiration. – True! – Alas, poor *Kisby*! – but, man, never fret – my honesty to a rotten egg – we bring her home sound. – We read a shocking account in the papers of a storm of rain at Richmond Gardens, and distress, &c. &c. – Is it true? If so, why did you not mention it? H—— sends her service to you, M—— his best respects – and all their best wishes to you and birds. – Your confounded epistle cost me seven pence; – deuce take you, why did not you enclose it? – So you do not like Eloisa – you are a noddy for that – read it till you do like it. – I am glad you have seen Cymon:[3] – that you like it – does but little credit to your taste – for every body likes it. – I can afford you no more time – for I have three letters to write besides this scrawl. – I hear nothing of moving as yet – pray God speed us southward! though we have fine weather – fine beef – fine ale – and fine ladies.

Lady Mary grows a little angel; – the Duchess gets pretty round – they all eat – drink – and seem pure merry – and we are all out of mourning this day[4] – farewell.

Yours, &c. &c.
I. SANCHO.

* Mr. Sancho was remarkably unwieldy and inactive, and never gave a greater proof of it than at this overset, when he and a goose-pye were equally incapable of raising themselves.

1. Now Kisby is in Richmond, and Sancho in Dalkeith, the
   situation of Letter 5 is reversed. Sancho has travelled north
   to the Scottish Highlands with some of his fellow servants,
   with one of whom, Miss H——, Kisby is in love, and whose
   figure, Sancho with mock sympathy tells the lovelorn Kisby,
   has in Edinburgh 'attracted universal admiration. – True!
   – Alas, poor Kisby.' It is not made clear by the letter. Why
   Sancho and the others had gone from Richmond to Dalkeith.
   Sancho does not expect a long visit: 'I hear nothing of
   moving as yet – pray God speed us southward! though we
   have fine weather – fine beef – fine ale – and fine ladies.' But
   the reason for the visit is almost certainly that the Montagu's
   daughter Elizabeth, Duchess of Buccleuch, is pregnant again,
   'pretty round', and already has a growing child to care for,
   Lady Mary, who had been born at the Montagu London
   residence on 21 May 1769. The second daughter, Elizabeth,
   with whom the Duchess was pregnant, was also to be born in
   London, on 10 October 1770, so the entourage may well
   have been sent by the Montagus to Dalkeith to accompany
   her to London for the birth. Moreover, as Sancho describes
   it, the visit seems more like a holiday, and since Miss Crewe's
   footnote to the letter tells us that he was already suffering
   seriously from the health problems which were to incapaci-
   tate him for his work by 1773, and plans were already being
   hinted at the following year in Letter 12 to give him
   assistance, and made explicit in Letter 16, with a view to his
   retiral, the visit to Dalkeith may have been intended not just
   as a household duty, but as something of a vacation for an
   ailing, elderly retainer, who would have known the Duchess
   from her childhood, and was himself conveniently acquainted with pregnancies from his own domestic experience, and so likely to provide mature advice and a beneficial
   influence.
2. Supple-Jack: a tropical climbing plant, in this case a walking
   stick made from one.
3. Pope, *'Eloisa to Abelard'*; possibly Dryden, *'Cymon and
   Iphigenia'* in *Fables*, though see 'Cymon' in Letter 84.
4. 'All out of mourning': see Letter 7. The son of the Montagus,
   Lord Monthermer, had died earlier in the year.

10

TO MISS L——.[1]

August 31, 1770.

Do not you condemn me for the very thing that you are guilty of yourself; – but before I recriminate – let me be grateful, and acknowledge that heart-felt satisfaction which I ever feel from the praise of the good. – Sterne says, Every worthy mind loves praise – and declares that he loves it too – but then it must be sincere. – Now I protest that you have something very like flattery; – no matter – I honestly own it pleases me – Vanity is a shoot from self-love – and self-love, Pope declares to be the spring of motion in the human breast. – Friendship founded upon right judgement takes the good and bad with the indulgence of blind love; – nor is it wrong – for, as weakness and error is the lot of humanity, real friendship must oft kindly overlook the undesigning frailties of undisguised nature. – My dear Madam, I beg ten thousand pardons for the dull sermon I have been preaching: – you may well yawn. So the noble! the humane! the patron! the friend! the good Duke leaves Tunbridge on Monday – true nobility will leave the place with him – and kindness and humility will accompany Miss L—— whenever she thinks fit to leave it. – Mrs. Sancho is pretty well, pretty round, and pretty tame! – she bids me say, Thank you, in the kindest manner possibly can – and observe, I say, Thank you kindly. – I will not pretend to enumerate the many things you deserve our thanks for: – you are upon the whole an estimable young woman – your heart is the best part of you – may it meet with its likeness in the man of your choice! – and I will pronounce you a happy couple. – I hope to hear in your next – (that is, if –) that you are about thinking of coming to town – no news stirring but politics – which I deem very unfit for ladies. – I shall conclude with John Moody's[2] prayer – 'The goodness of goodness bless and preserve you!' – I am dear Miss L——'s most sincere servant and friend,

IGN. SANCHO.

1. Miss L——: Lydia Leach. Her first name is Lydia since she is said to be the namesake of Sancho's daughter Lydia, Letter 20, n. 2. We can be fairly certain that Lydia's second name is Leach on the basis of baptismal records giving the full name of the Sancho's son William (Billy) as William Leach Osborne Sancho (see Appendix VII). William was given his

mother's maiden name, Osborne, and an additional name,
Leach, specifically identifying William's godmother, Miss
L——, Lydia Leach. It was common in the eighteenth
century to name children after godparents; in Letter 32,
addressed to Miss L——, little William is affectionately
referred to by Sancho as 'your foolish godson' and in Letter
33, again to Miss L——, Sancho gives a full report of
William's progress: 'He is the type of his father, fat, heavy,
sleepy, but, as he is the heir of the noble family, and your
godson, I ought not disparage him.' The name Leach occurs
in the St Margaret's registers and we know from Sancho's
letters that Miss L——'s family came from Tunbridge Wells
though an extensive study of the parish registers is required
to place the Leach family more firmly.

2. John Moody (1727?–1812): an actor and friend of Garrick.

11

TO MR. S'[IMO]'N.

Dalkeith, Sept. 15, 1770.

It was kindly done of my worthy old friend to give me the
satisfaction of hearing he was well and happy. – Believe me I very
often think of and wish to be with you; – without malice, I envy you
the constant felicity of being with worthy good children – whose
regards and filial tenderness to yourself – and christian behaviour to
each other – reflect honor to themselves and credit to you – But the
thing I have much at heart you are provokingly silent about – is my
sweet Polly married yet? has she made Mr. H—— happy? May they
both enjoy every comfort God Almighty blesses his children with!
And how comes it my dear Tommy does not give me a line? I hope
he is well – hearty – and happy, and honest downright Sally also;
– tell Tommy he has disappointed me in not writing to me. – I hope
Mrs. Sancho will be as good as her word, and soon pay you a visit.
– I will trust her with you, though she is the treasure of my soul.
– We have been a week in the Highlands, and a fine country it is.
– I hear nothing of coming home as yet – but I fancy it will not be
long now. – Mrs. H—— sends her love to you and yours – and I my
double love to self and the four young ones – with my best wishes
and respects to Mrs. B*unbury*,[1] tell her I am half a Methodist; – here
is a young man preaches here; one of those five who were expelled
from Oxford[2] – his name is M*iddleto*n, he has a good strong voice

– much passion – and preaches three times a day – an hour and a half each time; – he is well-built – tall – genteel – a good eye – about twenty-five – a white hand, and a blazing ring – he has many converts amongst the ladies; – I cannot prevail on Mrs. H—— to go and hear him – I have been four or five times, and heard him this day – his text was the epistle in the communion service. – I am, dear friend, yours sincerely, and all your valuable family's sincere well-wisher – and, were it in my power, I would add friend,

IGNATIUS SANCHO.

Their Graces are all well – and lady Mary grows every day – she is a sweet child. – Remember me to Mrs.——, and tell her Mrs. M—— is quite the woman of fashion: – she is pretty well in every thing except her eyes, which are a little inflamed with cold – and she does not forget they are so. Once more my cordial love to the girls, and to the worthies Tommy, Mr. H—— B—— and self. Adieu.

1. Mrs Bunbury: in 1771, as Catherine Horneck, she had married the artist Henry William Bunbury, younger brother of Sir (Thomas) Charles Bunbury, by whom Sancho's correspondents Mr Browne, Mr Rush and Mr Simon were employed, see Appendix VI. She and her sister Mary were 'The Horneck sisters painted as the Merry Wives of Windsor' by Daniel Gardner, see Letter 22, n. 4. Her husband was to engrave the vignette for the title page of Willliam Sancho's fifth edition of the Letters, see Appendix III. Oliver Goldsmith, in response to what he saw as an impertinent poem contained in a letter from her, which, he said, 'raises my indignation beyond the bounds of prose [and] inspires me at once with verse and resentment'. He included the poem in the letter; see 'Letter to Mrs Bunbury' in Arthur Friedman (ed.) *Collected Works of Oliver Goldsmith*, vol. IV, pp. 401–5. She is also referred to as 'Little Comedy' in Goldsmith's 'Verses in Reply to an Invitation to Dinner at Sir George Baker's' (Friedman, *Goldsmith*, vol. IV, pp. 384–5). Baker was friend and physician of Sir Joshua Reynolds. Sir Charles Bunbury is also mentioned in the 'Letter to Mrs Bunbury'. It is likely that Sancho met the Bunburys though Garrick, a friend and admirer of Henry William Bunbury the artist (see bibliography, Sir Thomas William Bunbury (ed.), *The Correspondence of Sir Thomas Hanmer* (1838) pp. 375–8).

2. 'Those five who were expelled from Oxford ... M.': the

reference is to what was called the St Edmund Hall Massacre. Six, not five students were sent down from St Edmund Hall for being over zealous in their Methodist evangelism. One of them was Erasmus Middleton (see J. S. Reynolds, *The Evangelicals at Oxford, 1735–1871*, (Blackwell, Oxford, 1953), pp. 34–42). I must thank my friend Professor Andrew Walls, of the Centre for the Study of Christianity in the Non-Western World, New College, Edinburgh, for this information. There is a fine account in Boswell's *Life* of Johnson's response to the expulsion:

> I talked of the recent expulsion of six students from the University of Oxford, who were Methodists, and would not desist from publickly praying and exhorting. JOHNSON. 'Sir, that expulsion was extremely just and proper. What have they to do at an University who are not willing to be taught, but will presume to teach? Where is religion to be learnt but at an University? Sir, they were examined and found to be mighty ignorant fellows.' BOSWELL. 'But, was it not hard, Sir, to expel them, for I am told they were good beings? 'JOHN-SON. 'Sir, I believe they might be good beings; but they were not fit to be in the University of Oxford. A cow is a very good animal in the field; but we turn her out of a garden.' Lord Elibank used to repeat this as an illustration uncommonly happy. (ed. R.W. Chapman, p. 490, 15 April 1772)

12

TO MRS. H——.

Richmond, Dec. 22, 1771.

You cannot conceive the odd agreeable mixture of pleasure and pain I felt on the receipt of your favor; – believe me, good friend, I honor and respect your nobleness of principle[1] – but at the same time greatly disapprove of your actions. – My dear Madam, bribery and corruption are the reigning topics of declamation; – and here, because I happen to be a well-wisher, you are loading us with presents. – One word for all, my good Mrs. H—— must not be offended when I told her it hurts my pride – for pride I have too much, God knows – I accept your present this time – and do you accept dame Sancho's and my thanks – and never aim at sending aught again. – Your daughter Kate brought me your letter – she

seemed a little surprised at my being favor'd with your correspondence – and I am sure wished to see the contents. – As I from my soul
honor filial feelings – it hurt me not to gratify her honest curiosity
– but I do not chuse to let her know any thing of the matter – to save
her the anxiety of hope and fear. She is very well, and rules over us
not with an iron sceptre – but a golden one – We tell her we love her
too well – in truth I can never return her a tithe of the kindnesses
she has shewn my family – But what's all this to you? – I shall tire
you with a jargon of nonsense, therefore I shall only wish you all
many happy returns of this season – good stomachs – good cheer
– and good fires. My kind remembrance to Madam Tilda – tell her, if
she's a good girl, I will try to recommend her to Mr. G—— the
painter,[2] for a wife; – he is really, I believe, a first-rate genius – and,
what's better, he is a good young man – and I flatter myself will do
honor to his science and credit to his friends. – Kitty looks like the
Goddess of Health – I am sure every drop of blood in her honest
heart beats for the welfare and happiness of her parents. – Believe
me ever your obliged servant and friend,

I. SANCHO.

1. In view of Sancho's next letter to Mrs H——, Letter 16,
   November 1773, the year Sancho was forced to retire
   because of ill-health, and opened his grocer's shop, it sounds
   from this letter as if the Montagus' plans to finance his
   retirement are already in progress through the good offices
   of Mrs H—— and her daughter Kate, another servant in the
   Montagu household, perhaps the Miss H—— with whom
   Kisby was in love according to Letter 9.
2. Mr G—— the painter: perhaps Daniel Gardner, see Letter
   22, n. 4.

13

TO MR. B'[ROWNE]'.
London, July 18, 1772.

MY DEAR FRIEND,
Nothing could possibly be more welcome than the favor of your
truly obliging letter, which I received the day before yesterday.
– Know, my worthy young man – that it's the pride of my heart
when I reflect that, thro' the favor of Providence, I was the humble

means of good to so worthy an object. – May you live to be a credit to your great and good friends, and a blessing and comfort to your honest parents! – May you, my child, pursue, through God's mercy, the right paths of humility, candour, temperance, benevolence – with an early piety, gratitude, and praise to the Almighty Giver of all your good – gratitude – and love for the noble and generous benefactors his providence has so kindly moved in your behalf! – Ever let your actions be such as your own heart can approve – always think before you speak, and pause before you act – always suppose yourself before the eyes of Sir William[1] – and Mr. Garrick. – To think justly – is the way to do rightly – and by that means you will ever be at peace within. – I am happy to hear Sir W—— cares so much about your welfare – his character is great – because it is good. – As to your noble friend Mr. Garrick – his virtues are above all praise – he has not only the best head in the world, but the best heart also; – he delights in doing good. – Your father and mother called on me last week, to shew me a letter which Mr. Garrick has wrote to you – keep it, my dear boy, as a treasure beyond all price – it would do honor to the pen of a divine – it breathes the spirit of father – friend – and christian! – indeed I know no earthly being that I can reverence so much as your exalted and noble friend and patron Mr. Garrick. – Your father and mother, I told you, I saw lately – they were both well, and their eyes overflowed at the goodness of your noble patrons – and with the honest hope you would prove yourself not unworthy of their kindness.

I thank you for your kindness to my poor black brethren – I flatter myself you will find them not ungrateful – they act commonly from their feelings: – I have observed a dog will love those who use him kindly – and surely, if so, negroes, in their state of ignorance and bondage, will not act less generously, if I may judge them by myself – I should suppose kindness would do any thing with them; – my soul melts at kindness – but the contrary – I own with shame – makes me almost a savage. – If you can with conveniency – when you write again – send me half a dozen cocoa nuts, I shall esteem them for your sake – but do not think of it if there is the least difficulty. – In regard to wages I think you acted quite right – don't seek too hastily to be independent – it is quite time enough yet for one of your age to be your own master. – Read Mr. Garrick's letter night and morning – put it next your heart – impress it on your memory – and may the God of all Mercy give you grace to follow his friendly dictates! – I shall ever truly rejoice to hear from you – and your well-doing will be a comfort to me ever; – it is not in your own power and option to command riches – wisdom and health are immediately the gift of God – but it is in your own breast to be good – therefore, my dear child, make the only right election – be good, and trust the rest to God; and remember he is about your bed, and about your path, and spieth out all your ways. – I am, with pride and delight,

Your true friend,
IGN. SANCHO.

1. Sir William: according to Stevenson's index, (Appendix VI), Browne was Steward to Sir Charles Bunbury, so this probably refers to the Rev Sir William Bunbury, bart. of Barton, the father of Sir Charles and Henry William Bunbury. That the Bunburys were familiar with Garrick is known from Sir Henry Bunbury (see his *Correspondence of Hanmer*, pp. 375–8), so it is not surprising that Garrick was also familiar with Browne, the Steward of the Bunbury estate.

14

TO MR. S'[OUBIS]'E.

Richmond, Oct. 11, 1772.

Your letter gave me more pleasure than in truth I ever expected from your hands – but thou are a flatterer;[1] – why dost thou demand advice of me? Young man, thou canst not discern wood from trees; – with awe and reverence look up to thy more than parents – look up to thy almost divine benefactors – search into the motive of every glorious action – retrace thine own history – and when you are convinced that they (like the All-gracious Power they serve) go about in mercy doing good – retire abashed at the number of their virtues – and humbly beg the Almighty to inspire and give you strength to imitate them. – Happy, happy lad! what a fortune is thine! – Look round upon the miserable fate of almost all of our unfortunate colour – superadded to ignorance, – see slavery, and the contempt of those very wretches who roll in affluence from our labours. Superadded to this woeful catalogue – hear the ill-bred and heart-racking abuse of the foolish vulgar. – You, *Soubise*, tread as cautiously as the strictest rectitude can guide ye – yet must you suffer from this – but armed with truth – honesty – and conscious integrity – you will be sure of the plaudit and countenance of the good. – If, therefore, thy repentance is sincere – I congratulate thee as sincerely upon it – it is thy birth-day to real happiness. – Providence has been very lavish of her bounty to you – and you are deeply in arrears to her – your parts are as quick as most men's; urge but your speed in the race of virtue with the same ardency of zeal as you have exhibited in error – and you will recover, to the satisfaction of your noble patrons – and to the glory of yourself. – Some philosopher – I forget who – wished for a window in his breast – that the world might see his heart; – he could only be a great fool, or a very good man: – I will believe the latter, and recommend him to your imitation. – Vice is a coward; – to be truly brave, a man must be truly good; – you hate the name of cowardice – then, So*ubise*, avoid it – detest a lye – and shun lyars – be above revenge; – if any have taken advantage either of your guilt or distress, punish them with forgiveness – and not only so – but, if you can serve them any future time, do it – You have experienced mercy and long-sufferance in your own person – therefore gratefully remember it, and shew mercy likewise.

I am pleased with the subject of your last – and if your conversion is real, I shall ever be happy in your correspondence – But at the same time I cannot afford to pay five pence for the honour of your letters;[2] – five pence is the twelfth part of five shillings – the forty-eighth part of a pound – it would keep my girls in potatoes two days. – The time may come, when it may be necessary for you to study calculations; – in the mean while, if you cannot get a frank, direct to me under cover to his Grace the Duke of ——. You have the best wishes of your sincere friend (as long as you are your own friend)

IGNATIUS SANCHO.

You must excuse blots and blunders – for I am under the dominion of a cruel head-ach – and a cough, which seems too fond of me.

1. Soubise had no mean talent for writing, tongue in cheek, a flattering, ironically obsequious letter. This is demon-strated by the sole survivor from his pen: see Edwards and

Dabydeen, *Black Writers in Britain*, pp. 81–2; or Edwards and Walvin, *Black Personalities in the Era of the Slave Trade*, pp. 234–5.

2. Before the days of the modern postal system, the writer paid for a 'frank', an earlier form of postage stamp, when sending a letter by carrier, otherwise the recipient had to pay. Soubise, not a man to pay cash if he could avoid it, had sent Sancho an unfranked letter. Letters could be sent unfranked under cover of the name of a member of one of the Houses of Parliament.

15[1]

TO MR. M'[EHEUX]'.

Nov. 8, 1772.

Bravo! my ingenious friend! – to say you exceed my hopes, would be a lye. – At my first knowledge of you – I was convinced that Providence had been partial in the talents entrusted to you – therefore I expected exertion on your side – and I am not disappointed. Go on, my honest heart, go on! – hold up the mirror to an effeminate gallimawfry – insipid, weak, ignorant, and dissipated set of wretches – and scourge them into shame – The pen – the pencil – the pulpit – oh! may they all unite their endeavours – and rescue this once manly and martial people from the silken slavery of foreign luxury and debauchery – Thou, my worthy M*eheux*, continue thy improvements; and may the Almighty bless thee with the humble mien of plenty and content! – Riches ensnare – the mediocrity is Wisdom's friend – and that be thine! – When you see *Soubise*, note his behaviour – he writes me word that he intends a thorough and speedy reformation. – I rather doubt him, but should be glad to know if you perceive any marks of it. – You do not tell me that you have seen Mr. G——; if you have not, I shall be angry with you – and attribute your neglect to pride. – Pray render my compliments most respectful and sincere to Mrs. H——, and the little innocent laughing rose-bud – My love to my son.[2] – I am heartily tired of the country; – the truth is – Mrs. Sancho and the girls are in town; – I am not ashamed to own that I love my wife – I hope to see you married, and as foolish.

I am yours sincerely, &c. &c.

IGN. SANCHO.

1. This is mis-numbered 14 in the original edition.
2. Sancho's 'love to my son' and 'the innocent laughing rose-bud' may refer to Sancho's first son, Jonathan William, evidence of whose birth has only recently come to light. See Letter 29, n. 3, and Appendix VII. Since Sancho often writes in fatherly fashion to young Meheux, 'love to my son' may simply refer to a friend's child.

16

TO MRS. H——.

Charles Street, Nov. 1, 1773.

MY DEAR AND RESPECTED MADAM,

I have sincere pleasure to find you honor me in your thoughts – To have your good wishes, is not the least strange, for I am sure you possess that kind of soul, that christian philanthropy, which wishes well – and, in the sense of Scripture, breathes peace and good-will to all. – Part of your scheme we mean to adopt – but the principal thing we aim at is in the tea, snuff, and sugar, with the little articles of daily domestic use[1] – In truth, I like your scheme, and I think the three articles you advise would answer exceeding well – but it would require a capital – which we have not – so we mean to cut our coat according to our scanty quantum – and creep with hopes of being enabled hereafter to mend our pace. – Mrs. Sancho is in the straw[2] – she has given me a fifth wench – and your worthy Kate has offered her the honor of standing for her sponsor, but I fear it must be by proxy. – Pray make my respects to Mrs. Matilda – I hope she enjoys every thing that her parents wish her. – shall dine with Mr. Jacob some day this week – I saw him at Dodd's chapel[3] yesterday – and if his countenance is to be believed, he was very well – I could not get at him to speak to him. – As soon as we can get a bit of house, we shall begin to look sharp for a bit of bread – I have strong hope – the more children, the more blessings – and if it please the Almighty to spare me from the gout, I verily think the happiest part of my life is to come – Soap, starch, and blue, with raisins, figs, &c. – we shall cut a respectable figure – in our printed cards.[4] – Pray make my best wishes to Mr. H——;[5] tell him I revere his whole family, which is doing honor to myself. – I had a letter of yours to answer, which I should have done before, had my manners been equal to my esteem. – Mrs. Sancho joins me in respectful love and thanks; I remain ever your much obliged servant to command,

IGNATIUS SANCHO.

1. The question of Sancho's fitness to continue his duties had already been hinted at in Letter 12. Now in 1773, as Jekyll confirms (pp. 23–4), Sancho received aid to set up shop.
2. In the straw: in childbed.
3. Dodd's chapel: William Dodd (1729–77), a popular preacher, had established at his own expense the fashionable Charlotte Chapel, named after the Queen, in Pimlico, London, and soon had a devoted congregation, Sancho being one, for whom Dodd could do no wrong. But Dodd spent lavishly, was involved in several scandals, and in due course was convicted of forgery in an attempt to defraud. For this he was hanged in 1777. The events of his life are given in Percy Fitzgerald, *A Famous Forgery, being the Story of the Unfortunate Dr. Dodd* (London, 1865). See also Letter 24.
4. Dr David Dabydeen has found one of Sancho's trade-cards, reproduced on p. xiv. Under the heading 'Tobacco', there is a note in *Notes and Queries*, VII, viii, p. 33 (1 June 1888) regarding a trade-card for 'Sancho's Best Tobacco'.
5. Mr and Mrs H—— and their daughter Kate, Miss H——, appear to be servants in the Montagu household given responsibility to see through the matter of Sancho's shop. Jacob is their son, a favourite of the Sancho children in later letters.

17

TO MRS. H——.

February 9, 1774.

It is the most puzzling affair in nature, to a mind that labours under obligations, to know how to express its feelings. – Your former tender solicitude for my well-doing – and your generous remembrance in the present order – appear friendly beyond the common actions of those we in general style good sort of people; – but I will not tease you with my nonsensical thanks – for I believe such kind of hearts as you are blest with have sufficient reward in the consciousness of acting humanely. – I opened shop[1] on Saturday the 29th January – and have met with a success truly flattering; – it shall be my study and constant care not to forfeit the good opinion of my friends. – I have pleasure in congratulating you upon Mrs. W——'s happy delivery and pleasing increase of her family; – it is the hope and wish of my heart, that your comforts in all things may multiply with your years – that in the certain great end – you may immerge without pain – full of hope – from corruptible pleasure – to immortal and incorruptible life – happiness without end – and past all human comprehension! – There may you and I – and all we love (or care for) meet! – the follies, the parties, distinctions – feuds of ambition – enthusiasm – lust – and anger of this miserable motley world – all totally forgot – every idea lost and absorbed in the blissful mansions of redeeming love!

I have not seen Sir Jacob[2] near a fortnight – but hope and conclude him well. – *Rush* is well, and grows very fat – An easy mind – full purse – and a good table – great health – and much indulgence – all these conduce terribly to plumpness. – I must beg when you see Mr.——, if not improper or inconvenient, that you will inform him – that where there is but little – every little helps; – I think he is too humane to be offended at the liberty – and too honest to be displeased with a truth. – I am, with grateful thanks to Mr. H——, your sincerely humble servant and poor friend,

I. SANCHO.

My best half and Sanchonetta's are all well.

1. Letters 12 and 16 have shown the part played by the H—— family in the preparations for Sancho's retirement and the opening of his grocer's shop on 29 January 1774, which had already achieved 'a success truly flattering'. But money was always a problem for Sancho – he needed more substantial resources – see Letter 38: 'if we can possibly achieve money – but we have somehow no friends'. Sancho had many friends, of course, but he is thinking here of those who might extend financial support and advice. He was to find such a friend in John Spink the Banker: his first letter to Spink is dated Christmas 1787, see Letter 57, though they probably met earlier through attendance at Dr Dodd's chapel, see Letter 21.

2. Sir Jacob: this cannot refer to Mrs H——'s son, named 'Mr Jacob' in Letter 16. Letter 131 to Mrs H. refers again to 'Sir Jacob', so I assume him to be another member of her family.

18

TO MR. S'[TEVENSON]'.
                                        Charles Street, Nov. 26, 1774.

Young says, 'A friend is the balsam of life' – Shakspeare says, – but
why should I pester you with quotations? – to shew you the depth
of my erudition, and strut like the fabled bird in his borrowed
plumage – In good honest truth, my friend – I rejoice to see thy
name at the bottom of the instructive page – and were fancy and
invention as much my familiar friends as they are thine, I would
write thee an answer – or try, at least, as agreeably easy – and as
politely simple. – Mark that; simplicity is the characteristic of good
writing – which I have learnt, among many other good things, of
your Honor – and for which I am proud to thank you. – In short,
I would write like you – think like you (of course); and do like you;
but as that is impossible, I must content myself with my old trick;
– now what that trick is – thou art ignorant – and so thou shalt
remain – till I congratulate you upon your recovery – *A propos*, you
begun your letter ill, as we do many things in common life; ten days
elapsed before you finished it – consequently you finished it well.
– My dear friend, may you, thro' God's blessing, ever finish happily
what you undertake – however unpromising the beginning may
appear to be! – I want you much in town – for my own sake – that's
a stroke of self-love. – And do you mean to bring any candles up
with you? – that's another! – I do not wonder at your making your
way amongst the folks of Hull – although there are four of the same
profession; – we love variety. – I will give them credit for admiring
the Artist; – but if they – that is two or three of them – have
penetration to look deeper – and love the Man – then I shall believe
that there are souls in Hull. – So – my cramp epistle fell into the
hands of thy good and rev. father[1] – *tant pis* – why he must think me
blacker than I am. – Mons. B—— goes on well: – I suppose you
know he has opened an Academy in St. Alban's Street[2] – at two
guineas a year – naked figures three nights a week – Mr. Mortimer –
and several eminent names upon his list – and room left for yours
– He hops about with that festivity of countenance – which denotes
peace and good-will to man. – I have added to my felicity – or
Fortune more properly has – three worthy friends – they are
admirers and friends of Mortimer and Sterne; – but of this – when
we meet. – You are expected at B*arton* House[3] upon your return
– and I hope you will call on them, if consistent with your time –

and agreeable to you. – My friend L—— is in town, and intends trying his fortune among us – as teacher of murder and neck-breaking – alias – fencing and riding. – The Tartars, I believe, have few fine gentlemen among them – and they can ride – though they have neither fencing nor riding masters; – and as to genteel murder – we are mere pedlars and novices – for they can dispatch a whole caravan – or a horde – and eat and drink – wench and laugh – and, in truth, so far they can match our modern fine gents.; – they have no acquaintance with conscience – But what's all this to you? – nothing – it helps to fill up the sheet – and looks like moralizing; – the good-natured partiality of thy honest heart will deem it – not absolutely nonsense. Alas! – thus it often happens – that the judgement of a good head is – bumfiddled[4] – and wrong biass'd by the weakness of a too kind heart. – Under that same weakness let me shelter my failings and absurdities – and let me boast at this present writing – that my heart is not very depraved – and has this proof of not being dead to virtue; – it beats stronger at the sound of friendship – and will be sincerely attached to *William Stevenson*, Esq. – while its pulsations continue to throb in the breast of your obliged

IGNATIUS SANCHO.

Do pray think about returning – The captain – the girls – the house – the court, stand all – just where they did – when you left them. – Alas! Time leaves the marks of his rough fingers upon all things – Time shrivels female faces – and sours small-beer – gives insignificance, if not impotency, to trunk-hose[5] – and toughness to cow-beef. – Alas! alas! alas! –

1. Some details of Stevenson's father are to be found in Appendix VI. Sancho's Letter 116 is addressed to him.
2. Mons B's Academy in St Albans Street: for Mortimer see Introduction, n. 10.
3. Barton House: or Barton Hall, the Bunbury family residence at Barton, between Mildenhall, Suffolk and Bury St Edmunds.
4. Bumfiddled: a Shandean whimsy for 'befuddled'.
5. Trunk-hose: stuffed breeches which went out of fashion during the previous century. Sancho is adopting his Shandean melancholy pose, and I take it he is saying that even when time fails to make yesterday's man impotent, it still makes him insignificant as well as outdated.

19

TO MRS. C'[OCKSEDGE]'.

Charles Street, July 4, 1775.

DEAR MADAM,

It would be affronting your good-nature to offer an excuse for the trouble I am going to give you – my tale is short. – Mrs. *Osborne*[1] is with us – she was, this day, observing poor Lydia with a good deal of compassion – and said she knew a child cured by roses boiled in new milk; – observed, that you had, at this very time, perhaps bushels of rose-leaves wasting on the ground. – Now my petition is – that you would cause a few of them to be brought you – (they will blush to find their sweetness excelled by your kindness) they are good dried, but better fresh – so when you come to town think of honest Lydia. – Mrs. *Osborne* this morning saw your picture in Bond Street.[2] – She approves much – and I fancy means to sit – she thinks that you enriched me with the strongest likeness – but the whole length the best. – I have the honor to transmit the compliments of Mesdames A*damson*[3] and Sancho – to which permit me to add mine, with the most grateful sensibility for the recent favor of favors. – I am, dear madam,

> Your most obliged
> humble servant,
> IGN. SANCHO.

1. Mrs Osborne was married to Mrs Sancho's brother, a West Indian, see Appendix VI. Lydia is one of the 'Sanchonettas' whose health is a constant source of worry to her parents, for example 'Lydia mends – she walks a little – we begin to encourage hope. Kitty is as lively as ever – and almost goes alone ...' (Letter 21). But it was Kitty who was to die early (Letter 88).

2. 'Your picture in Bond St': possibly at the Osbornes' home in Bond Street (Letter 80), where Sancho's friend Miss L——, also appears to reside (Letters 20, n. 3; 27; 33), and has just had her picture painted, too. There is another connection in Bond Street with the Sancho art circle: it was at Bretherton's well-known print shop at No. 134 that prints of paintings by Mr Bunbury were engraved. The picture of Mrs Cocksedge would be that painted by Mr Gardner (Letter 23) which 'hit off her likeness exceeding well' and is already known to be intended as a gift for Sancho, (Letter 22), 'she thinks that you enriched me with the strongest likeness'. It is to be given

a place of honour over Sancho's mantelpiece. Mrs Osborne is so impressed that she plans to have her own portrait done, 'She approves much – and I fancy means to sit.'

3. Mesdames ... Adamson: The Adamsons were a wealthy family with homes in Bury and London, and were friends of the Bunburys of Barton Hall; see Jane Fiske (ed.), *The Oakes Diaries*, vol. II, pp. 326–7.

20

TO MISS L——.

July 26, 1775.

DEAR MADAM,

I have just now had the pleasure of seeing a gentleman who is honored in calling you sister. – He suspended the pain in my foot for full five minutes, by the pleasing account he gave of your health. – I delivered my charge*[1] safe into his hands – he viewed it with an eye of complacency – from which I conclude he is not unworthy your sister's hand; – we commonly behold those with a sort of partiality – who bring good tidings from our friends – in that view I could not forbear thinking him a very good kind of man. I have to thank you for a very obliging and friendly letter – which I should have done much sooner, could I have complied with your kind wishes in giving a better account of myself. My better self has been but poorly for some time – she groans with the rheumatism – and I grunt with the gout – a pretty concert! – Life is thick-sown with troubles – and we have no right to exemption. – The children, thank God! are well – your name-sake gets strength every day – and trots about amazingly[2]. – I am reading Bossuet's Universal History, which I admire beyond any thing I have long met with: if it lies in your way, I would wish you to read it – if you have not already – and if you have, it is worth a second perusal. Mrs. Sancho rejoices to hear you are well – and intrusts me to send you her best wishes. – I hope you continue your riding – and should like to see your *etiquette* of hat, feather, and habit. – Adieu. – May you enjoy every wish of your benevolent heart – is the hope and prayer of your much obliged humble servant,

IGN. SANCHO.

* Miss L——'s picture.

If the Universal History of Bossuet[3] Bishop of Meaux, and Preceptor to Louis XV. should be difficult to find at Tunbridge – when you return to town, and give us the pleasure of seeing you – he will be exceeding proud of the happiness (and what Frenchman would not? – although a bishop) of riding to Bond Street in your pockets.

1. Sancho is an intermediary through whom a portrait of Miss L—— has been passed on to her brother-in-law, probably because, as a noted judge of the arts, Sancho's favourable opinion of her portrait would have been sought by his friend; and he in turn is pleased that the recipient views the portrait with 'an eye of complacency': that is, with satisfaction and approval.
2. 'Your namesake ... trots about amazingly': Miss L——'s first name was probably Lydia (see Letter 10, n. 1); Lydia herself was named after Sterne's daughter.
3. 'Universal History of Bossuet ... in your pockets': Jacques B. Bossuet (1627–1704), famous French orator and divine, was an important figure at the Court of Louis XIV, and tutor to the Dauphin. He became Bishop of Meaux, and published his *Discours sur l'histoire universelle* in 1681, a providentialist view, arguing divine intervention at all stages of history. A firm believer in divine providence, Sancho himself thought highly of Bossuet. Sancho means here that should Miss L—— be unable to find a copy, he intends to present her with one for her pocket. Miss L——'s family home is in Tunbridge (now spelt Tonbridge), but her town residence is in Bond Street, see Letter 19, n. 2.

21

TO MISS L——.

Charles Street, June 20, 1775.

I protest, my dear Madam, there is nothing so dangerous to the calm philosophic temper of fifty – as a friendly epistle from a pretty young woman; – but when worth – benevolence – and a train of amiabilities – easier felt than described – join in the attack, – the happy receiver of such an epistle must feel much in the same manner as your humble servant did this day. – But I did not mean to write a starch complimentary letter – and I believe you will think I have flourished rather too much. – Here then – I recover my wits – and the first use I make of them is to thank you, Mrs. Sancho's name, for your friendly enquiries – and to assure you, we both rejoice that you had so pleasant a passage – and that you enjoy your health. We hope also, that your young gallant will repay your humane attentions – with grateful regard – and dutiful attachment. – I beg your pardon, over and over, for my blundering forgetfulness of your kind order – it was occasioned by being obliged to say good-bye. – Taking leave of those we esteem is, in my opinion, unpleasant; – the parting of friends is a kind of temporary mourning. Mrs. Sancho is but indifferent – the hot weather does not befriend her – but time will, I hope; – if true worth could plead an exemption from pain and sickness – Miss L——— and Mrs. Sancho would, by right divine, enjoy the best health – But, God be blessed, there is a reward in store for both, and all like them – which will amply repay them for the evils and cross accidents of this foolish world. I saw Miss and Mrs. S*pink*, and Johnny,[1] at church last Sunday – they all looked pleasant, and told me they had heard you were well. – I would recommend a poem, which, if you have not – you should read, it is called Almeria;[2] I have not read it – but have heard such an account of it as makes me suspect it will be worth your notice. This end of the town is fairly Regatta-mad – and the prices they ask are only five shillings each seat. – They are building scaffoldings on Westminster-Hall – and the prayers of all parties are now for a fine evening. – May your evenings be ever fair – and mornings bright! I should have said nights happy – all in God's good time! which, you must be convinced, is the best time. – Lydia mends – she walks a little – we begin to encourage hope. – Kitty is as lively as ever – and almost goes alone – the rest are well. – Mrs. Sancho joins me in cordial wishes for your health and wealth. – I am, dear Madam,

Your most sincere friend,
and obliged humble servant,
IGN. SANCHO.

1. Probably the Spink family. In Letter 22 to Rush Sancho says that 'Johnny' is 'on the road for Bury', John Spink's home town (Letter 57).
2. Almeria: this is the name of the heroine of Congreve's *The Mourning Bride* (1697), still a popular play at the time. It contains two lines which have become famous quotations; 'Music hath charms to soothe the savage breast,' and 'Nor Hell a fury like a woman scorned.' I do not know of a poem of this name.

22

Undated[1]

MY DEAR FRIEND,

Thou hast an honest sympathizing heart – and I am sure will feel sorrow to hear poor Mr. W—— has paid the debt to Nature: – last Sunday heaven gained a worthy soul – and the world lost an honest man! – a Christian! – a friend to merit – a father to the poor and society – a man, whose least praise was his wit – and his meanest virtue, good humour. – He is gone to his great reward. – May you, and all I love and honor, in God's good time, join him! – I wish to hear about you – how you all do – when you saw Johnny – and whether Mrs. *Osborne* holds in the same mind – If so, she is on the road for London, and Johnny on the road for *Bury.* Pray have you heard from Mr. *Lincoln*[2]? A spruce Frenchman brought me a letter from him on Thursday; he left him well and in spirits – he wishes we would enquire for a place for him – he longs to be in England; – he is an honest soul, and I should feel true pleasure in serving him; pray remember he wants a place. – I know not what words to use in way of thanks to Mrs. *Cocksedge* for the very valuable present of her picture[3] – I have wrote to her – but my pen is not able to express what I feel – and I think Mr. Gardner[4] has hit off her likeness exceeding well – My chimney-piece now[5] – fairly imitates the times – a flashy fine outside – the only intrinsic nett worth, in my possession, is Mrs. Sancho – who I can compare to nothing so properly as to a diamond in the dirt – But, my friend, that is Fortune's fault, not mine – for, had I power, I would case her in gold. – When heard you from our friend Mr. J—— N——?[6] When you see or write to him – tell him we still care for him – and remember his easy good-nature and natural politeness. – I will trouble you with the inclosed without any ceremony – for I have been so often obliged to you, that I begin now to fancy I have a right to trouble you. Commend me to squire S——, and all worthy friends. – Lydia sends her love to you – she trots about amazingly – and Kitty imitates her, with this addition, that she is as mischievous as a monkey. – Mrs. Sancho, Mrs. *Meheux*, and Mrs. *Browne*, all think well of you, as well as yours,

I. SANCHO.

1. This letter is undated. Miss Crewe places it between a letter of 20 June 1775 and one of 31 July 1775. Sancho says he has written to thank Mrs Cocksedge for the painting, that is, Letter 19 of 4 July 1775, so Letter 22 should be dated July 1775. But again there is some uncertainty about the re-liability of Miss Crewe's dating, since Letters 19 and 20 dated July are placed before Letter 21, dated 20 June.

2. 'Mr Lincoln, an African' according to Stevenson's index. At this time it seems, he is resident in France. In Letter 31, Sancho hopes that he is on his way to England. In 1777, we learn from the wrongly dated Letter 1, he went out to India as ship's-bandsman, on the same ship as Soubise, to return again to England and sail for the Caribbean in 1779 (Letter 90, in which he is said to be from St Kitts.) He is back there with his family in Letter 153.

3. See Letters 19 and 23 for this picture of Mrs Cocksedge: also n. 5 below.

4. Mr Gardner: Daniel Gardner or Gardiner (1750?–1805) had studied with Reynolds, and became a popular minor painter in fashionable circles. According to his DNB entry, one of his paintings was entitled 'Mrs Gwyn and Mrs Bunbury, (the Horneck sisters), as the Merry Wives of Windsor', see note on Mrs. Bunbury, Letter 11, n. 1.

5. My chimney-piece: Sancho has hung the painting of Mrs Cocksedge in a position of honour over the fireplace; see Letter 23, n. 1.

6. Mr J—— N——: possibly James Norford, son of Dr William Norford, Sancho's physician at Bury.

23

TO MRS. C'[OCKSEDGE]'.

Charles Street, July 31, 1775.

DEAR MADAM,

If aught upon earth could make mortals happy – I have the best right to believe myself so – I have lived with the Great – and been favoured by beauty – I have cause to be vain – let that apologise for my boasting – I am to thank you for the best ornament of my chimney-piece. – Your picture,[1] which I had the joy to receive from Mr. Gardner, and which (exclusive of the partiality I have to your resemblance) I think a very good one; – it proves unquestionably three things; – your goodness – Mr. Gardner's skill – and my impudence! – in wishing so pleasing a prize. – If Kitty should live[2]

to woman's estate – she will exultingly tell folks – that's my
godmother's picture – and the next generation will swear the painter
was a flatterer – and scarce credit there was ever a countenance
so amiably sweet – in the days of George the Third – except
a Hamilton or Lady Sarah.[3] – Mrs. Sancho desires her thanks may
be joined with mine – as the thanks of one flesh. – Mr. M*eheux* is
well– and hopes, in concert with the Sanchos, that you had
a pleasant journey – and good health your companion. – That health
and pleasure – with love and friendship in its train – may ever
accompany you – is the wish, dear Madam, of your greatly obliged
humble servant,

IGNATIUS SANCHO.

1.   See Letters 19 and 22.
2.   'If Kitty should live': sadly, Kitty was not to live: her death is
     recorded in Letters 87 and 88. The phrase in Letter 21 'Kitty
     is lively as ever – and almost goes alone' expresses the
     Sanchos' hopes and fears.
3.   'A Hamilton or Lady Sarah': Elizabeth, 'La Belle' Hamilton
     (1641–1708), wife of the Compte de Grammont, a member
     of the earlier Montagu circle; and the forthright Lady Sarah,
     Duchess of Marlborough (1660–1744), mother of Lady Mary
     Churchill the wife of the 2nd Duke of Montagu, Sancho's
     first patron.

24

TO MISS. L——.

Charles Street, August 7, 1775.
I never can excuse intolerable scrawls – and I do tell you that for
writing conversable letters you are wholly unfit – no talent – no
nature – no style – stiff – formal – and unintelligible – take that – for
your apology – and learn to be honest to yourself. – The Duchess of
Kingston and Mr. Foote[1] have joined in a spirited paper-war – (I
should have said engaged) but I fear her Grace will have the worst of
it – Had she either the heart or head of our friend Miss L——,
I should pity her from my soul – and should muster up gallantry
enough to draw a pen (at least) in her defence; as it is – I think – in
principles they are well matched – but as her Grace appears to me
– to want temper – I think the Wit will be too hard for her. – I am
pleased with the Tunbridgians for their respectful loyalty – on his

Royal Highness's birth-day; – it is too much the fashion to treat
the Royal Family with disrespect. – Zeal for politics has almost
annihilated good-manners. – Mrs. Sancho feels the kindness of your
good wishes – but we hope you will be in town before she tumbles
in the straw, when a Benjamin mess of caudle[2] will meet your lips
with many welcomes. – Mrs. Sancho is – so, so – not so alert as
I have known her – but I shall be glad she holds just as well till she is
down. – My silly gout is not in haste to leave me – I am in my
seventh week – and in truth am peevish – and sick of its company.
– As to Dr. Dodd,[3] the last I heard of him – was that he was in
France; – he has not preached for these nine Sundays at Pimlico.
– You did not tell me the name of your Suffolk preacher – I fancy it
is Dr. Wollaston[4] – who is reckoned equal to Dodd; I am glad you
have him – as I would wish you to have every thing that God can
give you conducive to your love and pleasure. – Mrs. Sancho joins
me in respects and thanks – good wishes, &c. &c.

> I am, dear Madam
> Your ever obliged, humble servant,
> IGN. SANCHO.

1. The Duchess of Kingston and Mr Foote: Samuel Foote
   (1720–1777) was a playwright and theatre manager, whose
   productions were notorious for their slanderous implica-
   tions and often resulted in lawsuits or scandals. He went too
   far with the formidable Duchess of Kingston, when he let
   it be known that he intended to caricature her as Lady
   Crocodile in his play *The Trip to Calais*. She took the matter
   to court and had the play prohibited. The unseemly affair
   continued with a slanging match in the press. Foote, no
   friend of Garrick despite being one of his cronies, was no
   favourite of Sancho's either, as Sancho's satirical verses in
   Letter 25 and his jocular references to Foote's death in Letter
   54 show.
2. A Benjamin mess of caudle: a drink of gruel, with wine or ale
   spiced with an aromatic stimulant from the bark of a shrub
   called Benjamin, customarily given to women in childbirth
   ('in the straw') and their visitors; see letter 55, n. 3.
3. Dr Dodd: see Letter 16 and n. 3.
4. Dr Wollaston: Rev Dr Frederick Wollaston, (1735–1801),
   lecturer at St James' Church, Bury: see Fiske, *Oakes Diaries*,
   vol. II, p. 363.

25

TO MR. B'[ROWNE]'.

August 12, 1775.

DEAR SIR,

If I knew a better man than yourself – you wou'd not have had this application – which is in behalf of a merry – chirping – white tooth'd – clean – tight – and light little fellow; – with a woolly pate – and face as dark as your humble; – Guiney-born, and French-bred – the sulky gloom of Africa dispelled by Gallic vivacity – and that softened again with English sedateness – a rare fellow! – rides well – and can look upon a couple of horses – dresses hair in the present taste – shaves light – and understands something of the arrangement of a table and side-board; – his present master will authenticate him a decent character – he leaves him at his own (Blacky's) request: – he has served him three years – and, like Teague,[1] would be glad of a good master – if any good master would be glad to him. – As I believe you associate chiefly with good-hearted folks – it is possible your interest may be of service to him. – I like the rogue's looks, or a similarity of colour should not have induced me to recommend him. – Excuse this little scrawl from your friend, &c.

IGN. SANCHO.

'For conscience, like a fiery horse,
'Will stumble if you check his course;
'But ride him with an easy rein,
'And rub him down with worldly gain,
'He'll carry you through thick and thin,
'Safe, although dirty, to your inn.'[2]

1. Teague had become the type-name of the faithful Irish servant, from a character in a play, *The Committee*, by an Irish playwright Gorges Edmond Howard (1715–86).
2. This seems to be Sancho's own verse.

26

TO MRS. C'[OCKSEDGE]'.

August 14, 1775.

DEAR MADAM,

I am happy in hearing that the bathing and drinking has been of real service to you. – I imagine I see you rise out of the waves another Venus – and could wish myself Neptune, to have the honor of escorting you to land. – Mr. Priddie has sent me a pretty turtle,[1] and in very good condition. – I must beg you will do me the honor to accept of it – it will attend you at Privy Gardens,[2] where (had turtles a sense of ambition) it would think itself happy in its destination. – Pray my best respects to their honors R*ush* and Squire S*pink*. I live in hopes of seeing you all next week.

I am, dear Madam,
Your much obliged,
humble servant,
IGN. SANCHO.

1. Turtle: turtles were common enough as delicacies of the table in Bury at this time. See Fiske, *Oakes Diaries*, vol. I, p. 169 for a story of one which was carried from Liverpool to Bury on the top of a coach; also under Fiske's index of 'food', vol. II, p. 146. That this turtle is meant for eating (and is not a pet turtle-dove) is confirmed by Letter 31: 'the turtle pulled one way and a sweet loin of pork the other'. The 'pair of Antigua turtles', given by Mr P—— (possibly Priddie) to Kitty Sancho, noted in Letter 73, sounds in context like caged-birds, 'we having neither warmth nor room', but were probably sea-turtles, intended as a rich diet for the ailing Kitty.
2. Privy Gardens: the family house and its grounds of the 2nd Duchess of Montagu. On her death in 1751, the Privy Gardens passed to her second daughter, Mary, Lady Cardigan, whose husband adopted the title Duke of Montagu of the second creation. The Duke of Montagu was Sancho's employer; he died at Spring Gardens in 1790, and the line again became defunct. Mary was the mother of a daughter, Elizabeth, who became Duchess of Buccleuch, see Letter 9, n. 1.

27

TO MISS L———.

August 27, 1775.

Just upon the stroke of eleven – as I was following (like a good husband) Mrs. Sancho to bed – a thundering rap called me to the street-door – a letter from Tunbridge, Sir – thanks, many thanks – good night. – I hugged the fair stranger[1] – and – as soon as up stairs – broke ope the seal with friendly impatience – and got decently trimmed, for what? why, truly, for having more honesty than prudence. – Well, if ever I say a civil thing again to any of your sex – but it is foolish to be rash in resolves – Seriously, if aught at any time slips from my unguarded pen, which you may deem censurable – believe me truly and honestly – it is the error of uncultivated nature – and I will trust the candor of friendship to wink at undesigned offence; – not but I could defend – and would against any but yourself – the whole sad charge of flattery – But enough. – I paid a visit in Bond Street this morning. – Your sister looked health itself – she just returned from the country, and had the pleasure to hear from you at her first entrance.

Your friendly offer for the little stranger is in character – but if I was to say what my full heart would dictate – you would accuse me of flattery. – Mrs. Sancho is more than pleased – I won't say what I am – but if you love to give pleasure, you have your will. – Are you not pleased to find Miss Butterfield innocent?[2] – It does credit to my judgement, for I never believed her guilty – her trial proves undeniably that one half of the faculty are very ignorant. – I hear she intends suing for damages – and if ever any one had a right to recover, she certainly has; – and were I to decree them – they should not be less than 400l. a year for life, and 5000l. down by way of smart-money. – In my opinion, the *Duchess* of *Kingston*[3] is honored to be mentioned in the same paper with Miss Butterfield. – You should read the St. James's Evening papers for last week – you will easiy get them at any coffee-house – the affair is too long for a letter – but I will send you some black poetry[4] upon the occasion:

With Satire, Wit, and Humour arm'd,

   Foote opes his exhibitions;

High-titled Guilt, justly alarm'd,

   The Chamberlain petitions.

My Lord, quoth Guilt, this darling fiend

Won't let us sin in private;
To his presumption there's no end,
   Both high and low he'll drive at.
Last year he smok'd the cleric* gown'
   A Duchess now he'd sweat.
The insolent, for half a crown,
   Would libel all the Great!
What I can do, his Lordship cries,
   Command you freely may.
Don't license him, the Dame replies,
   Nor let him print his play.

Poor Lydia is exceedingly unwell. – They who have least sensibility are best off for this world. – By the visit I was able to make this morning – you may conclude my troublesome companion is about taking leave. – May you know no pains but of sensibility! – and may you be ever able to relieve where you wish! – May the wise and good esteem you more than I do – and the object of your heart love you – as well as you love a good and kind action! – These wishes – after the trimming you gave me in your last – is a sort of heaping coals on your head – as such, accept it from your sincere – aye – and *honest* friend,

IGN. SANCHO.

Mrs. Sancho says little – but her moistened eye expresses – that she feels your friendship.

* Dr. Dodd.

1. 'The fair stranger' from Tonbridge is probably the maid of Miss L——'s sister living in Bond Street. The letter is a not a wholly serious 'trimming' (a telling-off) from Miss L—— whose family home is in Tonbridge (Letter 20). Miss L——'s London residence is in Bond Street near Sancho's in-laws, the Osbornes: 'I paid a visit to Bond St. this morning. – Your sister looked health itself ...' Miss L—— is due to come up to London, as we know from Letter 33, written when she is on her way back to Tonbridge.
2. Miss Butterfield: Miss Jane Butterfield came before Lord Chief Baron Smythe, on Saturday 19 August 1775 in Croydon, charged with poisoning and causing the death of her benefactor, William Scawen. As Sancho's enthusiastic announcement demonstrates, Miss Butterfield was found not

guilty. Scawen's death was due to mercury poisoning as
a result of taking a quack remedy for rheumatism.
3.   The Duchess of Kingston and Mr Foote: see Letter 24, n. 1.
4.   The 'black poetry' must be Sancho's own.

28

TO MISS L——.

Sept. 12, 1775.

There is nothing in nature more vexatious than contributing to the
uneasiness of those, whose partiality renders them anxious for our
well-doing – the honest heart dilates with rapture when it can
happily contribute pleasure to its friends; – you see by this that I am
coxcomb enough to suppose me and mine of consequence – but if it
is so – it is such as you, whose partial goodness has grafted that folly
on my natural trunk of dullness. – I am, in truth, in a very unfit
mood for writing – for poor Lydia is very so, so – Mrs. Sancho not
very stout; – and for me, I assure you, that of my pair of feet – two
are at this instant in pain – This is the worst side – but courage!
Hope! delusive cheating Hope! beckons Self-love, and enlists him
of her side – and, together, use their friendly eloquence to persuade
me that better times are coming. – Your beloved wife (cries
Self-love) will have a happy time, and be up soon, strong and hearty.
– Your child (cries Hope) will get the better of her illness – and
grow up a blessing, and comfort to your evening life – and your
friend will soon be in town and enliven your winter prospects.
– Trust, trust in the Almighty – his providence is your shield – 'tis
his love, 'tis his mercy, which has hitherto supported and kept you
up. – See, see! cries Hope! look where Religion, with Faith on her
right – and Charity on her left – and a numerous train of blessings in
her rear, come to thy support. – Fond foolish mortal – leave
complaining – all will be right – all is right. – Adieu, my good friend
– write me something to chace away idle fears – and to strengthen
hope. – Too true it is, that where the tender passions are concerned,
our sex are cowards,

Yours, sincerely,
I. SANCHO.

Mrs. Sancho sends her best wishes.

29

Charles Street, Oct. 4, 1775.

Just as the twig is bent, the tree's inclin'd,
Tis education forms the tender mind.

So says POPE.[1]

Children like tender osiers take the bow,
And as they first are fashion'd, always grow.

DRYDEN.[2]

The sense of each is just the same, and they both prove an opinion,
which I have long been grounded in – that the errors of most
children proceed in great part from the ill cultivation of their first
years. – Self-love, my friend, bewitches parents to give too much
indulgence to infantine foibles; – the constant cry is, 'Poor little
soul, it knows no better!' – if it swears – that's a sign of wit and
spirit; – if it fibs – it's so cunning and comical; – if it steals – 'tis only
a paw trick – and the mother exultingly cries – My Jacky[3] is so
sharp, we can keep nothing from him! – Well! but what's all this to
you? – You are no mother. – True, my sincerely esteemed friend
– but you are something as good – you are perhaps better – much
better and wiser I am sure than many mothers I have seen. – You,
who believe in the true essence of the gospel – who visit the sick,
cover the naked, and withdraw not your ear from the unfortunate:
– but I did not intend to write your eulogium – it requires the pen of
one less interested – and perhaps less partiality and more judgement
would also be requisite. – Jacky S——[4] is the occasion of this
prefatory vast show of learning. I do believe him a fine child spoil'd
for want of proper management – he is just now in high disgrace
– he is wrong enough in all conscience, I believe – but are they, who
are about him, right? We will talk about this matter when I have the
pleasure of seeing you; – you shall forgive my impertinent meddling
– I will ask pardon and sin again – so we serve Heaven – so
complain, if you dare. – Mrs. Sancho is yet up; – if I pray at all, it's
for the blessing of a happy moment, with little pain for her; – as to
what she brings, I care not about its sex – God grant safety and
health to the mother – and my soul and lips shall bless his holy
name. – We cannot remove till after Mrs. Sancho is up – The house
will not be ready till towards Christmas, which is not the most

desirable time of the year for moving – but we must do as we can, not as we would.

At Charlotte Chapel – we had last Sunday a most excellent discourse from Mr. Harrison,[5] whom I suppose you have heard preach – if not, he is well worth hearing – to please me – or, to the best of my knowledge, he reads prayers better than most – Mr. Butler not excepted; – there is a dignity of expression in his Psalms, which catches the whole attention – and such an animated strength of devotion in his Litany, as almost carries the heart to the gates of Heaven – he is fine in the pulpit; – but comparisons are unfair – if Harrison reads prayers, and Dodd preaches at the same church – I should suppose greater perfection could not be found in England. I have to thank you for the honor of your correspondence – and can laugh in my sleeve like a Dutch Jew – to think that I get sterling sense for my farrago of absurdities – but you will, I hope, soon be in town. – Mrs. Sancho joins me in every sentiment of gratitude and sincerity. – I am, as much as a poor African can be, sincerely

Yours to command,

IGN. SANCHO.

We are in great hopes about poor Lydia. – An honest and ingenious motherly woman in our neighbourhood has undertaken the perfect cure of her – and we have every reason to think, with God's blessing, she will succeed – which is a blessing we shall owe entirely to the comfort of being poor – for had we been rich – the doctors would have had the honor of killing her a twelvemonth ago. ——Adieu.

1. Quotation: Alexander Pope, *Moral Essays: Epistle I, To Cobham*, ll. 149–50. Sancho quotes inaccurately; Pope's lines read: 'Tis education forms the common mind / Just as the twig is bent, the Tree's inclin'd.'
2. I have not been able to locate Dryden's lines.
3. My Jacky: this could be a reference to Sancho's recently identified first son. John Gurnett has identified a previously unknown 'Sanchonett', Jonathan William Sancho, whose birth is recorded at the St Margaret's Westminster parish office, March 1768, making him the fourth child born to the Sanchos. The ambiguous reference to 'My Jacky' may be an affectionate description of young Jonathan William Sancho, 'so sharp, we can keep nothing from him'. See Letter 15, n.

2 for another possible reference to this first Sancho son. No specific mention is made in the letters of the birth or death of Jonathan William Sancho, (though he probably died before his eighth birthday) before 14 December 1775, when, in Letter 33, William (Billy), is referred to as 'the heir of the noble family' (see Letter 33, n. 1); for details about the Sanchos' children see Appendix VII.

4.   Jacky S——: this is probably not a second reference to Jonathan Sancho, since Sancho's description seems to fit an older child or young adult who has made poor decisions about his companions. Sancho describes his own remarks about Jacky S—— as 'impertinent meddling', further suggesting his comments concern someone else's child, possibly John Spink's son.

5.   'Mr Harrison ... Mr Butler': the quality of his sermons and delivery at Charlotte Chapel (see Letter 16, n. 2 on Dr Dodd) is mentioned several times by Sancho, for example Letter 43. Mr Harrison is compared by Sancho to Weeden Butler the elder (1742–1823), who acted as amanuensis to Dodd, 1764–77. In 1776 Butler succeeded Dodd as morning preacher at Charlotte Chapel and officiated there until 1814.

30

TO MISS L——.

Thursday Morning, Oct. 16, 1775.

My worthy and respected friend, I hear, has protracted her stay. – I am greatly obliged to Miss L——'s goodness, who has given me this opportunity of addressing my good friend. – I am very low in heart. – Poor Mrs. Sancho is so indifferent – and Lydia, tho' upon the whole better, yet weak and poorly. – I am sufficiently acquainted with care – and I think I fatten upon calamity. – Philosophy is best practised, I believe, by the easy and affluent. – One ounce of practical religion is worth all that ever the Stoics wrote. – Mrs. Sancho smiles in the pains which it has pleased Providence to try her with – and her belief in a better existence is her cordial drop. – Adieu; bring health with you, and the sight of you will glad us all.

Yours,

I. SANCHO.

31

TO MR. R'[USH]'.

Oct. 18, 1775.

I begin to fear with you that our friend *Lincoln* is sick or married – or – what I would rather hope – is on his way to England.[1] – Thanks to our Suffolk friends – you take care we shall not starve. – I was for five minutes, when dinner was on table, suspended, in inclination, like the ass between the two loads of hay – the turtle pulled one way, and a sweet loin of pork the other[2] – I was obliged to attack both in pure self-defence; – Mrs. Sancho ate – and praised the pork – and praised the giver. – Let it not, my worthy *Rush*, mortify thy pride – to be obliged to divide praise with a pig; – we all echoed her – *Osborne* and *Rush* were the toasts – I know not in truth two honester or better men – were your incomes as enlarged as your hearts – you would be the two greatest fortunes in Europe; but I wrote merely to thank you – and to say Mrs. Sancho and Mrs. *Meheux* are both better than when I wrote last night – in short Mrs. *Meheux* is quite well – I pray God to send my dear Mrs. Sancho safe down and happily up – she makes the chief ingredient of my felicity – Whenever my good friend marries – I hope he will find it the same with him. – My best respects to Mesdames C. and C.[3] and take care of my brother. – I fear this will be a raking week. – Compliments to Master S—— and the noble Mr. B——

Yours, &c.

I. SANCHO.

1. Lincoln, see Letter 22, n. 2.
2. 'The turtle pulled one way, and a sweet loin of pork the other': see letters 26, n. 1 and 73, n. 1 for turtle-doves.
3. Mesdames C—— and C: probably Miss Crewe and either Mrs Crewe or Mrs Cocksedge. Master S—— and Mr B——: probably Spink and Browne.

32

TO MISS L——.

Friday, Oct. 20, 1775.

In obedience to my amiable friend's request – I, with gratitude to the Almighty – and with pleasure to her – (I am sure I am right) – acquaint her, that my ever dear Dame Sancho was exactly at half

past one, this afternoon, delivered of a – child.[1] – Mrs. Sancho, my
dear Miss L——, is as well as can be expected – in truth, better than
I feared she would be – for indeed she has been very unwell for this
month past – I feel myself a ton lighter: – In the morning I was crazy
with apprehension – and now I talk nonsense thro' joy. – This
plaguy scrawl will cost you I know not what – but it's not my fault
– 'tis your foolish godson's[2] – who, by me, tenders his dutiful
respects. I am ever yours to command, sincerely and affectionately,

I. SANCHO.

1. The child is William Leach Osborne Sancho (Billy); see the
   Introduction, p. 5, esp. n. 13, and Appendix VII. Sancho's
   letters give much loving detail about his little son Billy,
   providing a relatively rare record of a father's delights,
   worries and impressions of his young son. Though very little
   is known about the adult lives of Sancho's children, parish
   records and Sancho's own observations provide important
   information about family affections and domestic concerns,
   often an 'invisible' realm of experience.
2. Your foolish godson: see Letter 10, n. 1.

33

TO MISS L——.

Charles Street, Dec. 14, 1775.

There is something inexpressibly flattering in the notion of your
being warmer – from the idea of your much obliged friend's caring
for you; – in truth we could not help caring about you – our
thoughts travelled with you over night from Bond Street to the Inn.
– The next day at noon – 'Well, now she's above half way – Alas!
no, she will not get home till Saturday night – I wonder what
companions she has met with – There is a magnetism in good-nature
which will ever attract its like – so if she meets with beings the least
social – but that's as chance wills!' – Well, night arrives – and now
our friend has reached the open arms of parental love – excess of
delightful endearments gives place to tranquil enjoyments – and all
are happy in the pleasure they give each other. – Were I a saint or
a bishop, and was to pass by your door, I would stop, and say, Peace
be upon this dwelling! – and what richer should I leave it? – for
I trust where a good man dwells, there Peace makes its sweet abode.
– When you have read Bossuet, you will find at the end, that it was

greatly wished the learned author had brought the work down lower – but I cannot help thinking he concluded his design as far as he originally meant. – Mrs. Sancho, thank Heaven, is as well as you left her, and your godson thrives[1] – He is the type of his father – fat – heavy – sleepy – but, as he is the heir of the noble family, and your godson, I ought not to disparage him. – The duchess of Kingston is so unwell, that she has petitioned for a longer day – they say that her intellects are hurt; – though a bad woman, she is entitled to pity. – Conscience, the high chancellor of the human breast, whose small still voice speaks terror to the guilty – Conscience has pricked her – and, with all her wealth and titles, she is an object of pity. – Health attend you and yours! – Pleasure of course will follow. – Mrs. Sancho joins me in all I say, and the girls look their assent. – I remain – God forgive me! I was going to conclude, without ever once thanking you for your goodness in letting us hear from you so early – There is such a civil coldness in writing, a month perhaps after expectation has been snuffed out, that the very thought is enough to chill friendship – But you, like your sister Charity, as Thomson sweetly paints her (smiling thro' tears), delight in giving pleasure, and joy in doing good. – And now farewell – and believe us in truth, our dear miss L——'s

> Obliged and grateful friends,
> ANNE AND I. SANCHO.

1.   'Your godson thrives ... he is heir of the noble family': see Letter 10, n. 1 and Appendix VII.

34

TO MR. M'[EHEUX]'.

Jan. 4, 1776.

I know not which predominates in my worthy friend – pride or good-nature – Don't stare – you have a large share of both; – happy it is for you – as well as your acquaintance – that your pride is so well accompanied by the honest ardor of youthful benevolence. – You would, like the fabled pelican – feed your friends with your vitals – blessed Philanthropy! oh! the delights of making happy – the bliss of giving comfort to the afflicted – peace to the distressed mind – to prevent the request from the quivering lips of indigence!

But, great God! – the inexpressible delight – the not-to-be-described rapture in soothing, and *convincing* the tender virgin that *'you alone,'* &c. &c. (Prior's Henry and Emma see)[1] – but I think you dropp'd a word or two about flattery. – Sir – honest friend – know once for all – I never yet thought you a coxcomb – a man of sense I dare not flatter, my pride forbids it – a coxcomb is not worth the dirty pains. – You have (through the bounty of your great Creator) strong parts, and, thank the Almighty goodness, an honest sincere heart – yes, you have many and rare talents, which you have cultivated with success – you have much fire, which, under the guidance of a circumspect judgement, stimulates you to worthy acts – But do not say that I flatter in speaking the truth – I can see errors even in those I half reverence – there are spots in the Sun – and perhaps some faults in Johnny M*eheux* who is by far – too kind – generous – and friendly to his greatly obliged friend,

IGN. SANCHO.

P.S. I tell you what – (are you not coming to town soon?) – F——[2] and venison are good things, but by the manes of my ancestors – I had rather have the pleasure of gossipation with your sublime highness. – What sketches have you taken? – what books have you read? – what lasses gallanted? – The venison is exceeding fine, and the cleanest I ever saw – to-morrow we dress it – a thankful heart shall be our sweet sauce: – were you in town, your partaking of it would add to its relish. – You say I was not in spirits when you saw me at G——; why, it might be so – in spite of my philosophy – the cares and anxieties attendant on a large family and small finances sometimes over-cloud the natural cheerfulness of yours truly,

I. SANCHO.

N.B. A very short P—— S——

1. Prior's *Henry and Emma* (1709): this told a sentimental love-story based on the ballad *The Nut-brown Maid*, and was very popular in its time. It was translated into French prose and into Latin and parts of it were set to music by Dr Thomas Arne (see *The Literary Works of Matthew Prior* (eds.) H. B. Wright and M. K. Spears, Oxford, 1959, vol. I, p. 278 for text; vol. II, pp. 909–10 for notes.) Samuel Johnson had a low opinion of the poem however: 'The greatest of all

his amorous essays is *Henry and Emma*; a dull and tedious
dialogue, which excites neither esteem for the man nor
tenderness for the woman' (Samuel Johnson, *Lives of the
English Poets*, Open University Press, London, 1967).

2.   F——: fawn (young deer).

35

TO MR. R'[USH]'.

June 25, 1776.

You had a pleasant day for your journey – and after five or six miles
ride from town – you left the dust behind you – of course the road
and the country also improved as you drew nearer Barton.[1] I will
suppose you there – and then I will suppose you found Mrs.
Cocksedge well in health, and the better for the preceding day's
motion – She and Miss *Crewe* meet you with the looks of
a spring-morning. – I see you meet in fancy – I wish I could see you
in reality – but of that hereafter. – I want to know how Mrs.
Cocksedge does – and what Miss *Crewe* does – what you intend to
do – and what Mr. *Spink* will never do. – This letter is a kind of
much-ado-about – what – I must not say nothing – because the
ladies are mentioned in it. – Mr. and Mrs. *Browne* have a claim to
my best respects; – Pray say what's decent for me – and to the
respectable table also – beginning with my true friend Mrs.
Cocksedge, and then steering right and left – ending at last with
your worship. – Tell Mrs. *Cocksedge* that Kitty is as troublesome as
ever – that Billy gets heavier and stronger. – Mrs. Sancho remains,
thank God, very well – and all the rest ditto. – Let me know how
you all do – and how brother *Osborne* does. – As to news, all I hear
is about Wilkes[2] – he will certainly carry his point – for administration are all strongly in his interest – betts run much in his favor –
For my part, I really think he will get it – if he can once manage so
– as to gain the majority. ——I am, my dear R*ush*, yours – (much
more than Wilkes's – or indeed any man, *Osborne*'s excepted) in
love and zeal,

Ever faithfully,

I. SANCHO.

1.   Barton: a village on the edge of Mildenhall, a few miles north
     of Bury St Edmunds; Barton Hall was the home of the

Bunburys. The ladies would be Miss Crewe and Sancho's 'true friend' Mrs Cocksedge, a report being made of her godchild, Kitty, that she 'is as troublesome as ever', perhaps jokingly of her conduct, or, more probably, seriously of her health.

2. John Wilkes (1727–97), politician and journalist. His life swung between lavish expenditure and poverty. Initially a supporter of Pitt's administration, he was resentful at his lack of preferment, and also disagreed honestly with some of its policies. He damaged the government in a pamphlet of 1762, then founded the weekly journal, *The North Briton*, 1762–3, in which he made further attacks on the administration. In 1768 he was expelled from Parliament for libel and sentenced to a spell in the King's Bench Prison. But he remained popular as a defender of freedom of speech, continued to be active in local politics and became Lord Mayor of London in 1774. He regained his seat in Parliament, retiring in 1790 to the Isle of Wight, where he died.

36

TO MR STERNE.

July, 1776.

REVEREND SIR,

It would be an insult on your humanity (or perhaps look like it) to apologize for the liberty I am taking. – I am one of those people whom the vulgar and illiberal call '*Negurs.*' – The first part of my life was rather unlucky, as I was placed in a family who judged ignorance the best and only security for obedience. – A little reading and writing I got by unwearied application. – The latter part of my life has been – thro' God's blessing, truly fortunate, having spent it in the service of one of the best families in the kingdom. – My chief pleasure has been books. – Philanthropy I adore. – How very much, good Sir, am I (amongst millions) indebted to you for the character of your amiable uncle Toby! – I declare, I would walk ten miles in the dog-days, to shake hands with the honest corporal. – Your Sermons have touch'd me to the heart, and I hope have amended it, which brings me to the point. – In your tenth discourse, page seventy-eight, in the second volume – is this very affecting passage – 'Consider how great a part of our species – in all ages down to this – have been trod under the feet of cruel and capricious tyrants, who would neither hear their cries, nor pity their distresses. – Consider slavery – what it is – how bitter a draught – and how many millions are made to drink it!' – Of all my favorite authors, not one has drawn a tear in favor of my miserable black brethren – excepting yourself, and the humane author of Sir George Ellison. – I think you will forgive me; – I am sure you will applaud me for beseeching you to give one half-hour's attention to slavery, as it is at this day practised in our West Indies. – That subject, handled in your striking manner, would ease the yoke (perhaps) of many – but if only of one – Gracious God! – what a feast to a benevolent heart! – and, sure I am, you are an epicurean in acts of charity. – You, who are universally read, and as universally admired – you could not fail – Dear Sir, think in me you behold the uplifted hands of thousands of my brother Moors. – Grief (you pathetically observe) is eloquent; – figure to yourself their attitudes; – hear their supplicating addresses! – alas! – you cannot refuse. – Humanity must comply – in which hope I beg permission to subscribe myself,

Reverend Sir, &c.
IGN. SANCHO.

1. This Letter is discussed in the Introduction, pp. 5–7. Again, Miss Crewe's dating of the letter as July 1776 is badly out. It was in fact written on 27 July 1766.

37

TO MR. M'[EHEUX]'.
August 12, 1776.
'We have left undone the things we should have done,'[1]
&c. &c.
This general confession – with a deep sense of our own frailties – joined to penitence – and strong intentions of better doing – insures poor sinners forgiveness, obliterates the past, sweetens the present, and brightens the future; – in short, we are to hope that it reconciles us with the Deity – and if that conclusion is just, it must certainly reconcile us in part to each other. – Grant me that, dear *Meheux*, and you have no quarrel towards me for epistolary omissions; – look about you, my dear friend, with a fault-searching eye – and see what you have left undone! – Look on your chair –

those clothes should have been brushed and laid by – that linen
sent to wash – those shoes to be cleaned. – Zooks! why, you forget
to say your prayers – to take your physick – to wash your—— Pray
how does Mrs. H——? Lord, what a deal of rain! I declare I fear it
will injure the harvest. – And when saw you Nancy? – Has the cat
kittened? – I suppose you have heard the news: – great news! –
a glorious affair! (and is two ff's necessary[2]) – O! Lord, Sir! – very
little bloodshed – pity *any* shou'd – How! – do not you admire? –
How so? – Why this, Sir, is writing, 'tis the true sublime – and this
is stuff that gives my friend M*eheux* pleasure: – thou vile flatterer!
– blush! blush up to thine eyelids! – I am happy to think I have
found a flaw in thee – thou art a flatterer of the most dangerous sort,
because agreeable – I have often observed – there is more of value in
the manner of doing the thing – than in the thing itself – my
mind's-eye follows you in the selecting the pretty box – in arranging
the picked fruit. – I see you fix on the lid, drive the last nail, your
countenance lit up with glee, and your heart exulting in the pleasure
you were about giving to the family of the Sanchos – and then
snatch the hat and stick, and walk with the easy alacrity of a soul
conscious of good. – But hold, Sir, you were rather saucy in a part or
two of your letter – for which reason I shall not thank you for the
fruit – the good woman and brats may – and with reason, for they
devoured them – The box, indeed, is worth thanks, which, if God,
gout, and weather permit, you may probably hear something of on
Sunday next, from yours, with all your sins, &c. &c.

IGN. SANCHO.

1. Quotation: *Book of Common Prayer* (1661) (General Confession).
2. Sancho is playing games here in the manner of Sterne, but as
   the joke with Meheux is personal, the meaning is wrapped in
   obscurity: as Sancho says in the letter: 'There is more of
   value in the manner of doing the thing – than in the thing
   itself.' Out of the verbal mist it emerges that Meheux has sent
   the Sanchos a box of fruit. The 'Glorious affair' seems to
   refer to inflated reports of early successes in the American
   War – perhaps the meeting of the American Continental
   Congress in 17 May 1775, just after the Battle of Lexington,
   which was distinctly conciliatory in tone. At the time Letter
   37 was written, the English had taken New York City, and
   the war might have appeared to be going well: see Letter 55

for the defeat of 'Washintub's army' at Long Island (1776) and Brandywine Creek in 1777, but the optimism shown in Letter 37 appears to refer to events a year earlier. The question 'is two ff's necessary' appears to make a feeble pun on the word 'affair' ('a fair'), implying an easy victory, offensive in its complacency if that is its intention.

38

TO MR. K'[ISBY]'.

August 28, 1776.

MY WORTHY FRIEND,

I should have answered your billet, as soon as received – but I wanted to know the quantum that I was to wish you joy of – as nothing has yet for certainty transpired. – I will hope your legacy from Mrs. —— is handsome: – you can easily imagine the pleasure I felt – in finding she had so amply remembered poor Mrs. M*eheux*: that one act has more true generosity in it, aye, and justice perhaps, than any thing I ever knew of her in her long life: – it has removed an anxiety from me which (in spite of self-felt poverty – and the heart-felt cares of a large family) troubled me greatly. – As to myself, she used to promise largely formerly, that she would think of me: – as I never believed – I was not disappointed. – More and more convinced of the futility of all our eagerness after worldly riches, my prayer and hope is only for bread, and to be enabled to pay what I owe. – I labour up hill against many difficulties – but God's goodness is my support – and his word my trust. – Mrs. Sancho joins me in her best wishes, and gives you joy also; the children are all well – William grows, and tries his feet briskly – and Fanny goes on well in her tambour-work – Mary must learn some business or other – if we can possibly achieve money – but we have somehow no friends – and, bless God! – we deserve no enemies. Trade is duller than ever I knew it – and money scarcer; – foppery runs higher – and vanity stronger; – extravagance is the adored idol of this sweet town. – You are a happy being; – free from the cares of the world in your own person, you enjoy more than your master – or his master into the bargain. – May your comforts know no diminution, but increase with your years! – and may the fame happen, when it shall please God, to your sincere friend. I. Sancho and his family!

39

TO MR. M'[EHEUX]'.

September 1, 1776.

You have the happiest manner of obliging. – How comes it that – without the advantages of a twentieth generationship of noble blood flowing uncontaminated in your veins – without the customary three years dissipation at college – and the (nothing-to-be-done without) four years perambulation on the Continent – without all these needful appendages – with little more than plain sense – sheer good-nature – and a right honest heart – thou canst –

'Like low-born Allen, with an awkward shame,
'Do good by stealth, and blush to find it fame?'[1]

Now, by my grandame's beard – I will not thank you for your present – although my ears have been stunned with your goodness and kindness – the best young man! – and, good Lord! how shall we make him amends? &c. &c. – Pshaw! simpleton, quoth I, do you not plainly ken, that he himself has a satisfaction in giving pleasure to his friends which more than repays him? – So I strove to turn off the notion of obligation – though, I must confess, my heart at the same time felt a something, sure it was not envy – no, I detect it – I fear it was pride – for I feel within myself this moment, that could I turn the tables in repaying principal with treble interest, I should feel gratified – though perhaps not satisfied. – I have a long account to balance with you – about your comments upon the transcript; – you are a pretty fellow to dare put in your claim – to better sense – deeper thinking – and stronger reasoning than my wise self – To tell you the truth (tho' at my own expence) I read your letter the first time with some little chagrin; – your reasoning, tho' it hurt my pride – yet almost convinced my understanding. – I read it carefully a second time – pondered – weighed – and submitted – Whenever a spark of vanity seems to be glowing at my heart, I will read your letter – and what then? – Why, then, humbled by a proper sense of my inferiority – I shall still have cause for pride – triumph – and comfort – when I reflect that my valued Consort – is the true friend of his sincerely affectionate

IGN. SANCHO.

1. Quotation: Pope, *Epilogue to the Satires*, Dialogue I, ll. 135–6.

40

TO MR. M'[EHEUX]'.

Dec. 4, 1776.

I forgot to tell you this morning – a jack-ass would have shown more thought – (are they rationals or not?) The best recipe for the gout, I am informed – is two or three stale Morning-Posts; – Reclined in easy chair – the patient must sit – and mull over them – take snuff at intervals – hem – and look wise. – I apply to you as my pharmacopolist – do not criticize my orthography – but when convenient – send me the medicine – which, with care and thanks, I will return.

Yours,
Dismal SANCHO.

Pray how do ye do?

41

TO MR. M'[EHEUX]'.*

[J]anuary 4, 1777.

I have read, but have found nothing of the striking kind of sentimental novelty – which I expected from its great author – the language is good in most places – but never rises above the common pitch. – In many of our inferior tragedies – I have ever found here and there a flower strewn, which has been the grace and pride of the poetic parterre, and has made me involuntary cry out Bravo! – From dress – scenery – action – and the rest of playhouse garniture – it may show well and go down – like insipid fish with good sauce; – the Prologue is well – the Epilogue worth the whole – such is my criticism – read – stare – and conclude your friend mad – tho' a more Christian supposition would be – (what's true at the same time) that my ideas are frozen, much more frigid than the play; – but allowing that – and although I confess myself exceeding cold, yet I have warmth enough to declare myself yours sincerely,

I. SANCHO.

Love and many happy new years to the ladies.

* On reading the Tragedy of Semiramis, *from the French of Mons. Voltaire.*

42

TO MR. M'[EHEUX]'.

February 9, 1777.

Zounds! if alive – what ails you? if dead – why did you not send me word? – Where's my Tristram? – What, are all bucks alike? – all promise and no – but I won't put myself in a passion – I have but one foot and no head – go to – why, what a devil of a rate dost thou ride at anathematizing and reprobating poor ——! Pho! thou simpleton – he deserves thy pity – and whoever harbours a grain of contempt for his fellow creatures – either in the school of poverty or misfortune – that being is below contempt – and lives the scorn of men – and shame of devils. – Thou shalt not think evil of ——; nor shall he, either by word or thought, dispraisingly speak or think of *Meheux*.

In regard to thy *Nancy* thou art right – guard her well – but chiefly guard her from the traitor in her own fair breast, which, while it is the feat of purity and unsullied honor – fancies its neighbours to be the same – nor sees the serpent in the flowery foliage – till it stings – and then farewell sweet peace and its attendant riches.

I have only time to thank you for the leaves, and to lament your want of perspicuity in writing. – My love to George[1] when you see him – and two loves to Nancy – Tell her I could fold her to my bosom with the same tender pressure I do my girls – shut my eyes – draw her to my heart – and call her daughter! – And thou, monkey-face, write me a decent letter – or you shall have another trimming from yours,

I. SANCHO.

Look'ye, Sir, I write to the ringing of the shop-door bell – I write – betwixt serving – gossiping – and lying. Alas! what cramps to poor genius!

1. George: Meheux's brother.

42a

For THE GENERAL ADVERTISER.

The Outline of a Plan for establishing a most respectable Body of Seamen, to the Number of 20,000, to be ever ready for the manning a Fleet upon twelve Days' Notice.[1]

The proposer is humbly of opinion, that his plan is capable of many wholesome improvements, which he thinks would prove no unprofitable study, even to the Lords of the Admiralty.

Ift, Let the number of seamen, now upon actual service, be each man inrolled upon Her Majesty's books, at the rate of 5l. *per annum* for life; let them also receive the same quarterly, or half-yearly, upon personal application.

Ildly, Let books be opened for them in all His Majesty's different yards and sea-ports, and there their dwelling, age, time they have served, &c. to be fairly entered: each man to bring a certificate from his ship, signed by the captain, or some one he shall please to depute.

Illdly, As an encouragement to His Majesty's service, and population at the same time, let there be instituted in each of the ship-yards, or ports, &c. of these kingdoms, a kind of asylum, or house of refuge, for the sons of these honest tars, to be received therein at the age of six years; there to be taught navigation, or, after the common school learning, to be bound to such parts of ship-building as they by nature are most inclined to: such as choose sea service, to be disposed on board His Majesty's ships at fifteen years old, and to be enrolled upon the pension-books after ten years' faithful service, unless better provided for.

Might not there be some plan hit on to employ the daughters, as well as sons, of poor sailors? Do not our Fisheries (if they should ever happen to be attended to) open many doors of useful employment for both sexes?

To defray the above, I would advise the following methods:

First, The pension of 5l. *per* man for 20,000 amounts only to 100,000l.; let this be taken from the Irish list; it will surely be better employed than in the present mode for Pensioners of noble blood.

Secondly, Let the book- and office-keepers at the different yards, ports, &c. be collected from under-officers who have served with reputation: it will be a decent retreat for them in the evening of life, and only a grateful reward for past service.

May some able hand, guided by a benevolent heart, point out and strongly recommend something of this sort, that the honoured name of England may be rescued from the scandalous censure of man-stealing, and from the ingratitude also of letting their preservers perish in the time of peace!

I am, Sir, yours, &c.

AFRICANUS.

1. Plan for manning a fleet: this was a current concern of others, including Granville Sharp and General James Oglethorpe.

43

TO MR. M'[EHEUX]'.

July 27, 1777.

Go-to! – The man who visits church twice in one day, must either be religious – curious – or idle – whichever you please, my dear friend – turn it the way which best likes you – I will cheerily subscribe to it. – By the way, Harrison[1] was inspired this morning – his text was from Romans – chapter the – verse the – both forgot; – but the subject was to present heart, mind, soul, and all the affections – a living sacrifice to God; – he was most gloriously animated, and seemed to have imbibed the very spirit and manners of the great apostle. – Our afternoon orator was a stranger to me – he was blest with a good, clear, and well-toned articulate voice; – he preached from the Psalms – and took great pains to prove that God knew more than we – that letters were the fountain of our knowledge – that a man in Westminster was totally ignorant of what was going forward in Whitechapel – that we might have some memory of what we did last week – but have no sort of conjecture of what we shall do to-morrow, &c. &c. – Now Harrison's whole drift was that we should live the life of angels here – in order to be so in reality hereafter – The other good soul gave us wholesome matter of fact – They were both right – (but I fear not to speak my mind to my M*eheux* who, if he condemns my head, will, I am sure, acquit my heart). – You have read and admired Sterne's Sermons – which chiefly inculcate practical duties, and paint brotherly love and the true Christian charities in such beauteous glowing colours

– that one cannot help wishing to feed the hungry – clothe the naked, &c. &c. – I would to God, my friend, that the great lights of the church would exercise their oratorical powers upon Yorick's[2] plan: – the heart and passions once lifted under the banners of blest Philanthropy, would naturally ascend to the redeeming God – flaming with grateful rapture. – Now I have observed among the modern Saints – who profess to pray without ceasing – that they are so fully taken up with pious meditations – and so wholly absorbed in the love of God – that they have little if any room for the love of man. – If I am wrong, tell me so honestly – the censure of a friend is of more value than his money – and to submit to conviction, is a proof of good sense. – I made my bow to-night to Mrs. H——; the rest of the rogues were out – bright-eyed S—— and all. – Mrs. H—— says that you are hypped – Nonsense! – few can rise superior to pain – and the head, I will allow, is a part the most *sensible* if affected – but even then you are not obliged to use more motion than you like – Though I can partly feel the awkward sensations, and uneasy reflections, which will often arise upon the least ail of so precious a member as the eye – yet certain I am, the more you can be master of yourself (I mean as to cheerfulness, if not gaiety of mind) the better it will of course be with you. – I hope *George* is well – and that you ride often to see him I make no doubt – I like the monkey – I know not for why, nor does it signify a button – but sure he is good-tempered and grateful – but what's that to me? – Good night – the clock talks of eleven.

Yours, &c.

I. SANCHO.

1. Harrison: see Letter 29, n. 5.
2. Yorick: Sterne. See Letter 54, n. 2.

44

TO MR. M'[EHEUX]'.

July 23, 1777.

Yes – too true it is – for the many (aye, and some of those many carry their heads high) – too true for the miserable – the needy – the sick – for many, alas! who now may have no helper – for the child of folly poor S——[1] and even for thy worthless friend Sancho. – It is too true that the Almighty has called to her rich reward – she who, whilst on earth, approved herself his best delegate. – How blind, how silly, is the mortal who places any trust or hope in aught but the Almighty! – You are just, beautifully just, in your sketch of the vicissitudes of worldly bliss. – We rise the lover – dine the husband – and too oft, alas! lie down the forlorn widower. – Never so struck in my life! – It was on Friday night, between ten and eleven, just preparing for my concluding pipe – the Duke of *Montagu*'s man knocks – 'Have you heard the bad news?' – No – 'The Duchess of Queensberry² died last night.' – I felt fifty different sensations – unbelief was uppermost – when he crushed my incredulity, by saying he had been to know how his Grace did – who was also very poorly in health. – Now the preceding day, Thursday (the day on which she expired), I had received a very penitential letter from *Soubise*, dated from St. Helena; – this letter I enclosed in a long tedious epistle of my own – and sent to Petersham, believing the family to be all there. – The day after you left town her Grace died – that day week she was at my door – the day after I had the honor of a long audience in her dressing-room. – Alas! this hour blessed with health – crowned with honors – loaded with riches, and encircled with friends – the next reduced to a lump of poor clay – a tenement for worms. – Earth re-possesses part of what she gave – and the freed spirit mounts on wings of fire: – her disorder was a stoppage – she fell ill the evening of the Friday that I last saw her – continued in her full senses to the last. – The good she had done reached the skies long before her lamented death – and are the only heralds that are worth the pursuit of wisdom: – as to her bad deeds, I have never heard of them – had it been for the best, God would have lent her a little longer to a foolish world, which hardly deserved so good a woman: – for my own part – I have lost a friend – and perhaps 'tis better so. – 'Whatever is,' &c. &c. – I wish *Soubise* knew this heavy news, for many reasons. – I am inclined to believe her Grace's death is the only thing that will most conduce to his reform. – I fear neither his gratitude nor sensibility will be much hurt upon hearing the news – it will act upon his fears, and make him do *right* upon a *base* principle. – Hang him! he teases me whenever I think of him. – I supped last night with *Stevenson*; he called in just now, and says he has a right to be remembered to you. – You and he are two odd monkeys – the more I abuse and rate you, the better friend you think me. – As you have found out that your

spirits govern your head – you will of course contrive every method
of keeping your instrument in tune: sure I am that bathing – riding
– walking – in succession – the two latter not violent, will brace
your nerves – purify your blood – invigorate its circulation – Add to
the rest *continency* – yes, again I repeat it, *continency*; – before you
reply, think – re-think – and think again – look into your *Bible*
– look in *Young* – peep into your own breast – if your heart
warrants what your head counsels, act then boldly. – Oh! *apropos*
– pray thank my noble friend Mrs. H—— for her friendly present
of currant-jelly: it did Mrs. Sancho service, and does poor Billy
great good – who has (through his teeth) been plagued with a cough
– which I hope will not turn to the whooping sort. – The girls greet
you as their respected school-master. – As to your spirited kind
offer of a f*awn*,³ why when you please – you know what I intend
doing with it.

Poor Lady S——, I find, still lingers this side the world. – Alas!
when will the happy period arrive that the sons of mortality may
greet each other with the joyful news, that sin, pain, sorrow, and
death, are no more! skies without clouds, earth without crimes, life
without death, world without end! – peace, bliss, and harmony,
where the Lord – God – All in all – King of kings – Lord of lords
– reigneth – omnipotent – for ever – for ever! – May you, dear
M*eheux*, and all I love – yea the whole race of Adam, join with my
unworthy weak self, in the stupendous – astonishing – soul-cheer-
ing Hallelujahs! – where Charity may be swallowed up in Love –
Hope in Bliss – and Faith in glorious Certainty! – We will mix, my
boy, with all countries, colours, faiths – see the countless multitudes
of the first world – the myriads descended from the Ark – the
Patriarchs – Sages – Prophets – and Heroes! My head turns round at
the vast idea! – We will mingle with them and to untwist the vast
chain of blessed Providence – which puzzles and baffles human
understanding. Adieu.

Yours, &c.

I. SANCHO.

1. 'The child of folly poor S——': this must refer to the
   disgraced Soubise, see n. 2 below, and Letter 1, n. 6.
2. 'The Duchess of Queensberry ... a very penitential letter
   from Soubise, dated from St. Helena': reports of Soubise's
   disgrace for raping a maid of the Duchess were published in
   the *Morning Post* on 22 July 1777. Some time after this he

sailed to exile in India. Sancho's Letter 1, wrongly dated 14 February 1768, anticipates that its recipient will meet Soubise in India, so 1778 would appear to be the correct date of Letter 1. Soubise is said to have sailed for India on 15 July 1777: according to Letter 80, the Duchess died on 17 July 1777, 'just two days after you [Soubise] sailed from Portsmouth'. In Letter 44, Sancho says that he received a letter from Soubise from St Helena one day before 'the day on which she [the Duchess] expired'. Soubise would thus have been at sea only one day: clearly Sancho could not have received a letter from Soubise from St Helena. If there was a penitential letter from Soubise delivered at this time, it must have come from Portsmouth. Perhaps Sancho is confusing this letter with those he received from Soubise, sent not from St Helena but from Madeira and the Cape (Letter 80, 29 November 1778). Sancho had to delay the sad news of the Duchess's death until he knew Soubise's address in Madras, which he could not know until he had received Soubise's letter 'dated from Madras' to which Letter 80 is a reply. The long delay in correspondence probably affected the accuracy of Sancho's memory.

3. 'Your spirited kind offer of a 'f——' probably refers to the fawn (venison) of Letter 46: in Letter 34, Sancho writes 'F—— and venison are good things'.

45

TO MR. M'[EHEUX]'.

August 8, 1777.

'Know your own self, presume not God to scan;
'The only science of mankind, is man.'[1]

There is something so amazingly grand – so stupendously affecting – in the contemplating the works of the Divine Architect, either in the moral or the intellectual world, that I think one may rightly call it the cordial of the soul – it is the physic of the mind – and the best antidote against weak pride – and the supercilious murmurings of discontent. – Smoking my morning pipe, the friendly warmth of that glorious planet the sun – the leniency of the air – the cheerful glow of the atmosphere – made me involuntarily cry, 'Lord, 'what is man, that thou in thy mercy art so mindful of him! or what the son of man, that thou so parentally carest for him!' David, whose heart and affections were naturally of the first kind (and who indeed had experienced blessings without number), pours forth the grateful sentiments of his enraptured soul in the sweetest modulations of pathetic oratory. – The tender mercies of the Almighty are not less to many of his creatures – but their hearts, unlike the royal disposition of the shepherd King, are cold, and untouched with the sweet ray of gratitude. – Let us, without meanly sheltering our infirmities under the example of others – perhaps worse taught – or possest of less leisure for self-examination – let us, my dear Meheux, look into ourselves – and, by a critical examination of the past events of our lives, fairly confess what mercies we have received – what God in his goodness hath done for us – and how our gratitude and praise have kept pace in imitation of the son of Jesse. – Such a research would richly pay us – for the end would be conviction – so much on the side of miraculous mercy – such an unanswerable proof of the superintendency of Divine Providence, as would effectually cure us of rash despondency – and melt our hearts with devotional aspirations – till we poured forth the effusions of our souls in praise and thanksgiving. – When I sometimes endeavour to turn my thoughts inwards, to review the power or properties the indulgent all-wise Father has endowed me with, I am struck with wonder and with awe – worm, poor insignificant reptile as I am, with regard to superior beings – moral like myself. – Amongst, and at the very head of our riches, I reckon the power of reflection: – Where? where, my friend, doth it lie? – Search every member from the toe to the nose – all – all ready for action – but all dead to thought – It lies not in matter – nor in the blood – it is a party, which though we feel and acknowledge, quite past the power of definition – it is that breath of life which the Sacred Architect breathed into the nostils of the first man – image of his gracious Maker – and let it animate our torpid gratitude – it rolls on, although diminished by our cruel fall, through the whole race – 'We are fearfully and wonderfully made,'[2] &c. &c. were the sentiments of the Royal Preacher upon a self-review – but had he been blessed with the full blaze of the Christian dispensation – what would have been his raptures! – the promise of never, never-ending existence and felicity – to possess eternity – 'glorious dreadful thought!' – to rise, perhaps, by regular progression from planet to planet – to behold the wonders of immensity – to pass from good to better – increasing in goodness – knowledge – love – to glory in our Redeemer – to joy in ourselves – to be acquainted with prophets, sages, heroes, and poets of old times – and join in symphony with

angels! – And now, my friend, thou smilest at my futile notions –
Why preach to thee? – For this very good and simple reason, to
get your thoughts in return. – You shall be my philosopher – my
Mentor – my friend: – you, happily disengaged from various cares
of life and family, can review the little world of man with steadier
eye, and more composed thought, than your friend, declining fast
into the vale of years, and beset with infirmity and pain. – Write
now and then, as thought prompts, and inclination leads – refute my
errors – where I am just, give me your plaudit. – Your welfare is
truly dear in my sight – and if any man has a share in my heart, or
commands my respect and esteem, it is *James Meheux*.

Witness my mark,
I. SANCHO.

1. Pope, *Essay on Man* Ep. II, ll. 1–2. Sancho quotes inaccurately. For 'only science', read 'proper study'.
2. *Psalms* 139:14.

46

TO MR. M'[EHEUX]'.
August 14, 1777.

My dear M*eheux*, I know full well thy silence must proceed from ill
health. To say it concerns me, is dull nonsense – self-love without
principle will inspire even Devils with affection: – by so much less
as thou apprehendest thy friend has diabolical about him – so mayst
thou judge of his feelings towards thee. – Why wilt thou not part
with thy hair? Most assuredly I do believe it would relieve thee past
measure – Thou dost not fancy thy strength (like Samson's the
Israelite) lieth in thy hair. Remember, he was shorn thro' folly – he
lost his wits previous to his losing his locks – Do thou consent to
lose thine, in order to save thy better judgment. – I know no worse
soul-sinking pain than the head-ache, though (thank Heaven!) I am
not often visited with it. – I long to see thee – and will soon – if in
my power. – Some odd folks would think it would have *been* but
good manners to have thank'd you for the fawn[1] – but then, says the
punster, that would have *been* so like *fawn*-ing – which J. M*eheux*
loves not – *no*, nor Sancho either – 'tis the hypocrite's key to the

great man's heart – 'tis the resource of cowardly curs – and deceitful *bipeds*: – it is the spaniel's sort – and man's disgrace: – it is – In short, the day is so hot – that I cannot say at present any more about it – but that the fawn was large, fresh, and worthy the giver, the receiver, and the joyous souls that ate it. – Billy has suffered much in getting his teeth – I have just wished him joy by his mother's desire, who says that he took resolution at last, and walked to her some few steps quite alone: – albeit it gave me no small pleasure; – yet, upon consideration, what I approve of now perhaps (should I live to see him at man's estate) I might then disapprove – unless God's grace should as ably support him through the quick-sands, rocks, and shoals of life – as it has, happily, the honest being I am now writing to. – God give you health! – your own conduct will secure peace – your friends bread. – As to honors, leave it with titles – to knaves – and be content with that of an honest man,

    'the noblest work of God.'
Shave – shave – shave.

Farewell! Yours sincerely,
I. SANCHO.

1. 'Good manners to have thank'd you for the fawn': Sancho makes heavy weather of his puns on 'fawning'. The reader might infer from 'the joyous souls that ate it', that the 'fawn' was in fact venison.

47

TO MISS C'[REWE]'.

August 15, 1777.

I waited, in hopes that time or chance might furnish me with something to fill a sheet with better than the praises of an old man. – What have youth and beauty to do with the squabbling contentions of mad ambition? – Could I new-model Nature – your sex should rule supreme – there should be no other ambition but that of pleasing the ladies – no other warfare but the contention of obsequious lovers – nor any glory but the bliss of being approved by the Fair. – Now confess that this epistle opens very gallant, and allow this to be a decent return to one of the best and most sensible letters, that L—— Wells[1] has produced this century past. – I much wish for the pleasing hopes raised by your obliging letter, that my good friend's health is restored so fully, that she has by this time forgot what the pains in the stomach mean; – that she has sent all her complaints to the lake of Lethe – and is thinking soon to enliven our part of the world, enriched with health, spirits, and a certain bewitching benignity of countenance – which cries out, Dislike me if you can. – I want to know what conquests you have made – what savages converted – whom you have smiled into felicity, or killed by rejection – and how the noble Master of Ceremonies acquits himself, John *Spink*, Esq. I mean. – I hear my friend R*ush* will be in town this week, to my great comfort – for, upon my conscience, excepting my family, the town to me is quite empty. – Mrs. R*ush* is gone to Bury – and the good man is toiling, a lonely and forlorn object. – Mrs. Sancho joins in every good and grateful wish for your amiable friend,[2] with, dear Miss C*rewe*, your obliged friend and humble servant,

I. SANCHO.

1. L—— Wells: this is most likely to be Llandrindod Wells, a popular watering resort less costly than Bath though less highly fashionable, in Brecon, just over the Welsh border from Herefordshire and Shropshire: but also in Brecon are Llanwyrtd Wells and Llangummarch Wells. However, Sancho wrote a dance, presumably to celebrate the visit, called 'Lindindrod Lasses' to which he requested Mrs Cocksedge and friends to compose 'a figure', i.e. the dance-steps, in Letter 55, see n. 6.
2. Miss Crewe is accompanied by her 'amiable friend' Mrs Cocksedge, said in Letter 49 to have recently returned from a 'western expedition' for her health. Sancho writes here of 'the pleasing hopes raised by your obliging letter that my good friend's health is restored so fully …'.

48

TO MR. M'[EHEUX]'.

August 25, 1777.

JACK-ASSES.

My gall has been plentifully stirred – by the barbarity of a set of gentry, who *every* morning offend my feelings – in their cruel parade through Charles Street to and from market – they vend potatoes in the day – and thieve in the night season. – A tall lazy villain was bestriding his poor beast (although loaded with two panniers of potatoes at the same time), and another of his companions was good-naturedly employed in whipping the poor sinking animal – that the gentleman-rider might enjoy the two-fold pleasure of blasphemy and cruelty – This is a too common evil – and, for the honor of rationality, calls loudly for redress. – I do believe it might be in some measure amended – either by a hint in the papers, of the utility of impressing such vagrants for the king's service – or by laying a heavy tax upon the poor Jack-asses – I prefer the former, both for thy sake and mine; – and, as I am convinced we feel instinctively the injuries of our *fellow creatures*, I do insist upon your exercising your talents in behalf of the honest sufferers. – I ever had a kind of sympathetic (call it what you please) for that animal – *and do I not love you?* – Before Sterne had wrote them into respect,[1] I had a friendship for them – and many a civil greeting have I given them at casual meetings – What has ever (with me) stamped a kind of uncommon value and dignity upon the long-ear'd kind of the species, is, that our blessed Saviour, in his day of worldly triumph, chose to use that in preference to the rest of his own blessed creation – 'meek and lowly, riding upon an ass.' I am convinced that the general inhumanity of manking proceeds – first, from the cursed false principle of common education – and, secondly, from a total indifference (if not disbelief) of the Christian faith, – A heart and mind impressed with a firm belief of the Christian tenets, must of course exercise itself in a constant uniform general philanthropy – Such a being carries his heaven in his breast – and such be thou! Therefore write me a bitter Philippick against the misusers of Jack-asses – it shall honor a column in the Morning Post – and I will bray – bray my thanks to you – thou shalt figure away the champion of poor friendless asses here – and hereafter shalt not be ashamed in the great day of retribution.

Mrs. Sancho would send you some tamarinds. – I know not her reasons; – as I hate contentions, I contradicted not – but shrewdly suspect she thinks you want cooling. – Do you hear, Sir? send me some more good news about your head. – Your letters will not be the less welcome for talking about *John Meheux*, but pray do not let vanity so master your judgment, to fancy yourself upon a footing with George for well-looking – If you were indeed a proof sheet, you was marred in the taking off – for George (ask the girls) is certainly the fairest impression.

I had an order from Mr. Henderson[2] on Thursday night to see him do Falstaff – I put some money to it, and took Mary and Betsy with me – It was Betty's first affair – and she enjoyed it in truth – Henderson's Falstaff is entirely original – and I think as great as his Shylock: – he kept the house in a continual roar of laughter: – in some things he falls short of Quin[3] – in many I think him equal. – When I saw Quin play, he was at the height of his art, with thirty years judgment to guide him. Henderson, in seven years more, will be all that better – and confessedly the first man on the English stage, or I am much mistaken.

I am reading a little pamphlet, which I much like: it favours an opinion which I have long indulged – which is the improbability of eternal Damnation – a thought which almost petrifies one – and, in my opinion, derogatory to the fullness, glory, and benefit of the blessed expiation of the Son of the Most High God – who died for the sins of all – all – Jew, Turk, Infidel, and Heretic; – fair – sallow – brown – tawny – black – and you and I – and every son and daughter of Adam. – You must find eyes to read this book – head and heart, with a quickness of conception, thou enjoyest – with many – many advantages – which have the love – and envy almost of yours,   I. SANCHO.

Respects in folio to Mrs. H——.

1. Jackasses: a favourite topic of Sterne, see *Tristram Shandy*, vol. IV, ch. 20. 'I'll not hurt the poorest jackass upon the king's high-way'; vol. VII, ch. 32, 'God help thee, Jack! said I, thou hast a bitter breakfast on't – and many a bitter day's labour.' The reference in Sancho is probably to the famous chapter 'The Dead Ass' in *A Sentimental Journey*: 'Shame on the world! said I to myself. – Did we but love each other as this poor soul loved his ass – 'twould be something.'
2. John Henderson (1747–1805): an actor known as 'the Bath Roscius'. He was a friend of Gainsborough, and on the stage came next to Garrick in public esteem. Garrick was jealous of him.
3. James Quin (1693–1766): as an actor of the older generation he was Garrick's great rival in reputation. On his death Garrick composed an epitaph for his tomb at the Abbey Church, Bath.

49

TO MR. R'[USH]'.

August 27, 1777.

DEAR FRIEND,

Whether this finds you officially parading on Newmarket turfs – or in the happier society of the good geniuses of Barton House – may it find you well – in good joyous spirits – gay, debonair – happy at heart – happy as I have seen my meaning express'd in the countenance of my friend Mrs. *Cocksedge*, where humanity – humility – and good-will – have outshone beauty – in one of the finest faces of your country – But this between ourselves: and pray how does the aforesaid lady do? – Does she ride, walk, and dance, with moderation? – and can you tell me that she continues as well as when she first went down? – and still finds good from her western expedition? – And the little Syren[1] Miss *Crewe*? – Have there no letters, sent by Cupid's post, sticking on the arrow's point, been picked up about your grounds, blown by western breezes across the country? – Tell her nothing can ever hurt her but Love and Time. – May Love bring her happiness, and Time honour! – As to wealth – may she have no more than she can manage with comfort and credit! Monsieur L——'s letter is a good one – and I think it would make one laugh even in the gout. – God bless his old boy – for he is a true type of beggarly pride – cunning – narrow-hearted – vain and mean – one of Satan's dupes – who do his dirty work for a little worldly trash – and cheat themselves at last. – I know a man who delights to make every one he can happy – that same man treated some honest girls with expenses for a Vauxhall evening.[2] – If you should happen to know him, you may tell him from me – that last night – three great girls – a boy – and a fat old fellow – were as happy and pleas'd as a fine evening – fine place – good songs – much company – and good music could make them. – Heaven and Earth! – how happy, how delighted were the girls! – Oh! the pleasures of novelty to youth! – We went by water – had a coach home – were gazed at – followed, &c. &c. – but not much abused.[3] – I must break off before I have half finished – for Mr. —— is just come in – You are not the first good friend that has been neglected for a fop.

IGN. SANCHO.

1. The 'Little Syren' would be Miss Crewe, elsewhere associated by Sancho with the temptations of love: 'Oh, Miss Crewe! beware – beware of the little god,' (Letter 70). Miss Crewe had been Mrs Cocksedge's companion on the 'western expedition' to Llandrindod Wells, see Letter 47, n. 2.
2. The Vauxhall or New Spring Gardens, a famous public pleasure park in London, close to the Thames near Lambeth Palace.
3. 'Not much abused' has been interpreted as racial abuse, but it would not have been uncommon for anyone riding by coach in a party to be subject to a degree of mockery by London street urchins. Sancho does not sound much offended, more amused; see the Introduction, p. 9.

50

TO MR. M'[EHEUX]'.
September 3, 1777.

I feel it long since I heard from you – very long since I saw you – and three or four days back had some notion I should never, in this paltry world, see thee again – But (thanks to the Father of Mercies!) I am better, and have a higher relish of health and ease, from contrasting and blessings with the pains I have endured. – Would to God you could say that your dizzy dismal head-achs were flown to the moon, or embarked for Lapland – there to be tied up in a witch's bag – and sold to Beelzebub with a cargo of bad winds – religious quarrels – politics – my gout – and our American grievances! – But what are you about in your last (where you dropped the candid friend and assumed the flatterer). – You hinted as if there was a chance of seeing you in Charles Street: I wish it much, – My friend, I have had a week's gout in my hand, which was by much too hard for my philosophy. – I am convinced, let the Stoics say what they list – that pain is an evil: – in short, I was wishing for death – and little removed from madness – But (thank Heaven!) I am much better – my spirits will be mended if I hear from you – better still to see you. – I find it painful to write much, and learn that two hands are as necessary in writing as eating. – You see I write, like a lady, from one corner of the paper to the other. – My respects – and love – and admiration – and compliments – to Mrs. ——, and Mrs. and Miss —— Tell Mitchell, he kept his word in calling to see us before he left town! – I hope confound the ink! – what a blot![1] Now don't you dare suppose I was in fault – No Sir, the pen was diabled[2] – the paper worse, – there was a concatenation of ill-sorted chances – all – all – coincided to contribute to that fatal blot – which has so disarranged my ideas, that I must perforce finish before I had half disburthened my head and heart. – But is N*ancy* a good girl? – And how does my honest George do? Tell Mrs. H—— what you please in the handsome way of me. – Farewell, I will write no more nonsense this night – that's flat.

                                                        IGN. SANCHO.

How do you like the print? – Mr. D—— says, and his wife says the same, that your are exceedingly clever – and they shall be happy to do any thing which is produced by the same hand which did the original – and if Mr. D—— can be of any service to you in the etching, you may command him when you please.

1. An example of Sterne-like game-playing with the text, the whimsical introduction of an irrelevant digression, by making his topic a blot on the page.
2. Diabled: bedevilled.

51

TO MR. M'[EHEUX]'.
                                                    September 16, 1777.
Sir, he is the confounded'st dunderhead – sapscull – looby – clodpate – nincompoop – ninnyhammer – booby-chick – farcical – loungibuss – blunderbuss[1] – this good day in the three kingdoms! – You would bless yourself, were it possible for you to analyse such a being – not but his heart is susceptible of a kind of friendly warmth – but then so cursed careless – ever in a hurry – ever in the wrong, at best but blundering about the right. – Why now, for example, when you sent the pig, I can make oath, if need be, that the dunce I speak of longed more for a letter than the animal – The basket was searched with hurry – not care; – No letter! – Well it can't be help'd – his head ach'd – he had not time, &c. &c. – The pig was disengaged from the basket – the straw consigned to the chimney. – This being rather a coolish morning, a little fire was

thought necessary – and in raking up the loose dirty waste stuff under the grate, there appeared a very bloody letter, which seemed unopened: – your hand-writing was discernible through the dirt and blood: – curiosity and affection ran a race to pick up and examine it – when, behold, it proved to be the companion of the pig! but so effaced with blood – that very – very little of my friend's good sense could be made out. – Your poor letter is a type of what daily happens – merit oppressed and smothered by rubbish. – Alas! poor letter, it shared the fate, the poor world, which we inhabit, will hereafter undergo – one bright gleam of imitation of the mind that dictated it – some few sparks. Alas! alas! my poor letter – pass but a few years – perhaps a few months – thy generous friendly compost may – thy friend whose heart glows while he writes – who feels thy worth – yea and reveres it too. – Nonsense – Why we know the very hinges of our last cradles will rust and moulder; – and that, in the course of another century, neither flesh, bone, coffin, or nail – will be discernible from mother earth. – Courage – While we live, let us live – to Virtue – Friendship – Religion – Charity – then drop (at death's call) our cumbrous (you are thin) load of flesh, and mount in spirit to our native home. – Bless us, at what a rate have I been travelling! – I am quite out of breath – Why, my friend, the business was to thank you for the pig. – Had you seen the group of heads – aye, and wise ones too – that assembled at the opening of the fardel – the exclamations – Oh! the finest – fattest – cleanest – why, sir, it was a pig of pigs; – the pettitoes[2] gave us a good supper last night – they were well dressed – and your pig was well eat – it dined us Sunday and Monday. – Now, to say truth, I do not love pig – merely pig I like not – but pork corned – alias – salted – either roast or boiled – I will eat against any filthy Jew naturalized – or under the bann. – On Saturday-night the newsman brought me the two papers of J—— 13th and 20th; – right joyful did I receive them – I ran to Mrs. Sancho – with I beg you will read my friend's sensible and spirited defence of – of, &c. – She read – though it broke in upon her work – she approved; – but chance or fortune – or ill-luck – or what ever you mean by accident – has played us a confounded trick – for since Saturday they have – both papers – disappeared – without hands – or legs – or eyes – for no one has seen them. – Bureau – boxes – cupboards – drawers – parlour – chamber – shop – all – all has been rummaged – pockets – port-folio – holes – corners – all been searched. – Did you see them? – did you? – Where can they be? – I know not – nor I – Nor I – but God does! – Omnipotence knoweth all things. – It has vexed me – fretted dame Sancho ... teased the children – but so it is. – Hereafter I suppose they will be found in some obvious (though now unthought of) place; and then it will be, Good Lord, who could have thought it!

Where is the *Jack-ass* business? – Do not be lazy – I feel myself a party concerned – and when I see you, I have a delicious morsel of true feminine grace and generosity to shew you. – I shall not apologize for this crude epistle – but mark and remark – I do thank you in the name of every Sancho, but – self – They ate and were filled; – I have reason to thank you – but – as I do not affect pig – in a piggish sense – I hold myself execpted; – and, although I did eat – and did also commend, yet I will not thank you, that's poz.[3]

I. SANCHO.

The papers are found, as you will see – Here is one and a piece – it has suffered through ignorance; – but what cannot be cured must be endured.

1. Another imitation of Sterne's whimsicality of style, going back to the rhetorical catalogues of objects and attributes, of which there are several instances in this one letter. To give an example from *Tristram Shandy*, 'Fool, coxcomb, puppy — give him but a NOSE – Cripple, Dwarf, Driviller, Goosecap –' (vol. IV, ch. 20). In this letter, as is common too with Sterne, a trivial subject, here the gift of a joint of pork, is made the subject of a comic semi-melancholic digression on nothing in particular, for which reason the meaning of the letter is inevitably unclear.
2. Pettitoes: pig's trotters.
3. Poz: positive.

52

TO MR. R'[USH]'.

Sept. 17. 1777.

MY RESPECTED FRIEND.

I feel myself guilty of an unmannerly neglect – in delaying to give my good Mrs. *Cocksedge* some account of the little commissions she honored me with. – You must exert your friendly influence, in making my peace with her – not but that I well know mercy has the blest preponderancy in her scale – nor can kindness or mercy be lodged in a fairer breast. – In faith I am scarce half alive – yet what really is alive about me – hungers to hear news from *Bunbury*: first how Mrs. *Cocksedge* got down – and her good companion – how her health is. Tell her, I hope she left all her pains behind her – If so, I believe I have taken possession of them all – Alas, my friend, I never was but half so bad before – both feet knocked up at once, plenty of excruciating pains, and great lack of patience – Mrs. Sancho has had a blessed week of it – for my companion did not contribute much to the sweetening my temper – It was the washing-week, which you know made it a full chance and half better. – She was forced to break sugar and attend shop. – God bless her and reward her! – she is good – good in heart good in principle – good by habit – good by Heaven! God forgive me, I had almost sworn. – Tell me how the ladies got down – how they do? and what they do? – how you do? – and how —— feels now the broom is hung on his door-top. – The certainty that *Bunbury* and its connexions are all alive and merry will be a cure for my gout – and thou shalt be sole doctor – as well as first friend to thy ever obliged true friend,

I. SANCHO.

53

TO MR. M'[EHEUX]'.

September 20, 1777,

'What Reason warrants, and what Wisdom guides,
'All else is towering phrensy, or rank folly.'[1]

So says ADDISON
And so well knoweth my friend J. M*eheux* Well, and what then? Why, if follows of course – that, instead of feeling myself delighted and gratefully thankful, for – I will and must speak out – yet if these kindnesses cost the pocket of my friend – they are not kindnesses to the Sanchos. – For innate goodness of heart – greatness of spirit – urbanity – humanity – temperance – justice – with the whole sweet list of Heaven-born manly virtues – I do, without flattery, give thee (and with pride do I avouch it) credit – I respect thy person, and love thy principles; – but, my good M*eheux*, there is

a prior duty – which I dare believe you will never willingly be deficient in – and yet your generosity of soul may let even such a worm as I break into it. – Now, that should not be – for take me right – I do not mean any thing derogatory to your rank in the world – or to the strength of your finances – What Sterne said of himself, that think I of you – that you are as good a gentleman as the King – but not quite so rich. – I honor thy feelings – and am happy that I can honestly say, that I conceive them. – The joy of giving and making happy is almost the attribute of a God – and there is as much sweetness conveyed to the senses by doing a right well-natured deed, as our frame can consistently bear – *So much for chastisement – a pretty way of thanking.* – Well, I have critically examined thy song – some parts I like well – as it is a maidenhead it should be gently treated – But why N——?[2] Oh! Nature, a true passion is jealous even of the initials of its mistress's name. – Well, N—— let it be – I will certainly attempt giving it a tune – such as I can – the first leisure – but it must undergo some little pruning when we meet. – I have had another little visit from the gout – and my hand yet remembers the rough salute; – my spirits have been rather low. – Young's ninth night, the Consolation,[3] has been my last week's study – it is almost divine: – how many times has it raised, warmed, and charmed me! – and is still new. – I hope you found your mother and honest George as well as you wished – and had the full enjoyment of maternal and filial affections. – The girls are rampant well – and Bill gains something every day. – The rogue is to excess fond of me – for which I pity him – and myself more. – My respect and kind enquiry to your old horse. – Tell him I wish him better – and am a real friend to honest brutes – some I could almost envy. – To say I am rejoiced to hear you are better, is telling you no news —— Be but as well as I wish you – as rich – and as good – Sampson, Solomon, and the Duke de Penthievre, will never be comparisons more. – Adieu!

Yours, &c.
I. SANCHO.

I am as melancholy – as a tea-kettle when it sings (as the maids call it) over a dead fire.

Oh! – but is it N*ancy* indeed? – Now don't you be after humming[4] me – Believe me, honey, if I never find out the truth, I shall know it for all that.

1. I have not been able to find the source for Addison's words.
2. It appears that Meheux has sent a poem designating his girl-friend Nancy only by her initial: Sancho jests that the practice of using initials is a sign of jealousy, and intends to set the poem to music, after he has carried out some 'pruning'.
3. Edward Young, *Night Thoughts* (1752–5). 'The Consolation' is the name of the ninth Book or 'Night' of the poem, and concerns the Day of Judgement. The poet cannot be the Edward Young of Letter 7, since he had died five years before.
4. Humming: humbugging, trying to delude, also a pun on humming a tune, and humming like a honey-bee.

54

TO MR. S'[TEVENSON]'.

October 24, 1777.

I deny it – That I ought to have acknowledged your favor two weeks ago I confess – but my silence was not so long – nor broad – nor rusty – nor fusty as yours. – Blithe health – festive hours – and social mirth – be thine, my friend! – Thy letter, though late, was truly welcome – it unbended the brow of care – and suspended, for some hours, disagreeable thoughts. – By St. Radagunda! quoth I – (ramming my nostrils with Hardham)[1] he has catched the mantle. – Alas, poor Yorick![2] – Oh! that thou hadst, by divine permission, been suffered a little – little longer, amongst the moon-struck children of this namby pamby world! – Father of light and life! thy will be done: – but surely – half the wit – half the good sense – of this present age – were interred in Sterne's grave. – His broad philanthropy, like the soul-cheering-rays of the blessed Sun, invested his happy spirit, and soared into Heaven with it – where, in progressive rise from bliss to bliss, he drinks-in large draughts of rapture, love and knowledge, and chants the praises of redeeming love, with joy unbounded and unceasing vigour. – Your invocation has mounted me, Merry Andrew-like,[3] upon stilts. – I ape you, as monkeys ape men by walking upon two. – That you have recovered the true tone of your health and spirits, I rejoice – To be happy in despite of fortune shows the Philosopher – the Hero – the Christian. – I must confess, my fortitude (which is wove of very flimsy materials) too oft gives way in the rough and unfriendly jostles of life: – Madam Fortune, who by the way is a bunter[4] – (and such I love not) has been particularly cross and untoward to me since you left us – They say she is fond of fools – 'Tis false and scandalous – She hates me – and I have the vanity to say and believe – that if folly, sheer folly, had any charms, I should stand as fair in her esteem as A.B. C.D. E.F. – or any of Folly's family through the whole alphabet. – You halted at Burleigh – You did just what I wished you to do – and left it, I trust, as well in health as you entered that sweet mansion – Stopp'd at Retford – and found your venerable parents well – and contributed to their happiness – increased their felicity by the many nice little attentions of filial love – which the good heart delights in – and even angels approve. – And how do the worthy souls of Hull and its environs? – Do they credit themselves by esteeming a good-enough kind of mortal? – You cannot imagine what hold little Billy gets of me – he grows – prattles – every day learns something new – and by his good-will would be ever in the shop with me – The monkey! he clings round my legs – and if I chide him or look sour, he holds up his little mouth to kiss me. – I know I am the fool – for parents' weakness is child's strength: – truth orthodox – which will hold good between lover and lovee – as well as ... Mrs. Sancho is so so – The virgins are as well as youth and innocence – souls void of care and consciences of offence can be. – Dame Sancho would be better if she cared less. – I am her barometer – If a sigh escapes me, it is answered by a tear in her eye. – I oft assume a gaiety to illume her dear sensibility with a smile – which twenty years ago almost bewitched me: – and *mark!* – after twenty years enjoyment – constitutes my highest pleasure! – Such be your lot – with a competency – such as will make œconomy a pleasant acquaintance – temperance and exercise your chief physician – and the virtues of benevolence your daily employ – your pleasure and reward! – And what more can friendship wish you – but to glide down the stream of time – blest with a partner of congenial principles, and fine feelings – true feminine eloquence – whose very looks speak tenderness and sentiment – your infants growing – with the roseate bloom of health – minds cultured by their father – expanding daily in every improvement? – Blest little souls! – and happy – happy parents! – Such be thy lot in life – in marriage! – But take a virgin – or a maiden to thy arms; – but – be that as thy fate wills it. – Now for news. – Two hours ago (in tolerable health and cheery spirits), considering his journey not so fatigued as might be expected – followed by four superb carriages – their Royal Highnesses the Duke and Duchess of Gloucester arrived in town. – As to America, if you know any thing at Hull, you know more than is known in London. – Samuel Foote, Esq.[5] is dead – a leg was burried some years since – and now the whole *foote* follows. – I think you love a pun. – Colman[6] is the gainer, as he covenanted to give him 1600l. *per annum*, for his patent. – In short, Colman is happy in the bargain – and I trust Foote is no loser. – I have seen poor Mr. de Groote[7] but once – and then could not attend to speak with him – as I had customers in the shop. – I waited by appointment for Mr. ——, to get your honor's address – and then three weeks before I could get the franks – a fortnight since for Mr. —— writing to you – I call this a string of beggarly apologies. – I told M*eheux* you expected a line from him – He wanted faith. – I made him read your letter – and what then? 'Truly, he was not capable – he had had no classical education – You write with elegance – ease – propriety.' – Tut, quoth I, pr'ythee give not the reins to pride – Write as I do – just the effusions of a warm though foolish heart: – friendship will cast a veil of kindness over thy blunders – they will be accepted with a complacent smile – and read with the same eye of kindness – which indulges now the errors of his sincere friend,

IGN. SANCHO.

A true genius will always remember to leave a space – unwritten – to come in contact with the wax or wafer – by which means the reader escapes half an hour's puzzle to make out a sentence; – and ever while you live – never omit – no – not that – What? – what! – Dates! Dates! – Am not I a grocer? – pun the second.

1. Hardham: a brand of snuff.
2. 'Catched the mantle ... Yorick!': caught the quality of Sterne in his letter. Yorick was a fictional clergyman of Danish extraction supposedly a descendant of Hamlet's jester, invented by Sterne for *Tristram Shandy* – see vol. I, ch. 12. For *A Sentimental Journey*, Sterne adopted the name as his own pseudonym.
3. Merry-Andrew: a clownish entertainer.
4. Bunter: a female rag-picker, and by extension any woman of low habits.
5. For Foote, see Letter 24, n. 1.
6. 'Colman is the gainer ... Foote is no loser': George Colman

the elder (1732–94), dramatist and friend of Garrick, Dr
Johnson and Bunbury to name only a few, owned and
managed the Covent Garden Theatre for seven years, until
he resigned because of poor health in May 1774. Two years
later the Haymarket Theatre was transferred from Foote to
Colman; Colman was 'the gainer' because Foote's death on
21 October 1777 relieved Colman from an annuity of 1,600*l*,
which was part of the transaction.

7.   De Groote: see Letter 56, n. 2; Letter 62a, notes 1 and 3.

55

TO MRS. C'[OCKSEDGE]'.
                              Charles Street, Nov. 5, 1777.

Now, whether to address – according to the distant, reserved, cold,
mechanical forms of high-breeding – where polished manners, like
a horse from the manege, prances fantastic – and, shackled with the
rules of art, proudly despises simple nature; – or shall I, like the
patient, honest, sober, long-ear'd animal – take plain nature's path
– and address you according to my feelings? – My dear friend – you
wanted to know the reason I had never addressed a line to you: – the
plain and honest truth is, I thought writing at – was better than
writing to you – that's one reason. – Now a second reason is
– I know my own weakness too well to encounter with your little
friend – whom I fear as a critic – and envy as a writer. – Another
reason is – a case of conscience – which some time or other you may
have explained. – Reason the fourth – a secret – and so must be – till
the blessed year 1797[1] – and then if you will deign to converse with
an old friend – you shall know all. – Kitty sends her respects to
Nutts[2] – and her duty to her godmother. – Billy looks wisely by
turns – and will speak for himself – if you should ever come to town
[a]gain. – The girls all improve in appetite. – Mrs. Sancho is
tolerably well – and I am yours, very seriously,

                                                      I. SANCHO.

P.S. I wrote to my friend *Rush*, and then made some modest
demands upon your good-nature. – There are a sort of people in the
world (one or two in a large extent of country) rare enough to meet
with – and you are one – whom nature hath left entirely defenceless
to the depredations of knaves – For my part, I own I have no

remorse when I tax your good-nature – which proceeds from your having obliged me so much – that I think with the street paupers – when they cry – 'Good your ladyship, give me something '– you always used to remember your poor old 'woman.' – Well, but to conclude – We courtiers are all alive upon this great good news – the Queen, God bless her! safe; – another Princess³ – Oh the cake and caudle! – Then the defeat of Washintub's army⁴ – and the capture of Arnold and Sulivan⁵ with seven thousand prisoners – thirteen countries return to their allegiance. – All this news is believed – the delivery of her Majesty is certain – Pray God the rest may be as certain – that this cursed carnage of the human species may end – commerce revive – sweet social peace be extended throughout the globe – and the British empire be strongly knit in the never-ending bands of sacred friendship and brotherly love! – Her good Grace of P—— is just arrived – the Gardens would look as they were wont – but for you. – But to conclude – the little dance (which I like because I made it) – I humbly beg you will make Jack play – and amongst you contrive a figure.⁵ – The Duchess of —— visits the Queen this evening – which being a piece of news you may credit – and of the utmost consequence – I close my very sensible decent epistle with – and so God bless you! – Pray tell Mr. *Rush* my thanks for his obliging letter – and that I join him and all his friends in honest gladness – upon his brother's account. – I fear, also, he has had, and still has, too much practice. – I have this opinion of him – that his humanity will ever be found equal to his skill – and that he will be a credit to his profession – as well as a blessing to his patients. – My humble respects and best wishes attend Miss —— and Messieurs B—— and S——, &c.

The great news is not yet officially authenticated – as no express is yet arrived from the Howes⁷ – the Isis man of war, which is supposed to have the dispatches, not being got in; – but the King and Cabinet believe the news to be true, though brought by hear-say – at sea.

1. The mysterious event of 1797: I have been unable to identify the event to which Sancho refers.
2. Nutts: the Crewe's pet spaniel.
3. 'Another Princess – Oh the cake and caudle': Princess Sophia was born on 3 November 1777. Sancho mentioned a caudle drink in Letter 24 (see n. 2), also in relation to childbirth. Six different types of caudles are recognised, including recipes

for 'rich' luxurious caudles which contained cream, ground almonds, sugar and rose or orange water added to the gruel and wine or ale. 'Poor' caudle would omit expensive spices and sugar, adding an egg or a small amount of wine and ale to the gruel. See Moira Buxton, 'Hypocras, caudels and possets', in *Liquid Nourishment: Potable Foods and Stimulating Drinks*, (ed.) C. Anne Wilson, (Edinburgh University Press; forthcoming).

4.   'The defeat of Washintub's army': news of successes during the previous year led the patriotic Sancho to be over-sanguine about the outcome of the American War. Washington had been defeated at Long Island (1776) and Brandywine Creek (1777) and British forces under General William Howe (see n. 7 below) had taken New York, capturing Generals Arnold and Sullivan (see n. 5 below). The reservations of Sancho's last paragraph were justified, as Letter 56 shows. Despite early successes, Burgoyne's plan to march on New England from Canada ended in defeat at Saratoga (1777). From December 1777 to June 1778, despite a terrible winter and fears of mass defection, Washington held his army together at Valley Forge, and then the French came into the war, tipping the scales on the American side. In Letter 56, the bad news of the war is starting to reach London. But for all his patriotism Sancho was never an enthusiast for this 'cursed carnage of the human species'. In fact, the war went the Americans' way until the defeat of Cornwallis (1781) virtually ended it in their favour, though peace was only officially declared at the Treaty of Paris in 1783.

5.   Arnold and Sullivan: Benedict Arnold, 1714–1801, was a general in the American Colonist's army. He served with distinction in the defeat of Burgoyne at the Battle of Saratoga in 1777, a battle which changed the course of the war (see Letter 56, n. 1) but was later court-martialled and admonished by Washington for various offences. He was placed in charge of West Point, but schemed to hand it over to the British. He then defected, was appointed a general in the British Army and spent the rest of his life mainly in London. In the United States his name is a byword for a traitor, but, at this time, he was to the patriotic Sancho one of the enemy. John Sullivan, 1740–95, was an American general commanding in Canada, where Burgoyne launched his initially successful march on New England in 1777.

6.   The little dance: since Sancho wrote this dance for the pleasure of his Suffolk friends, it could well be the one entitled 'Lindrindod Lasses', celebrating the visit of Mrs Cocksedge and Miss Crew to Llandrindod Wells. It is to be found in Sancho's collection, *Twelve Country Dances for the*

Year 1779, included in Josephine Wright, *Sancho*, p. 56. The text gives both the music and the dance figure, perhaps the one Sancho asks in the letter for Mrs Cocksedge and the others to 'contrive'.

7. The Howes: Richard Howe (4th Viscount Howe, 1726–99) was commander-in-chief of the British navy in North America. He resigned in 1777 under pressure from the government for being too lenient in his dealings with the colonists, with whom he was determined to promote a negotiated settlement. Richard Howe served again 1782–3 as commander-in-chief of the channel fleet. Richard's brother, Sir William Howe (5th Viscount Howe, 1729–1814), was commander-in-chief of the British Army in North America, 1775–8. He was a master of light-infantry tactics. Like his brother Richard, William came under criticism for oscillation and leniency toward the Americans and eventually resigned his command. The *Isis* was an active ship throughout the American war.

56

TO MR. S'[TEVENSON]'.

December 20, 1777.

With the old story of the season, &c. &c. most sincerely, and amen.

When Royal David – in the intoxication of success – and fullness of pride – imprudently insisted upon the numbering of his people – we are told, the Prophet was sent to announce the Divine displeasure – and to give him the choice of one of the three of the Almighty's heaviest punishments: – in his choice – he showed both wisdom and true piety – you know the rest. – Now, my friend, thou knowest my weakness; – I sincerely believe the Sacred Writ – and of course look upon war in all its horrid arrangements as the bitterest curse that can fall upon a people – and this American one – as one of the very worst – of worst things: – that it is a just judgement, I do believe – that the eyes of our rulers are shut – and their judgements stone-blind – I believe also. – The Gazette will give you a well-drest melancholy account – but you will see one thing in it which you will like – and that is, the humane solicitude of General Burgoyne[1] – for the safety and good treatment indiscriminately of all his camp-artificers and attendants. – He is certainly a man of feeling – and I regard him more for the grandeur of his mind in adversity – than I should in all the triumphal pomp of military madness. – But let me return, if possible, to my senses. – For God's sake! what has a poor starving Negroe, with six children, to do with kings and heroes, and armies and politics? – aye, or poets and painters? – or artists – of any sort? quoth Monsier S——. True – indubitably true. – For your letter, thanks – it should have come sooner – better late, &c. &c. – What have I to do with your good or evil fortune – health or sickness – weal or woe? – I am resolved, from henceforth, to banish feelings – Misanthrope from head to foot! – *Apropos* – not five minutes since I was interupted, in this same letter of letters, by a pleasant affair – to a man of no feelings. – A fellow bolted into the shop – with a countenance in which grief and fear struggled for mastery. – 'Did you see any body go to my cart, sir?' – 'No, friend, how should I? You see I am writing – and how should I be able to see your cart or you either in the dark?' – 'Lord in heaven pity me!' cries the man, 'what shall I do? oh! what shall I do? – I am undone! – Good God! – I did but go into the court here – with a trunk for the lady at Captain G——'s (I had two to deliver), and somebody has stole the other. – What shall I do? – what shall I do?' – 'Zounds, man! – who ever left their cart in the night with goods in it, without leaving some one to watch?' – 'Alack, sir, I left a boy, and told him I would give him something to stand by the cart, and the boy and trunk are both gone!' – Oh nature! – oh heart! – why does the voice of distress so forcibly knock at the door of hearts, but to hint to pride and avarice our common kindred – and to alarm self-love? – Mark, I do think, and will maintain it – that self-love alone, if rightly understood, would make man all that a dying Redeemer wills he should be. – But this same stolen trunk: – the ladies are just gone out of my shop – they have been here holding a council – upon law and advertisements. – God help them! – they could not have come to a worse – nor could they have found a stupider or sorrier adviser: – the trunk was seen pending between two in the Park – and I dare say the contents by this time are pretty well gutted. – Last Sunday I met, coming from church, Mr. C——: he looks well, better than when you left him. – I took occasion, as we were prating about and about your worship – to pin Mr. de Groote's[2] interest upon the skirts of his feelings: – he desired, when I saw him next, I would send him into Crown-street – which I religiously performed – but have not seen Mr. de Groote since. – In truth, there is (despite of his note) so much of the remains of better times – somewhat of the gentleman and artist in ruins – something creative of reverence as well as pity – that I have wished to do more than I ought – though at the same time too little for such a being to receive – without insult – from the hands of a poor negroe – (Pooh, I do not care for your prancings, I can see you at this distance) – We have agreed upon one thing; – which is, I have undertaken to write to Mr. Garrick for him, in the way of local relief; – I will wager a tankard of porter I succeed – in some sort. – I will aim at both sides of him – his pity and his pride – which, alas! – the last I mean, finds a first-floor in the breast of every son of Adam. – S—— called on me this day, and left a picture for you at your lodgings – and a very spirited head in miniature, of your own doing, with me – which I like so well – you will find it difficult to get it from me – except you talk of giving me a copy – Self-love again. – How can you expect business in these hard times – when the utmost exertions of honest industry can scarce afford people in the middle sphere of life daily provisions? – When it shall please the Almighty that things shall take a better turn in America – when the conviction of their madness shall make them court peace – and the same conviction of our cruelty and injustice induce us to settle all points in equity – when that time arrives, my friend, America will be the grand patron of genius – trade and arts will flourish – and if it shall please God to spare us till that period – we will either go and try our fortunes there – or stay in Old England and talk about it. – While thou hast only one mouth to feed – one back to clothe – and one wicked member to indulge – thou wilt have no pity from me – excepting in the argument of health – may that cordial blessing be thine – with its sweet companion ease! – Peace follows rectitude – and what a plague would'st thou have more? – Write soon if thou dar'st – retort at thy peril. – Boy – girls – and the old Duchess, all pretty well – and so so is yours,

I. SANCHO.

1. The war in America had been rumoured to be going successfully for the English, see Letters 37 and 55. But despite the appearances of early success, General Burgoyne, second-in-command of the English forces, was unhappy about troop numbers and administration, and returned temporarily to London. A plan was drafted in which he was to move south from Canada with a large force and cut off New England. At first he was successful, despite lacking the troops he had been promised. He surrounded Ticonderoga

and captured it after a siege of less than a week, giving rise
to the optimism of Sancho's previous letters on the war.
The King had wanted to award Burgoyne the Order of the
Garter, but was dissuaded by Lord Derby, and Burgoyne
was promoted to Lieutenant General instead. The inade-
quacy of the English force became apparent: it moved far too
slowly on New England, finding itself confronted and
outnumbered by Washington's army which surrounded it at
Saratoga, where it surrendered. Burgoyne was courteously
allowed to return to London, where he was bitterly de-
nounced for not remaining a prisoner with his army. He in
turn grew bitter against the Tory administration, and was
supported in Parliament only by the leading Whigs, Charles
James Fox and Sheridan. In this Letter, news of Burgoyne's
defeat has arrived, and Sancho is making the best of it by
stressing the General's humaneness and 'the grandeur of his
mind' (Burgoyne was an able general badly served by the
administration, and also a playwright of considerable talent)
rather than the 'military madness' of the war; but, as 'a poor
starving negro, with six children' (he was hardly starving,
though no doubt as usual short of money) whatever patriotic
enthusiasm he had displayed is drowned in a surge of
semi-comic-melancholic irony. In the final part of the letter
he expresses high hopes for the future of America, once it has
recovered from its own 'madness' in the face of what Sancho
admits to be 'our cruelty and injustice' and is still in patriotic
expectation of an English victory, 'when it shall please the
Almighty that things shall take a better turn in America
– when the conviction of their madness shall make them
court peace'.

2. De Groote: the ever-solicitous Sancho seeks the help of both
the unidentified C—— and Garrick on behalf of the
impoverished scholar de Groote. There is some success to
report in Letter 62a.

57

TO J. S'[PINK]'. Esq.
Charles Street, December 26, 1777.
I had the favor of a letter – replete with kindness which I can never
deserve – and have just now received the valuable contents – of
which said letter was harbinger – without either surprise or emotion
– save a kind of grateful tickling of the heart – the child of respect –
and I believe twin-brother of gratitude. – Now had I heard of an

Archbishop (at this sacred season especially) – gladdening the hearts of the poor, aged, and infirm – with good cheer – informing the minds of the young with Christian precepts – and reforming his whole See by his pious example – that would have surprised me: – had I been informed of a truly great man – who, laying aside party and self-interest – dared to step forth the advocate of truth – and friend to his country; – or had any one told me of a lord – who was wise enough to live within bounds – and honest enough to pay his debts – why it would have surprised me indeed. – But I have been well informed there is a Mr. S—— at Bury – and I think I have seen the gentleman – who lives in a constant course of doing beneficent actions – and, upon these occasions, the pleasure he feels constitutes him the obliged party. – You, good sir, ought of course to thank me – for adding one more to the number you are pleased to be kind to – So pray remember, good sir, that my thanks (however due in the eye of gratitude) I conceive to be an act of supererogation – and expect that henceforth you will look upon the Sanchos – as a family that have a rightful call upon your notice. – Mrs. Sancho joins me in repetition of the customary wishes. – Give me credit for having a heart which feels your kindness as it ought. – That Heaven may lengthen your days for the good of mankind – and grant every wish of your heart – is the true conclusion of

> Your greatly obliged and
> respectful humble servant,
> I. SANCHO.

58

TO MR. F'[ISHER]'.[1]
Charles Street, January 27, 1778.

Full heartily and most cordially do I thank thee, good Mr. *Fisher*, for your kindness in sending the books – That upon the unchristian and most diabolical usage of my brother Negroes – the illegality – the horrid wickedness of the traffic – the cruel carnage and depopulation of the human species – is painted in such strong colours – that I should think would (if duly attended to) flash comviction – and produce remorse in every enlightened and candid reader. – The perusal affected me more than I can express; – indeed I felt a double or mixt sensation – for while my heart was torn for

the sufferings – which, for aught I know – some of my nearest kin
might have undergone – my bosom, at the same time, glowed with
gratitude – and praise toward the humane – the Christian – the
friendly and learned Author of that most valuable book. – Blest be
your sect! – and Heaven's peace be ever upon them! – I, who, thank
God! am no bigot – but honour virtue – and the practice of the great
moral duties – equally in the turban – or the lawn-sleeves – who
think Heaven big enough for all the race of man – and hope to see
and mix amongst the whole family of Adam in bliss hereafter –
I with these notions (which, perhaps, some may style absurd) look
upon the friendly Author – as a being far superior to any great name
upon your continent. – I could wish that every member of each
house of parliament had one of these books. – And if his Majesty
perused one through before breakfast – though it might spoil his
appetite – yet the consciousness of having it in his power to facilitate
the great work – would give an additional sweetness to his tea. –
Phyllis's poems[2] do credit to nature – and put art – merely as art
– to the blush. – It reflects nothing either to the glory or generosity
of her master – if she is still his slave – except he glories in the *low
vanity* of having in his wanton power a mind animated by Heaven
– a genius superior to himself. – The list of splendid – titled –
learned names, in confirmation of her being the real authoress
– alas! shows how very poor the acquisition of wealth and
knowledge is – without generosity – feeling – and humanity. – These
good great folks – all know – and perhaps admired – nay, praised
Genius in bondage – and then, like the Priests and the Levites in
sacred writ, passed by – not one good Samaritan amongst them.
– I shall be ever glad to see you – and am, with many thanks,

Your most humble servant,
IGNATIUS SANCHO.

1. Mr F. must be Jabez Fisher from Philadelphia, see Letter 83,
    n. 1.
2. Sancho's remarks on the poet Phillis Wheatly are discussed
    in the Introduction, pp. 9–10.

59

TO MR. W'[INGRAV]'E.
Charles Street, March 12, 1778.

Will you forgive me, if I take the liberty to trouble you with getting
my enclosed plan inserted in the General Advertiser, or Morning
Intelligencer, as speedily as they conveniently can, if, after you have
perused it, you think it admissible? – If not, destroy it; for I have
not yet vanity sufficient to think whatever I privately approve must
of course be approvable – I send you the copy of what real affection
made me draw up for the late unfortunate Dr. Dodd* (which, as it
never was inserted, I must believe the learned editor thought it too
insignificant for the laudable service it was meant to help. – My
respects attend your whole family. – I am, dear Sir,

Yours, &c. &c.
I. SANCHO.

I prefer Mr. Parker's paper for many reasons: – let me have your
opinion of my plan – for in serious truth I think it ought to be put
into execution.

* Mr. Sancho also wrote to Dr. Dodd when in prison.

59a

For THE GENERAL ADVERTISER.
Palace-Yard, March 12, 1778.

SIR,

The Romans were wont to decree public honors on the man who
was so fortunate as to save the life of a citizen – a noble act of policy,
founded on true humanity, to stimulate the endeavours of every
individual towards acts of benevolence, and brotherly regard for
each other. Actuated by zeal to my prince, and love to my country,
I mean to deserve well of both, by publishing, through the channel
of your paper, a plan for greatly diminishing the national debt, or,
in case a war with the house of Bourbon[1] should be inevitable,
for raising three or four years' supplies, without oppressing the
merchant, mechanic, or labouring husbandman; in short, without

abridging one needful indulgence, or laying any fellow-subject under the least self-denying restraint.

Mr. Editor, we all know that in noble families plate is merely ideal wealth – and in very many houses of your first connections and over-grown fortunes, there are vast quantities of it old and useless, kept merely for the antiquity of its fashion, and the ostentatious proof of the grandeur of ancestry. Our neighbours the French (if I mistake not), in the last war, had the spirit (when the treasures of their Grand Monarque were nearly exhausted) to send their plate generously to the Mint, in aid of national honour and security. Their churchmen have often showed the laity the glorious example of aiding the state. We, to our immortal honor, have never yielded them the palm in courage, wisdom, or gallantry. Let every gentleman, whose landed property exceeds 500l. *per annum*, give up, without reserve, his useless family plate, all except knives, forks, and spoons, which may be deemed useful and necessary. I trust, such is the exalted spirit of the British nobility and gentry, that they will resign with cheerfulness what they can so very well do without. Should this meet (as I hope it will) with the cheerful assent of the public, let the quantities, so nobly given, be printed against the names of the patriotic donors, as a lasting testimony of their zeal for the public good, and a glorious proof of the internal riches of this queen of isles!

AFRICANUS.

1. The national debt had been brought about by the American war, in which England was now facing defeat. The French ('the house of Bourbon') became involved in the war as America's allies after Burgoyne's defeat at Saratoga.

59b

To the Editor of the MORNING POST.

SIR,

I am one of the many who have been often edified by the graceful eloquence and truly Christian doctrine of the unfortunate Dr. Dodd:[1] – as a Divine, he had, and still has, my love and reverence; his faults I regret; but, alas! I feel myself too guilty to cast a stone: Justice has her claims – but – Mercy, the anchor of my hope, inclines me to wish he might meet with Royal clemency – His punishments have already been pretty severe – the loss of Royal favor – the cowardly attacks of malicious buffoonery – and the over-strained zeal for rigid justice in the prosecution. – Oh! would to God the reverend bishops, clergy, &c. would join in petitioning the Throne for his life! – It would save the holy order from indignity, and even the land itself from the reproach of making too unequal distinctions in punishments. He might, by the rectitude of his future life, and due exertion of his matchless powers – be of infinite service – as chaplain to the poor convicts on the river – which would be a punishment, and, at the same time, serve for a proof or test of his contrition – and the sincerity of a zeal he has often manifested (in the pulpit) for the service of true Religion – And he may rise the higher by his late fall – and do more real service to the thoughtless and abandoned culprits, than a preacher whose character might perhaps be deemed spotless. If this hint should stimulate a pen, or heart, like the good Bishop of Chester's, to exert itself in the behalf of a man who has formerly been alive to every act of Heaven-born charity – the writer of this will have joy, even in his last moments, in the reflection that he paid a mite of the vast debt he owes Dr. Dodd as a preacher.

I—— s——

1. Like many of its congregation, Sancho's faith in Dr Dodd and his Pimlico chapel remained unabated, despite Dodd's execution for forgery and fraud in 1777 when this plea for clemency by Sancho must have been written, though Miss Crewe places it between letters dated March and April 1778. Dr Johnson was another of many who made such a plea.

60

TO MRS. H——.

Charles Street, April 9, 1778.

DEAR MADAM,

I have to thank you for repeated favors – and I do most sincerely. – You have a pleasure in doing acts of kindness – I wish from my soul that your example was more generally imitated. – I have given to the care of Mr. W—— one of Giardini's benefit tickets – which I present not to you – Madam – but to Mr. H——, that he may judge of fiddlers' taste and fiddlers' consequence in our grand metropolis – The ticket was a present from the great Giardini[1] – to the lowly Sancho – and I offer it as a tribute of musical affection to thy worthy partner – and with it – to both the sincerest best wishes and respects of their much obliged servant,

IGN. SANCHO.

1.   Felice Giardini, 1716–96: a composer, impresario and virtuoso violinist who had close associations with the London music scene over nearly half a century. He was co-manager of the London Opera for several sessions in the 1750s and 1760s, leader of the Three Choirs Festival 1770–6, and during the same period directed musical entertainments at Carlisle House, Soho.

61

TO MR. J'[ACK]' W'[INGRAV]'E.

May 4, 1778.

MY DEAR WINGRAVE,

Your short letter gave me much pleasure – which would have been enlarged had your epistle been longer – But I make allowances – as I ought – for the number of friends who wish equally with me – and expect to be gratified. You are greatly fortunate in enjoying your health – for which I doubt not but you are truly thankful to the Almighty Giver. – As to your success, it is the best comment upon your conduct; – for rectitude of principle and humble deportment, added to strict attention and good-nature, must make even fools and knaves wish you well – though envy will mix itself with the transient kindness of such – But with such noble natures as you went out happily connected with, you are every day sowing the good seeds of your future fortune. – I hope to live to see you return – the comfort and honor of your good father and family. – But observe – I do not wish you half a million – clogged with the tears and blood of the poor natives: – no – a decent competence got with honesty – and that will keep increasing like the widow's cruse,[1] and descend down to posterity with accumulated blessings. – You desire to transfer your share in me to your brother Joe: – now be it known to you – Joe has interest sufficient in his own natural right with me, to secure him every attention in my poor power – But you flatter

– my good friend – though your flattery carries a good excuse with it – you flatter the poor.

I say nothing of politics – I hate such subjects; – the public papers will inform you of mistakes – blood – taxes – misery – murder – the obstinacy of a few – and the madness and villainy of a many. – I expect a very, very long letter from you – in answer to a sermon I wrote you last year. – Miss —— is still divinely fair; – she's a good girl, but no match for Nabobs. – Mrs. *Cocksedge* is as handsome as ever – and *Rush* as friendly. God bless them! feasting or fasting – sleeping or waking! – May God's providence watch over and protect them – and all such! – Your brother Frank is a sweet boy: – a painter who would wish to draw a cherub will find no fitter subject. – The C——ds – but what have I to do with good people, who will of course all write for themselves? – So let them. – Your father – Oh Jack! what a cordial! – what a rich luxury is it to be able to contribute, by well-doing, to a father's, nay a whole family of kindred love, and heart-felt affection! what a bliss to add to all their happiness – and to insure your own at the same time! – May this high pleasure be thine! and may the God of truth and fountain of all good enrich thy heart and head with his spirit and wisdom – crown your labours with success – and guard you from avarice – ambition – and every Asiatic evil[2] – so that your native land may receive you with riches and honor – your friends with true joy – heightened with sincere respect! So wishes – so prophesies – thy true friend and obliged servant,

I. SANCHO.

1. The widow's cruse: I Kings xvii: 12–16. Elijah, starving in the desert, receives a message from the Lord that he should seek sustenance from a widow in Zarephath. She fears that her cruse of oil and barrel of meal will fail, but miraculously they are made inexhaustible. Later Elijah, with the Lord's help, restores by a miracle the life of the widow's dead son. This letter might be read as a prologue to Letter 68, in which Sancho contrasts the greed of the 'Christian navigators' who have exploited oriental and African trade, with those who practise true Christian commerce with its divinely appointed benefits under the benevolence of the Lord. Sancho's belief in 'Christian Commerce' is discussed in some detail in the Introduction, pp. 10–14.
2. Every Asiatic evil: Sancho thinks of the danger of British virtues being corrupted by residence in India, and the

'knavery' and 'treachery' to be encountered in local life. See
Letter 68 and my comments on this in the Introduction,
pp. 10–11.

62

TO MISS C'[REWE]'.

Charles Street, May 9, 1778.

The Sanchos – in full synod – humbly present their respectful
compliments to the good Mrs. *Cocksedge* and Miss *Crewe* What
a *Crewe*! are happy in hearing they got well into Suffolk – that they
continue so – and enjoy the beauties of this sweetest of seasons
– with its attendant dainties – fresh butter – sweet milk – and the
smiles of boon nature – on hill and dale – fields and groves
– shepherds piping – milk-maids dancing – and the cheerful
respondent carolings of artless joy in the happy husbandmen.
– Should you perchance rise early in pursuit of May-dew –
I earnestly make it my request – you will save – and bring to town
a little bottle of it for my particular use. – Happy – thrice happy
nymphs – be merciful to the poor hapless swains! – The powerful
little god of mischief and delight now at this blest season prunes his
beauteous wings – new feathers and sharpens his arrows – tight
strings his bow – and takes too sure his aim. – O lads, beware the
month of May! – For you, blest girls! Nature decked out as in
a birth-day suit courts you with all its sweets – where-e'er you
tread, the grass and wanton flowerets fondly kiss your feet – and
humbly bow their pretty heads to the gentle sweepings of your
under-petticoats – The soft and amorous southern breezes toy with
your curls – and uncontroul'd steal numberless kisses. – The
blackbirds and thrushes suspend their songs – and eye beauty and
humanity with pleasure; – and, could their hearts be read – thank
most sincerely the generous fair hands that fed them in the winter
– The cuckoo sings – on every tree – the joys of married life – the
shrubbery throws out all its sweets to charm you – though, alas! an
unlucky parciplepliviaplemontis[1] seizes my imagination – my brains
are on the ferment. – Miss *Crewe* will excuse me. – Make my best
wishes to Mrs. *Cocksedge*: tell her I hope she rides and walks in
moderation – eats heartily, and laughs much – sleeps soundly,
dreams happily – That she – you – my *Rush* and your connections

– may enjoy the good of this life without its evil – is the true Black-a-moor wish of

I. SANCHO.

Now mark, this is not meant as a letter – no – it is an address to the ladies. – Pray our best respects to Mr. and Mrs. B*unbury*: – It is an address to Spring-birds and flowers – and when you see Johnny,[2] our loves – It is a caution to the swains against the popery of Love. – The King and Queen are just now returned from Portsmouth. – I said nothing in regard to the month – by way of advice to the ladies. – The Spectator – blessings on his memory – has – They say the Royal chaise was covered with dirt – even the very glasses. – Quistus Quirini was found very late last night. – Nothing broke – except the hemmings of advantage. – They say – the Queen never look'd better. – But what amazed most people – both the Royal postillions rode the off horses – which it is expected the Gazette of this night will explain. – Adieu.

Is not that – *a good one?*

1. Parciplepliviaplemontis: a Shandean pseudo-scholarly word which seems to be composed of obscure and contradictory elements such as parcity, frugality; plenitude, fullness; plemmirulate, overflowing; and the Latin montis, mountain; it could be any words which the reader may imagine it to be composed of.
2. 'Johnny' here may be John Rush Sr., or John Spink, the banker from Bury (who appears to be called 'Johnny' in Letters 20 and 21).

62a

From the PUBLIC ADVERTISER of
May 13th, 1778.
[Inserted unknown to Mr. Sancho.]
TO MR. B'[ROWNE]'.

DEAR SIR,
I could not see Mr. de Groote[1] till this morning – He approached the threshold – poor man – in very visible illness; – yet, under the pressure of a multitude of infirmities – he could not forget his recent

humane benefactor. – With faltering speech he inquired much who you were – and, in conclusion, put up his most earnest petitions to the Father of mercies in your behalf – which (if the prayers of an indigent genius have as much efficacy as those of a fat bishop) I should hope and trust you may one day be the better for. – He is in direct descent from the famous Hugo Grotius[2] by the father's side. – His own mother was daughter to Sir Thomas Hesketh.[3] – He married the widow Marchioness de Malaspina. – His age is 86, he had a paralytic stroke – and has a rupture. – His eyes are dim, even with the help of spectacles. – In truth, he comes close to Shakespeare's description in the last age of man – 'sans teeth – sans eyes – sans taste – sans every thing.'

He has the honor to be known to Doctor Johnson – and the luck to be sometimes remembered by Mr. Garrick. – If you help him – you do yourself a kindness – me a pleasure – and he, poor soul, a good – which he may one time throw in your teeth – in that country where good actions are in higher estimation than stars – ribbons – or crowns.

Yours, most respectfully,
IGNATIUS SANCHO.

He lodges at No 9, New Pye-Street, Westminster.

1. Isaac de Groote (1694?–1799): referred to earlier, Letters 54 and 56, as the object of Sancho's charitable efforts. Sancho wrote on his behalf to Garrick, who paid his rent (Letter 69). Later he was to be granted a place in the Charterhouse hospice (Letter 79). The provision of his place was largely due to the efforts of Dr Johnson, who contacted the Archbishop of Canterbury by way of Archdeacon Vyse of Lambeth, to whom Johnson wrote, 'Let it not be said that in any lettered country, a nephew of Grotius asked for charity and was refused,' Boswell, *Life*, (ed.) R. W. Chapman (1970), pp. 814–5 (19 July 1777).
2. Hugo Grotius (1583–1645): Dutch statesman and law-scholar; Dutch Ambassador to England, in 1613 he was charged with conspiracy by the Dutch and sentenced to life imprisonment. He escaped, and served Queen Christina of Sweden as her Ambassador to France. His great work of legal scholarship is *De Jure Belli et Pacis* (1625), a fundamental text in the establishment of international law.
3. Sir Thomas Hesketh: no source has been traced which substantiates Sancho's link between de Groote's parentage

and the name Hesketh. If Sancho is correct, Sir Thomas
Hesketh would have been de Groote's maternal grandfather,
but the dates are out by a generation or more, casting doubt
on Sancho's claim. Sources for Hesketh focus on Sir Thomas
Hesketh, who died in 1778, making him younger than de
Groote; sources also focus on Sir Thomas's wife, Lady
Harriet Hesketh (1753–1807), cousin and favourite correspondent of the poet William Cowper. Lady Harriet was born
when de Groote was middle-aged, again showing a discrepancy in dates. Sancho may have had in mind Sir Thomas's
father, Thomas Hesketh, but he and his wife Martha had no
daughters whom we might link to de Groote, either as his
mother, as Sancho claims, or in any other filial relationship.

63

TO MR. R'[USH]'.

[undated]

My good friend, take my thanks for your kind attention – and
believe me, I am exceedingly mortified at being thus thrust forward
in the public prints.[1] – You may observe, by what has happened to
me, how very difficult it is to do even a right thing – so as to escape
uneasiness. – Trust me, this same letter (though wrote, I dare say,
with the kindest intention imaginable) will do me hurt in the
opinion of many – I therefore repeat, I like it not – and dare own to
my friend *Rush* it hurts my pride. – You may laugh – but it's truth.
– The drawing was gone to my friend S——, but I recovered it in
time.[2] – Hope the ladies are well – and that it will amuse them for
a few moments. The young man who invented the design is no artist
– but I think he has genius.

1. Sancho is embarrassed at being publicly seen to seek charity
   for de Groote in the previous letter, written privately to
   Browne, inserted in *The Public Advertiser* without Sancho's
   (or presumably de Groote's) permission. In Letter 56, his
   tact makes him fear that to make public any charity towards
   de Groote might seem a condescension, 'too little for such
   a being to receive – without insult'.
2. Sancho is characteristically giving aid and advice to Matthew
   Darly, a young artist, presumably the one who appears in
   Letter 65.

64

May 14, 1778.

What terms shall I find to express my gratitude to the obliging, the friendly Miss *Crewe*, for the pleasure we enjoyed from the contents of the best letter that has been wrote this good year? – You, who delight to please, will also feel high satisfaction in knowing you have succeeded. – We hope the change of weather has had no ill effect upon our friend – and that she will adhere to her promise in remembering how ill she has been – and that it is too probable any cold got by over-exertion or fatigue may occasion a relapse. – We have had much thunder and rain this morning – and, if old saws say true,[1] we are to expect a continuance of about thirty-seven days good ducking weather. – We will leave it to the all-wise Disposer of events – with this comfortable reflection – that whatever he wills – is best. – We are happy to hear so good an account of the ——s, she especially, as very likely a good course of fatigue, sweetened with gain, may contribute as much to her health as her pleasure – and re-establish her perfectly. – We have nothing stirring in the news way, or any other way – the town is literally empty, saving a few sharks of both sexes, who are too poor to emigrate to the camps or watering-places, and so are forced to prey upon one another in town. – I protest, it is to me the most difficult of things to write to one of your female geniuses – there is a certain degree of clever-ality (if I may so call it), an easy kind of derangement of periods, a gentleman-like – fashionable – careless – see-saw of dialogue – which I know no more of than you do of cruelty. – I write as I think – foolishly – and you write well – Why? – Because you think well. – So much for praise – compliment – flattery, &c. – My respects attend Mr. B—— and Mrs. S—— and Mrs. ——; tell Miss A——s, one of us will come to see her – perhaps. – I have received a kind letter from my good friend the doctor – and one also from the surgeon to the guards, dated New York, June 12: – he thinks the Commissioners[2] might have saved themselves the trouble – as they are like to come back – just as wise as they went. – The Panton-Street good folks are well for what I know – not having seen them since I last had the honor of addressing Mrs. C——.[3] Adieu! – Our best respects – with Kitty's and Billy's in particular – attend Monsieur Nuts[4] – Pray tell him so – with all civility – He deserves it

on the force of his own merits – Were it not even so – yet surely,
I think, we should regard him for the sake of our friend.

Mrs. Sancho joins me in every thing to Self and Co.

Yours, dear Miss *Crewe*,
with zeal and esteem,
I. SANCHO.

1. This letter is dated 14 May. The 'old saw' applies to St
   Swithin's Day, 15 July. It is said that if it rains on St Swithin's
   Day, it will rain for forty days afterwards, so one would
   expect the letter to be dated 17 May. Either Sancho's folklore
   or Miss Crewe's editing appears to be at fault about the date.
   Since Sancho says in the same letter that he has just received
   a letter from New York, dated 12 June, some such confusion
   seems likely.
2. The Commissioners: Lord North formed a Peace Commission sent to America to investigate and report on the
   progress of the war. The Commission was placed in the
   hands of Admiral William Howe and his brother, General
   Richard Howe (see Letter 55, n. 7 for details about the Howe
   brothers).
3. I am unable to say who 'the Panton St. good folks' are.
   Mrs. C—— here is probably Mrs Crewe, but may refer to
   Mrs Cocksedge.
4. A favorite spaniel. Miss Crewe's note.

65

TO MR. I'[RELAND]'.

May 22, 1778.

DEAR SIR,

I claim your indulgence – and modestly insist upon your help. – The
companions to this billet are the hobby horses of a young man[1] that
I respect – Darly has used him with less attention than he ought
– having kept the press affair above a month – and done nothing – so
he is (of course) out of favor. – I want first your approbation – That
gained – I wish your interest to get them speedily into the world.
– There are some inaccuracies in both – which any regular artist will
amend. – As my friend is self-taught, his errors must be excused
– I wish I could wait upon you – but my stiff joint – my leg – is so
unwell, that at present I must give up any hopes of that pleasure. –

I hope Mrs. *Ireland's* health is perfectly restored. – I should wish to win her over to our interests in the affairs before you. – In good faith, I like the subject myself – and can fancy I discern something like wit in both of them. – Forgive and assist yours faithfully,

SANCHO the Big.

1. 'The companions to this billet' would be some drawings of the young man referred to here and in Letter 63 as being 'no artist – but I think he has genius'. Matthew Darly was an engraver and artists' colourman, best known as a caricaturist, who published some of Henry Bunbury's early sketches. I do not know what 'the press affair' is, over which Darly has been remiss.

66

TO MR. H——.

Charles Street, Westminster, May 31, 1778.

The Sanchonian chapter of inquiries, dictated by an esteem nearly bordering upon affection (perhaps as warmly sincere as most modern friendships) runs thus – How do you do? Are you the better for your journey? Did the exercise create any amendment of appetite? Was your travelling party agreeable? And how did you find the good couple? – the sweet sensations arising from the sight of those we love, the reviewing the places, either houses, fields, hedges, stiles, or posts of our early morn of life acquaintance, the train of pleasurable ideas awakened, are more salutary than the whole college of grave faces. – Tell me much about yourself – and more about your honored parents, whom I hope you found as well as you wished – your kindred at Lancaster, to whom my hearty wishes – and to all who have charity enough to admit dark faces into the fellowship of Christians.[1] – Say much for me to your good father and mother – in the article of respect thou canst not exaggerate – Excepting conjugal, there are no attentions so tenderly heart-soothing as the parental. – Amidst the felicity of thy native fields mayst thou find health, and diffuse pleasure round the respectable circle of thy friends! – No news – but that Keppel[2] is in chace of De Chartres.

Yours truly,

I. SANCHO.

If you can afford a line, enclose it in the enclosed. Mrs. Sancho
and girls wish you every pleasure.

1. 'Charity enough to admit dark faces': one of many hints
    which do not quite conceal traces of ironically controlled
    racial bitterness. Mr H—— is said to have 'kindred at
    Lancaster', and Mrs H—— in Letter 91 to be 'an honest and
    very agreeable northern lady'. According to Stevenson's list
    of Sancho's correspondents, Appendix VI., she is the same
    Mrs H—— who, as a senior servant with the Montagus,
    helped make the arrangements for the opening of Sancho's
    grocer's shop. Her son Jacob is said to be a popular visitor
    with the Sanchos and their children in Letter 93.
2. Keppel, Viscount Augustus (1725–86): Keppel engaged the
    French fleet in the Channel on 27 July 1778, the French
    having by now joined in the war on the American side. But
    the action, if it can be called such, was ineffectual and
    inconclusive, for which Keppel was court-martialled in
    January 1779 and acquitted. In 1782 he was appointed First
    Lord of the Admiralty. Sancho probably refers to him in
    Letter 105, 'at home Admirals that do not choose to fight'.

67

TO MR. M'[EHEUX]'.

June 10, 1778.

'"Tis with our judgements as our watches – none
Go just alike – yet each believes his own."[1]

POPE.

So, my wise critic – blessings on thee – and thanks for thy sagacious
discovery! – Sterne, it seems, stole his grand outline of character
from Fielding – and whom did Fielding plunder? thou criticizing
jack ape! – As to S——,[2] perhaps you may be right – not absolutely
right – nor quite so very *altogether* wrong – but that's not my affair.
– Fielding and Sterne both copied nature – their palettes stored with
proper colours of the brightest dye – these masters were both great
originals – their outline correct – bold – and free – Human Nature
was their subject – and though their colouring was widely different,
yet *here* and *there* some features in each might bear a little
resemblance – some faint likeness to each other – as, for example
– in your own words – Toby and All-worthy – The external

draperies of the two are as wide as the poles – their hearts – perhaps – twins of the same blessed form and principles. – But, for the rest of the Dramatis Personæ, you must strain hard, my friend, before you can twist them into likeness sufficient to warrant the censure of copying. – Parson Adams is yet more distant – his chief feature is absence of thought – The world affords me many such instances – but in the course of my reading I have not met with his likeness, except in mere goodness of heart – in that perhaps Jack M—— may equal him – but then he is so confounded jingle-headed! – Read boy, read – give Tom Jones a second *fair* reading! – Fielding's wit is obvious – his humour poignant – dialogue just – and truly dramatic – colouring quite nature – and keeping chaste. – Sterne equals him in every thing, and in one thing excels him and all mankind – which is the distribution of his lights, which he has so artfully varied throughout his work, that the oftener they are examined the more beautiful they appear. – They were two great masters, who painted for posterity – and, I prophesy, will charm to the end of the English speech. – If Sterne has had any one great master in his eye – it was Swift, his countryman – the first wit of this or any other nation. – But there is this grand difference between them – Swift excels in grave-faced irony – whilst Sterne lashes his whips with jolly laughter. – I could wish you to compare (after due attentive reading) Swift and Sterne – Milton and Young – Thomson and Akenside – and then give your free opinion to yours ever,

I. SANCHO.

I want a handful or two of good fresh peach leaves – contrive to send me them when opportunity serves – and word, at the first leisure period, how Miss *Anne Sister-like – George Grateful-look*[3] – Mrs. &c. &c. – and how your worship's hip does. – You had set up my bristles in such guise – in attacking poor Sterne – that I had quite forgot to give you a flogging for your punning grocery epistle – But omittance is no quittance. – Swift and Sterne were different in this – Sterne was truly a noble philanthropist – Swift was rather cynical. What Swift would fret and fume at – such as the petty accidental *sourings* and *bitters* in life's cup – you plainly may see, Sterne would laugh at – and parry off by a larger humanity, and regular good will to man. I know you will laugh at me – Do – I am content: – if I am an enthusiast in any thing, it is in favor of my Sterne.

1. Quotation: Pope, *Essay on Criticism*, ll, 9–10.
2. S——: in view of the way the letter continues, this is probably Swift.
3. Anne ... George: names probably given in private jest to common acquaintances of Sancho and Meheux.

68[1]

TO MR. J'[ACK]' W'[INGRAV]'E.

1778.

Your good father insists on my scribbling a sheet of absurdities, and gives me a notable reason for it, that is, 'Jack will be pleased with it.' – Now be it known to you – I have a respect both for father and son – yea for the whole family, who are every soul (that I have the honor or pleasure to know any thing of) tinctured – and leavened with all the obsolete goodness of old times – so that a man runs some hazard in being seen in the *Wingrave*'s society of being biassed to Christianity. I never see your poor father but his eyes betray his feelings for the hopeful youth in India – A tear of joy dancing upon the lids is a plaudit not to be equalled this side death! – See the effects of right-doing, my worthy friend – Continue in the track of rectitude – and despise poor paltry Europeans – titled, Nabobs – Read your Bible – As day follows night, God's blessing follows virtue – honor and riches bring up the rear – and the end is peace. – Courage, my boy – I have done preaching. – Old folks love to seem wise – and if you are silly enough to correspond with gray hairs, take the consequence. – I have had the pleasure of reading most of your letters, through the kindness of your father. – Youth is naturally prone to vanity – Such is the weakness of human nature, that pride has a fortress in the best of hearts – I know no person that possesses a better than Johnny *Wingrave*: – but although flattery is poison to youth, yet truth obliges me to confess that your correspondence betrays no symptom of vanity – but teems with truths of an honest affection, which merits praise – and commands esteem.

In some one of your letters which I do not recollect – you speak (with honest indignation) of the treachery and chicanery of the

Natives*. – My good friend, you should remember from whom they learnt those vices: – The first Christian visitors found them a simple, harmless people – but the cursed avidity for wealth urged these first visitors (and all the succeeding ones) to such acts of deception – and even wanton cruelty – that the poor ignorant Natives soon learnt to turn the knavish and diabolical arts – which they too soon imbibed – upon their teachers.

I am sorry to observe that the practice of your country (which as a resident I love – and for its freedom, and for the many blessings I enjoy in it, shall ever have my warmest wishes, prayers, and blessings): I say it is with reluctance that I must observe your country's conduct has been uniformly wicked in the East – West-Indies – and even on the coast of Guinea. – The grand object of English navigators – indeed of all Christian navigators – is money – money – money – for which I do not pretend to blame them – Commerce was meant by the goodness of the Diety to diffuse the various goods of the earth into every part – to unite mankind in the blessed chains of brotherly love, society, and mutual dependence: – the englightened Christian should diffuse the Riches of the Gospel of peace, with the commodities of his respective land – Commerce attended with strict honesty, and with Religion for its companion, would be a blessing to every shore it touched at. – In Africa, the poor wretched natives – blessed with the most fertile and luxuriant soil – are rendered so much the more miserable for what Providence meant as a blessing: – the Christians' abominable Traffic for slaves – and the horrid cruelty and treachery of the petty Kings – encouraged by their Christian customers – who carry them strong liquors, to enflame their national madness – and powder and bad

---

*   Extracts of two Letters from Mr. Wingrave to his Father,
              dated Bombay, 1776 and 1777.
       '1776. I have introduced myself to Mr. G——, who
     'behaved very friendly in giving me some advice, which was
     'very necessary, as the inhabitants, who are chiefly Blacks,
     'are a set of canting, deceitful people, and of whom one must
     'have great caution.'
       '1777. I am now thoroughly convinced, that the account
     'which Mr. G—— gave me of the natives of this country is
     'just and true, that they are a set of deceitful people, and have
     'not such a word as Gratitude in their language, neither do
     'they know what it is – and as to their dealings in trade, they
     'are like unto Jews.'

fire-arms, to furnish them with the hellish means of killing and kidnapping. – But enough – it is a subject that sours my blood – and I am sure will not please the friendly bent of your social affections. – I mentioned these only to guard my friend against being too hasty in condemning the knavery of a people who, bad as they may be – possibly – were made worse by their Christian visitors. – Make human nature they study, wherever thou residest – whatever the religion, or the complexion, study their hearts. – Simplicity, kindness, and charity be thy guide! – With these even Savages will respect you – and God will bless you.

Your father, who sees every improvement of his boy with delight, observes that your handwriting is much for the better – In truth, I think it as well as any modest man can wish. – If my long epistles do not frighten you – and I live till the return of next spring – perhaps I shall be enabled to judge how much you are improved since your last favor – Write me a deal about the natives – the soil and produce – the domestic and interior manners of the people – customs – prejudices – fashions – and follies. – Alas! we have plenty of the two last here – and, what is worse, we have politics – and a detestable Brothers' war – where the right hand is hacking and hewing the left – whilst Angels weep at our madness – and Devils rejoice at the ruinous prospect.

Mr. R*ush* and the ladies are well. – Johnny R*ush*[2] has favoured me with a long letter – He is now grown familiar with danger – and can bear the whistling of bullets – the cries and groans of the human species – the roll of drums – clangor of trumpets – shouts of combatants – and thunder of cannon – All these he can bear with soldier-like fortitude – with now and then a secret wish for the society of his London friends – in the sweet blessed security of peace and friendship.

This, young man, is my second letter – I have wrote till I am stupid, I perceive – I ought to have found it out two pages back. – Mrs. Sancho joins me in good wishes – I join her in the same – in which double sense believe me,

Yours, &c. &c.

I. SANCHO.

Very short.

POSTSCRIPT.

It is with sincere pleasure I hear you have a lucrative establishment – which will enable you to appear and act with decency – Your

good sense will naturally lead you to proper œconomy – as distant
from frigid parsimony, as from a heedless extravagancy – But as
you may possibly have some time to spare upon your hands for
necessary recreation, give me leave to obtrude my poor advice. –
I have heard it more than once observed of fortunate adventurers
– they have come home enriched in purse, but wretchedly barren in
intellects – The mind, my dear Jack, wants food – as well as the
stomach – Why then should not one wish to increase in knowledge
as well as money? – Young says – 'Books are fair Virtue's advocates
and friends' – Now my advice is – to preserve about 20l. a year for
two or three seasons – by which means you may gradually form
a useful, elegant, little library – Suppose now the first year you send
the order, and the money, to your father, for the following books
– which I recommend from my own superficial knowledge as
useful. – A man should know a little of Geography – History –
nothing more useful, or pleasant.

Robertson's Charles the Fifth, 4 vols.

Goldsmith's History of Greece, 2 vols.

Ditto, of Rome, 2 vols.

Ditto, of England, 4 vols.

Two small volumes of Sermons useful – and very sensible – by one
Mr. Williams, a dissenting minister – which are as well as fifty – for
I love not a multiplicity of doctrines – A few plain tenets, easy,
simple, and directed to the heart, are better than volumes of
controversial nonsense. – Spectators – Guardians – and Tatlers
– you have of course. – Young's Night-Thoughts – Milton – and
Thomson's Seasons were my summer companions for near twenty
years – They mended my heart – they improved my veneration of
the Deity – and increased my love to my neighbours.

You have to thank God for strong natural parts – a feeling
humane heart – You write with sense and judicious discernment
– Improve yourself, my dear Jack, that, if it should please God to
return you to your friends with the fortune of a man in upper rank,
the embellishments of your mind may be ever considered as greatly
superior to your riches – and only inferior to the goodness of your
heart. I give you the above as a sketch – Your father and other of
your friends will improve upon it in the course of time – I do indeed
judge that the above is enough at first – in conformity with the old
adage—— 'A few Books and a few Friends, and those well chosen.'

Adieu, Yours,

I. SANCHO.

1. This letter is discussed in some detail in the Introduction, pp. 10–11.
2. Johnny Rush, son of Sancho's friend, John Rush, Sir Charles Bunbury's valet, serving with the English forces in the American War is the Mr J—— R—— of Letter 72. He is 'still in New York with the Guards' in Letter 127.

69

TO MR. M'[EHEUX]'.

July 26, 1778.

DEAR M——,

S*** is a riddle[1] – I will serve him if I can – Were I rich, he should have not reason to despise me – but he must learn to try to serve himself – I wish you would throw your good sense upon paper for him – Advice from one of his own years would sink deeper than the fusty phlegmatic saws of an old man – Do in charity give him half an hour's labour – I do really think that you and S*** have sense enough for a dozen young fellows – and if it pleased God it were so divided they would each be happier, wiser, and richer than S*** or M——. And this by the way of thanking you – Pooh – I will do that when I see you – and if that never happens, a good action thanks itself. – Mr. Garrick called upon S—— on Tuesday night, and won his heart: he called to pay poor De Groote's lodgings,[2] sat with him some time, and chatted friendly.

I admire your modesty in grudging me two letters for one – and greasing me with the fulsoms of sneering praise – Sirrah, be quiet – What, you Snoodlepoop! have you any care, wife, or family? You ought to write volumes – It gives expansion to your thoughts – facility to your invention – ease to your diction – and pleases your Friend,

SANCHO.

Write, Knave – or – or – or –

1. S*** is a riddle to me, too.
2. S—— is probably John Spink: that is the initial by which he is designated in Stevenson's index, and, being a banker, he may well have helped to arrange Garrick's payment of the impoverished de Groote's rent.

70

TO MRS. C'[OCKSEDGE]'.

July 23, 1778.

DEAR MADAM,

Shall I acknowledge myself a weak superstitious fool? Yes, I will tell
the honest truth – You have this foolish letter in consequence of
a last night's dream – Queen Mab has been with me – aye, and with
Mrs, Sancho too – For my part, I dare not reveal half my dream
– But upon telling our night's visions over the tea-table at breakfast,
it was judged rather uncommon for us all to dream of the same
party. – Now I own I have great reason to dream of you waking
– for you have been a very true and uncommon friend to me and
mine – Neither have I the least objection to these nightly visits, so as
I have the pleasure to meet you (though but in vision) in good
health – Thy health is the very thing that I doubt about – therefore
graciously let us know by the next post that you are well, and mean
to take every prudent step so to continue – That you have left off
tea, I do much approve of – but insist that you make your visitors
drink double quantity – that I may be no loser – I hope you find
cocoa agree with you – It should be made always over night, and
boiled for above fifteen minutes – But you must caution Miss
Crewe not to drink it – for there is nothing so fattening to little
folks – The R——ns way-laid my friend *Rush*, and pressed Dame
Sancho and self into the service last Sunday – We had a good and
social dinner, and Mrs. Sancho forced me to stay supper – I think
the Doctor looks as well as I ever saw him – Indeed I could read in
his cheerful countenance that he left you well – I do not doubt but
you have paid a visit to the camp – and seen brother *Osborne* in his
glory[1] – I hope he will have regard to his health: and for profit, I do
think it must answer better to him than to (almost) any other man in
the country – Pray be so kind to make our best respects to Miss
A——s,[2] and to every one who delighteth in Blackamoor greetings.
– We have no news but old lies – scoured and turned like misers'
coats – which serve very well. We gape and swallow – wonder and
look wise – Conjurors over a news-paper, and blockheads at home.
– Adieu! Let me hear that you are very well. It will please Mrs.
Sancho, and, if I know any thing of her husband, it will be no less
pleasing to your much obliged humble servant and friend,

IGN. SANCHO.

N.B. I walk upon two legs now.

Our best respects to Miss *Crewe*; hope she is intent upon camp fashions; but caution her in my name to be on her guard: Cupid resides in camp by choice. Oh, Miss *Crewe*! beware – beware of the little God.

I. S.

Now this is writing to Miss *Crewe*.

1. Sancho's West Indian brother-in-law John Osborne, resident in Bond Street, has been summoned, either as a member or agent of the militia, to military exercises at a camp at Cavenham, as we learn from Letter 99, only a few miles from the Bunbury home, Barton Hall, between Mildenhall, Suffolk and Bury St Edmunds. The entry of the French into the American war resulted in a flurry of such activity, and King George III viewed parades at Coxheath and Warley camps. The arrival of the military near a town for exercises was also an occasion for dances and flirtations likely to cause a flutter among the young ladies (see, for instance, events in *Pride and Prejudice*). Thus, later in the letter, Sancho expresses to Miss Crewe the hope that 'she is intent upon camp fashions … Cupid resides in camp', etc. One of Sancho's musical pieces in his *Twelve Country Dances* (1779) called 'Culford Heath Camp' may have been written for this occasion. It is included in Josephine Wright's collection of Sancho's music.
2. Miss A——s: probably another reference to Sarah Adamson.

71

TO MR. K'[ISBY]'.

July 28, 1778.

I received yours with satisfaction, as it gave me a certainty of your being (upon the whole) much better. As to your saying you are not girlishly inclined[1] – why, I give you credit for it – Thou must watch – and – pray – for Satan is artful, and knoweth all our weak parts – and that dirty little blind feathered-shouldered scoundrel of a boy, master Cupid, lurks couchant in the pupil of an eye – in the hollow of a dimple – in the cherry-ripe plumpness of a pair of lips – in the artfully timid pressure of a fair hand – in the complimentary squeeze of a farewell – in short, and in one word, watch – watch.

So you forgot all I said about Charles the Fifth. Well, you give

144 The Letters of Ignatius Sancho

your reasons – But when you have got through your sugar works,[2] I hope you will give due attention to Robertson: – his first volume is the most learned, and the dryest, yet absolutely necessary to be read with great attention, as it will render the other much more easy, clear, and intelligible. Make yourself tolerably acquainted with the feudal system of Europe, which you will find explained in his first volume – the rest will amply reward you – I recommend to you to make extracts upon the passages which strike you most – It will be of infinite use to you – as I trust you will find it as much a history of Europe during two centuries, as of Charles the Fifth. After all – I shall fume and scold if you do not read this work – and abuse you, if you do not relish it. – You flatter my vanity very agreeably, in ever supposing that any hints of mine should conduce to the culture of your little farm. – Be that as it may – I am happy in the certainty of never intentionally misleading or misadvising any male youth – I wish I could say Virgin! – farewell! – Read, reflect! then write, and let me have your opinions.

Yours sincerely,

I. SANCHO.

1. When last met in the letters, Kisby was 'girlishly inclined', in love with Miss H—— (Letter 9).
2. Suddenly, Sancho drops his frivolity and returns to a favourite topic: serious reading. He had recommended Robertson's *Charles the Fifth* to Jack Wingrave in Letter 68, and has done the same to young Kisby, in an attempt to steady and improve his mind. But Kisby seems to prefer 'sugar works', probably romances more suited to his amorous temperament. At the time of the earlier letter, Kisby was a servant in the household of the Montagu family at Richmond, so the reference to his 'little farm' is unclear, perhaps a private joke, as is Sancho's coy innuendo, that he is sure he is not guilty of ever 'intentionally misleading or misadvising any male youth – I wish I could say Virgin!'

72

TO MR. R'[USH]'.

July 31, 1778.

DEAR FRIEND,

Thanks for your very valuable letter, and its obliging companion – Your brother writes in good spirits – but I fear the minority members were right in their predictions of the success of the Commissioners[1] – Alas! what desolation, destruction, and ruin, bad hearts or bad heads have brought upon this poor country! – I must, however, give Mr. *Johnny Rush* another letter, he fluctuates so terribly in his opinions[2] – as you will see by the contents of his letter to me – which I hope you will soon enable me to show you. – Yes, I must and will give him a flogging, which you will say is extremely grateful, and a civil return for his kindness in thinking of me. – I have had a very kind and good letter from the little wren. – We were pleased to hear Mrs. *Cocksedge* had enjoyed so great a share of health. She, who is lovely even in sickness, with the additional roseat bloom of health and flow of spirits, will be almost too much for mere mortals to bear – Tell her from me to get sick before she comes up, in pity to the beaux. – Mrs. Sancho is better. Poor Kitty goes on after the old sort – The happiest, my *Rush*, in this life, have something to sigh for – Alas! I have enough. – I feel much pleasure in the happy view Mr. and Mrs. R——n have before them – I have no sort of doubt that they will be successfully happy – I should have true pleasure to see my friend Mr. J. *Rush* in as likely a road – I have spoke and wrote to Mr. W—— to look out sharp – Time, which ripens revolutions, and murders empires, Time will, I hope, produce happiness and content to us all. – Your coming to town will give me spirits; for, large as the town is, I cannot say I have more than one friend in it – Come, you and I shall be rich indeed; for I believe few of the sons of Adam can boast of having more than two real friends. – The best respects to Mrs. *Cocksedge*, and the amiable little *Crewe*,

From yours, &c.
IGNATIUS SANCHO.

1. The Commissioners: see Letter 64, n. 2.
2. Letter 68 told how Sancho has heard from Johnny Rush Jr., at the American war.

73

Sept. 4, 1778.

For this month past we have wished to hear something about you – and every day for these two past weeks have I had it in serious contemplation to put the question – not to the amiable Miss *Crewe*, but to my friend *Rush*, who, notwithstanding your friendly excuse, is, I do think, rather culpable for his silence. – But hang recrimination – your goodness is more than sufficient to exculpate a thousand such sinners. We thank you, with heart-felt pleasure, for the information of our and your dear friend Mrs. *Cocksedge*'s health – which I hope she will be careful of for our and many sakes – I have a favour to beg of her, through your mediation, which is this – I have a pair of Antigua turtles – the gift of Mr. *Priddie*, who kindly burthened himself with the care of them – The true property is vested in Kitty – but so it is – we having neither warmth or room, and Kitty's good godmother[1] having both – and that kind of humanity withal which delighteth in doing good to orphans – I, in the name of Kate and her doves, do through you – our trusty council – petition Mrs. *Cocksedge* in behalf of said birds – Were I poetically turned – what a glorious field for fancy flights! such as the blue-eyed Goddess with her flying car – her doves and sparrows, &c. &c. – Alas! may imagination is as barren as the desert sands of Arabia – But in serious truth – the shop (the only place I have to put them in) is so cold, that I shall be happy to billet them to warmer quarters – which shall be done – as soon as Mrs. *Cocksedge* announces her consent – and empowers Molly to take them in. – As to news – we have none worth heeding – Your camps have ruined all trade – but that of hackney-men. – You much surprise us in the account of your late fair visitant – but pleased us more in the account of *Osborne*'s success[2] – The season has been, through God's blessing, as favourable as his friends – He is a lucky soul. – The *Spinks* are both well, I hope – to whom pray be so kind to remember us. – As to friend *Rush*, tell him, that whatever censure his omissions in writing may draw upon him – when the goodness of his heart and urbanity of soul are flung into the other scale, the faulty scale kicks the beam – We forgive, because we love – and love sees no faults.

Mrs. Sancho joins me in love and good wishes to both of you –

Kitty has been very poorly for above a month past, and continues but very so so – Betsy mends fast – Billy needs no mending at all – The rest are well – and all join in respects and compliments to Nutts.

I am
Dear Miss *Crewe* and Co's
Most obliged
humble servant,
IGN. SANCHO.

1. Mrs Cocksedge was said in Letter 22 to be godmother to Kate (Kitty) Sancho. Molly would be one of her servants who is to take charge of Mr Priddie's gift to Kitty of the inconvenient Antigua turtles. P—— was probably the 'Mr Priddie' who had made a similar gift earlier, see Letter 26.
2. Sancho's brother-in-law John Osborne, was said to be 'in his glory' at the camp (see Letter 70). His 'success' here refers to this, and may represent a promotion or more probably some financial wizardry. In Letter 75 Sancho writes of Osborne, 'his harvest has, I hope, been plentiful' which sounds more like a business venture than a military success. Perhaps he was a quartermaster and engaged in provisioning.

74

TO MR. M'[EHEUX]'.

Sept. 16, 1778.

DEAR *MEHEUX*,

Yours just received – and by great good luck I have found Mr. *Browne's* list; which I inclose – and God speed your labours! Poor —— sets off this evening for —— to take one parting look of his ——, and on Monday sets off fresh for ——. Mr. H——'s anxieties end in good luck at last – he also on Monday enters in one of the best houses in the city.[1] – On Thursday I hope you will succeed in your affair – and then my three Geniuses will be happy – I have had plague and perplexity enough with two of you. – When do you think of coming to town? In my last was some of the best poetry – that has – or was – aye, aye. Pray, Sir read it over once more. Well, what do you, or can you, say to it? Oh, envy – envy! – But, Mr. Monkey, the wit and true poetry of that billet must make amends for the shortness of it. – This is Saturday night – consequently it must be esteemed a favour that I write at all – My head aches – and, though my invention teems with brilliancies, I can only remember that I am very much

Yours,

I. SANCHO.

1. 'One of the best houses': a City of London business house. Mr H—— is called 'a very silly fellow' in Letter 88, but is being hard worked (Sancho calls it 'worked sweetly') by his 'house' in Letter 77, 'what with his office late hours'.

75

TO MISS C'[REWE]'.

October 1, 1778.

It is recorded of some great personage – I forget who – that they had so pleasing a manner in giving a refusal – that the *Refused* has left *them* with more satisfaction under a rejection – than many have experienced from receiving a *favour* conferred with perhaps more kindness than *grace*. – So it fares with me – I had anticipated the future happiness of my new friends – the comforts of warmth – the pleasures of being fed and noticed, talked to and watched, by the best heart and finest face within a large latitude – But I am content – I am certain of the *inconveniency* – and my best thanks are due, which I pray you make with our best wishes. – I am sorry both for *Osborne*'s and my friend's sake that the camp breaks up so soon.[1] – As to brother *Osborne*, his harvest has, I hope, been plentiful and well got in. – My friend, poor *Spink*, like most modest men of merit, is unlucky – He set out before I got either my friend *Rush*'s or your letter – His best way is to turn about; – and may good luck over-take him – detain him – fill his pockets – and send him in glee home again! – This is more to be wished than expected – If he falls in your way, I shall envy him – he will meet hospitality and the graces. – Betsy and Kitty are both invalids. – Mrs. Sancho is well, and joins me in every good wish. – Next month I hope brings you all to town – Bring health and spirits with you. – We have no news – no trade! consequently no money or credit.

Give Mr. *Rush* my thanks for his friendly letter in your kindest manner – and say all to our worthy esteemed friend Mrs. *Cocksedge*

that gratitude can conceive and friendship dictate – in the names of
all the Sanchos – and at the head place

Yours, &c. &c.

I. SANCHO.

1. Sancho is sorry for Miss Crewe's ('my friend's') sake that the
   camp may break up sooner than wished; the romantic
   excitements he warned her of earlier will be coming to an
   end. So apparently will be the profit to Osborne, though
   Sancho does not make clear exactly what the source of that
   profit is – obviously it has been a good camp for Osborne.
   Spink, the banker, has had a less profitable time, but the
   camp may yet help to fill his pockets. Sancho hopes that the
   end of autumn will bring all of them to London and then
   he can make a profit on his shop sales. For Sancho, the
   excitements of the camp appear to be more a matter of
   business and balls than preparations for battle.

76

TO MR. S'[PINK]'.

Yours just received Thursday,
Oct. 4, 1778.

'Whatever is – s right – The world, 'tis true,
'Was made for Cæsar – and for Billy too.'[1]
Poverty and Genius were coupled by the wisdom of Providence for
wise and good ends, no doubt – but that's a mystery. – I feel for and
pity you – A pox upon pity and feelings! say I: they neither fill the
belly, nor clothe the body – neither will they find lodging – or
procure an inside birth[2] in a rascally stage – Thee and I too well
know all this – But as I am at this present moment – thank fortune!
not quite worth ten shillings – pity – cursed foolish pity – is, with as
silly wishes, all I have to comfort you with. – Were I to throw out
my whole thoughts upon paper, it would take a day's writing, and
thou wouldst be a fool to read it – One dawn of hope I enjoy from
the old saw – that 'gloomy beginnings are for the most part blessed
with bright endings:' – may it be so with you, my friend! – At the
worst you can only face about – and your lodgings and old friends
will cordially receive you – For my part, I have use for every mite of
my philosophy – my state at present is that of suspense – God's will
be done!

This letter will reach you by the hands of a friend indeed – the best and truest I ever found – a man who, if the worth of his heart were written in his face, would be esteemed by the whole race of Adam – He will greet you kindly from the benevolence of his nature – and perhaps will not dislike you the more for the attachment which for thee is truly felt by thy sincere friend,

I. SANCHO.

Mrs. Sancho is well – Kitty mends very slow – Billy improves in sauciness – The girls are pretty good – Monsieur H—— rides uneasily – his saddle galls him – his beast is restive – I fear he will never prosecute long journeys upon him – he is for smoother roads – a pacing tit – quilted saddle – snaffle bridle, with silken reins, and gold stirrups. – So mounted we all should like; but I query albeit, though it might be for the ease of our bodies, whether it would be for the good of our souls. Adieu!

Should you be so lucky as to see *Barton*,[3] the house of the worthy Baronet Sir *Charles Bunbury*; mind I caution thee to guard thy heart: – you will there meet with sense that will charm exclusive of beauty – and beauty enough to subdue – even were sense wanting – add to this, good-nature, and all the charities, in one fair bosom. – Guard! guard thy heart!

1. Quotation: a variation on Pope's 'whatever IS, is RIGHT' from the *Essay on Man, Ep. I*, l, 294. I do not recognise the rest of the quotation: it may be Sancho's own words.
2. Inside birth: a variant spelling of 'inside berth', with reference to an inside seat in a stage-coach.
3. Barton House near Mildenhall, a few miles north-west of Bury St Edmunds. The lavish compliments paid to the house sound more like compliments to female charm. One of its great attractions was the beautiful widow Mrs Cocksedge, so admired by Sancho. She was a regular visitor to the house and is said by Stevenson to have married Sir Charles Bunbury (see Appendix VI).

77

TO MR. S'[TEVENSON]'.
October 15, 1778.

You want a long letter – where am I to find subject? My heart is sick with untoward events – Poor Kitty is no better – the Duke of Queensberry ill[1] – dangerously I fear – the best friend and customer I have. M*eheux* is just now come in – nay he is at my elbow – You know I wish you well – and that we all are well, Kitty excepted – so let M*eheux* conclude for your loving friend,

I. SANCHO.

The above you are to consider as bread and cheese: M*eheux* will give you goose stuffed with grapes*. Mr. H—— called here last night, and read yours: – he is worked sweetly – what with his office late hours,[2] and his family's odd humours – But all is for the best.

---

*   Alluding to Mr. *Stevenson*'s last letter, wherein he had informed Mr. Sancho, that the epicurean morsel was one of the many dishes with which he had been regaled at a place where he had lately dined.

1.   The Duke of Queensberry is dangerously ill: Sancho refers to the Duke's serious leg injury resulting from an accident when alighting from his carriage. The injury led to the Duke of Queensberry's death, recorded in Letter 79.
2.   'He is worked sweetly …' see Letter 74, n. 1.

78

TO MR. R'[RUSH]'.
October 16, 1778.

MY DEAR FRIEND,

Accept my thanks, my best thanks, for your kind readiness in obliging and serving my friend *Stevenson*.[1] He has sense, honour, and abilities – These we should naturally suppose would insure him bread – But that is not always the case: – in the race of fortune, knaves often win the prize – whilst Honesty is distanced – But then, mark the end – whilst the knave full often meets his deserved punishment, Honesty yoked with Poverty hugs Peace and Content in his bosom. – But truce with moralizing – though in serious truth my heart and spirits are low – The noble and good duke of Queensberry is, I fear, very dangerously ill. Exclusive of gratitude for past favours, and my own interest in the hope of future, I grieve for the public loss in him – a man who ennobled his titles, and made greatness lovely by uniting it with goodness: – If he dies, his gain is certain, for he has served a master who will not wrong him – but the world will lose a rare example! and the poor a friend! – He never knew a day's illness till now for fifty years past – His regularity of life and serenity of mind are in his favor – but his advanced life is against him – 80 odd – The great fear is a mortification in his leg – The King and Queen paid him a visit, as the prints must have informed you – He came to town on purpose to present himself at the levee – to thank them for the honor done him – He was taken ill the Sunday after their majesties' visit, and came to town the Tuesday after – I have been or sent daily to inquire about him – and was there about two hours ago – The faculty are pouring in the bark[2] – and allow his grace strong wines as much as he can drink – *God's will be done!*

Mr. *Stevenson* writes in raptures of you all. – I wonder not at him – I only wish for the good of mankind such characters as *Bunbury* house contains were more plenty – Poor Kitty continues much the same – The rest are, thank God, well. – Mrs. Sancho joins me in cordial wishes to self and ladies. Adieu,

Yours sincerely and gratefully,

I. SANCHO.

1. Rush's service must refer to the visit of Stevenson to the Bunbury household at Barton Hall, where Rush was valet to Sir Charles, and would have been responsible for ensuring appropriate domestic assistance to Stevenson.
2. The faculty: the medical profession. Infusions of tree-bark were often used as medicines. See Letter 24, n. 2 for an example of tree-bark used in 'a Benjamin drink of caudle', an infusion given at childbirth.

79

TO MR. S'[TEVENSON]'.

October 22, 1778.

MY DEAR FRIEND,

Have you never beheld a bust with double – no, not double – but with two very different profiles? one crying – and one laughing – That is just my situation at present – for poor de Groote – huzza! – is presented to the Charter-house[1] – by – bless him! the good archbishop of Canterbury – But, by a standing law, he cannot be admitted till a fresh quarter begins – and, as he says, he may be dead by that time – We will hope not – Well, this is the laughing side. – The duke of Queensberry died this morning.[2] – Alas! 'I ne'er shall look upon his like again!' – the clearest head, and most humane of hearts – I have in common with many – many – a heavy loss – I loved the good duke – and not without reason – He is gone to reap a reward which St. Paul could not conceive in the flesh, and which I will be bold to say they both perfectly enjoy at this moment – God of his mercy grant, that thee and I – and all I love – yea, and all I know – may enter eternity with as promising hopes – and realize the happiness in store for such as the duke of Queensberry!

Lord Lincoln[3] died on his passage – the news came last night – but he has left a son and daughter – T —— is well – but still plagued with his uncouth kinsfolk.

Adieu, Yours, &c. &c.
I. SANCHO.

Kitty very poorly, the rest all well.

1. Charterhouse: a charitable institution founded in London in 1611, on the site of a Carthusian monastery, to aid the deserving poor. It is now a famous London public school.
2. The Duke of Queensberry died in London on 22 October 1778, aged 80, and was buried at Durisdeer.
3. Lord Lincoln: Henry Fiennes Pelham Clinton. Lord Lincoln died in France on 18 October 1778, four days before Sancho's news of the death. Lord Lincoln and his wife, Lady Frances Seymour Conway, had two children, as Sancho records: a son who died on 23 September 1779, and a daughter.

80

TO MR. S'[OUBISE]'.

Charles Street, Westm. Nov. 29, 1778.

DEAR SOUBISE,

Yours, dated from Madras, came safe to hand – I need not tell you that your account pleased me – and the style of your letter indicated a mind purged from its follies – and a better habit of thinking, which I trust happily preceded a steadier course of action – I know not whether or not Providence may not in your instance produce much good out of evil – I flatter myself you will yet recover, and stand the firmer in your future life from the reflection (bitter as it is) of your former. – I have no doubt but you received my letter charged with the heavy loss of your great, your noble, friendly benefactress, and patroness, the good duchess of *Queensbury*; she entered into bliss, July 17, 1777,[1] just two days after you sailed from Portsmouth. I have now to inform you, that his Grace followed her October 21st this year; just fifteen months after his good duchess – full of years and honors – He is gone to join his duchess, and share in the rewards of a righteous God, who alone knew their merits, and alone could reward them.

Thus it has pleased God to take your props to himself – teaching you a lesson at the same time, to depend upon an honest exertion of your own industry – and humbly to trust in the Almighty.

You may safely conclude now, that you have not many friends in England – Be it your study, with attention, kindness, humility, and industry, to make friends where you are – Industry with good-nature and honesty is the road to wealth. – A wise œconomy – without avaricious meanness, or dirty rapacity, will in a few years render you decently independent.

I hope you cultivate the good-will and friendship of *Lincoln*[2]. He is a jewel – prize him – love him – and place him next your heart – He will not flatter or fear you – So much the better – the fitter for your friend – He has a spirit of generosity – Such are never ungrateful – He sent us a token of his affection, which we shall never forget. – Let me counsel you for your character's sake, and as bound in honor, the first money you can spare, to send over 20l. to discharge your debt at Mr. P——'s, the sadler – It was borrowed money, you know. – As for me, I am wholly at your service to the extent of my power – But whatever commissions you send over to me – send money – or I stir none – Thou well knowest my poverty – but 'tis an honest poverty – and I need not blush or conceal it. – You also are indebted to Mr. *Osborne*, Bond-street – What little things of that kind you can recollect – pay as soon as you are able – It will spunge out many evil traces of things past, from the hearts and heads of your enemies – create you a better name – and pave the way for your return some years hence into England – with credit and reputation. – Before I conclude, let me, as your true friend, recommend seriously to you to make yourself acquainted with your Bible. – Believe me, the more you study the word of God, your peace and happiness will increase the more with it. – Fools may deride you – and wanton youth throw out their frothy gibes: – but as you are not to be a boy all your life – and I trust would not be reckoned a fool – use your every endeavour to be a good man – and leave the rest to God. – Your letters from the Cape, and one from Madeira, I received; they were both good letters, and descriptions of things and places. – I wish to have your description of the fort and town of Madras – country adjacent – people – manner of living – value of money – religion – laws – animals – fashions – taste, &c. &c. – In short, write any thing – every thing – and above all, improve your mind with good reading – converse with men of sense, rather than with fools of fashion and riches – be humble to the rich – affable, open, and good-natured to your equals – and compassionately kind to the poor. – I have treated you freely in proof of my friendship – Mrs. *Sancho*, under the persuasion that you are really a good man, sends her best wishes – When her handkerchief is washed, you will send it home – The girls wish to be remembered to you, and all to friend Lincoln.

Yours, &c. &c.
I. SANCHO.

1. The Duchess of Queensberry died at Queensberry House, London, aged 76 and was buried at Durisdeer; see Letter 44, n. 2.
2. Charles Lincoln: the West Indian musician, see Letter 22, n. 2. For Soubise himself, see Letter 1, n. 6 and Letter 44, n. 2.

81

TO MR. I'[RELAND]'.

Jan. 1, 1779.

In compliance with custom, I beg leave to wish Mr. and Mrs. I*reland* happy years – many or few, as the Almighty shall think fit – but may they be happy! – As I wish it sincerely, their obligation is of course the greater – and to oblige them yet more, I will put it in their power to oblige me – which they can do by lending me the volume of Annual Registers[1] (I think it is that of 1774) which has Goldsmith's Retaliation[2] in it. – I hope Mr. and Mrs. I*reland* have no complaints – but the general one, extreme coldness of the weather – which, though happily exempted themselves from much suffering, by good fires and good cheer, yet I am sure their sympathizing hearts feel for the poor. – I find upon inquiring, that ten o'clock in the morning will best suit Mr. L——. I will be in Privy Gardens[3] just five minutes before Mr. and Mrs. I*reland* and Mr. Mortimer – I hope Mrs. I*reland* will not pretend to repent – Sunday is a lazy morning. If Mrs. I*reland* has not read Ganganelli,[4] it is time she should. I therefore take the liberty to send them – *Them*, Mr. I*reland* will say, is bad grammar – He is, madam, a good-natured critic – I address myself to you, therefore, because my heart tells me you will be a successful advocate for the blunders of a true Blackamoor. – I have had the confidence to mark the passages that pleased me most in my post-haste journey through the good Pontiff's letters – and I shall be vain if Mrs. I*reland* should like the same passages – because it would give a sanction to the profound judgment of her most obedient servant,

I. SANCHO.

Note – The sixteenth letter, 1st verse, is a kind of stuff which would almost turn me to the Romish – there is every thing in it which St. Paul had in his heart.

1. *Annual Register:* an annual review of events of the year, founded by the publisher Dodsley and the parliamentarian, Edmund Burke, in 1758 (for Burke see Letter 133, n. 3).
2. Goldsmith's *Retaliation*: this poem grew out of an epigram competition between Goldsmith and Garrick, in which each was to write the other's epitaph. As well as to Garrick, it refers to others in Sancho's circle, including Richard Cumberland and Dr William Dodd. Other poems by

Goldsmith refer to friends of Sancho, for instance Sir
Charles Bunbury and his sister-in-law, Mrs Bunbury, the
former Catherine Horneck, see Letter 11, n. 1. The text of
the poem with a detailed introduction and notes is to be
found in Friedman, *Goldsmith's Collected Works* (1966), vol.
IV, pp. 343–59.

3. Privy Gardens: see Letter 26, n. 2.
4. Ganganelli: the family name of Pope Clement XIV (1705–74)
    whose *Dominus ac Redemptor noster* (1773) was directed
    against the authority of the Jesuits.

82

TO J'[OHN]' S'[PINK]', ESQ.
                                         Charles Street, Jan. 1779.

'Beyond the fix'd and settled rules
'Of Vice and Virtue in the schools,
'Beyond the letter of the Law,
'Which keeps mere Formalists in awe,
'The better sort do set before 'em
'A grace – a manner – a decorum;
'Something that gives their acts a light;
'Makes 'em not only just – but bright,
'And sets 'em in such open fame,
'Which covers *Quality* with shame.'[1]

Judiciously elegant Prior has befriended me – and described my
honored friend Mr. *Spink*. I wish I knew which way to shew my
gratitude – The only method I can think of, is to enjoy the benefits
with a thankful heart, and leave God in his own good time to
reward you.

I should last night have gratefully acknowledged the receipt of
your letter and note – but I hoped for a frank – I am disappointed,
and a longer delay would be unpardonable. – Be assured, dear Sir
I shall (with all the alacrity of a heavy man) bestir myself in the
execution of your generous order. – I hope Mrs. *Spink* and every
one of your family enjoy health and every good – Mrs. Sancho joins
me in respects and thanks to Mrs. *Spink* and yourself.

                                         I remain, dear Sir,
                                         Your very obliged
                                         and faithful servant,
                                         I. SANCHO.

1. Quotation: the opening lines of Prior's 'Paolo Purgante and
    His Wife'. The poem contains a passing reference, lines
    131–3, to de Groote's uncle, the great jurist Hugo Grotius,
    see Letter 62a, n. 2. The comic subject of the poem, a wife's
    eagerness for sex with her tired scholarly husband, seems to
    have been one to amuse and appeal to the uxorious Sancho,
    as it did to Dr Johnson. Asked by Boswell whether he
    thought the poem improper, Johnson replied: 'Sir, there is
    nothing there but that his wife wanted to be kissed when
    poor Paolo was out of pocket. No, Sir, Prior is a lady's book.
    No lady is ashamed to have it standing in her library.'
    Boswell, *Life*, (ed.) R. W. Chapman, 1970, p. 869, (22
    September 1777). Sancho misquotes the poem several times:
    the main changes are to l. 4, in Prior, 'Which keeps our Men
    and Maids in Awe', and l. 10, completely rewritten by
    Sancho, in Prior, 'Which willing Malice cannot blame.'

83

TO IGNATIUS SANCHO.
Bath, April 20, 1779.

MY WORTHY THOUGH UNKNOWN FRIEND,

Notwithstanding we have not any personal knowledge of each
other, yet I flatter myself thou wilt excuse this address from one
who equally loves and reveres a virtuous character, in whatever
name, society, or class of men it is found, without distinction. I am
fully persuaded that the great God, who made all the nations that
dwell upon earth, regards the natives of Africa with equal com-
placence as those of this or any other country; and that the rewards
annexed to virtue will accompany it in all ages and nations, either in
this life, or in a future happier world which is to come.

The principal view I have in addressing thee by letter, is to inform
thee that there have lately fallen into my hands two letters of thy
writing, the one to a gentleman in the East Indies, the other to my
friend Jabez Fisher from Philadelphia.[1]

I am so much pleased with these letters, on account of the
humanity and strong good sense they contain, that I am very
desirous of gaining thy permission to print them in a collection of
Letters of Friendship,[2] which I think of publishing in autumn. I have
thy two letters in my possesion, but did not think it would be acting
candidly to publish them without thy consent, which I am very

solicitous to obtain. If, in transcribing, any little inaccuracy in point of grammar has crept in, I will take care to correct it: there is nothing in them that can do thee the least discredit: on the contrary, the sentiments they contain do thee great honour; and, if published, may convince some proud Europeans, that the noblest gifts of God, those of the mind, are not confined to any nation or people, but extended to the scorching deserts of Guinea,[3] as well as the temperate and propitious climes in which we are favoured to dwell.

I shall be happy if thou wilt oblige me with a reply as soon as is convenient, and still more so if thou wilt write such an one as thou art willing to have appear with the other two in my collection.

Be assured, my friend, that I *feel* the regard I *profess:* and should rejoice were it in my power to put an end to the slavery, or lessen the misery, of *one* of thy poor countrymen.

Mercy knows no distinction of colour; nor will the God of mercy make any at the last day. Adieu, my good Friend! and believe me to be, with great esteem.

Thine in all ready services,
EDMUND RACK.

1. Jabez Fisher of Philadelphia: included only as an otherwise unidentified initial in Stevenson's index; he is the Mr F. of Letter 58, who sent Sancho anti-slavery works from America, including the poems of Phillis Wheatley.
2. Edmund Rack, *Letters of Friendship:* I have not found any trace of these letters being published. Rack published several books, among them *Essays, Letters and Poems* (Bath, 1781), and a *Life of Penn* (1771).
3. 'Scorching deserts of Guinea': the word 'desert' is used here in its eighteenth-century sense of 'wilderness', and as such could be used to describe a rain forest.

83a

THE ANSWER.[1]

SIR,

I have just received your favor of the 20th instant. As to the letters in question, you know, Sir, they are not *now* mine, but the property of the parties they are addressed to. – If you have had their permission, and think the simple effusions of a poor Negro's heart worth mixing with better things, you have my free consent to do as you please with them; – though, in truth, there wants no increase of books in the epistolary way – nor indeed in any way – except we could add to the truly valuable names of Robertson, Beattie, and Mickle, some new *Youngs, Richardsons,* and *Sternes.*

Accept my best thanks for the very kind opinion you are so obliging to entertain of me – which is too pleasing (I fear) to add much to the humility of,

Dear Sir,
Yours, &c.
I. SANCHO.

1. Sancho's 'Answer': Sancho's modest reluctance to acknowledge his letters as worthy of publication is the conventionally polite response: he is in fact clearly pleased by Rack's admiration, as he had every right to be, and would have had no objection to adding his name to the 'truly valuable' ones listed. This might lead us to reconsider Miss Crewe's prefatory note, Appendix V, which claimed that Sancho had no ambition to publish his letters, also discussed in Appendix I.

84

TO MRS. I'[RELAND]'.

Charles Street, Jan. 21, 1797.[1]

DEAR MADAM,

My wife wishes to see Cymon[2] – and my wishes (like a civil husband) perfectly correspond with hers – I had rather be obliged to you than any good friend I have; – for I think you have an alacrity in doing good-natured offices – and so I would tell the Queen – if she dared dispute it. – You are not so great indeed – but I am sure you are as good – and I believe her to be as rich in goodness as she is high in rank – If my request is within the limits of your power, you will favor us with the order[3] soon in the day. – I have looked abroad for the wonder you wished to be procured for you – but have met with nothing likely hitherto.

Yours most gratefully,
I. SANCHO.

1. Printer's error. The date should be 1779.

2. Cymon: perhaps a copy of Dryden's fable, 'Cymon and Iphigenia'. I do not know of another work of this name, which was mentioned earlier in Letter 9.
3. The expression 'you will favour us with the order' suggests that the Irelands are in the book trade, like Sancho's friend and correspondent Wingrave, and the adult Billy Sancho. Sancho orders a print from them and returns a book in Letter 96 (see n. 3).

85

TO MRS. H———.

Charles Street, Feb. 9, 1779.

DEAR MADAM,

I felicitate you in the first place on the pleasing success of your maternal care, in restoring your worthy son[1] to good health – He looks now as well, fresh, and hearty, as love and friendship can wish him. – Mrs. Sancho joins me in hearty thanks for your kind attention to our well-doing – and your goodness in the very friendly order[2] – which I have endeavoured to execute with attention and honesty. – As to news, there is none good stirring – trade is very dull – money scarce beyond conception – Fraud! perfidy! villainy! from the highest departments to the lowest – The King God bless him, is beset with friends – which he ought to fear.[3] – I believe he has one true friend only – and that is the Queen, who is the ornament and honor of her sex. – Pray, dear Madam, make my best respects to your good son and daughter, Mr. J———, and all I have the honor to know. Our best thanks and wishes attend Mr. H—— and yourself, and believe me

Yours, &c.

I. SANCHO.

1. The 'worthy son' of Mrs H—— is named Jacob, as we learn from Letter 93. Her daughter, also mentioned by Sancho in this letter, named Kate in Letter 12, was probably the young lady who had captured Kisby's heart, and whose figure 'attracted universal admiration' in Edinburgh, according to Letter 9.
2. It might be recalled that Mrs H—— was a principal agent in the establishment of Sancho's grocery business on his retirement, see Letters 12 and 16. We learn that she continues

to encourage business by ordering her groceries from Sancho's shop.

3. The King: along with his Prime Minister, Lord North, to whose daughter Sancho was to dedicate his collection, *Twelve Country Dances* (1779) King George III received much of the blame for the loss of the American war, which led to the fall of North's administration. For North, see Letter 115, n. 4 and Letter 133, n. 7.

86

TO MR. G——.[1]

Feb. 1779.

SIR,

The very handsome manner in which you have apologized for your late lapse of behaviour does you credit. – Contrition, the child of conviction, serves to prove the goodness of your heart – The man of levity often errs – but it is the man of sense alone who can gracefully acknowledge it. – I accept your apology – and if in the manly heat of wordy contest aught escaped my lips tinged with undue asperity, I ask your pardon, and hope you will mutually exchange forgiveness with

IGN. SANCHO.

1. Sancho refers to a Mr G—— on several occasions, apparently not always to the same person. I do not know who this particular G—— was, or the nature of his offence.

87

TO J'[OHN]' S'[PINK]', ESQ.

March 9, 1779.

It has given me much concern, dear Sir, the not having it in my power to make my grateful acknowlegments sooner for your very kind letter, and friendly present which accompanied it. – My first thanks are due to heaven – who for the example, as well as service, of mortals, now and then blesses the world with a humane, generous being. – My next thanks are justly paid to you – who are pleased to rank me and mine in the honored class of those you wish to serve: – for these six past weeks, our days have been clouded by the severe illness of a child – whom it has pleased God to take from us;[1] and a cowardly attack of the gout at a time when every exertion was needful – I have as yet but very little use of my hand – but I am thankful to have sufficient to exculpate me from the vice of ingratitude – which my long silence might lay me under the imputation of. – Mrs. Sancho begs me to express her sense of your kindness – and joins me cordially in the most respectful sensations and best wishes to Mrs. *Spink* and yourself. I am, dear Sir,

> (and with very great reason)
> Your much obliged
> humble servant,
> I. SANCHO.

1. The child who died was Kitty, who had been ill for some time. Letter 88 also concerns her death.

88

TO MR. S'[TEVENSON]'.

March 11, 1779.

DEAR FRIEND,
I received yours about three hours since – I give you due credit for your sympathizing feelings on our recent very distressful situation – For thirty nights (save two) Mrs. Sancho had no clothes off – but you know the woman. Nature never formed a tenderer heart – Take her for all in all – the mother, wife, friend – she does credit to her sex – She has the rare felicity of possessing true virtue without arrogance – softness without weakness – and dignity without pride – She is S——'s full sister[1] without his foibles – and to my inexpressible happiness, she is my wife – and truly best part – without a single tinge of my defects. – Poor Kitty! happy Kitty I should say, drew her rich prize early – Wish her joy! and joy to Mortimer![2] – He left life's table (before he was cloyed or surfeited with dull sickly repetitions) – in prime of years – in the meridian of character as an artist – and universally esteemed as a man – he winged his rapid flight to those celestial mansions – where Pope – Hogarth – Handel – Chatham – and Garrick, are enjoying the full sweets of beatific vision – with the great Artists – Worthies – and

Poets of time without date. – Your father has been exceeding kind – This very day Mr. W——, of Retford, called on me – a goodly-looking gentleman: he inquired after you with the anxious curiosity of a friend – told me your father was well – and, by his account, thinks by much too well of me. – Friend H—— shall produce the things you wot of – and brother *Osborne* bring them in his hand. – H—— is a very silly fellow – he likes silly folks – and, I believe does not hate Sancho. – Tomorrow night I shall have a few friends to meet brother *Osborne*. We intend to be merry[3] – Were you here, you might add to a number, which I think too many for our little room. – So I hear that the —— No, hang me! if I say a word about it – Well; and how do you like the company of Monsieur Le Gout? – Shall I, in compliance with vulgar custom, wish you joy? Pox on it, my hand aches so, I can scrawl no longer. – Mrs. Sancho is but so so – the children are well – Do write large and intelligible when you write to me – I have fine hands and fine language – Write plain honest nonsense, like thy true friend,

I. SANCHO.

1. 'She is S——'s full sister': the meaning of this is unclear. Mrs Sancho was in fact Osborne's sister, so perhaps this is a misprint for O——, as Osborne is usually designated. But this may refer to Stevenson himself, meaning that she could be his sister, having similar virtues without his small faults, a roundabout compliment to Stevenson, in which the reference to his 'foibles' is intended in Sancho's jesting Shandean manner to be affectionate, not to be taken seriously.
2. Mortimer: John Hamilton Mortimer the artist (see the Introduction, n. 10) who died in 1779.
3. Sensibly, Sancho and his wife intend to gather for drinks with her brother Osborne and a few friends, to 'be merry', probably as good a way as any to help come to terms with Kitty's death, by holding some kind of 'wake' with those who knew and loved her.

89

TO MR. W'[INGRAV]'E.
Charles Street, March 31, 1779.

You wish me to write a consolatory letter to Mrs. *Wingrave*, my good friend.[1] – What can I possibly write but your good sense must have anticipated? The soul-endearing soothings of cordial love have the best and strongest effects upon the grief-torn mind. – You have of course told her that thanks are due – greatly so! – to a merciful God – who might have bereaved her of a child, instead of a worthy cousin – or that she ought to feel comfort – and to acknowledge divine mercy – that it was not her husband: – that to lament the death of that amiable girl, is false sorrow in the extreme. – Why lament the great bliss and *choice prize* of what we love? – What is it she has not gained by an early death! – You will say, she was good, and will suppose that in the tender connexions of wife, friend, and mother, she would have been an honored and esteemed example. – True – she might – and it is as true – she might have been unhappily paired – ill-matched to some morose, ill-minded, uneven bashaw – she might have fell from affluence to want – from honor to infamy – from innocence to guilt. – In short, we mistake too commonly the objects of our grief – the living demand our tears – the dead (if their lives were virtuous) our gratulations. – In your case all that can be said is – earth has lost an opening sweet flower (which, had it lasted longer, must of course soon fade) – and heaven has gained an angel – which will bloom for ever. – So let us hear no more of grief – we all must follow: – no! let us rejoice with your worthy friend Mrs.——*, joy to the good couple! may they each find their respective wishes! may he find the grateful acknowledgment of obliged and pleasing duty! – and she, the substantial, fond, solid rewards due to a recitude of conduct – marked strongly with kindness and wisdom! and may you, my friend! – but my leg aches – my foot swells – I can only say, my love to the C——ds, and to poor Joe and Frank. – Read this to Mrs. *Wingrave*. My silly reasoning may be too weak to reach her; but, however, she may smile at my absurdities – If so, I shall have a comfort – as I ever wish

---

*   This union was remarkable for disparity of years; the bridegroom being 78, the bride in the bloom of youth.

to give pleasure to her dear sex – and the pride of my heart is ever to please one – alas! – and that one a – wife. – So writes thy true friend,

I. SANCHO.

Mr. W*ingrav*e comes as far as Privy Gardens – but cannot reach Charles Street.[2]
    How's that?
I hear my scheme of taxation was inserted directly, and should be glad to see the paper, if easily got.[3]
    Vanity!

1. The subject of how to cope with bereavement continues. Wingrave wants Sancho to comfort his wife with a letter of condolence on the death of her cousin. Sancho says, with perhaps an acid touch in view of his loss of Kitty, that Mrs Wingrave is lucky it was not her husband or child. Sancho insists that true faith in the Christian message means mourning for the dead is unreasonable if we really believe they have reached the bliss of Heaven: 'Why lament the great bliss and choice prize of what we love?'
2. Sancho would often meet his friends at Privy Gardens, the mansion with its associated park which was the Montagus' London residence, but would prefer Wingrave to visit him at his own home in Charles Street.
3. Sancho's scheme of taxation appeared in a letter to *The General Advertiser* over a year earlier, Letter 59a. It seems that Sancho's letter on the subject had been republished, though I have not been able to trace it.

90

TO MR. L'[INCOLN]'.[1]

May 4, 1779.
MY DEAR CHILD,
I am truly sorry to address this letter to you at this season in the English channel – The time considered that you have left us, you ought in all good reason to have been a seasoned creole of St. Kitt's; – but we must have patience – what cannot be cured must be endured. – I dare believe you bear the cruel delay with resignation – and make the best and truest use of your time, by steady reflection and writing. – I would wish you to note down the occurrences of

every day – to which add your own observation of men and things – The more you habituate yourself to minute investigation, the stronger you will make your mind – ever taking along with you in all your researches the word of God – and the operations of his divine providence. – Remember, young man – nothing happens by chance. – Let not the levity of frothy wit, nor the absurdity of fools, break in upon your happier principles – your dependence upon the Deity – Address the Almighty with fervor – with love and simplicity – carry his laws in your heart – and command both worlds. – But I meant mere fatherly advice, and I have wrote a sermon. – Dear boy, 't is my love preaches. – N—— begged me to write a line for him, as he said you wanted news – I have none but what you know as well as myself – such as the regard and best wishes of Mrs. Sancho, the girls, and myself – such as wishing a happy end to your long-protracted voyage – and a joyful meeting with your worthy and respectable family: – and in order to leave room for friend N——, I here assure you I am your affectionate friend,

I. SANCHO.

1. Mr. Lincoln: Charles Lincoln, see Letter 22, n. 2.

91

TO MR. R'[USH]'.

May 1779.

MY DEAR WORTHY R*USH*,
Your letter was a real gratification to a something better principle than pride – it pleased my self-love – There are very few (believe me) whose regards or notice I care about – Yourself, brother, and *Osborne*, with about three more at most, form the whole of my *male* friendly connections. – Your brother is not half so honest as I thought him – he promises like a tradesman, but performs like a lord. – On Sunday evening we expected him – the hearth was swept – the kettle boiled – the girls were in print – and the marks of the folds in Mrs. Sancho's apron still visible – the clock past six – no Mr. R*ush*. Now to tell the whole truth, he did add a kind of clause, that in case nothing material happened of hospital business,[1] he would surely do himself the &c. &c. &c. – So, upon the whole, I am

not quite clear that he deserves censure – but that he disappointed us of a pleasure I am very certain. – You don't say you have seen Mr. P——.[2] I beg you will, for I think he is the kind of soul congenial to your own. – *Apropos*, the right hand side (almost the bottom of Gray-Street), there is a Mrs. H——, an honest and very agreeable northern lady,[3] whom I should like you to know something of – which may easily be done – if you will do me the credit just to knock at her door when you go that way – and tell her, there is a Devil that has not forgot her civilities to him, and would be glad to hear she was well and happy. – Mr. R*ush* called on me in the friendly style – when I say that, I mean in the R*ush* manner – He asked a question, bought some tea, looked happy, and left us pleased: – he has the graces. – The gout seized me yesterday morning – the second attack – I looked rather black all day. – Tell Mrs. *Cocksedge*, I will lay any odds that she is either the handsomest or ugliest woman in Bath – and among the many trinkets she means to bring with her, tell her not to forget health.[4] May you all be enriched with that blessing – wanting which, the good things of this world are trash. – You can write tiresome letters! Alas! will you yield upon the receipt of this? – If not, that palm unquestionably belongs to your friend,

I. SANCHO.

1. The Mr Rush who has not turned up for tea is the addressee's brother, George, a medical man with 'hospital business', the Dr Rush of Letter 156, who attended the dying Sancho.
2. Mr. P—— is probably the Mr P—— of Letter 26, given his full name Priddie in Letter 73, on both occasions associated with gifts of edible turtles or pet turtle-doves.
3. Mrs H——'s northern connections are said to be with Lancaster, see Letter 66 to her husband.
4. This is another example of Sancho's jesting Shandean 'curmudgeonly' manner, in which one shows friendship by a critical remark that cannot possibly be taken seriously. Sancho is almost obsessed by Mrs Cocksedge's beauty and she knows it, having been complimented by him so often. He also seems much concerned with her health; his attitude to her sometimes approaches that of a lover rather than a close friend.

92

TO '[JOHN]' S'[PINK]', ESQ.[1]

Charles Street, June 16, 1779.

DEAR SIR,

In truth, I was never more puzzled in my life than at this very
present writing – The acts of common kindness, or the effusions of
mere common good-will, I should know what to reply to – but, by
my conscience, you act upon so grand a scale of urbanity, that a man
should possess a mind as noble and a heart as ample as yourself,
before he attempts even to be grateful upon paper. – You have made
me richer than ever I was in my life[2] – Till this day I thought a bottle
of good wine a large possession. Sir, I will enjoy your goodness with
a glad heart – and every deserving soul I meet with shall share a glass
with me, and join in drinking the generous donor's health. Mrs.
Sancho's eyes betray her feelings – She bids me thank you for her
– which I do most sincerely, and for myself,

IGNATIUS SANCHO.

1. This Letter and Letter 94, according to Stevenson's index to
   John Spink, are addressed to Mr I. S——, so this is a printer's
   error, presumably arising from a similarity between the
   letters 'I' and 'J' in Sancho's hand. We can see this in the
   reproduction of a manuscript letter by Sancho in the article
   by R. W. Willis, 'New light on Ignatius Sancho', *Slavery and
   Abolition*, (1.)3, (1980), p. 355.
2. I do not know what was Spink's generous act 'upon so grand
   a scale', but it appears from the next letter that it included the
   whole community. As a banker, Spink has perhaps been able
   to solve Sancho's recurrent worries about money.

93

TO MRS. H——.

June 17, 1779.

DEAR MADAM,

Your son, who is a welcome visitor wherever he comes,[1] made
himself more welcome to me by the kind proof of your regard he
brought in his hands. – Souls like yours, who delight in giving
pleasure, enjoy a heaven on earth; for I am convinced, that the

disposition of the mind in a great measure forms either the heaven or hell in both worlds. – I rejoice sincerely at the happiness of Mrs. W——: and may their happiness increase with family and trade! – and may you both enjoy the heartfelt delight of seeing your children's children walking in the track of grace! – I have, to my shame be it spoken, intended writing to you for these twelve months past[2] – but in truth I was deterred through a fear of giving pain. – Our history has had little in it but cares and anxieties – which (as it is the well-experienced lot of mortality) we struggle with it, with religion on one hand, and hope on the other.

Mr. W——, whose looks and address bespeak a good heart and good sense, called on me. – I will not say how much I was pleased – Pray make my kindest respects to your good partner, and tell him, I think I have a right to trouble him with my musical nonsense.[3] – I wish it better for my own sake – Bad as it is, I know he will not despise it, because he has more good-nature. – I hear a good report of Mr. S*pink*, and that his humanity has received the thanks of a community in a public manner.[4] – May he! and you! and all I love, enjoy the blissful feelings of large humanity! – There is a plaudit as much superior to man's as heaven is above earth! Great God, in thy mercy and unbounded goodness, grant that even I may rejoice through eternity with those I have respected and esteemed here! – Mrs. Sancho joins me in love to yourself and Mr. H——. Your son Jacob is the delight of my girls – Whenever he calls on us, the work is flung by, and the mouths all distended with laughter: – he is a vile romp with children. – I am, dear madam, with true esteem and respect,

Your obliged servant,

IGN. SANCHO.

1. The son of Mrs H—— is said in Letter 85 to have recovered from an illness. Here, he is a 'welcome visitor' and Sancho gives his name: 'your son Jacob is the delight of my girls'.
2. Either Sancho or Miss Crewe is unreliable with dates here: Sancho had written to Mrs H—— well within 'these twelve months past', see Letter 85 of 9 February 1779. Since both this and Letter 93 make reference to her lively and popular son, it seems unlikely that there are two Mrs H—— with whom Sancho is corresponding. Stevenson's index confirms this.
3. 'Musical nonsense': earlier, Sancho sent Mrs Cocksedge a piece of music for dancing which was later to appear in his

collection of *Twelve Country Dances for the Year 1779* (Letter 55, n. 6.); and Sancho also wrote a piece for the camp attended by Osborne (see Letter 70, n. 1.). It looks as if another of the pieces written for the collection is being tried out here among his friends in the Bury St Edmunds community.

4. I do not know what act of generosity Sancho refers to, but it extended beyond the community to himself personally, as Letters 92 and 94 show.

94

TO '[JOHN]' 'S[PINK]', ESQ.

June 29, 1779.

A little fish – which was alive this morn – sets out this eve for Bury – ambitious of presenting itself to Mrs. S*pink*. If it should come good,[1] the Sanchos will be happy – In truth, Mr. S*pink* ought not to be displeased – neither will he, I trust, if he considers it – as it really is – a grain of salt – in return for favors received of princely magnitude – and deeply engraven in the hearts of his much obliged and faithful servants,

He and She SANCHOS.

1. Sancho hopes the small fresh fish will 'come good', i.e. arrive in good condition. But again we hear of Spink's 'favours of a princely magnitude' which sounds more like substantial financial aid than mere good advice.

95

TO MR. M'[EHEUX]'.

August 1, 1779.
Coat and Badge.[1]

Bravo! So you think you have given me the retort courteous – I admit it – Go to! you are seedy, you are sly – true son in the right direct line of old Gastpherious Sly. – Your letter to S——n makes ample amends for your impudence in presuming to mount my hobby – Yes, I do affirm it to be a good, yea, and a friendly letter – The leading-string thought is new, and almost poetic; – I watched him while he read it – he read it twice – I judge he felt the force of your argumentation: – may he avail himself of your friendly hints! and may you have the heart-felt satisfaction of finding him a wiser being than heretofore! How doth George's mouth? – I honor you for humane feelings – and much more for your brotherly affection: – but do not Namby-Pamby with the manly exertions of benevo-lence – What I mean is – ah me! poor George – to be sure 'tis well its no worse – but then the loss of a tooth, and a scar, are so disfiguring – Pooh, simpleton, if his heart is right, and God blesses him with health, his exterior will ever be pleasing in spite of the gap in his gums – or scar above his chin. – G—— is likely – the rogue has a pleasing, cheery phiz – neither so old – nor so mouldy as some folks – Not having been rocked in the cradle of flattery – he has consequently more modesty than his elders. – I could easily fill the sheet in contrasting the merits of the two lads – but then it would (I plainly foresee) turn out so much to the disadvantage of Prince Jacky, that in mere charity I forbear – and shall conclude with wishing both your heads to agree, as well in good health as in the many good qualities which I have not time to enumerate.

Mrs. Sancho is pretty well – the girls and Billy well – I am sometimes better – sometimes so so – I should have answered you sooner – but yesterday was obliged to write all day – though fast asleep the whole time – Perhaps you will retort, that it is the case with me at this present writing – False and scandalous. – I declare I was never more awake – Remember me to Mr. S——, the ladies, and to thyself, if thou knowest him.

Farewell. Thine, &c. &c. &c.

I. SANCHO.

1. Coat and Badge: a pub or inn outside London where Sancho wrote this letter.

96

TO MR. I'[RELAND]'.

August 3, 1779.

DEAR SIR,

I much wish to hear that Mrs. I*reland* is quite recovered – or in the best possible way towards it. – I have next to thank you for your princely present – and to say I feel myself rich and happy in the splendid proofs I have of your regard.

You love a pun almost as well as Dennis – I shall contrive to be in your debt as long as I live – and settle accounts hereafter – where I know no more than the pope. – But if you, Sterne, and Mortimer, are there, sure I am, it will be the abode of the blest. – But to business – I am commissioned to get as good an impression as possible of St. Paul preaching to the Britons[1] – shall esteem it a fresh obligation, if you will be kind enough to chuse one, and send by the bearer. – I return faith for pudding – and Mr. Sharpe's strictures upon slavery[2] – The one may amuse, if not edify: the other I think of consequence to every one of humane feelings. – Do pray let me know how Mrs. *Ireland* does – With thanks, respects, and why not friendship?

I am, dear Sir,
Yours, &c.
I. SANCHO.

1. St Paul preaching to the Britons: this refers to a print of J. H. Mortimer's painting *St Paul Converting the Britons*, which won a prize in 1770 for the best historical painting. The request to purchase it comes from Meheux, according to Letter 107.
2. 'Mr Sharpe's strictures upon slavery': this might be any one of many abolitionist publications by Granville Sharp (1735–1815), all of which are listed in Prince Hoare's *Memoir of Granville Sharp* (London, 1820). His *Essay on Slavery* (1776) is probably the one Sancho refers to here.

97

TO MR. M'[EHEUX]'.

August 14, 1779.

You kindly gave me liberty to bring Mr. S——. The proposal did honor to your heart, and credit to your judgment; – but an affair has rendered that part of your invitation inadmissible – Now, pox take bad quills – and bad pen-makers! – Sir, it was fifty pound to a bean-shell, but that you had had a blot as big as both houses of parliament[1] in the very fairest, yea, and handsomest part of this epistle – My pen, like a drunkard, sucks up more liquor than it can carry, and so of course disgorges it at random. – I will that ye observe the above simile to be a good one – not the cleanliest in nature, I own – but as pat to the purpose as dram-drinking to a bawd – or oaths to a serjeant of the guards – or – or – dulness to a Black-a-moor – Good – excessive good! – And pray what? – (oh! this confounded pen!) what may your Worship's chief employ have been? – You have had your Devils dance – found yourself in a lazy fit – the inkstand, &c. staring you full in the face – You yawned – stretched – and then condescended to scold me for omitting what properly – and according to strict rule – you should have done yourself a month ago. – Zounds! – God forgive us! – this thought oversets the patience – coat and lining – of your right trusty friend,

IGN. SANCHO.

1. 'A blot as big as both houses of parliament': we are back with Shandyism, Sterne's art of the essay on nothing in particular. This time the whole letter plays with the idea of writing a letter about writing a letter.

98

TO MR. M'[EHEUX]'.

August 20, 1779.

In all doubtful cases it is best to adhere to the side of least difficulty. – Now, whether you ought to have shown the *politesses* of the *Ton* in making enquiry after my Honor's health – and travels – or whether my Honor should have anticipated all enquiry – by sending a card of thanks for more than friendly civilities – is a very nice point, which, for my part, I willingly leave to better casuists; – and as I honestly feel myself the obliged party – so I put pen to paper as a testimonial of the same. – I will suppose your head improved – I mean physically: I will also hope your heart light – and all your combustible passions under due subordination – and then adding the fineness of the morning – from these premises I will believe that my good friend is well and happy.[1]

I hope George[2] effected his wish in town. If he has to do with people of feeling, there is a something in his face which will command attention and love – The boy is much handsomer than ever you were; and yet you never look better than when you look on him – Would to God you were as well settled!

The stage contained five good souls, and one huge mass of flesh*. – They, God bless them, thought I took up too much room – and I thought there was too little – We looked at each other, like folks dissatisfied with their company – and so jolted on in sullen silence for the first half-hour; – and had there been no ladies, the God or Goddess of Silence would have reigned the whole way. – For my part, quoth I to myself, I have enjoyed true pleasure all day – the morning was bright, refreshing, and pleasant, the delicious bowl of milk, the fresh butter, sweet bread, cool room, and kind hostess – the friendly converse, the walk – the animated flow of soul in I—— M——,[3] – the little but elegant treat high-seasoned with welcome – Oh! Sancho, what more could luxury covet, or ambition wish for? True, cries Reason – then be thankful. – Hold! cries Avarice with squinting eyes and rotten stumps of teeth – hungry, though ever cramming – it cost thee one shilling and nine pence, one shilling and nine pence I say. – What of that? cries Œconomy. We ate fairly half a crown's worth. – Aye, cries Prudence, that alters the case – Od-so, we are nine pence in pocket, besides the benefit of fresh air, fresh scenes, and the pleasures of the society we love. – The sky was cloudless, and, to do me a particular favor, the moon chose to be at full – and gave us all her splendor – But our envious Mother Earth (to mortify our vanity) rose up – rolling the whole way in clouds of dust. – Contention flew in at the coach-windows, and took possession of both the females: – 'Madam, if you persist in drawing up the glass, we shall faint with heat.' – 'Oh dear! very sorry to offend your delicacy; but I shall be suffocated with dust – and my clothes –' 'I have clothes to spoil as well as other folks, &c. &c. &c.' – The males behaved wisely, and kept a stricter neutrality than the French with the Americans. – I chewed the cud of sweet remembrance, and with a heart and mind in pretty easy plight, gained the castle of peace and innocence[4] about nine o'clock. – Well, Sir, and how do you find youself by this time? – I sweat, I protest – and then the bright God of day darts his blessings full upon my shop-window – so intensely, that I could fancy myself St. Bartholomew broiling upon a gridiron.

---

*   Mr. Sancho was remarkable for corpulency.

Oh! thou varlet – down – down upon thy knees, and bless thy indulgent stars for the blessings – comforts – beauties, &c. – of thy situation, The Land of Canaan in possession – milk and honey – shady trees – sweet walks covered with the velvet of nature – pleasant views – cool house – and the superintendency of the sweet girls – to whom my love and blessings – And, sirrah! mark what I say, and obey me without reply: – There is a plump good-natured looking soul – I think you called her Patty – my conscience tells me, that I owe her something more than kind words and cool thanks; – therefore tell her, a man that notes particularly the welcome of the eye – and saw plainly good-will and good-nature in the expression of her honest countenance – sends her a dish of tea – which she must sweeten by her cheery acceptance of it – from one who knows not how to return the many, many obligations he has received from the he's and she's of P—— house[5] – exclusive of what he owes – and shall be content ever to owe – the saucy rogue he addresses.

Farewell. Yours, &c.

I. SANCHO.

1. Another letter amiably inconsequential in the manner of Sterne, in which Sancho chattily thanks Meheux for his company.
2. George is Meheux's brother. Once again Sancho adopts light-hearted personal abuse as a mode of expressing affection. George is mentioned again in Letter 103.
3. I——M——: John Meheux. Sancho is referring to their conversation. Once again the printer has mistaken Sancho's handwritten 'J' for an 'I', see Letter 92, n. 1 above.
4. 'Castle of peace and innocence': Sancho's home at 20 Charles Street.
5. P—— house: Meheux's home, the full name of which I cannot identify.

99

TO MRS. C'[OCKSEDGE]'.

Charles Street, Aug. 25, 1779.

MA CHERE AMIE,

In the visions of the night – behold I fancied that Mrs. Sancho was in Suffolk – that she saw strange places – fine sights – and good people – that she was at *Barton* amongst those I love and honor

– that she was charmed and enraptured with some certain good
folks who shall be nameless – that she was treated, caressed, and
well pleased – that she came home full of feasts – kindness – and
camps – and in the conclusion dunned me[1] for a whole month to
return some certain people thanks – for what? – Why, for doing as
they ever do – contrive to make time and place agreeable – truly
agreeable to those who are so lucky as to fall in their way: – in truth,
so much has been said, and description has run so high – that now
I am awake – I long for just such a week's pleasure – But time and
chance are against me. – I awake to fears of invasion, to noise,
faction, drums, soldiers, and care: – the whole town has now but
two employments – the learning of French – and the exercise of
arms[2] – which is highly political – in my poor opinion – for, should
the military fail of success – which is not impossible – why, the
ladies must take the field, and scold them to their ships again. – The
wits here say our fleet is outlawed – others have advertised it – The
republicans teem with abuse, and the *King*'s friends are observed
to have long faces – every body looks wiser than common – the
cheating shop-counter is deserted, for the gossiping door-threshold
– and every half hour has its fresh swarm of lies. – What's to become
of us? We are ruined and sold, is the exclamation of every mouth –
the moneyed man trembles for the funds – the land-holder for his
acres – the married men for their families, old maids – alas! and old
fusty batchelors, for themselves – For my part, I can be no poorer
– I have no quarrel to the Romish religion[3] – and so that you come
to town in health and spirits, and occupy the old spot – so that
the camp at Cavendish breaks not up to the prejudice of Johnny
Osborne, and my worthy *Rush* is continued clerk at Newmarket: in
short, let those I love be uninjured in their fortunes, and unhurt in
their persons – God's will be done! I rest perfectly satisfied, and
very sincerely and cordially,

Dear Madam, Yours,
and my sweet little Miss *Crewe*'s,
most obedient
and obliged servant,
I. SANCHO.

I should have said a deal about thanks and your kindness – but
I am not at all clear it would please you. – Mrs. Sancho certainly
joins me in every good wish – The girls are well – and William

thrives – Our best respects attend Mr. *Browne* and his good Lady – Mr. and Mrs. *Spink*. Adieu!

Pray make Mr. William Sancho's and my compliments acceptable to Nutts. – We hope he is well, and enjoys this fine weather unplagued by flies, and unbitten by fleas.

1. Dunned me: pestered me.
2. 'The exercise of arms': now that the French had joined forces with the Americans, there had been a burst of military activity, the King visiting several of the camps set up for exercises. The one attended by Osborne was situated at Cavenham, just to the south of Mildenhall, the home of the Bunburys. It provides the principal 'employment' of the town, which reinforces the view that Osborne's 'glory' of Letter 70 was, in fact, not military, but a profitable business opportunity. Sancho implies this when he hopes that 'the camp at Cavenham breaks not up to the prejudice of Johnny Osborne'.
3. The Romish religion: the dominant religion of France. Sancho's tolerance towards Roman Catholicism will be seen later in the letters on the Gordon Riots, see Letters 134 and 135.

100

TO MR. S'[TEVENSON]'.

August 31, 1779.

You have made ample amends for your stoical silence – insomuch that, like Balaam – I am constrained to bless – where peradventure I intended the reverse. – For hadst thou taken the wings of the morning – and searched North, East, South, and West – or dived down into the sea, exploring the treasures of old Ocean – thou couldst neither in art or nature have found aught that could have made me happier – gift-wise – than the sweet and highly finished portrait of my dear Sterne![1] – But how you found it – caught it – or came by it – heaven and you know best. – I do fear it is not thy own manufacturing. – Perhaps thou hast gratified thy finer feelings at an expence which friendship would blush for. – 'But what have you to do with that?' True – it may appear impertinent; but could aught add to the value of the affair, it would be its having you for its father. – But I must hasten to a conclusion. – I meant this – not as an epistle

of cold thanks – but the warm ebullitions of African sensibility. –
Your gift would add to the pride of Cæsar – were he living, and
knew the merits of its original – It has half turned the head of
a Sancho – as this scrawl will certify. Adieu! The hen and chicks
desire to be remembered to you – as I do – to all! – all! – all!

I. S.

1. It was in all probability with gratitude for this gift of Sterne's
   portrait in mind, that Elizabeth Sancho presented her father's
   portrait by Gainsborough to Stevenson in 1820, see Appendix II. Sancho also owned a cast of a bust of Sterne by the
   sculptor Nollekins. See the Introduction, esp. n. 12.

101

TO MR. I'[RELAND]'.

Sept. 2, 1779.

In truth, I know myself to be a very troublesome fellow – But as it
is the general fate of good-nature to suffer through the folly they
countenance, I shall not either pity or apologize. – I have to beg you
just to examine my friend Laggarit's petition.[1] – Mr. P—— does not
seem to approve of it – but is for expunging almost the best half.
– My friend has tried to get the great *Edmund* Burke's opinion – but
has met with a negative – he being too busy to regard the distresses
of the lowly and unrecommended. – For my part, I have as much
faith in Mr. *Ireland*'s judgement as in ——, and a much higher
opinion of his good-will; – and as Mr. P—— may be partly hurried
away by leaning rather too much to republican modes – I dare say, if
he finds that your opinion coincides with the sense of the petition as
it now stands, he will not be offended as its being presented without
his mutilations. – Mr. Laggarit is fearful of offending any way – and
has every proper sense of Mr. P——'s zeal, and good-will. – I dare
say it will strike you as it does me – that in the petitionary style
every term of respect is necessary; and although some of the titles
are rather profane, and others farcical – yet custom authorizes the
use, and it is a folly to withstand it.

Yours to command,
I. SANCHO.

I hope Mrs. *Ireland* is as well as you would wish her.

1. Laggarit's petition: I have been unable to trace this reference.

102

TO MR. S'[TEVENSON]'.
                              Charles Street, Sept. 2, 1779.

MY DEAR FRIEND,

You can hardly imagine how impatient I was to hear how they behaved to you at B——u.[1] I must confess you give a rare account of your travels. I am pleased much with all the affair, excepting the cellar business[2] – which I fear you repented rather longer than I could wish. – I had a letter from my honest L*incol*n,[3] who takes pride to himself in the honor you did him, and says Mr. S—— pleases himself in the hope of catching you on your return – when they flatter themselves the pictures will merit a second review: – but beware of the cellar! – I hope you are as well known at Scarborough as the Wells,[4] and find more employment than you want, and that you get into friendly chatty pieces for the evenings. – If I might obtrude my silly advice – it should be to dissipate a little with the girls – but for God's sake beware of sentimental ladies! and likewise be on thy guard against the gambling Dames, who have their nightly petites parties at quadrille – and with their shining faces and smooth tongues, drain unwary young men's pockets, and feminize their manners. – But why do I preach to thee, who art abler to instruct gray-hairs – than I am to dust my shop? – Vanity! which has gulled mighty states-men, misled poor me, and for the sake of appearing wiser than I am – I pray you – 'set me down an ass!' I enclosed a petulant billet to your Reverend Sire[5] – which I hope he did not send you. – There is no news worth talking about in town, excepting that it rains frequently, and people of observation perceive that the days are shorter. – Mrs. Sancho and children all well – and I dare swear – wish you so – in which they are heartily seconded by

                                        Yours sincerely,
                                        IGNATIUS SANCHO.

How shall I know whether you get this scrawl, except you send me word?

1. B——u: It would make sense if this were a misprint B——y, for 'Bury'.
2. Sancho gives scarcely any clue as to what 'the cellar business'

refers to, but he enjoyed wine, as is testified by his gout. The phrases 'which I fear you repented' and 'beware of the cellar' suggest that it has something to do with a bout of excessive drinking, but the meaning remains obscure.

3. L——n: Charles Lincoln, the West Indian musician. Letter 90 was addressed to him 'in the English Channel'. He must have returned from India, where he was bound in 1778 (Letter 1, wrongly dated), spent some time in England, and been laid up (Letter 90) at one of the Channel ports, bad weather having delayed his 'long protracted voyage' home to St Kitts. It appears from Letter 102 that the delay had given him time to write to Sancho telling him of his 'pride … in the honour' Stevenson has done him, perhaps by painting his portrait. By the time Sancho received his letter, Lincoln was probably at sea again, to reach St Kitts, according to Letter 153, 'after a long tedious voyage'.

4. 'As well known at Scarborough as the Wells': Stevenson's northern connections have been mentioned in other letters; his parents live in Retford, Nottinghamshire, and he has associations with Hull (Letter 18), so Sancho sees Stevenson as a painter known beyond his home in East Anglia, both in the north (for example, Scarborough) and the fashionable Wells or health resorts in the south familiar to the Sancho circle (for example, Bath, Wells, Tunbridge, Cheltenham, Llandrindod).

5. The Rev Mr Stevenson of Letter 116; see Appendix VI for further details.

103

TO MR. M'[EHEUX]'.

Sept. 4, 1779.

The *Lamb** just now kindly delivered to the *Bear*† the *Monkey's*‡ letter. – I am glad at heart that the forced exercise did thy hip no hurt – But that N*ancy* of thine – I do not like such faces – if she is half what she looks, she is too good for any place but heaven – where the hallelujahs are for ever chanting by such cherub-faced sluts as she – Thank God! she is neither daughter nor sister of mine – I should live in perpetual fear.¹ – But why do I plague myself

*   Mr. Me*heux*'s Sister.
†   Meaning himself.
‡   Mr. Me*heux*, to whom he often gave that title. [Miss Crewe's notes.]

about her? She has a protector in you – and foul befall the being (for no man would attempt it) that wishes to injure her! – Mrs. D—— I could like so well, that I wish to know but very little of her. Strange, but true – and when you have been disappointed in your schemes of domestic happiness, and deceived in your too hasty-formed judgements, to the age of fifty, as oft as your friend, you will fully enter into my meaning.

She looks open, honest, intelligently sensible – good-natured, easy, polite, and kind – knowledge enough of the world to render her company desirable – and age just sufficient to form her opinions, and fix her principles: – add to all this an agreeable face, good teeth, and a certain *je ne sai quoi* – (forgive the spelling, and do not betray me) – But I say again and again – when one has formed a great opinion of either male or female – 'tis best, for that opinion's sake, to look no further – There, rogue!

I shall take no notice of the tricking fraudulent behaviour of the driver of the stage – *as how* he wanted to palm a bad shilling upon us – and *as how* they stopped us in the town, and most generously insulted us – and *as how* they took up a fat old man – his wife *fat* too – and child – and after keeping us half an hour in sweet converse of the – of the *blasting* kind – how that the fat woman waxed wroth with her plump master, for his being serene – and how that he caught choler at her friction, tongue-wise – how he ventured his head out of the coach-door, and swore liberally – whilst his ——, in direct line with poor *Steven*son's nose, entertained him with *sound* and sweetest of exhalations. – I shall say nothing of being two hours almost on our journey – neither do I remark that *Steven*son turned sick before we left Greenwich, nor that the child *pissed* upon his legs: – in short, it was near nine before we got into Charles Street.

Sir, the pleasures of the day made us more than amends for the nonsense that followed. – Receipt in full.

I. SANCHO.

My best respects to Mr. Y——; and my love, yea, cordial love to Nancy – Tell her – No – if I live to see her again, I will tell her myself.

Observe, we were seven in the coach – The breath of the old lady, in her heat of passion, was not rose-scented: – add to that, the warmth naturally arising from crowd – and anger – you will not wonder at *Steven*son's being sick. – And he *Steven*son wanted to be in town rather sooner. – My compliments to George. – Mr. L—— is so kind to promise to call for this scrawl – Thank him for me, as well as for thyself. – Adieu. – Mrs. *Sancho* is pretty well, the two Fannys and Kitty[2] but indifferent.

1. 'Thank God! she is neither daughter nor sister of mine': Letter 103 is perplexing; like a number of the letters, it reflects Sancho's ambiguous attitude towards women: 'When you have been disappointed in your schemes of domestic happiness and deceived in your too hasty formed judgements, to the age of fifty, as oft as your friend, [Sancho] you will fully enter into my meaning.' Is Sancho, like Sterne in *The Sentimental Journey*, 'playing the rake' according to the fashion of the age? (See Letter 104, n. 1.) Would it be to take it all too solemnly to ask what disappointments and cross-currents of desire the pious and domesticated soul of Sancho might have concealed? Sancho characteristically presents himself as a faithful husband and father, which no doubt he was, but passages in the letters reveal a man with an eye for the girls, and a nervous sense of his own vulnerability to women. In Letter 102, he has advised Stevenson to 'dissipate a little with the girls – but for God's sake beware of sentimental ladies'.

   Sancho is insistent that women need protection, but he also finds them dangerous. His ambivalence is brought out by, for example, 'that Nancy of thine – I do not like such faces – if she is half what she looks, she is too good for any place but heaven', though Heaven appears to be populated by 'such cherub-faced sluts as she'. Miss Crewe is pretty but harmless: 'sweet little Miss Crewe' (Letter 99) or the 'little wren', 'the amiable little Crewe' (Letter 72), while Mrs Cocksedge is spoken of in terms closer to those of a would-be lover. For example, Sancho's adoration of Mrs Cocksedge in Letter 147, 'But how does my good, my half-adored Mrs. Cocksedge,' and even more so in Letter 72, 'She who is lovely in sickness, with the additional roseate bloom of health and flow of spirits, will be almost too much for mere mortals to bear – Tell her from me to get sick before she comes up, in pity to the beaux.' This passage is followed by the lame comment, 'Mrs. Sancho is better', a reference to Ann Sancho's health. When Mrs Cocksedge makes a gift to Sancho of her portrait by Gardner, Sancho writes 'my pen is not able to express what I feel' and the portrait is granted a place of honour above the domestic fireplace, 'My chimney piece now – fairly imitates the times – a flashy fine outside,' while Sancho declares his truest attachment to be to his wife 'the only intrinsic nett worth in my possession, is Mrs.

Sancho – who I can compare to nothing so properly as to
a diamond in the dirt ... had I power I would case her in
gold' (Letter 22). Sancho then returns to the subject of the
painting, 'The next generation will swear the painter was
a flatterer – and scarce credit there was a countenance so
amiably sweet ... Mrs Sancho desires that her thanks may be
joined with mine – as the thanks of one flesh' (Letter 23).
What Ann Sancho made of her husband's adoration of Mrs
Cocksedge we do not know because she is silent in Sancho's
letters, spoken on behalf of, and about, by her husband; the
reader might wonder how Sancho and his women would
have been represented by Ann Sancho had she written
letters. For a study of relationships between black and white
women in the late eighteenth and early nineteenth centuries,
see Clare Midgley, *Women Against Slavery: the British
Campaigns 1780–1870* (Routledge, London and New York,
1992).

2. Kitty: Sancho may have mistakenly inserted the name of his
young daughter who died six months earlier (Kitty's death is
recorded in Letter 87); see Letter 108, n. 2 and Letter 125,
n. 4. Other references to Kitty after her death suggest Miss
Crewe wrongly dated some letters, see Appendix I.

104

TO MRS. W'[INGRAV]'E.
Charles Street, Sept. 5, 1779.

DEAR MADAM,
Your wonder will be equal to your indignation – when (after due
apologies for the liberty of this address – and a few good-natured
protestations of friendship and so forth – with an injunction to strict
secrecy) I inform you that it is absolutely necessary for your
immediate setting out for Red-lion Court. – Your good man is only
running after all the young gipsies about the neighbourhood – All
colours – black or fair[1] – are alike – This is the effect of country air
– and your nursing. – The good man made his appearance on
Thursday evening last – the glow of health in his face – joy in his
eyes. – 'Wife, Joe, and little Frank all well, and myself never better in
my life!' – A pretty girl he led by the hand – and as if one petticoat
plague was not enough, he insisted upon taking away two of mine
– and carried his point against every reasonable odds. – Away they
all went to the play – and God only knows where else – I threatened

him with a modest report to Melchbourn,[2] but he seemed to care very lightly about it. – So I humbly advise, as your best method of taming him, either to insist upon his speedily coming down to you – or else your immediate setting out for home. – At present he only attempts our daughters – but should you be absent a month longer, I tremble for our wives. – For my part, I have some reason, for here both wife and daughters are as fond of Mr. *Wingrave* as they dare own. – Seriously, I think, you should coax him down, if only for a fortnight; – for it is amazing how much better he is for the short time he was absent – and this I take to be the pleasantest and wholesomest time for the country – if the evening dews are carefully guarded against – I shall advise him strongly to take the other trip – and I trust your documents with the innocent simplicity of all around him – fine air – exercise – new milk – and the smell of new hay – will make him ten thousand times worse than he is – You won't like him the worse for that. My love attends cousins I—— and F——.

I am, dear Madam,
Most sincerely yours to command,
IGNATIUS SANCHO.

Mrs. Sancho joins me in every thing but the abuse of Mr. *Wingrave*.

1. Black or fair: probably means 'dark or fair', since black was often used of brown- or black-haired women, without reference to race.
2. Melchbourn: probably Melchbourne, due west from Cambridge into Bedfordshire. Wingrave was a bookseller in London (see Appendix VI); the shop, it appears from this letter, was in Red-lion Court. He has been recovering his health in the country with his wife and younger sons, and Sancho is telling tales to Mrs Wingrave of her husband's fondness for the 'gipsy' girls of the neighbourhood now he is back in London. Sancho does not exempt himself from this extramarital spree, 'as if one petticoat plague was not enough ... he insisted upon taking away two of mine'. These revelations do not appear to be intended all that seriously, as the final comment of Mrs Sancho indicates. Perhaps they represent a way of 'playing the rake' typical of Sterne: see the article 'Pope plays the rake', in *The Art of Alexander Pope*, (eds) Howard Erskine-Hill and Anne Smith (Vision Press, London, 1979).

105

TO MR. R'[USH]'.

Sept. 7, 1779.

DEAR FRIEND,

We are all in the wrong – a *little*.[1] – Admiral Barrington[2] is arrived from the West-India station – and brings the pleasant news, D'Estaing fell in with five of our ships of the line – with the best part of his fleet. We fought like Englishmen, unsupported by the rest: – they fought till they were quite dismasted and almost wrecked – and at last gave the French enough of it – and got away all, though in plight bad enough: – but the consequence was, the immediate capture of the Grenadas. – Add to this – Sir Charles Hardy[3] is put into Portsmouth, or Gosport; – and although forty-odd strong in line-of-battle ships, is obliged to give up the sovereignty of the channel to the enemy. Lord S*andwich*[4] is gone to Portsmouth, to be a witness of England's disgrace – and his own shame. – In faith, my friend, the present time is rather *comique*. – Ireland[5] almost in as true a state of rebellion as America. – Admirals quarrelling in the West-Indies – and at home Admirals that do not choose to fight.[6] – The British empire mouldering away in the West – annihilated in the North – Gibraltar going[7] – and England fast asleep. – What says Mr. B——[8] to all this? – He is a ministerialist. – For my part, it's nothing to me – as I am only a lodger – and hardly that. – Give my love and respect to the ladies – and best compliments to all the gentlemen – with respects to Mr. and Mrs. I*reland*.

Give me a line to know how you all do – The post is going – only time to say God bless you. – I remain

Your affectionate

I. SANCHO.

Past eleven at night.

1. 'We are all in the wrong – a *little*': this letter is discussed in more detail in the Introduction p. 9.
2. Admiral Barrington: Samuel Barrington (1729–1800) was sent out in May 1778 as commander-in-chief of the West Indies, involved in skirmishes with the French commander D'Estaing late in 1778 and 1779. In January 1779, Barrington was superseded by Vice-Admiral Byron, though Barrington

remained as second-in-command of the fleet, and was active against D'Estaing at Granada. D'Estaing took St Vincent in June and Grenada 4 July, and defeated Admiral Byron off Grenada on 6 July 1779. Sancho looked back to a summer when command of the sea in the Leeward Islands had passed, temporarily, to the French. Returning to Britain in September, Barrington was 'radiating gloom about the state of the fleet and broadcasting his view that every island which the enemy attacked would fall'. See Piers Mackesy, *The War for America 1775–1783* (London, Longmans, Green and Co., 1964), p. 306.

3. Sir Charles Hardy: Sir Charles Hardy (1716?–80) was appointed by Lord Sandwich (see below, n. 4) commander-in-chief of the Channel Fleet following Keppel's resignation (for Keppel, see Letter 66, n. 2). By July 1779 an invasion of the south coast of England by combined French and Spanish forces looked imminent. Thirty thousand troops were concentrated at Harve and St Malo to seize the Portsmouth area and the Bourbon fleets were in the Channel to protect their crossing, but the British Channel fleet was far to the westward and ignorant of the enemy's presence. Hardy had under his command no more than forty-five ships, as Sancho remarks, 'forty-odd strong line-of-battle ships', though British ships had the advantage of increased efficiency. The British were unaware of the formidable enemy presence in the channel until 15 August when the combined fleet was sighted. Four days before Sancho wrote this letter, Hardy had retreated to the narrower waters of the channel where the larger and less-well-equipped combined fleet would be at a disadvantage. The enemy did not follow, but the situation seemed grim, and invasion panic seized towns such as Plymouth. By mid-September the feared invasion was no longer a threat; the combined fleet had retreated to return to Brest as winter approached, disadvantaged by the difficulties of the French and Spanish admirals working together, and the poor condition of the combined fleet and crew.

4. Lord Sandwich: First Lord of the Admiralty from 12 January 1771 to March 1782. By the end of August Hardy's ships desperately needed supplies, particularly water, so the fleet came up to Spithead. On the request of the King, Sandwich arrived in Portsmouth on 5 September to see the condition of the Channel fleet and speed its provisioning. Much of the activity at Portsmouth was misdirected since the combined fleet was ordered home on the day Hardy anchored at Spithead, effectively ending the threat of invasion (see above, n. 3). Sancho's view of Hardy 'obliged to give up the sovereignty of the channel to the enemy' and of 'England's disgrace' reflects the negative public opinion of

activities in the Channel which politicians feared: 'Hardy's
retreat up the Channel, though fully justified, had created
the image of a British fleet flying before the enemy; and the
withdrawal to Spithead did nothing to improve appearances,'
Mackesy, *The War for America*, p. 297.

5. 'Ireland ... America': Irish trade with America had been
badly effected by the embargo of February 1776 which
forbade the exportation of almost all provisions to all
countries other than Great Britain and the loyal colonies.
The embargo was at the root of Irish protests which
'inevitably invited comparisons with revolutionary America
... The "armed associations" of Irish patriotism, the Volun-
teers, grew to an estimated 40,000 by the end of 1779, while
within the blossoming non-importation movement, both
inside and outside the Irish Parliament, the slogans of
revolutionary America found a rhetorical home in Volunteer
resolutions and reviews.' Maurice J. Bric, 'The American
Revolution and Ireland', in *The Blackwell Encyclopedia of
the American Revolution* (eds.) Jack P. Greene and J. R.
Poole (Basil Blackwell, London, 1991) p. 506; see Letter 111,
n. 1.

6. 'Admirals that do not choose to fight': probably a reference
to the inconclusive action for which Viscount Keppel was
court-martialled in 1779. See Letter 66, n. 2.

7. 'Gibraltar going': Gibraltar was besieged June 1779, exacer-
bating Sancho's uneasy sense of Britain's apparent decline.
See Letter 142, n. 1 for the relief of Gibraltar.

8. Mr. B——: probably Sancho's friend Browne (steward to Sir
Charles Bunbury, and so Rush's colleague at Barton House).
See Appendix VI.

106

TO MISS L——.

Charles Street, Sept. 18, 1779.

I cannot forbear returning my dear Miss L—— our united thanks
for her generous present – which came exactly in time to grace poor
Marianne's[1] birth-day, which was yesterday. – The bird was good,
and well dressed: – that and a large applepye feasted the whole
family of the Sanchos. Miss L—— was toasted; and although we
had neither ringing of bells, nor firing of guns, yet the day was
celebrated with mirth and decency – and a degree of sincere joy and
urbanity seldom to be seen on *Royal* birth-days. Mary, as queen of
the day, invited two or three young friends – Her breast filled with

delight unmixed with cares – her heart danced in her eyes – and she looked the happy mortal. – Great God of mercy and love! why, why, in a few fleeting years are all the gay day dreams of youthful innocence to vanish? Why can we not purchase prudence, decency, and wisdom, but at the expense of our peace? Slow circumspect caution implies suspicion – and where suspicion dwells confidence dwells not. – I believe I write nonsense – but the dull weather, added to a dull imagination, must, and I trust will, incline you to excuse me. – If I mistake not, writing requires – what I could tell you, but dare not – for I have smarted once already. – In short, I write just what I think – and you know Congreve says somewhere, that

'Thought precedes the will,'
and
'Error lives ere Reason can be born.'[2]

Now Will – Reason – and Gratitude, all three powerfully impel me to thank you – not for your goose – nor for any pecuniary self-gratifying marks of generosity – but for the benevolent urbanity of your nature – which counsels your good heart to think of the lowly and less fortunate. – But what are my thanks, what the echoed praises of the world, to the heart-approving sensations of true charity! – which is but the prelude to the divine address at the last day – 'Well done, thou good,' &c. &c. – That you and all I love – and even poor me – may hear those joyful words, is the prayer of

Yours, &c. &c.
I. SANCHO.

1. Poor Marianne: Sancho's daughter, also called Mary, whose birthday it is said to be. The birth on 2 August 1763 of Ann Alice Sancho, the daughter who must have been known as Marianne or Mary, is recorded at St Margaret's, Westminster, though I cannot account for the discrepancy in birth dates. The word 'poor' marks Sancho's melancholy at fleeting youth, and his sense of the vulnerability of his daughters to mortality (Kitty) and recurrent ill-health (Lydia); see Letter 127, n. 4 where the death of 'Poor M——' is mentioned, possibly another reference to Sancho's daughter.
2. Quotation: Congreve, *The Mourning Bride*, Act 3, Sc. 1, ll. 33–5.

107

TO MR. I'[RELAND]'.

October 3, 1779.

DEAR SIR,

You will make me happy by procuring me an order from Mr. Henderson[1] for three any night this week[2] – 'Tis to oblige a worthy man who has more wants than cash – Believe me, there is more of vanity than good-nature in my request – for I have boasted of the honor of being countenanced by Mr. I*reland*, and shall ostentatiously produce your favor – as a proof of your kindness – and my presumption. – Thanks over and over for Sir H—— Freeman's Letters,[3] which I will send home in a day or two. – I return the Sermons, which I like so well, that I have placed a new set of them by Yorick's,[4] and think they will not disagree. – I pray you to send by the bearer the bit of honored Mortimer[5] you promised for friend M——, who, though he called some few mornings since on purpose – yet was so plagued with the *mauvaise hondt*[6] (I believe I spell it Yorkshirely, but you know what I mean), that the youth could not for his soul say what he was looking after – If you accompany it with the sea-piece you kindly offered me, I shall have employment in cleansing and restoring beauties which have escaped your observation – and I shall consider myself

Your much more obliged

I. SANCHO.

1. That Mr Ireland was a seller of books, prints and paintings is confirmed in this letter. He also appears to have had access to theatre tickets. Mr Henderson is the leading actor after Garrick, see Letter 48, n. 2.
2. The order for three theatre tickets is for a performance by Henderson of the role of Richard III, according to Letter 109.
3. Freeman's Letters: I cannot trace Sir H—— Freeman or his letters.
4. Yorick's sermons: Sterne's sermons.
5. 'The bit of honored Mortimers': the print of *St Paul Converting the Britons*. See Letter 96, no. 1.
6. 'Mauvaise hondt': bashfulness, spelt 'honte'.

108

TO MR. M'[EHEUX]'.
                                    October 5, 1779.

You mistake – I am neither sick – idle – nor forgetful – nor hurried – nor flurried – nor lame – nor am I of fickle mutable disposition. – No! I feel the life-sweetening affections – the swell of heart-animating ardor – the zeal of honest friendship – and what's more – I feel it for thee. – Now, Sir, what have you to say in humble vindication of your hasty conclusions? What, because I did not write to you on Monday last – but let a week pass without saying (what in truth I know not how to say, though I am now seriously set about it) – In short, such hearts and minds (if there be many such, so much the better), such beings, I say, as the one I am now scribbing to – should make elections of wide different beings than Blacka-moors for their friends. – The reason is obvious – from Othello to Sancho the big – we are either foolish – or mulish – all – all without a single exception. – Tell me, I pray you – and tell me truly – were there any Blackamoors in the Ark?[1] – Pooh! – Why there now I see you puzzled – Well – Well – be that as the learned shall hereafter decide. – I will defend and maintain my opinion – simply – I will do more – wager a crown upon it – nay, double that – and if my simple testimony faileth – Mrs. Sancho and the children five-deep[2] will back me – that Noah, during the pilgrimage in the blessed Ark, never with wife and six children set down to a feast upon a bit of finer – goodlier – fatter – sweeter – salter – well-fed pork;[3] we eat like hogs.

When do your Nobles intend coming home? – the evenings get long, and the damps of the park after sun-set – But a word to the wise.

Oh! I had like to have almost forgot – I owe you a dressing for your last letter. There were some saucy strokes of pride in it – ebullitions of a high heart – and tenderly over-nice feelings – Go to – what have I found you? My mind is not rightly at ease – or you should have it – And so you would not give me a line all the week – because – But what? I am to blame – A man in liquor – a man deprived of reason – and a man in love – should ever meet with pity and indulgence: – in the last class art thou! – Nay, never blush – plain as the nose in thy face are the marks – refute it if you are able – dispute if you dare – for I have proofs – yea, proofs as

undeniable as is the sincerity of the affection and zeal with which
thou art ever regarded by thy

IGNATIUS SANCHO.

How do the ladies – and Mr. M——? Mind, I care not about
——[4] so tell her, and lye. – You may tell George the same story –
but I should like to hear something about you all.

1. Sancho is cheerfully mocking the stereotyping of black
    people. The reference to the Ark is to the old belief, about
    which there was much pseudo-learned debate, that the
    African race was made black as a punishment laid upon the
    ancestral Cham, son of Noah, for disobeying God's instruc-
    tion to refrain from sex while in the Ark, so that no child
    should be born to claim the earth after the flood: so God
    ordained 'that a sunne be born ... who not only it selfe but al
    his posteritie after him should be so blacke and lothsome,
    that it might remaine a spectacle of disobedience to al the
    worlde'. See George Best, *Discourse*, 1578, quoted in Ed-
    wards and Walvin, *Black Personalities*, p. 8.
2. 'Children five deep': since Kitty's death there have been five
    Sancho children, but in the same sentence, Sancho appears to
    have forgotten this and writes of six. See Letter 103, n. 2 and
    Letter 125, n. 4.
3. Sancho is making play with the idea of the patriarchal
    Hebrew Noah eating pork.
4. 'I care not about——': the blank space is probably another
    reference to Meheux's lady friend Nancy, see Letter 103.
    George is Meheux's brother.

109

TO MR. M'[EHEUX]'.

October 9, 1779.

My friend Mr. I*reland*, who, *like* a simple fellow with a palish phiz
– crazy head – and hair of a pretty colour – an awkward loon –
whom I do sometimes care about – who has more wit than money
– more good sense than wit – more urbanity than sense – and more
pride than some princes – a chap who talks well – writes better – and
means much better than he either speaks or indites. A careless son of
nature, who rides without thinking – tumbles down without hurt
– and gets up again without swearing – who can – in short, he is

such an eccentric phizpoop – such a vessel! – a new skin full of old
wine is the best type of him – know you such a one? No! I guessed
as much – Nay, nay – if you think for a twelvemonth and a day, you
will never be a jot the nearer – Give it up, man. – Come, I will solve
the mystery – His name is ——. I will tell you anon – But as I was
saying – for I hate prolixity – as I was saying above Mr. *Ireland* (in
imitation of the odd soul I have laboured to describe) wishing to do
me honor as well as pleasure – came in person twice, to insist
accompanying *he* and *she* and two more, to see Mr. Henderson take
possession of the throne of Richard[1] – into the boxes – (I believe
box is properer) – We went – the house as full, just as it could be,
and no fuller – as hot as it was possible to bear – or rather hotter.
– Now do you really and truly conceive what I mean? – Alas! there
are some stupid souls, formed of such phlegmatic, adverse materials,
that you might sooner strike conception into a flannel petticoat – or
out of one – (now keep your temper, I beg, sweet Sir) than convince
their simple craniums that six and seven make thirteen. – It was
a daring undertaking – and Henderson was really awed with the
idea of the great man, whose very robes he was to wear – and whose
throne he was to usurp. – But give him his due – he acquitted
himself well – tolerably well – He will play it much better next time
– and the next better still. Rome was not built in six weeks – and,
trust me, a Garrick will not be formed under seven years. – I supped
with his Majesty[2] and Mr. and Mrs. *Ireland*, where good-nature and
good-sense mixed itself with the most cheerful welcome.

And pray, how is your head by this time? – I will teach you to
wish for pleasure from Blackamoor dunderheads. – Why, Sir, it is
a broken sieve to a ragged pudding-bag – By the time you have
gone through this scrawl you will be as flat, dull, and tedious, as
a drunken merry-andrew – or a methodist preacher – or a tired poor
devil of a post-horse; – or, to sum up all in one word, as your most
– what you please,

I. SANCHO.

Is pesorpher Quidois.

Your true friend and so forth.

Zounds, Sir! send me a good handsome epistle – such as you were
wont to do in peaceful days before * * * had warped your faculties,
and made you lazy. – Why, you – but I will not put myself in
a passion. – Oh! my *Meheux*, I would thou wert in town – But 'tis

no matter – I am convinced in our next habitation there will be no care – love will possess our souls – and praise and harmony – and ever fresh rays of knowledge, wonder, and mutual communication will be our employ. Adieu.

The best of women – the girls – the boy – all well. I could really write as long a letter on a taylor's measure, as your last hurry-begotten note.

1. Mr. Henderson ... Richard: Henderson was performing *Richard III*, but Sancho has in mind the theatrical rivalry between 'the King' (Garrick) and the Pretender (Henderson).
2. His Majesty: Garrick, with whom Sancho and the Irelands had supper after the play.

110

TO MR. M'[EHEUX]'.

October 17, 1779.

No! You have not the least grain of genius – Alas! description is a science – a man should in some measure be born with the knack of it. – Poor blundering Meheux, I pity thee – Once more I tell thee, thou art a bungler in every thing[1] – ask the girls else. – You know nothing of figures – you write a wretched hand – thou hast a nonsensical style – almost as disagreeable as thy heart – Thy heart, though better than thy head – and which I wish from my soul (as it now is) was the worst heart in the three kingdoms – thy heart is a silly one – a poor cowardly heart – that would shrink at mere trifles – though there were no danger of fine or imprisonment. – For example – come, confess now – could you lie with the wife of your friend? could you debauch his sister? could you defraud a poor creditor? could you by gambling rejoice in the outwitting a novice of all his possessions? – No. – Why then thou art a silly fellow – incumbered with three abominable inmates; – to wit – Conscience – Honesty – and Good-nature – I hate thee (as the Jew says[2]) because thou art a Christian.

And what, in the name of common sense, impelled thee to torment my soul with thy creative pen drawing of sweet A–r–bn–s?[3] I enjoyed content at least in the vortex of smoke and vice – and lifted my thoughts no higher than the beauties of the park or

—— gardens. – What have I to do with rural deities? with parterres – fields – groves – terraces – views – buildings – grots – temples – slopes – bridges – and meandering streams – cawing rooks – billing turtles – happy swains – the harmony of the woodland shades – the blissful constancy of rustic lovers? – Sir, I say you do wrong to awaken ideas of this sort: – besides, as I hinted largely above, you have no talent – no language – no colouring – you do not groupe well – no relief – false light and shadow – and then your perspective is so false – no blending of tints – Thou art a sad fellow, and there is an end of it.

Stevenson, who loves fools (he writes to me) – but mum; Stevenson wishes to have the honor of a line from quondam friend Meheux. Now Meheux is an ill-natured fellow – But were it contrariwise, and Meheux would indulge him – I would enclose it in a frank – with something clever of my own to make it more agreeable. – Sirrah! refute if you dare – I will so expose thee – do it – 'tis I command you. – Stevenson only entreats – You have need of such a rough chap as Sancho to counterpoise the pleasures of your earthly paradise. – Pray take care of your Eve[4] – and now, my dear Meheux, after all my abuse, let me conclude

Yours affectionately,

I. SANCHO.

POSTSCRIPT.

The tree of knowledge has yielded you fruit in ample abundance: – may you boldly climb the tree of life, and gather the fruits of a happy immortality! – in which I would fain share, and have strong hope, through the merits of a blessed Redeemer, to find room sufficient for self – and all I love – which, to say what I glory in, comprehends the whole race of man – and why not? Namby-Pamby.[5] Meheux cannot write to Stevenson till I have your letter to enclose to him – If there is any delay, the fault is not mine.

1. The letter opens with a typical bout of comic insults, which resolve into compliments, then revert again to friendly abuse.
2. 'As the Jew says': Shylock in *The Merchant of Venice*, Act I, Sc. 3, l. 43, 'I hate him for he is a Christian.'
3. A——r——bn——s: I cannot identify this place-name.
4. 'Your Eve': probably Meheux's friend Nancy again.
5. 'Namby-Pamby': silly sentimentality.

111

October 20, 1779.

Zounds, Sir! would you believe? Ireland has the * * * to claim the advantages of a free unlimited trade – or they will join in the American dance! – what a pack of * * * are * * *! I think the wisest thing Administration can do (and I dare wager they will) is to stop the exportation of potatoes – and repeal the act for the encourage-ment of growing tobacco * * *. It is reported here (from excellent authority) that the people at large surrounded the Irish parliament,[1] and made the members – the courtiers – the formists and non-cons – cats – culls – and pimpwhiskins – all – all subscribe to their – Well, but what says your brother? – No better news, I much fear, from that quarter. – Oh, this poor ruined country! – ruined by its success – and the choicest blessings the Great Father of Heaven could shower down upon us – ruined by victories – arts – arms – and unbounded commerce – for pride accompanied those blessings – and like a canker-worm has eaten into the heart of our political body. – The Dutch have given up the Serapis and the Scarborough, and detained Paul Jones twenty-four hours after their sailing:[2] – how they will balance accounts with France, I know not; but I do believe the Mynheers[3] will get into a scrape.

Tell Mr. B—— the Pyefleets[4] fluctuate in price like the stocks, and were done this morning, at Billingsgate 'change, at 1*l.* 6*s.* 8*d. per* bushel; but I have sent them this evening properly directed – also a book of *Cognoscenti dilitanti divertimenti.*[5] – As for the ladies, I cannot say any thing in justice to their merits, or my own feelings: – therefore I am silent. – Write soon – a decent, plain, and intelligible letter – a letter that a body may read with pleasure and improvement – none of your circumroundabouts for

I. SANCHO.

1. 'Ireland ... Irish parliament': North introduced free trade concessions late in 1779, following events in Dublin when mobs 'protested against government policy and decorated the cannons outside the Irish Parliament with the legend "free trade or else"'. Irish opposition to the 1776 embargo (see Letter 105, n. 5) enlivened the patriot movement and, in Edmund Burke's words, changed 'a mere question of commerce into a question of state'. See Bric, 'The American

Revolution and Ireland', in *The Blackwell Encyclopedia* (eds) Greene and Poole, p. 506.

2. John Paul Jones (1747–92), originally John Paul from Kirkudbrightshire, Scotland, took the surname Jones when he fled to America to conceal his identity after twice being accused of murdering members of his ships' crew, having been cleared of only one of the charges. In his ship the *Bonhomme Richard*, Jones defeated the *Serapis* (under Captain Richard Pearson) and the *Countess Scarborough* off the east coast of England on 23 September 1779. Jones's ship the *Bonhomme Richard* sank, but not before Pearson had surrendered the *Serapis*.

3. Mynheers: Dutchmen.

4. Pyefleets … Billingsgate 'change: Sancho's word 'Pyefleets' cannot be traced, but 'Pyflet' or 'pikelet' can refer to a small young fish; this makes sense since Sancho locates the commodity whose price he quotes 'at Billingsgate [ex] change', a fish market, where fish would normally be sold by the barrel. Letter 94 describes how Sancho sends fresh fish to friends, 'A little fish … sets out this evening for Bury.'

5. A book of *Cognoscenti dilitanti divertimenti*: Sancho is sending a loose collection of light reading for general amusement, the title of which is intended to flatter the receiver, Mr Rush. The materials sent by Sancho may have included some of his own musical compositions. *Divertimenti* suggest an easy-going musical composition; perhaps it also included work by one or more of the young artists mentioned in other letters who sought Sancho's opinion and support.

112

TO MR. R'[USH]'.

Nov. 1, 1779.

DEAR FRIEND,
I should on Saturday night have acknowledged your kindness, but was prevented by weakness! – idleness! – or some such nonsense! – Were you here, Mrs. Sancho would tell you I had quacked myself to death. – It is true, I have been unwell – from colds and from a purging! – which disorder prevails much in our righteous metropolis – and perhaps from quacking: – but of this when we meet. I was much pleased with my letter from Sir John[1] – in which there is very little news – and less hope of doing any thing to the

purpose, either in the conquering or conciliating mode, than in any letter I have been favored with. – He makes no mention of receiving any packets from me, and I have wrote six or eight times within the last twelve months – so you see plainly the packets are either lost, or his letters stopt. – I shall give him a line by Wednesday's post – and let it try its fortune. – I enclose you some American congress notes – for he does not say he has sent you any – though he mentions the news-papers.

We talk of sending over a vast force next spring. Why Govern ment will so madly pursue a losing game is amongst the number of things that reason can never account for – and good sense blushes at. – It is reported in the city, that our safety this summer was purchased of D'Orvilliers and Monsieur Sartine.[2] – It is certain (although a vote of credit was granted for a million) that there is no money in the Exchequer – and that the civil list is 800,000l. in arrears. – This looks dark – whilst Ireland treats us rather loconic – Scotland not too friendly – America speaks but too plainly: – but what a plague is all this to you and me? I am doomed to difficulty and poverty for life – and let things go as they will, if the French leave us Newmarket, they will not ruin my friend. – I hope the good ladies are well, and preparing for London Squire S——[3] and his good woman well also – he in the enjoyment of his gun, and she in the care of the sweet children. – My best respects to Mr. and Mrs. B——, and I should be a beast to neglect my worthy friend Mr. S——. Now I have a scheme to propose to the electors of Great Britain, to take Sir C—— and Mr. S——[4] for their patterns – and at the general election (if they can find as many) to return 300 such – It would immortalize them in the annals of this country for their wisdom of choice – and what's much better, it would perhaps (with God's blessing) save Old England. – We want, alas! only a few honest men of sound principles and good plain understandings – to unite us – to animate with one mind! – one heart! – one aim! – and to direct – the roused courage of a brave people properly – then we might hope for golden times – and the latter end of the present reign emulate the grand close of the last.

I got a very pretty young lady to choose this inclosed ticket[5] – meaning to baffle ill-luck; for, had I chose it myself, I am certain a blank would have been the consequence. – May it be prosperous! – Mrs. Sancho joins me in every thing – Love to *Osborne.* The girls giggle their respects to Mr. R*ush*. Billy joins in silence, but his love to Nutts is plain. How does he do?

Yours,
IGN. SANCHO.

1. Sir John: this could be Johnny Rush or John Osborne.
2. D'Orvilliers and Monsieur Sartine: Admiral D'Orvilliers commanded French ships in the combined fleet; Gabriel de Sartine was the French minister of war.
3. Squire S——: probably John Spink, who was married and had children. See Letter 82.
4. Sir C—— and Mr S——: Sancho refers to Sir Charles Bunbury and possibly Mr Stevenson as model citizens; see Letter 147, n. 1 for Bunbury's 1780 election victory.
5. 'The inclosed ticket ... May it be prosperous!': probably a lottery ticket. During the eighteenth century the British government annually raised large sums of money in lotteries. The prizes were in the form of terminable or perpetual annuities. There was an interval of at least forty days between the sale and the drawing of tickets; during this time tickets changed hands and shopkeepers attracted custom by offering the chance of a fractional share in a ticket.

113

TO MR. S'[TEVENSON]'.

Nov. 14, 1779.

DEAR FRIEND,

Yours by my brother gave me money – and, what was more pleasing to me, a tolerable account of your success – the lateness of the season considered. – Come, brighten up: my brother P—— has left us much happier than he found us. – We have succeeded beyond our expectation – Humility is the test of Christianity – and parent of many, if not of all the virtues. – But we will talk this over when you return from grape-stuffed geese and fine girls[1] H—— seems to be in better favor with her goddessship lady Fortune – His affair will do – He will stand a fair chance of rising. – I wish from my soul something good in the same line was destined for you – But have courage – Time and patience conquer all things. – I hope you will come home soon, and leave a foundation for better fortune next year at B*arton*, and its friendly neighbourhood. Kitty is very

poorly[2] – God's will be done! – I have a horrid story to tell you
about the – Zounds! I am interrupted. – Adieu! God keep you!

Yours, &c. &c.
I. SANCHO.

Mrs. Sancho, and girls, and Billy, send their compliments, &c. and
pray all our respective loves and best wishes to the friendly circle at
B*arton*, and every where else.

1. Grape-stuffed geese and fine girls: see Appendix I and Letter
   77.
2. Kitty's death is recorded in Letter 87, 9 March 1789, so
   Letter 113 is probably wrongly dated by Miss Crewe and
   should be dated closer to Letter 77. See Appendix I.

114

TO MR. S'[TEVENSON]'.

Nov. 16, 1779.

You have missed the truth by a mile – aye and more – It was not
neglect – I am too proud for that – it was not forgetfulness, Sir, I am
not so ungrateful – it was not idleness, the excuse of fools – nor
hurry of business, the refuge of knaves – It is time to say what
it was. Why, Mrs. D—— in town from Tuesday till Monday
following – and then – and not till then – gave me your letter – and
most graciously did I receive it – considering that both my feet were
in flannels – and are so to this luckless minute. – Well, Sir, and what
have you to say to that? Friend H—— has paid for them. – I pay
him again – and shall draw upon you towards Christmas – Never
poorer since created – But 'tis a general case – Blessed times for
a poor Blacky grocer to hang or drown in! – Received from your
good reverend parent (why not honored father?) a letter, announcing the approach of a hamper of prog[1] – which I wish you was near
enough to partake. – Your good father feels a satisfaction in doing
– I think a wrong thing – His motive is right – and, like a true
servant of Christ, he follows the spirit – not the letter – He will be
justified in a better world – I am satisfied in this – and thou wilt in
thy feelings be gratified. – Huzza! – we are all right – but your

father pays the piper. How doth Squire G—— ?[2] odso – and his pretty daughter? – Kiss the father for me – and drink a bottle with the fair lady. – I mean as I have wrote – so tell them – and do what's best in thy own and their eyes. – When you see brother *Osborne*, my love to him and his household. – I have no spirits when the gout seizes me – pox on him! – Great news from Sir Charles Hardy[3] – Huzza for ever! – all mad – nothing but illuminations – out with your lights – bells ringing, bonfires blazing – crackers bouncing – and all for what? – what? – The girls open-mouthed – Billy stares – Mrs. Sancho rubs her hands – The night indeed is cold, but Billy must go to bed – The noisy rogues with the Gazette extra – stun our ears. Adieu!

Yours, &c. &c.
I. SANCHO.

I should have enclosed a paper, but it will cost the devil and all – My family all join in customary customs.

1. Prog: provision for a journey or excursion, or, in this case, simply food. In Letter 116, Sancho writes to thank Rev Stevenson for his 'bountiful treat'.
2. Squire G … his pretty daughter. Letters 126, 128 and 129 also refer to Mr G—— and/or his daughter; this is probably not the Mr G—— to whom the rather formal Letter 86 is addressed.
3. Great news: it was October before the British government knew that the combined fleet had returned to Brest for the winter and thus no longer posed a threat. See Letter 105, n. 3 and n. 4

115

TO '[JOHN]' S'[PINK]', ESQ.[1]
Charles Street, Nov. 21, 1779.

DEAR SIR,

We are happy to hear by brother *Osborne* that you and Mrs. *Spink* enjoy good health – May God preserve it, and increase your every comfort!

I am far from being sorry that you have not been in town this autumn – for London has been sickly – almost every body full of complaint – add also that the times are equally full of disease – Luxury! Folly! Disease! and Poverty! you may see daily riding in the same coach – the doors ornamented with the honors of a virtuous ancestry topped with coronets; surrounded with mantle ermined – and, alas! Corruption for the supporters.

Now, my good Sir, you can have no real pleasure but what must arise from your own heart were you amongst us – and that would be in pitying our weakness, and fighting over distresses your benevolence of heart could not alleviate. – And yet I fear, if you keep from town till times mend, I shall have no chance of seeing you this side eternity. You should come up for a day or two, were it only to be witness to the roguery of M*iniste*rs and lottery-office-keepers[2] – and the madness of the dupes of each. – I have much to thank you for – which I will not forget in a better world, if I see you not in this. – We have eat your turkey today – it is a joke to say it was good – bad things seldom, if ever, come from Mr. *Spink*. Mrs. Sancho joins me in thanks to Mrs. *Spink*. who we hope will not be always unknown. – The customary wishes of the approaching sacred season to you and all your connexions. – Pray excuse blunders, for I am forced to write post – as I expect O*sborne* every moment. As I write first, and think afterwards, my epistles are commonly in the Irish fashion. You, who prefer the heart to the head, will overlook the error of the man who is, and ever will be, very sincerely and gratefully,

Your much obliged
friend and servant,
IGN. SANCHO.

It is expected the whole M*inistry* will run from their posts before Friday next, Lord S*andwich*[3] and Lord N*ort*h excepted.[4] Now I have a respect for Lord N*ort*h; he is a good husband, father, friend, and master – a real *good man* – but I fear a bad *m*inister.

1. Once again the printer has mistaken Sancho's handwritten 'J' for an 'I'. See Letter 92, n. 1.
2. 'Lottery office keepers': see Letter 112, n. 5 and Letter 120, n. 1.
3. Lord Sandwich: see Letter 105, n. 4.
4. Lord North: Frederick North (1732–92) British statesman. North was a Lord of the Treasury (1759–65), Joint Paymaster-General (1766–7), Chancellor of the Exchequer

(1767–82) and the First Lord of the Treasury (Premier) (1770–82). Sancho's view of North as a decent man but a 'bad m[iniste]r' is an apt summary. North was a charming man of culture; he was a good manager of the House of Commons who defended his Ministry in Parliament against a fierce opposition. But North's political skills were those of peace, not war. North himself stated 'upon military matters I speak ignorantly, and therefore without effect'. In 1778 North proposed conciliatory offers to the American colonies which, if made in 1775, might have averted the war and American independence. He resigned in March 1782 when faced with an imminent vote of no confidence in the Commons. He succeeded his father as 2nd Earl of Guilford in 1790. For some details of the domestic political storms he faced, see Letter 133, n. 7.

116

TO THE REV. MR. S'[TEVENSON]'.

Dec. 5, 1779.

REV. AND HON. SIR,

I have just now received your too valuable favor[1] – Forgive me, good Sir, if I own I felt hurt at the idea of the trouble and cost you (from a spirit too generous) have been put to – and for what, my good Sir? Your son shewed me many kindnesses – and his merits are such as will spontaneously create him the esteem of those who have the pleasure of knowing him – It is honoring me to suppose I could be of service to him. – Accept then, good Sir, of my thanks, and Mrs. Sancho's – and be assured you have sevenfold overpaid any common kindness I could render your deserving son and my friend. – I wish he was here to partake of your bountiful treat – for well do I know his filial heart would exult, and his eyes beam with love and respect. – Mrs. Sancho joins me in respectful acknowledgments and thanks to Mrs. *Stevenson* and self.

We are, dear Sir,
Your most obliged servants,
IGN. and A. SANCHO.

1. 'Your too valuable favor': the Sancho family have received the 'hamper of prog' which Rev Stevenson announced would arrive, see Letter 114, n. 1.

117

Dec. 14, 1779.

SIR,

I expect an answer.

Yours,

I. S.

Our friend H———'s[1] head and heart are fully occupied with
schemes, plans, resolves, &c. &c. in which (to his immortal honor)
the weal and welfare of his *Stevenson* are constantly considered. The
proposal which accompanies this letter, from what little judgment
I have, I think promises fair. – You will, however, give it a fair
examination – and of course determine from the conviction of right
reason. – If as a friend I might presume to offer my weak opinion,
I freely say, I think in every light it seems eligible. – The circle of
your acquaintance is at present circumscribed – I mean in the artist
line. – Now, in case you connect yourself in a business which
requires constant daily perambulation – the chances are on your
side for forming acquaintance – perhaps friendships – with men of
genius and abilities, which may happily change the colour of your
fortunes – The old proverb is on your side – 'Two heads,' &c. – And
very fortunately in your case, where in fact one has *wit*, and the
other *judgment* – the *chair* of *interest* will have its complete
furniture in the two top ornaments – and *honesty* for its *basis.* So
much for Mons. H———, and now I have to reckon with you. How
could you be so preposterously wrong to trouble the repose of your
worthy father and mother about me? Surely you must think me
exceedingly interested – or your heart must be a very proud one. If
either – in the first instance you did me a wrong – in the last perhaps
I may wrong you – Be it as it may, I know it gave me real vexation.
– Your father sent such a basket,[2] as ten times rapid the trifling
service I had the honor as well as pleasure of rendering a man of
merit, and my friend: – believe me, I never accepted any present
with so ill a will. – With regard to them, every thankful acknowledgment was due – I wrote a very embarrassed letter of thanks, with
a resolution to give you a chastisement for laying me under the
necessity. – I hear with pleasure that you have enough to do. H———
declares he is sorry for it – as he wants and wishes you in town. Pray

give my best wishes to Mess. B—— and S——w, and my love to O——. If you should happen to know a Miss A——, a rich farmer's daughter, remember me to her – Were you not widow-witched, she or some other heavy-pursed lass might be easily attainable to a man of your – Aye, aye, but that, says ——, will not be, I fear. – For I verily believe that * * * * * for the * * * * and by the same token do you not * * * * * * *? But this is matter of mere speculation.[3] God bless you! Yours sincerely – cordially – and sometimes offensively – but always friendly,

IGN. SANCHO.

1. Our friend H——: see Appendix VI, Letter 74, n. 1 and Letter 77, n. 2.
2. A basket: the 'hamper of prog' mentioned in Letter 114 and acknowledged as received in letter 116.
3. Mere speculation: it is not clear precisely what Sancho means, though it would seem to have something to do with female companionship for Stevenson; see Letter 103, n. 1.

118

TO D—— B——E, ESQ.

Dec. 17, 1779.

GOOD SIR,

A stranger to your person (not to your virtues) addresses you – will you pardon the interested intrusion? I am told you delight in doing good. – Mr. Wingrave (who honors me with his friendships, by whose persuasion I presume to trouble you) declares – you are no respecter of country or colours – and encourages me further by saying, that I am so happy (by the good offices of his too partial friendship) to have the interest and good wishes of Mr. B——e.[1]

Could my wish be possibly effected to have the honor of a General-post-office[2] settled in my house, it would certainly be a great good – as (I am informed) it would emancipate me from the fear of serving the parish offices – for which I am utterly unqualified through infirmities – as well as complexion. – Figure to yourself, my dear Sir, a man of a convexity of belly exceeding Falstaff – and a black face into the bargain – waddling in the van of poor thieves and pennyless prostitutes – with all the supercilious mock dignity of little office – what a banquet for wicked jest and wanton wit – as

needs must, when, &c. &c. – Add to this, my good Sir, the chances
of being summoned out at midnight in the severity of easterly winds
and frosty weather – subject as I unfortunately am to gout six
months in twelve – the consequence of which must be death –
death! Now I had much rather live – and not die – live indebted to
the kindness of a few great and good – in which glorious class, you,
dear Sir, have the pre-eminence – in the idea of

Your most respectful
and obliged humble servant,
IGN. SANCHO.

1.   Mr. B——e: Stevenson's index does not identify this correspondent, see Appendix VI. Sancho says Mr B——e is
friend to Mr Wingrave, so perhaps he too was a bookseller;
see Letter 130 where Sancho suggests B——e might print
a friend's pamphlet.

2.   A general post office: as one who both wrote and received
many letters, and who was proprietor of a grocer's shop,
Sancho's request that 20 Charles Street act as a Post Office
seems a reasonable one. William Dockwra's London Penny
Post allowed letters and parcels to be carried, registered and
insured for a penny; Dockwra established sorting and
district houses, receiving-houses and hourly collections with
a maximum of ten daily deliveries in central London and
a minimum of six for the suburbs. In *Survey of London and
Westminster* (1735) we learn that there were 'above 600
Houses that receive for the Penny Post, there being one in
most great streets; at the door or window of which is
commonly hung up a printed Paper in a Frame with these
words in large letters, PENNY POST LETTERS AND
PARCELS ARE TAKEN IN HERE'. The service seems
little changed by the eighteenth century when Defoe, in *Tour
Through the Whole Island of Great Britain* (1727), observed
that letters could be sent 'with the utmost Safety and
Dispatch ... almost as soon as they can be sent by messenger,
and that Four, Five, Six to Eight times a day ... We see
nothing of this at Paris, at Amsterdam, at Hamburgh or
any other City, that ever I have seen or heard of.' Street
letter boxes were not introduced in London until the mid-
nineteenth century. Sancho suggests that acting as a receiving house would provide a community service, one more
appropriate to a man of his 'infirmities as well as complexion' than, for example, 'serving the parish offices' or
other duties which might require the gout-stricken Sancho
to be 'summoned out at mid-night'. Letter 123 records
Sancho's gracious acceptance of B——e's refusal.

119

DEAR SIR,

The Park guns are now firing, and never was a poor devil so puzzled as your humble Sancho is at this present moment. – I have a budget of fresh news – aye, and that of consequence – and a million of stale thanks, which perhaps you will think of no consequence. – Impelled by two contrary passions, how should a poor Negro know precisely which to obey? Your turkey and chine[1] are absolutely as good, as fine, and as welcome – as nobly given, and as gratefully accepted – as heart can wish, or fancy conceive – Then, on the other hand – the news is as glorious,[2] as well-timed and authenticated, as pleasing, as salutary in the ministerial way, as much wanted, and as welcome – as the turkey and chine – to a certain set I mean – of king's friends and national * * * * *. The said turkey and chine will keep fresh and good, and chear some honest hearts (I trust) on Christmas-day. – The news, good as it is, may half of it prove false by Christmas – and the true part will be stale news by that time – much of it will be liable to doubt and malicious disquisition. – Now, on the other hand, the turkey and its honest fat companion are bettering every day – and feast us by anticipation. – But again, the news will come with a handsome face – attested by a Gazette extraordinary, garnished by the happy flourishes of news-paper invention – Then there is the speech of the noble Sir C——; I meant to say much upon the score – You have read it without doubt – so have I more than once or twice – and I find the same fault with it that the majority and minority do – which is neither more nor less than what's exceeding natural to both parties – The majority detest it for its truth – the minority would have better liked it – had it not been so da*m*n'd *honest.* Now (between ourselves) I do confess to you, my worthy friend, strip this famed speech of its truth and honesty, there will very little worth notice remain – excepting candour, a spice of benevolence, and perhaps too much charity: – but as the above are the vices only of a very few, we may the better endure it in Sir C——. There is certainly an express arrived this day with very comfortable news – plenty of killed and wounded – plenty of prisoners – and (as it always happens) with little or no loss on our side. – But dear me – how I have run on! – I protest the sole business of this letter was to ease my mind, by unburthening my head and heart of some weighty thanks, which, for aught I know, except very decently managed, are more likely to give pain than pleasure to some odd-constructed minds, men who fatten upon doing good, and feel themselves richer in proportion to their kindness: such beings are the *Stevensons*, the *Bunburys*, the *Rushs*, *Osborns*, &c. &c. – whom God mend – in the next world I mean. – So wishing you every felicity in this, and every comfort attendant on the approaching festival, with love and good-will to all friends, especially to Mrs. *Browne*, the worthy Mr. *Spink's* family, Squire S——ns, and his mate, in which Mrs. Sancho claims her full share, I remain, dear Sir, (I fear I tire you)

Your most obliged
humble servant,
I. SANCHO.

1. Chine: a joint of meat – mutton, beef or pork – consisting of the whole or part of the backbone of an animal and the adjoining flesh.
2. 'The news is glorious ... the noble Sir C——': news of Britain's activities in the Channel, information about which could have been conveyed in a speech by Sir Charles Hardy (for Hardy, see Letter 105 n. 3). Sir Charles's death is recorded in Letter 125.

120

TO MR. B'[ROWNE]'.

Dec. 24, 1779.

Losers have the privilege to rail[1] – I was taking the benefit of the act, upon my seeing Johnny *Osborn*, when he abruptly (and not disagreeably) stopped my mouth with saying, he had just loaded a stout lad, in the name of Mr. B——, and dispatched him to Charles Street. – Now this same spirit of reparation may suit well with both the in- and out-side of Mr. B——; and those who know the man will not marvel at the deed. – For my own part, I have been long convinced of the blindness, and more than Egyptian stubbornness, of repiners of every sect – for how can we say but that seeming evils in the seed, with the cultivation of benevolence – mark that – may yield an abundant crop of real substantial good? – The confounded lurches, and four by honors, trimmed me of ten pieces.

– Ten pieces! quoth I, as I was preparing for bed – better been at home. – Ten pieces! quoth Prudence. You had no business to play. – So much good money flung away! cries Avarice. – Avarice is a lying old grub – I have pork worth twice the money – and the friendly wishes of a being who looks hospitality and good-will. – The blessings of the season attend you! – May you have the pleasure and exercise of finding out want, and relieving it! – and may you feel more pleasure than the benefited! – which I believe is mostly the case in souls of a kind, generous, enlarged structure. – My respects attend the gun and dog of Squire S——,[2] which being the things of most consequence, I name before Mrs. S—— or himself. – They and every one connected with *Barton* house have my best wishes – and you, my good Sir, the thanks of

Your most humble servant,
I. SANCHO.

1. 'Losers have the privilege to rail': Sancho has lost some money, possibly on the lottery. When Sancho purchased a lottery ticket for his friend Mr Rush, and sent it to him with the wish 'may it be prosperous!', he also may have purchased one for himself, and lost 'ten pieces' as a result. See Letter 112, n. 5. The lottery drawing extended at least as long as the period of time between letters 112 and 120. Sancho loved to gamble; in Letter 112 the superstitious gambler 'got a very pretty young lady to choose this inclosed ticket — meaning to baffle ill-luck'. As a young man in his early twenties, during his period of employment with the Montagu family, Sancho lost his clothes playing cribbage, but even this embarrassing loss does not appear to have been enough to cure Sancho of his passion for gambling. See Peter Fryer, *Staying Power: the History of Black People in Britain*, p. 94.
2. Squire S——: probably John Spink. See Letter 112, n. 3.

121

TO MRS. M'[EHEUX]'.

Christmas-Day, 1779.

May this blest season bring every pleasure with it to my kind and worthy Mrs. Me*heux*! and may the coming year bless the good and happy man of her heart with the possession of her person! and may every future one, for a long period of time, bring an increase to her joys and comforts! – So pray the Sanchos – and also join in thanks to Mrs. M*eheux* for her friendly present. – Will Mrs. M*eheux* be so kind to say all that's civil and thankful to Mrs. W*ingrave*, for her kindness in sending me a bottle of snuff? – and also make my respectful compliments to Mr. L——? God keep you all!

Yours I remain, much
obliged and thankful,
IGN. SANCHO.

122

TO MR. W'[INGRAVE]'.
Dec. 26, 1779.

It is needless, my dear Sir, to say how pleasingly the news of your great good fortune affected us.– For my part, I declare (self excepted) I do not know, in the whole circle of human beings, two people whom I would sooner wish to have got it; – neither, in my poor judgment, could it have fallen with a probability of being better used in any other hands. The blessings of decent competency you have been used to from early childhood – your minds have been well cultivated. Virtuous and prudent in your conduct, you have enjoyed the only true riches (a good name) long. – Your power of doing good will certainly be amply increased; but, as to real wealth, I will maintain it, you were as rich before. – You must now expect a decent share of envy – for, as every one thinks pretty handsomely of self, most of the unfortunate adventurers of your acquaintance will be apt to think how much pleasanter it would have been to have had twenty thousand pounds to themselves. – Avarice will groan over his full bags, and cry, 'Well, I never had any luck!' Vanity will exclaim, 'It is better to be born lucky than rich!' whilst Content, sheltered in her homely hovel, will cry, 'Blessings on their good hearts! Aye, I knew their good parents – they were eyes to the blind, and feet to the lame, and made the orphan's and the widow's hearts sing for joy. God will prosper the family.' – But while I am prating away, I neglect to thank you, which was the chief business of this letter – to thank you, and to admire that rectitude of temper which could in the full tide of worldly good fortune remember the obscure, the humble old friend – Accept my thanks, and the plaudit also of a heart too proud to court opulence, but alive to the feelings of truth, sacred friendship, and humanity. – Mine and Mrs. Sancho's thanks for your genteel present attend you, Mrs. W*ingrave*, and the worthy circle round! – May every year be productive of new happiness in the fullest sense of true wisdom – the riches of the heart and mind! – So wishes thy obliged sincere friend,

I. SANCHO.

123

TO D. B——E, ESQ.

Dec. 30, 1779.

HONORED SIR,

Permit me to thank you – which I do most sincerely – for the kindness and good-will you are pleased to honor me with. – Believe me, dear Sir, I was better pleased with the gracious and soothing manner of your refusal[1] – than I have been in former times with obligations less graciously conferred. – I should regret the trouble I have given you, but that my heart feels a comfort, and my pride a gratification, from the reflection, that I am cared for, and not unnoticed, by a gentleman of the first worth and highest character. I am, dear Sir, with profound respect and gratitude,

Your most obliged
and humble servant,
I. SANCHO.

1. Sancho's request for a 'General-post-office' is refused, see Letter 118, n. 2.

124

TO MR. I'[RELAND]'.

Dec. 1779.

DEAR SIR,

The bearer of this letter[1] gives himself a very good report – he is certainly the best judge – he can cook upon occasion – dress and shave – handle a salver with address – and clean it too: – he is but

little in make, and I hope not great in opinion. – Examine his morals
– if you can see through so opaque a composition as a Bengalian. –
Was he an African – but 'tis no matter, he can't help the place of his
nativity. I would have waited upon the worthy circle yesterday, but
the day was so unfriendly I had not the heart to quit the fire-side.
– I hope you and Mrs. *Ireland* have as much health and spirits as
you can manage – I have had a pretty smart engagement with the
gout, of which I can give a better account than Sir Charles Hardy[2]
can of the combined fleet. – I wish to place you, Sir, in the Censor's
chair – for the which purpose I most pressingly beg the favor of
your company to-morrow, Friday the 19th, in the afternoon – to
meet a young unfledged genius of the first water – who, as well as
myself, is fool enough to believe you possess as much true taste as
true worth. – Be that as God pleases – If you delight to do me
honor, comply with this request, and imagine Sterne would have
done as much for

                                                        I. SANCHO.

1. 'The bearer of this letter': see Letter 132, n. 2.
2. Sir Charles Hardy ... the combined fleet: see Letter 105,
    n. 3 and Letter 114, n. 3.

125

TO MR. R'[USH]'.
                                              Last Day, 1779.

DEAR FRIEND,
I wish I could tell you how much pleasure I felt in the reading your
cheerful letter – I felt that you was in good health, and in a flow of
cheerfulness, which, pray God, continue to you. – I shall fancy
myself amongst you about the time you will get this – I paint in my
imagination the winning smiles, and courteously kind welcome, in
the face of a certain lady, whom I cannot help caring for, with the
decent pleasingly demure countenance of the little C——,[1] Squire
Bunbury, with the jovial expression of countenance our old British
freeholders[2] were wont to wear – the head and heart of Addison's
Sir Roger de Coverley; *Simon* tipsy with good will, his eyes dancing
in his head, considering within his breast every species of welcome

to do honor to his noble master, and credit to the night; and, lastly, my friend looking more kindness than his tongue can utter and present to every individual, in offices of love and respect. – My R*ush*, what would I give to steal in unseen – and be a happy spectator of the good old English hospitality – kept up by so few – and which in former times gave such strength and consequence to the ancestry of the present frivolous race of Apostates! – Honored and blest be Sir *Charles*[3] and his memory, for being one of those golden characters that can find true happiness in giving pleasure to his tenants, neighbours, and domestics! – Wherever such a being moves, the eyes of love and gratitude follow after him – and infant tongues, joining the voice of youth and maturer years, fill up the grand chorus of his praise. – I inclose without apology a billet for ——: he well knows how prone I naturally am to love him. – But love is untractable, there is no forcing affections. – But I perhaps too quickly feel coldness. —— has a noble soul – and he has his foibles. – For me, I fling no stone – I dare not; for, of all created beings, I know none so truly culpable, so full of faults, as is your very sincere friend and obliged servant,

I. SANCHO.

As we commonly wish well to ourselves, you may believe that we cordially join in wishing every good, either in health, wealth, or honor, to the noble owner of *Barton* Hall – to the thrice dearly respected —— guess who! to you and all – and all and you. Billy loves flesh – Kitty[4] is a termagant – Betsy talks as usual – the Fannys work pretty hard. Adieu! I conclude 1779 with the harmony of love and friendship.

1. Little C——: possibly Miss Crewe.
2. 'Our old British freeholders ... Sir Roger de Coverley': Squire Bunbury is compared to the fictional Sir Roger de Coverley, Addison's gregarious squire, who features as a member of the fictitious Spectator Club in a number of Addison's *Spectator* essays. Sir Roger is a symbolic representation of the landed gentry, in contrast to fellow club member Sir Andrew Freeport, who represents 'the middle condition' between the landed gentry and the poor. Freeholders were principally but not exclusively land-owning Tory voters. In Addison's minor work *The Freeholder*, Sir Roger de Coverley features as the archetypal Tory fox hunter.

3. 'Honored and blest be Sir C——': the death of Charles
   Hardy; see Letter 105, n. 3.
4. Kitty: Sancho may have mistakenly inserted the name of his
   young daughter who died nine months earlier (Kitty's death
   is recorded in Letter 87); see Letter 103, n. 2, and Letter 108,
   n. 2. Other references to Kitty after her death suggest Miss
   Crewe wrongly dated some letters, see Appendix I.

126

TO —— MR. S'[TEVENSON]'.

1780, January the 4th day.

MY DEAR FRIEND,

You have here a kind of medley, a hetrogeneous, ill-spelt, heteroclite,[1] (worse) eccentric sort of a – a –; in short, it is a true Negroe
calibash of ill-sorted, undigested chaotic matter. What an excellent
proem! what a delightful sample of the grand absurd! – sir – dear Sir
– as I have a soul to be saved (and why I should not would puzzle
a Dr. Price[2]), as I have a soul to be saved I only meant to say about
fifteen words to you – and the substance just this – to wish you
a happy New-year – with the usual appendages – and a long et
cetera of cardinal and heavenly blessings. A propos, blessings –
never more scanty – all beggars by Jove – not a shilling to be got in
London: – if you are better off in the country, and can afford to
remit me your little bill, I inclose it for that good end. – H—— is
– but he can better tell you himself what he is – for in truth I do
think he is in love, which puts the pretty G——[3] into my head – and
she brings her father in view. – My love and respects to each. – Mrs.
Sancho joins me, and the girls her – and God keep you!

Yours sincerely,
I. SANCHO.

1. Heteroclite: a word in common usage in the seventeenth and
   eighteenth centuries denoting irregularity, abnormality,
   eccentricity.
2. Dr Price: Richard Price (1723–91), liberal pamphleteer,
   a Presbyterian clergyman and an author on various subjects.
   Though Price was friends with the liberal theologian Dr
   Priestley, they took opposite views on the great questions of
   morals and metaphysics: Price argued against Priestley, in

published correspondence between them, for the free agency of man and the unity and immateriality of the human soul. Price wrote in defence of the rights of the American colonies; his *Observations on the Nature of Civil Liberty* (1776) enjoyed wide readership in Britain and America. He also became well-known for his writing on financial and political questions, in particular his *Appeal to the Public on the Subject of the National Debt* (1771).

3. 'Pretty G ... her father': see Letter 114, n. 2.

127

TO MR. '[JACK]' W'[INGRAV]'E.[1]
Charles Street, Jan. 5, 1786.[2]

DEAR *WINGRAVE*,

Were I as rich in worldly commodity as in hearty will, I would thank you most princely for your very welcome and agreeable letter; – but, were it so, I should not proportion my gratitude to your wants: – for, blessed be the God of thy hope! thou wantest nothing more than what's in thy possession, or in thy power to possess. – I would neither give thee *Money* – nor *Territory* – *Women* – nor *Horses* – nor *Camels* – nor the height of Asiatic pride, *Elephants*; – I would give thee *Books* –

'*Books*, fair Virtue's advocates and friends!'[3]

But you have books plenty – more than you have time to digest – After much writing – which is fatiguing enough – and under the lassitude occasioned by fatigue, and not sin – the cool recess – the loved *book* – the sweet pleasures of imagination poetically worked up into delightful enthusiasm – richer than all your fruits, your spices, your dancing girls, and the whole detail of eastern, effeminate foppery – flimsy splendour, and glittering magnificence. – So thou thinkest – and I rejoice with thee and for thee. Shall I say what my heart suggests? No – you will feel it praise – and call it flattery – Shall I say, Your worthy parent read your filial letter to me, and embalmed the grateful tribute of a virtuous son with his precious tears. – Will you believe! – he was for some minutes speechless through joy. – Imagine you see us – our heads close together – comparing notes; – imagine you hear the honest plaudits of love and friendship sounding in thy ears – 'Tis glory to be proud on such occasions – 'tis the pride of merit – and as you allow me to counsel you with freedom, I do strongly advise you to love praise – to court praise – to win it by every honest, laudable exertion – and be oft, very often jealous of it: – examine the source it proceeds from – and encourage and cherish it accordingly; – Fear not – mankind are not too lavish of it – censure is dealt out by wholesale, while praise is very sparingly distributed – Nine times in ten mankind may err in their blame – but in its praises the world is seldom, if ever, mistaken. – Mark – I praise thee *sincerely*, for the *whole* and every *part* of thy *conduct*, in regard to my two sable brethren*. I was an ass, or else I might have judged, from the national antipathy and prejudice through custom even of the Gentoos towards their woolly-headed brethren, and the well-known dignity of my Lords the Whites, of the impropriety of my request – I therefore not only acquit thee honourably – but condemn myself for giving thee the trouble to explain a right conduct. – I fear you will hardly make out this scrawl, although it is written with a pen of thy father's – a present, mended from a parcel of old quills by his foreman, or brother C——d. – Your honest brother Joseph came post with your letters – good-will shining in his face – joy in his innocent eyes: – he promises to be as much a *Wingrave* as his Indian brother. – You flatter my vanity in supposing my friendship of any utility to Joe. – He has in his good father Moses and the Prophets – which you have had – and availed yourself well of the blessing – and I trust Joe will do the same – besides having precept and example from a worthy and loving brother. – Poor M——,[4] your favourite – I scarce knew her – she was as pure within, as amiable without – she enriches the circle of the blest – and you have a friend in heaven.

I hope you sometimes – aye often – consult with Dr. Young's Night Thoughts[5] – carry him in your pockets – court him – quote him – delight in him – make him your own – and laugh at the wit, and wisdom, and fashion of the world. – That book well studied will make you know the value of death – and open your eyes to the

---

*   Mr. *Wingrave* having wrote word, that if any European in India associated with those of that complexion, it would be considered as a degradation, and would be an obstacle to his future preferment: he laments in very strong terms the cruelty of such an opinion, hopes not to forfeit Mr. Sancho's good opinion from being compelled to comply with the custom of the country, – with repeated assurances of serving them, if in his power; though he must remain unknown to them.

snares of life: – its precepts will exalt the festive hour – brighten and bless the gloom of solitude – comfort thy heart, and smooth thy pillow in sickness – and gild with lustre thy prosperity – disarm death itself of its terrors – and sweetly soften the hour of dissolution. – I recommend all young people, who do me the honor to ask my opinion – I recommend, if their stomachs are strong enough for such intellectual food – Dr. Young's Night-Thoughts – the Paradise Lost – and the Seasons; – which, with Nelson's Feasts and Fasts – a Bible and Prayer-book – used for twenty years to make my travelling library – and I do think it a very rich one. I never trouble my very distant friends with articles of news – the public prints do it so much better – and then they may answer for their untruths – for among the multitude of our public prints, it is hard to say which lyes most.

Your enclosed trust was directly delivered to the fair hands it was addressed to. – I have the authority to say, it gave great pleasure to both the ladies and your friend Mr. R——, who wears the same cordial friendly heart in his breast as when you first knew him. – Your friend Mr. John Rush is still at New York with the Guards – where he is very deservedly honored, loved, and esteemed: – he corresponds with his old acquaintance, and does me the honor to remember me amongst his friends. – Our toast in Privy Gardens is often the three Johns: *Rush*, *Wingrave*, and *Osborne*, an honest – therefore a noble triumvirate.

I feel old age insensibly stealing on me – and, alas! am obliged to borrow the aid of spectacles, for any kind of small print. – Time keeps pacing on, and we delude ourselves with the hope of reaching first this stage, and then the next – till that ravenous rogue Death puts a final end to our folly.

All this is true – and yet I please and flatter myself with the hope of living to see you in your native country – with every comfort possessed – crowned with the honest man's best ambition – a fair character. – May your worthy, your respectable parents, relations, and friends, enjoy that pleasure! and that you may realize every fond hope of all who love you, is the wish of

Your sincere friend,
IGNATIUS SANCHO.

POSTSCRIPT.

This letter is of a decent length – I expect a return with interest. – Mrs. Sancho joins me in good wishes, love, and compliments.

1. Printer's error (as in Letter 92 to John Spink); the hand-written 'J' has been misread as an 'I'.
2. This letter is misdated by Miss Crewe six years after Sancho's death; it should be 1780. See Appendix I.
3. I have been unable to identify this quotation.
4. 'Poor M—— ... in heaven': this could be a record of the death of the Sanchos' daughter, 'Poor Marianne', of Letter 106, where her birthday celebrations are described. Sancho's observation 'I scarce new her' might suggest that the 'poor M——' of this letter refers to the death of a friend or relation of Jack Wingrave, but the remark might also be read as a comment on the suddenness of a beloved daughter's death and Sancho's sense of loss; see Letters 87 and 88 for Kitty's death and the Sanchos' bereavement, and Appendix VII.
5. 'Dr Young's Night Thoughts': Edward Young, *Night Thoughts* (1752–5). See Letter 53, n. 3.

128

TO MR. S'[TEVENSON]'.
Charles Street, Jan. 11, 1780.

MY DEAR FRIEND,

Mr. R*ush* faithfully discharged his commission – paid me the desirable – and intrusted me with ten guineas – to pay on demand – And here he comes, 'faith – as fresh as May, and warm as friendly zeal can make mortality – to demand the two letters – which he will deliver himself – for his own satisfaction. – I wish from my soul that Chancellors, Secretaries of State, Kings, aye and Bishops, were as fond of doing kind things – But they are of a higher order – Friend R*ush* is only a Christian. – I give you credit for your promises of reformation in the epistolary way – and very glad am I to hear of your success. – Know your own worth – Honor yourself – not with supercilious pride, but with the decent confidence of your own true native merit – and you must succeed in almost any thing you choose to undertake – So thinks Sancho. – As to what you request me to do by way of inspecting your goods and chattels in your late lodging, I must beg to decline it – as I feel it awkward to insinuate the least deficiency in point of attention to your interests in such a heart as H——'s – a heart which to my knowledge feels every sentiment of divine friendship for you – a heart animated with the strongest zeal and flowing ardor to serve you, to love you.

The kindness[1] of you and your two friends exceedingly embarrasses me – I would not wish to appear to any one either arrogant, vain, or conceited – no – nor servile, mean, or selfish. – I grant your motive is friendly in the extreme – and those of your companions as nobly generous – But – but what – Why this – and the truth – Were I rich, I would accept it, and say Thank ye, when I chose it. – As I am poor, I do not choose to say Thank ye but to those I know and respect. – You must forgive me – and call it the error of African false principle – Call it any thing but coldness and unfeeling pride, which is in fact ingratitude in a birth-day suit. – As to the Grand Turk of Norfolk – if it comes, we will devour it, and toast Don S—— and the unknown giver. – Thou, my *Stevenson*, hast (oh! prostrate, and thank the giver) a noble and friendly heart, susceptible of the best, the greatest feelings. H—— is thy twin brother – Perhaps he has more fire in his composition. – Woman apart, he is a glorious fellow – * * * * Apart – alas! alas! alas! – * * * * apart, what might not be hoped, expected – from * * * * * * So the poor boy flew his kite – but the tail was lost. – Poor H—— has a book and a fair-one to manage – ticklish – very ticklish subjects either – and your worship has a book to castrate, and a fandango to dance – with a *Tol de le rol, de le lol.* – Your reason for postponing your journey to town is wisely great, or greatly wise; – it does you honor, because it is founded in equity. I am glad to hear the Rev. Mr. S(*tevenson*] is better – I love and venerate that good man; – not because he begat you, but for his own great parts and many virtues – (By the bye) I know more of him than you think for. – Tell brother *Osborne* I am glad to hear he is well, and Mrs. *Osborne* better; – and tell him, the name of the Bishop's lady's dog (that was lost, and has been missing these two months) is Sherry* When you see Mr. S——, the good, the friendly, generous Mr. S——, my and mine make the respects of – we wish him many happy years and his family. – To Mr. G——[2] and his amiable daughter, say all that's right for me. – And now to conclude, with thanks, &c. &c. I and we – that's spouse and self – remain, &c. &c. &c. &c. &c. &c.

I. SANCHO.

* Mr. *Osborne* had promised Mr. Sancho two months before to send him immediately a present of sherry.

1. 'The kindness ... The Grand Turk of Norfolk': Sancho seems to be acknowledging a generosity other than the expected

arrival of 'The Grand Turk of Norfolk', presumably
a reference to a turkey.

2.   Mr G ... and daughter: see Letter 114, n. 2.

129

TO MR. S'[TEVENSON]'.
Charles Street, Jan. 17, 1780.

MY DEAR FRIEND,

I received, as you taught me to expect, last week, a very fine * * *,[1]
and after it as kind a letter, in name of a Mr. E—— W—— of
Norfolk, near Houghton-Hall, &c. – I have bespoke a frank, and
mean to thank him, as I also thank you, whom I look upon as the
grand friendly mover of the generously handsome act. – You have
your reward, for you had a pleasure in doing it; – and Mr. W——
has his, if he believes me honest. – Could I any way retaliate, I
should feel lighter; – that's pride – I own it – Humility should be
the poor man's shirt, and thankfulness his girdle – be it so – I do
request you to thank Mr. W—— for me, and tell him he has the
prayers – not of a raving mad whig, nor fawning deceitful tory – but
of a coal-black, jolly African, who wishes health and peace to every
religion and country throughout the ample range of God's creation!
and believes a painter may be saved at the last day, maugre all the
Miss G——s and widows in this kingdom. I have done nothing in
the shoe affair yet, for which I ought to ask poor C——'s pardon as
well as yours: – the rogue has left the court, and gone to live in
Fish-market, Westminster-bridge; – I shall ferret him out, and make
him bless his old master.

I inclose your receipts in proof of my honesty – a rare virtue as
times go! M—— has wrote to you – left his letter with me – and I,
like a what you please, let it slip into the fire, with a handful of
company he had no business to be amongst: – he shall write you
another – you will both be angry – but you will both forgive, as
good Christians ought, accidents – I am sorry. – I will say no more
than God keep you and direct your goings!

Yours, &c. &c.
I. SANCHO.

When you see the honorable Mr. B——, give our loves and best

wishes to him and Mrs. B——, and Squire S—— and his good dame also. – Salute the home of G—— for me.

1. 'A very fine ***': probably the arrival of the turkey sent by William Stevenson. See Letter 128, n. 1.

130

TO MR. W'[INGRAV]'E.
Charles Street, March 1, 1780.

MY GOOD FRIEND,
I wish to interest you in behalf of the inclosed book[1] wrote by a greatly-esteemed friend, a young man of much merit, and a heart enriched with every virtue. – The book I beg you will snatch time to read with attention – it is an answer (as you will see) to a flaming bigoted Mongrel against Toleration; – Swift says, 'Zeal is never so pleased as when you set it a tearing.'[2] He says truly. Could you get the pamphlet (whose title I forget), you would be better enabled to judge of the force, truth, and strength of my friend's answer: – For my part, I love liberty in every sense, whilst connected with honesty and truth. – It has been shown a bookseller, but he happened to be the very man who had just published a flimsy answer to the same – consequently would not encourage my friend's, lest it should injure the sale of his other. – Understand, my good friend, that the author is very ill-calculated for booksellers' and printers' jockey-ship; which, to a liberal mind, fraught with high and generous ideas, is death and the devil.

I own I was guilty of teazing him into the finishing this little work, with a view of having it printed – Now my friend is not richer than poets commonly are – and, in short, will not run any risks. – I would gladly stand the expense of printing, but I am not richer than he; – I want it printed – and request of you, if, upon perusing it, you do not find it inimical either to Religion, Country, or Crown, that you contrive to push it into the world without delay; but if, upon mature deliberation, you find it dangerous, with washed hands send it me back, and set me down for an ass in the trouble I have given thee and myself. – Perhaps, jaundiced by prejudice, I behold it with too partial eyes; for I verily believe it will not discredit the printer – Suppose you shew it in confidence to the greatly amiable, the good Mr. B——e.[3] I mention him in particular, for, sure I am, his nobly-benevolent soul would start at the bare idea of religious persecution: – he would, I trust, feel the full force of my friend's reasoning – and his good opinion would be the best sanction for endeavouring to push the work forward.

I had the pleasure of meeting a gentleman in our street one day last week, who seemed to be so goodly a personage – that I said to myself, there's Sir Charles Grandison – his figure was noble, his eye brightened with kindness; the man of fashion and of sense was conspicuous in him – Think how I stared, when the gentleman accosted me – said, he knew me through my friend W*ingrave*; – his name was * * * *. I bowed and stammered some nonsense – I was taken by surprize. – I am in such a hurry, and the pen is naught, that I fear you will scarcely understand this scrawl. – Remember I give you full powers over this work – do what you can, but do it soon, and make your report to your friend,

I. SANCHO.*

*   The book alluded to in this letter was printed under the title of 'An Answer to the Appeal from the Protestant Association.'

1.   As Crewe's note explains, the book is *An Answer to the Appeal from the Protestant Association*. Sancho's letter, explaining that a similar pamphlet had already been published, demonstrates that pamphlets and sermons were popular forms of communication through which the public were informed and engaged in the controversy raised by the Catholic Act of 1778, the repeal of which led to the Gordon Riots (see Letters 134–7): 'the Protestant Associations kept the fear and hate of Popery burning with the distribution of pamphlets as ill-written as they were grotesque'. See Christopher Hibbert *King Mob: The Story of Lord George Gordon and the Riots of 1780* (London, 1958) p. 21.

2.   Quotation: I have been unable to identify the source of Swift's words.

3.   Mr B——e: see Letter 118, n. 1.

131

Charles Street, March 23, 1780.

DEAR MADAM,

I and mine have a thousand things to thank you for – Shall I say the plain truth, and own I am proud to know that you care for me and my little ones? your friendly attention to our interests proves it – but mortals of your cast are oftener envied than loved: – the majority, who are composed chiefly of the narrow-minded or contracted hearts, and of selfish avidity, cannot comprehend the delight in doing as they would be done by – and consequently cannot love what they do not understand – Excuse my nonsense, I ever write just what I think – My business was to give you some account why I delayed the teas, and to thank you for your very noble order. – Sir Jacob[1] was here this afternoon, and if his looks tell truth, he is exceeding well. – H—— desires his love to you and the worthy partner of your heart, to whom I join with my spouse in wishing every earthly felicity – heavenly, you have both insured by being faithful stewards. – Sir Jacob hath sent a parcel, which accompanies the teas, which I hope will reach you safe and right, as they set out to-morrow noon. – Tell Mr. H——, I pray you, that the winter has used me as roughly as it has him – I never have been so unwell for these four months past; – But, alas! one reason is, I do believe, that I am past fifty – But I hope with you, that spring will set us all right. – As to complaints in trade, there is nothing else – we are all poor, all grumblers; all preaching œconomy, and wishing our neighbours to practice it – but no one but the quite undone begin at home. We are all patriots, all politicians, all state quacks,[2] and all fools – The ladies are turned orators,[3] and declaim in public; expose their persons, and their erudition, to every jackanapes[4] who can throw down half-a-crown – As to the men, they are past saving. – As I can say no good, I will stop where I am. – And is my good friend Mr. S—— unmarried still? fie, fie upon him! how can he enjoy any good alone? He should take a partner, to lead him gently down the hill of life – to superintend his linen and his meat – to give sweet poignancy to his beverage – and talk him to sleep on nights. – Pray tell him all my say – and also that the majority are killing up the minority as fast as they can – Nothing but duels, and rumours of duels. – But is it not time to finish? Dear Madam, forgive all my impertinences; and, believe me, dame Sancho and self have a true sense of your goodness, and repeatedly thank you both for your kindness to,

Yours in sincerity,
and greatly obliged friends,
ANNE and IGN. SANCHO.

1. Sir Jacob: see Letter 17, n. 2.
2. Quacks: charlatans.
3. 'The ladies are turned orators': Sancho may refer to women's presence in public gatherings just before the Gordon Riots (see Letters 134–7); see Hibbert's account of the riots in which illustrations show women's involvement, *King Mob* (1958) facing p. 84; p. 85; p. 100. 'The ladies who 'expose their persons ... to every Jackanapes who can throw down a half-crown' carries suggestions of prostitution and begging, hardly suitable topics in a letter to a female friend, but such suggestive overtones register criticism of a vocal female presence in the public domain (see n. 4 below). Iain McCalman, *Radical Underworld: Prophets, revolutionaries and pornographers in London 1795–1840* (Cambridge University Press, 1988) includes details of radical eighteenth-century women; Clare Midgley, *Women Against Slavery: the British Campaigns 1780–1870* (Routledge, London and New York, 1992) is an excellent study of black and white women's roles in eighteenth-century anti-slavery activities.
4. Jackanapes: the etymology of the word is uncertain, though its origin is linked to the Duke of Suffolk whose badge was an ape's clog and chain, such as was attached to a tame ape. Jackanapes also denotes a roguish rascal (see Letter 67 for the similar 'jack ape'). The *Oxford English Dictionary* gives an example of its usage in a sixteenth-century medical text, 'Women that have as much knowledge in phisick or surgery as hath Jackanapes' which clearly suggests the derogatory attitude towards women in Sancho's use of the word (see n. 3 above). In both contexts, jackanapes is used to belittle female presence in the public domain.

132

For the GENERAL ADVERTISER.

April 29, 1780.

FRIEND EDITOR,

'In the multitude of Counsellors there is wisdom.'[1] sayeth the preacher – and at this present crisis of national jeopardy, it seemeth to me befitting for every honest man to offer his mite of advice[2] towards public benefit and edification. – The vast bounties offered for able-bodied men sheweth the zeal and liberality of our wise lawgivers – yet indicateth a scarcity of men. Now, they seem to me to have overlooked one resource (which appears obvious); a resource which would greatly benefit the people at large (by being more usefully employed), and which are happily half-trained already for the service of their country by being – *powder proof* – light, active, young fellows: – I dare say you have anticipated my scheme, which is to form ten companies at least, out of the very numerous body of hair-dressers. They are, for the most part, clean clever, young men – and, as observed above, the utility would be immense: – The ladies, by once more getting the management of their heads into their own hands, might possibly regain their native reason and œconomy – and the gentlemen might be induced, by mere necessity, to comb and care for their own heads – those (I mean) who have heads to care for. – If the above scheme should happily take place, among the many advantages, too numerous to particularize, which would of course result from it – one, not of the least magnitude, would be a prodigious saving in the great momentous article of time; – people of the *ton* of both sexes (to speak within probability) usually losing between two or three hours daily on that important business. – My plan, Mr. Editor, I have the comfort to think, is replete with good – it tends to serve my king and country in the first instance – and to cleanse, settle, and emancipate from the cruel bondage of French as well as native friseurs,[3] the heads of my fellow-subjects.

Yours, &c.

AFRICANUS.

1. Quotation: Proverbs, 11:14.
2. Sancho puts forward a comical scheme to form a company of hairdressers, punning on 'powder proof' to suggest both

gunpowder and cosmetic grooming powder. The hairdressing habits of men and women are linked to 'French
bondage', a reference to the war with France. In Letter 139
Sancho reports that citizens previously encouraged to arm
themselves against a French invasion are being asked to give
up their arms. In Letter 25 Sancho lists hairdressing and
shaving among the numerous skills of a black servant and, in
Letter 124, Sancho mentions a Bengali messenger boy who
'can cook … dress and shave'. Both men were among the
many skilled blacks in eighteenth-century London who
worked as hairdressers and grooms. Among them was
Olaudah Equiano who, after purchasing his freedom, returned to England in 1767 and was apprenticed to a
hairdresser; for Equiano, see the Introduction, p. 1, and Peter
Fryer, *Staying Power*, chapters 4 and 5.

3.   Friseurs: frisure: curling the hair; curls or ringlets.

133

TO MRS. H——.
Charles Street, May 20, 1780.

DEAR MADAM,

Your goodness is never tired with action – how many, very many
times, have I to thank you, for your friendly interesting yourself in
our behalf! – You will say, thanks are irksome to a generous mind
– so I have done – but must first ask pardon for a sin of omission.
I never sent you word, that your good son, as friendly as polite, paid
me the note directly – and would not suffer it to run its sight. They
that know Sir Jacob[1] will not wonder, for he is a Christian – which
means, in my idea, a gentleman not of the modern sort. – Trade is at
so low an ebb, the greatest are glad to see ready money – In truth,
we are a ruined people – let hirelings affect to write and talk as big as
they please – and, what is worse, religion and mortality are vanished
with our prosperity – Every good principle seems to be leaving us;
– as our means lessen, luxury and every sort of expensive pleasure
increases – The blessed Sabbath-day is used by the trader for
country excursions – tavern dinners – rural walks – and then,
whipping and galloping through dust and over turnpikes, drunk
home. – The poorer sort do any thing – but go to church – they take
their dust in the field, and conclude the sacred evening with riots,
drunkenness, and empty pockets: – The beau in upper life hires his

whisky and beast for twelve shillings; his girl dressed *en militaire* for half-a-guinea, and spends his whole week's earnings to look and be thought *quite the thing*. – And for upper tiptop high life – cards and music are called in to dissipate the chagrin of a tiresome, tedious Sunday's evening – The example spreads downwards from them to their domestics; – the laced valet and the livery beau either debauch the maids, or keep their girls – Thus profusion and cursed dissipation fill the prisons, and feed the gallows. – The clergy – hush! I will not meddle with them – God forbid I should! they are pretty much the same in all places; – but this I will affirm, wherever a preacher is in earnest in his duty, and can *preach*, he will not want for crowded congregations. – As to our politics[2] – now don't laugh at me – for every one has a right to be a politician; so have I; and though only a poor, thick-lipped son of Afric! may be as notable a Negro state-botcher as * * * * *, and so on for five hundred – I do not mean *Burke*,[3] *Saville*,[4] *Bute*,[5] nor *Dunning*,[6] mind that – no, nor *North*,[7] *Grenville*,[8] *Jenkinson*,[9] nor *Wedderburne*,[10] names that will shine in history when the marble monuments of their earthly flatterers shall be mouldering into dust. – I have wrote absolute nonsense – I mean the monuments of *North*, *Grenville*, &c. and not of their flatterers. – But it is right I should give you an apology for this foolish letter. – Know then, my dear Madam, I have been seriously and literally fast asleep for these two months; – true, upon the word of a poor sufferer, a kind of lethargy – I can sleep standing, walking, and feel so intolerably heavy and oppressed with it, that sometimes I am ready to tumble when walking in the street. – I am exceeding sorry to hear Mr. H—— is so poorly – and hope, through God's mercy, the waters will have the wished effect – For my own part, I feel myself ten years older this year than the last – Time tries us all – but, blessed be God! in the end we shall be an over-match for Time, and leave him, scythe and all, in the lurch – when we shall enjoy a blessed Eternity. – In this view, and under the same hope, we are as great – yea, as respectable and consequential – as Statesmen! Bishops! Chancellors! Popes! Heroes! Kings! actors of every denomination – who must all drop the mark when the fated minute arrives – and, alas! some of the very high be obliged to give place to Mr. and Mrs. H——. May you and yours enjoy every felicity here! every blessing hereafter! wish thy much obliged friends!

The SANCHOS.

1. Sir Jacob: see Letter 17, n. 2.
2. 'As to our politics': people whose 'names that will shine in history' were active in politics during the Reform Movement (1714–1830), taking leading roles in the great political storms of 1780 during the North Administration (for North see n. 7 below). Challenges to the status quo included proposed changes in duration of Parliaments, reformed constituencies, demands for increased representation of the people in Parliament, and control of the King's household expenditure.
3. Burke: Edmund Burke (1729–97), British statesman and philosopher. Burke wrote lengthy works on philosophy and was a parliamentary speaker of great eloquence. In 1780–2 Burke was a leading advocate of economical reform and piloted through the House of Commons the Establishment Act abolishing a number of offices tenable with a seat in the Commons.
4. Savile: Sir George Savile (1726–84) the last male representative of an old and distinguished Yorkshire family with a parliamentary ancestry dating back to the sixteenth century. For most of his political life Savile, like Burke, was closely connected with Lord Rockingham, though Savile never belonged to a party and tried to judge questions on their merits. He became one of the most respected men in the commons. Savile stood as a candidate for Yorkshire in 1753, and was returned again in 1759. In 1779 The Yorkshire Association was formed to campaign for parliamentary reform and, in 1780, Savile introduced the Yorkshire Petition, demanding an inquiry into the pension list, the reduction of exorbitant salaries and the abolition of sinecures.
5. Bute: John Stuart, 3rd Earl of Bute (1713–92), was elected a Scottish representative peer in April 1737. He took his seat in the House of Lords for the first time in January 1738, but did not take part in the debates and was not re-elected to the 1741, 1747 or 1754 Parliaments. He spent much of his time at the Island of Bute where he studied agriculture, botany and architecture, and enjoyed performing in masquerades and plays with friends and relatives. Bute was a favourite of the King, which laid the foundation of his political career. He was made Secretary for the Northern Department 1761–2 and followed Newcastle as First Lord of the Treasury in 1762, resigning office in 1763. He recommended and was followed by George Grenville as his successor (for Grenville, see n. 8 below). Bute, who was deeply unpopular during his administration, is something of the odd man out in Sancho's list; he may be mentioned here for his taste in literature, the fine arts and acting (interests shared and much admired by Sancho) as well as for his political career.

6. Dunning: John Dunning (1731–83) began his legal career in the office of his father, a country attorney, and ended as the foremost advocate of his day. Dunning was appointed Solicitor-General in 1768; like Burke, Dunning was an advocate of economical reform and he played an important role for the Opposition in parliamentary battles. After the defeat of Burke's Economical Reform Bill in March 1780, Dunning took the lead in the Commons of the movement to reduce the influence of the Crown.

7. North: Lord North: Frederick North, Head of Administration (1770–82). Lord North spent almost the whole of his political life in the House of Commons and was its leader for nearly fifteen years. During the American war North was head of the Treasury Board, Leader of the House of Commons and, at the age of thirty-seven, First Minister (for details concerning North's handling of the American war and his abilities as a statesman see Letter 85, n. 3 and Letter 115, n. 4). The day before Sancho wrote this letter, Charles Jenkinson (see n. 9, below) wrote to the King and said of North: 'his labours are immense and such as few constitutions could bear'. Though North ranks among the greatest parliamentarians of the eighteenth century, he was forced to contend with virtually insoluble problems and his career was disastrous. North was forty-nine years old when his administration ended.

8. Grenville: male members of the Grenville family were active in politics during the Reform Movement (1714–1830). George Grenville's (1712–70) administration followed that of Bute (see n. 5 above). During his administration Grenville was First Lord of the Treasury and Chancellor of the Exchequer (1763–5). He went into opposition in July 1765 with a number of followers; though unpopular, Grenville was recognised as an able and knowledgeable man in the House of Commons and by 1768 he was its foremost senior statesman. Though Grenville died ten years before this letter was written, Sancho may have had him in mind as one whose name 'will shine in history'. Other Grenvilles active in politics during the Reform Movement included George Grenville's brothers, Henry (1717–84), and James (1715–83), his sons George (1753–1813), Thomas (1755–1846) and William Wyndham (1759–1834) and his nephews James (1742–1825) and Richard (1742–1823). The Grenvilles voted steadily in opposition in the crucial divisions before the fall of North.

9. Jenkinson: Charles Jenkinson (1729–1808), later Earl of Liverpool, belonged to a younger branch of an old Oxfordshire family. Jenkinson occupied an important 'behind the scenes' place at the centre of government and was consulted

by Lord North and George III on important government business. Jenkinson was private secretary to Bute (see n. 5 above) and became a Secretary to the Treasury under Grenville (see n. 8 above). By 1778 Jenkinson belonged to an inner circle of North's confidential advisers and succeeded Lord Barrington as Secretary at War.

10. Wedderburn: Alexander Wedderburn (1733–1805) came from a distinguished Scottish legal family; he made a reputation for himself at the Scottish bar and in the general assembly of the Church of Scotland and he entered Parliament in 1761. Wedderburn supported the Bute and Grenville Administrations (see n. 5 and 8 above) and in July 1765 followed Grenville into opposition until Grenville's death. Wedderburn accepted the office of Attorney-General in 1778, and was appointed Chief Justice of the Common Pleas. He was given a peerage in 1780.

134

TO J'[OHN]' S'[PINK]', ESQ.
Charles Street, June 6, 1780.

DEAR AND MOST RESPECTED SIR,

In the midst of the most cruel and ridiculous confusion, I am now set down to give you a very imperfect sketch of the maddest people that the maddest times were ever plagued with. – The public prints have informed you (without doubt) of last Friday's transactions; – the insanity of Lord George Gordon,[1] and the worse than Negro barbarity of the populace; – the burnings and devastations of each night you will also see in the prints: – This day, by consent, was set apart for the further consideration of the wished-for repeal; – The people (who had their proper cue from his lordship) assembled by ten o'clock in the morning – Lord N*orth*, who had been up in Council at home till four in the morning, got to the house before eleven, just a quarter of an hour before the associators reached Palace-yard: – But, I should tell you, in Council there was a deputation from all parties; – The *Shelburne* party were for prosecuting Ld *George* and leaving him at large; – The A*ttorney General* laughed at the idea, and declared it was doing just nothing; – The M*inority* were for his expulsion, and so dropping him gently into insignificancy; – that was thought wrong, as he would still be industrious in mischief; – The R*ockingha*m party, I should suppose, you will think counselled best, which is, this day to expel him the house – commit him to the Tower – and then prosecute him at leisure – by which means he will lose the opportunity of getting a seat in the next parliament, and have decent leisure to repent him of the heavy evils he has occasioned. – There is at this present moment at least a hundred thousand poor, miserable, ragged rabble, from twelve to sixty years of age, with blue cockades in their hats[2] – besides half as many women and children, all parading the streets – the bridge – the Park – ready for any and every mischief. – Gracious God! what's the matter now? I was obliged to leave off – the shouts of the mob – the horrid clashing of swords – and the clutter of a multitude in swiftest motion – drew me to the door – when every one in the street was employed in shutting up shop. – It is now just five o'clock – the ballad-singers are exhausting their musical talents with, the downfall of Popery, *Sandwich*, and North. – Lord *Sandwich* narrowly escaped with life about an hour since; the mob seized his chariot going to the house, broke his glasses, and, in struggling to get his lordship out, they somehow have cut his face – The guards flew to his assistance – the light-horse scowered the road, got his chariot, escorted him from the coffee-house, where he had fled for protection, to his carriage, and guarded him bleeding very fast home. This – this – is liberty! genuine British liberty! – This instant about two thousand liberty boys are swearing and swaggering by with large sticks – thus armed, in hopes of meeting with the Irish chairmen[3] and labourers – All the guards are out – and all the horse; – the poor fellows are just worn out for want of rest, having been on duty ever since Friday. – Thank heaven, it rains; may it increase, so as to send these deluded wretches safe to their homes, their families, and wives! About two this afternoon, a large party took it into their heads to visit the King and Queen, and entered the Park for that purpose – but found the guard too numerous to be forced, and after some useless attempts gave it up. – It is reported, the house will either be prorogued, or parliament dissolved, this evening, as it is in vain to think of attending any business while this anarchy lasts.

I cannot but felicitate you, my good friend, upon the happy distance you are placed from our scene of confusion. – May foul Discord and her cursed train never nearer approach your blessed abode! Tell Mrs. *Spink*, her good heart would ach, did she see the anxiety, the woe, in the faces of mothers, wives, and sweethearts, each equally anxious for the object of their wishes, the beloved of their hearts. – Mrs. Sancho and self both cordially join in love and gratitude, and every good wish – crowned with the peace of God, which passeth all understanding, &c.

I am, dear Sir,
Yours ever by inclination,
IGN. SANCHO.

POSTSCRIPT,

The Sardinian ambassador[4] offered 500 guineas to the rabble to save a painting of our Saviour from the flames, and 1000 guineas not to destroy an exceeding fine organ: The gentry told him, they would burn him if they could get at him, and destroyed the picture and organ directly. – I am not sorry I was born in Afric. – I shall tire you, I fear – and, if I cannot get a frank, make you pay dear for bad news. – There is about a thousand mad men, armed with clubs, bludgeons, and crows, just now set off for Newgate, to liberate, they say, their honest comrades. – I wish they do not some of them lose their lives of liberty before morning. It is thought by many who discern deeply, that there is more at the bottom of this business than merely the repeal of an act[5] which has as yet produced no bad consequences, and perhaps never might. – I am forced to own that I am for an universal toleration. Let us convert by our example, and conquer by our meekness and brotherly love!

Eight o'clock. – Lord George Gordon has this moment announced to my Lords the mob – that the act shall be repealed this evening: – Upon this, they gave a hundred cheers – took the horses from his hackney-coach – and rolled him full jollily away: – They are huzzaing now ready to crack their throats.

Huzzah.

I am forced to conclude for want of room – The remainder in our next.

1. For a discussion of this letter, see the Introduction pp. 15–16. In December 1779 Lord George Gordon (1751–93) accepted the presidency of the Protestant Association, and led it in a campaign to repeal the Catholic Act of 1778. A mass lobby of Parliament to present a petition on 2 June against the relief of Roman Catholics from certain minor disabilities led to the worst rioting of the century, witnessed and described

in letters by Sancho. The mob attacked Roman Catholic chapels and property, the homes of prominent public figures and then prisons, businesses and the Bank of England in just less than a week. As Sancho records, arson and pillaging were widespread; Lord Sandwich was attacked on his way to the House of Lords; Lord Mansfield's house in Bloomsbury was set on fire and his library destroyed (see Letter 136); Sir John Fielding's house was also burnt. Prisons and other buildings were burnt; prisoners, who joined the angry mob, were released, as Sancho reports in Letter 135. By 8 June, twenty-thousand troops brought the rioters under control. Three hundred people were killed; one hundred and ninety-two rioters were convicted and twenty-five executed. On 9 June Gordon was sent to the Tower and kept there for eight months. He was tried for high treason in the King's Bench on 5 February 1781 and acquitted.

2. In May 1780 an advertisement appeared in a number of newspapers under the heading 'Protestant Association' calling a meeting on 2 June in St George's Fields 'to consider the most prudent and respectful manner' to present their petition to Parliament (see n. 1 above). All those participating were advised to 'wear blue cockades in their hats to distinguish them from Papists and those who approve of the late act in favour of Popery'; the Protestant Association made free blue cockades available for those who arrived without their knot of ribbons. Following the riots, a handbill was circulated requesting people to abstain from wearing blue cockades, now associated with the rioters and riotous behaviour generally; another handbill asked employers not to employ people wearing blue cockades. See Hibbert, *King Mob* (1958), pp. 31–2; 115.

3. 'Irish chairmen': carriers of sedan chairs.

4. Sardinian ambassador: B. Cardiff (1779–83). The rioting crowd destroyed everything in the ambassador's chapel. Sancho reports the destruction of a painting and an organ; vestments, altar ornaments and pews were passed into the streets and burned. The pregnant wife of the ambassador was so terrified she collapsed.

5. The Catholic Act of 1778, see n. 1 above.

135

Charles Street, June 9, 1780.

MY DEAR SIR,

Government is sunk in lethargic stupor – anarchy reigns – When I look back to the glorious time of a George II. and a Pitt's administration, my heart sinks at the bitter contrast. We may now say of England, as was heretofore said of Great Babylon – 'The beauty of the excellency of the Chaldees is no more;'[1] – The Fleet prison, the Marshalsea, King's-Bench, both Compters, Clerkenwell, and Tothill Fields, with Newgate, are all flung open;[2] – Newgate partly burned, and 300 felons from thence only let loose upon the world. – Lord Mansfield's house in town suffered martyrdom; and his sweet box at Caen Wood escaped almost miraculously, for the mob had just arrived, and were beginning with it, when a strong detachment from the guards and light-horse came most critically to its rescue – The liberty, and, what is of more consequence, papers and deeds of vast value, were all cruelly consumed in the flames. – Lord North's house was attacked; but they had previous notice, and were ready for them. The Bank, the Treasury, and thirty of the chief noblemen's houses, are doomed to suffer by the insurgents.[3] – There were six of the rioters killed at Lord Mansfield's, and, what is remarkable, a daring chap, escaped from Newgate, and condemned to die this day, was the most active in mischief at Lord Mansfield's, and was the first person shot by the soldiers: so he found death a few hours sooner than if he had not been released. – The ministry have tried lenity, and have experienced its inutility; and martial law is this night to be declared – If any body of people above ten in number are seen together, and refuse to disperse, they are to be fired at without any further ceremony – so we expect terrible work before morning. – The insurgents visited the Tower, but it would not do – They had better luck in the Artillery-ground, where they found and took to their use 500 stand of arms; a great error in city politics not to have secured them first. – It is wonderful to hear the execrable nonsense that is industriously circulated amongst the credulous mob – who are told his M*a*jest*y* regularly goes to mass at Lord P——re's chapel[4] – and they believe it, and that he pays out of his privy purse Peter-pence to Rome. Such is the temper of the times – from too relaxed a government – and a King

and Queen on the throne who possess every virtue. May God in his
mercy grant that the present scourge may operate to our repentance
and amendment! that it may produce the fruits of better thinking,
better doing, and in the end make us a wise, virtuous, and happy
people! – I am, dear Sir, truly Mrs. *Spink*'s and your most grateful
and obliged friend and servant,

I. SANCHO.

The remainder in our next.

Half-past nine o'clock.

King's-Bench prison is now in flames, and the prisoners at large;
two fires in Holborn now burning.

1. For a discussion of this letter, see the Introduction, p. 16, and
   Letter 134, n. 1.
2. 'The fleet prison ... Newgate': prisons attacked by rioters,
   see Letter 134, n. 1.
3. 'The Bank ... insurgents': after initial assaults on Roman
   Catholic targets, the mob attacked the Bank of England.
   Jack Wilkes, formerly commander of the Buckinghamshire
   Militia, wrote in his diary, 'fired six or seven times at the
   rioters ... Killed two rioters directly opposite to the Great
   Gate of the Bank; several others in Pig Street and Cheapside'.
   See Hibbert, *King Mob* (1958), p. 102.
4. Lord P——re's chapel: probably Lord Petre, a spokesman
   for Roman Catholics leading up the riots.

136

TO J'[OHN]' S'[PINK]', ESQ.

June 9, 1780.

DEAR SIR,

Happily for us the tumult begins to subside – Last night much was
threatened, but nothing done, except in the early part of the evening,
when about fourscore or a hundred of the reformers got decently
knocked on the head; – they were half killed by Mr. Langdale's
spirits[1] – so fell an easy conquest to the bayonet and but-end. –
There is about fifty taken prisoners, and not a blue cockade to be
seen: – the streets once more wear the face of peace – and men seem
once more to resume their accustomed employment! – the greatest
losses have fallen upon the great distiller near Holborn-bridge, and
Lord Mansfield; the former, alas! has lost his whole fortune – the

latter, the greatest and best collection of manuscript writings, with one of the finest libraries in the kingdom. – Shall we call it a judgment? – or what shall we call it? The thunder of their vengeance has fallen upon gin and law – the two most inflammatory things in the Christian world. – We have a Coxheath and Warley of our own;[2] Hyde Park has a grand encampment, with artillery park, &c. &c. St. James's Park has ditto, upon a smaller scale. The Parks, and our West end of the town, exhibit the features of French government. This minute, thank God! this moment Lord George Gordon is taken. Sir F. Molineux has him safe at the Horse-guards. Bravo! he is now going in state in an old hackney-coach, escorted by a regiment of militia and troop of light horse to his apartments in the Tower.

Off with his head – so much for Buckingham.[3]

We have taken this day numbers of the poor wretches, insomuch we know not where to place them. Blessed be the Lord! we trust this affair is pretty well concluded. – If any thing transpires worth your notice, you shall hear from

Your much obliged, &c. &c.
I. SANCHO.

Best regards attend Mrs. *Spink*. His lordship was taken at five o'clock this evening – betts run fifteen to five Lord George Gordon is hanged in eight days – He wished much to speak to his Majesty on Wednesday, but was of course refused.

1. 'Mr Langdale's spirits … the great distiller': Langdale was a Roman Catholic who owned one of the largest distilleries in London. Rioters set Langdale's distillery on fire; wind carried the flames to surrounding buildings and houses down Holborn towards Fleet Market. The fire was fed by a fire engine mistakenly pumping gin from the stills in Langdale's cellar on to the flames. The heat caused the stills to burst and overflow; unrectified gin flowed in the streets and men and women who drank it were made violently ill or were killed. As Sancho remarks, 'they were half killed by Mr Langdale's spirits'. Others were trapped and killed by flames and smoke in the cellar and warehouse. Langdale's losses were estimated at more than one hundred thousand pounds.

2. A reference to military camps established at Cavenham, Coxheath and Warley when the French joined forces with the Americans (see Letter 70, n. 1, and Letter 99, n. 2). Militia

regiments brought to London from the country were
camped in St George's Fields, St James Park, Hyde Park and
in the gardens of the British Museum.
3. Quotation: Colley Cibber (1671–1757), *Richard III* (1700)
Act 4, adapted from Shakespeare, *Richard III* (1591), Act 3,
Sc. 4, l. 74: 'Talk'st thou to me of "ifs"? Off with his head!'

137

TO J'[OHN]' S'[PINK]', ESQ.

June 13, 1780.

MY DEAR SIR,

That my poor endeavours have given you information or amusement, gratifies the warm wish of my heart; – for as I know not the
man to whose kindness I am so much indebted, I may safely say,
I know not the man whose esteem I more ardently covet and
honour. – We are exceeding sorry to hear Mrs. *Spink*'s indisposition,
and hope, ere this reaches you, she will be well, or greatly mended.
– The spring with us has been very sickly – and the summer has
brought with it sick times. Sickness! cruel sickness! triumphs
through every part of the constitution: – the state is sick – the
church (God preserve it!) is sick – the law, navy, army, all sick – the
people at large are sick with taxes – the Ministry with Opposition,
and Opposition with disappointment. – Since my last, the temerity
of the mob has gradually subsided; – numbers of the unfortunate
rogues have been taken: – yesterday about thirty were killed in and
about Smithfield, and two soldiers were killed in the affray. – There
is no certainty yet as to the number of houses burnt and gutted, for
every day adds to the account – which is a proof how industrious
they were in their short reign. Few evils but are productive of some
good in the end: – the suspicious turbulence of the times united the
royal brothers;[1] – the two Dukes, dropping all past resentments,
made a filial tender of their services: – His Majesty, God bless him!
as readily accepted it – and on Thursday last the brothers met –
They are now a triple cord – God grant a blessing to the union!
There is a report current this day, that the mob of York city have
rose, and let 3000 French prisoners out of York-castle – but it meets
with very little credit, I do not believe they have any thing like the
number of French in those parts, as I am informed the prisoners are
sent more to the western inland counties, – but every hour has its

fresh cargo of lies. The camp in St. James's Park is daily increasing – that and Hyde Park will be continued all summer. – The King is much among them, walking the lines, and examining the posts – He looks exceeding grave. Crowns, alas! have more thorns than roses.

You see things, my dear Sir, with the faithful eye which looks through nature up to nature's God – the sacred page is your support – the word of God your shield and armour – well may you be able so sweetly to deduce good out of evil – the Lord ordereth your goings – and gives the blessing of increase to all your wishes. For your kind anxiety about me and family, we bless and thank you. – I own, at first I felt uneasy sensations – but a little reflection brought me to myself. – Put thy trust in God, quoth I. – Mrs. Sancho, whose virtues outnumber my vices (and I have enough for any one mortal) feared for me and for her children more than for herself. – She prayed too, I dare say – and her prayers were heard.

America seems to be quite lost or forgot amongst us; – the fleet is but a secondary affair – Pray God send us some good news, to chear our drooping apprehensions, and to enable me to send your pleasanter accounts; – for, trust me, my worthy friend, grief, sorrow, devastation, blood, and slaughter, are totally foreign to the taste and affection of

Your faithful friend
and obliged servant,
I. SANCHO.

Our joint best wishes to Mrs. Spink, self and family.

1. The royal brothers: King George III's brothers, William Henry, Duke of Gloucester (1743–1805) and Henry Frederick, Duke of Cumberland (1745–90) both married women whom the King considered unsuitable. This led to a rift between the King and his brothers.

138

TO J'[OHN]' S'[PINK]', ESQ.

June 15, 1780.

DEAR SIR,

I am exceeding happy to inform you, that at twelve this noon Lord Lincoln arrived express from Sir Henry Clinton,[1] with the pleasing news, that, on the 12th of April, Charles Town with its dependencies capitulated to his Majesty's arms, with the loss of only 200 men on our side – By which fortunate event, five ships of war, besides many frigates, and one thousand seamen, were captured; and seven thousand military which composed the garrison. – You will have pleasure, I am sure, in finding so little blood shed – and in the hope of its accelerating the so much wished for peace. Inclosed is a list of the prisoners, which is from Lord Lincoln's account – at least I am confidently told so – And, more than that, it is said the late terrible riot was on a plan concerted between the French and Americans – upon which their whole hope of success was founded – They expected universal bankruptcy would be the consequence, with despair and every sad concomitant in its train. – By God's goodness, we have escaped – May we deserve so great mercy,

Prays sincerely yours,
I. SANCHO.

The Gazette will not be out in time, but you shall have one to-morrow without fail. – As soon as this news was announced, the Tower and Park guns confirmed it – the guards encamped in the Parks fired each a grand *feu de joye* – To-night we blaze in illuminations, and to-morrow get up as poor and discontented as ever. – I wish, dear Sir, very much to hear Mrs. *Spink* is quite recovered – It would indicate more than a common want of feeling, were not my wife and self anxious for the health and repose of such very rare friends. – Indulge us, do, dear Sir, with a single line, that we may joy in your joy upon her amendment, or join our wishes with yours to the God of mercy and love for her speedy recovery. – I inclose you an evening paper – there is not much in it. – Upon consideration, I have my doubts concerning the French and Americans being so deep in the plan of our late riots: – there requires, I think, a kind of supernatural knowledge to adjust their motions so critically – But you can judge far better than my weak intellects; – therefore I will not pretend to affirm any thing for truth, except my sincere desire to approve myself most gratefully

Your obliged servant,
IGN. SANCHO.

1. 'Sir Henry Clinton ... Charles Town': Sir Henry Clinton

(1730–95) was commander-in-chief of the British Army in
North America, succeeding General Howe (see Letter 55,
n. 7). The fall of Charleston fuelled new hope that the long
American struggle would result in a British victory. That
hope is registered by Sancho who views the fall of 'Charles
Town' as decisive, 'accelerating the so much wished for
peace', and, in Letter 139, 'the fate of America will soon be
decided'. In February Clinton landed with 12,000 men,
attacked Charleston, and, following a long, prudent siege,
captured the town and 5500 patriots on 12 May 1780. In
Letter 144 Sancho reports news of the consolidation of
Clinton's victories in the South. Though Clinton was an able
tactician and strategist, he lacked confidence to be a successful commander in the American war; he resigned his commission in 1782 and returned to England.

139

TO J'[OHN]' S'[PINK]', ESQ.

June 16, 1780.

DEAR SIR,

As a supplement to my last, this is to tell you a piece of private news
– which gives ministry high hopes in the future. General Washington, who was anxiously watching Sir H. Clinton, no sooner saw
with certainty his intention, but he struck his camp, and made the
most rapid march to New York – They expected it; – but as he was
in superior force they felt their danger. – Sir H. Clinton, as soon as
he could possibly settle the garrison of Charles Town, embarked
with seven thousand men, and got to New York in time to save it;
– and if he can possibly bring Washington to a battle, it is thought
the fate of America[1] will be soon decided. – Thank God! the sky
clears in that quarter; – but we look rather lowering at home –
Ministry wish now too plainly to disarm the subjects. – Last year,[2]
under dread of a French invasion, the good people were thanked for
their military fervor – Master tradesmen armed their journeymen
and apprentices – and the serjeants of the guards absolutely made
little fortunes in teaching grown gentlemen of all descriptions their
exercise. – In fancied uniforms, and shining arms, they marched to
the right, wheeled to the left, and looked battle-proof; – but now it
seems they are not only useless, but offensive. – How the affair will
end, God only knows! – I do not like its complexion – Government

has ordered them to give up their arms: – if they do, where is British liberty? if they refuse, what is administration? Many are gentlemen of large property – Inns of Court Members, Lawyers, &c. – dangerous people. – Time will unveil the whole. – May its lenient powers pour the balm of healing councils on this once glorious spot! – and make it as heretofore the nurse of freedom – Europe's fairest example – the land of truth, bravery, loyalty, and of every heart-gladdening virtue! That you and Mrs. *Spink* may, surrounded with friends, and, in the enjoyment of every good, live to see the completion of my wishes – is the concluding prayer of,

Dear Sir,
Yours ever, &c.
I. SANCHO.

1. The fate of America: for details see Letter 138, n. 1.
2. 'Last year … God knows!': Sancho's description, 'in fancied uniforms, and shining arms, they marched to the right, wheeled to the left, and looked battleproof' is reminiscent in tone of his comical proposal for a company of hairdressers published in *The General Advertiser*. See Letter 132, n. 2.

140

TO J'[OHN]' S'[PINK]', ESQ.

June 19, 1780.

DEAR SIR,

I am sorry to hear by brother *Osborne* that Mrs. *Spink* yet continues but poorly – May she be soon perfectly well – and health attend you both! We remain pretty quiet – the military are so judiciously placed, that in fact the whole town (in despite of its magnitude) is fairly overawed and commanded by them. – His *Majesty* went this day to the House, and gave them the very best speech, in my opinion, of his whole life: I have the pleasure to inclose it. If I err in judgment, I know you more the true candid friend, than the severe critic, and that you will smile at the mistake of the head, and do justice to the heart, of

Your ever obliged,
I. SANCHO.

There is a report that the Quebec Fleet, escorted by two frigates, are entirely captured by a French squadron. I hope this will prove premature.

141

Charles Street, Westm. June 23, 1780.
MY DEAR FRIEND,

How do you do? is the blessing of health upon you? do you eat moderately, drink temperately, and laugh heartily, sleep soundly, converse carefully with one eye to pleasure, the other fixed upon improvement? The above is the hope and wish of thy friend, friend to thy house, and respector of its character. – You, happy young man, by as happy a coincidence of fortune, are like to be the head of the W*ingrave* family – May riches visit you, coupled with honour and honesty! – and then sweet peace of mind shall yield you a dignity which kings have not power to confer: – then will you experience that the self-ennobled are the only true noble: – then will you truly feel those beautiful lines of Pope's,

> One self-approving hour whole years outweighs
> Of idle starers, or of loud huzzas;
> What can ennoble sots, or slaves or cowards?
> Alas! not all the blood of all the Howards.[1]

Your father, I trust, will send you some public prints, in which you will see the blessed temper of the times – We are (but do not be frightened) all, at least two-thirds of us, run mad – through too much religion; – Our religion has swallowed up our charity – and the fell dæmon Persecution is become the sacred idol of the once free, enlightened, generous Britons. – You will read with wonder and horror the sad, sad history of eight such days as I wish from my soul could be annihilated out of Time's records for ever.

That poor wretched young man[2] I once warned you of is, I find (from under his own hand), now resident at Calcutta – 'Tis not in the power of friendship to serve a man who will in no one instance care for himself – so I wish you not to know him – but whatever particulars you can collaterally glean of him, I shall esteem it a favor if you would transmit them to

Your sincere friend,
IGNATIUS SANCHO.

Mrs. Sancho joins me cordially in every wish for your good.

1. Sancho quotes from two sections of Pope's *An Essay on Man, Epistle IV.* 'One self-approving hour ... loud huzzas;' lines 255–6; 'What can enoble sots ... all the Howards', lines 215–16.
2. 'That poor wretched young man': Julius Soubise. See Letter 1, n. 6 and Appendix I, n. 3.

142

TO J'[OHN]' S'[PINK]', ESQ.

June 27, 1780.

DEAR SIR,

There is news this day arrived, which, I believe, may be depended upon – that Rodney[1] brought the French admiral to a second engagement about the 26th of May; it unluckily fell calm, or the affair would have been decisive. – The van of Rodney, however, got up to Mons. Guichen's fleet's rear, and gave it a hearty welcome. – Rodney still keeps the seas, and prevents the French fleet getting into Martinique. – The account says, the enemy had the advantage of six ships of the line more than Rodney – and a report runs current, that Walsingham[2] has fallen-in with the Dominica fleet, consisting of thirty merchantmen and two frigates, and taken most of them – but this wants confirmation. – Dear Sir, I hope Mr. *Spink* is better than mending – quite well – to whom our most sincere respects. – Your order, good Sir, is completed, and, please God, will be delivered to tomorrow's waggon.

Excuse my scrawling hand – in truth my eyes fail me. I feel myself since last winter an old man all at once – the failure of eyes – the loss of teeth – the thickness of hearing – are all messengers sent in mercy and love, to turn our thoughts to the important journey which kings and great men seldom think about; – it is for such as you to meditate on time and eternity with true pleasure; – looking back, you have very much to comfort you; – looking forward, you have all to hope. – As I have reason to respect you in this life, may I and mine be humble witnesses in the next of the exceeding weight of bliss and glory poured out without measure upon thee and thine!

I. SANCHO.

1. Sir Rodney: George Brydges Rodney (1719–92). In October 1779 Rodney was appointed commander-in-chief of the Leeward Islands. On 16 January 1780, on his way to take up his command, Rodney captured a Spanish fleet and effected the relief of Gibraltar (see Letter 105, n. 7). Sancho's versions of events in the West Indies once again demonstrates his patriotic zeal and optimism concerning Britain's achievements in the theatre of war. The British and French fleets were balanced in number and though Britain had a fair opportunity of winning, results were inconclusive because of poor communications, Walsingham's late arrival with additional ships and inadequate signalling during battle (for Walsingham, see n. 2 below). Two encounters took place off Martinique: the first occurred in mid-April, when inconclusive results lead to recriminations which enraged Rodney; following the 'second engagement' between 10–21 May, Rodney maintained that an additional five ships would have given him a decisive victory.

2. Walsingham: Commodore Walsingham commanded four of the twelve ships committed to the West Indies, and was given orders in March to sail to Jamaica in case Guichen attacked there, while Rodney took five ships to meet the French at Martinique (see n. 1 above). Three of Walsingham's ships were later ordered to join Rodney, but Walsingham was wind-bound at Torbay as late as 17 April; the delay meant Walsingham did not reach Rodney until after the second encounter with the French.

143

TO MR. O'[SBORNE]'.

July 1, 1780.

DEAR BROTHER,

Shall I rejoice or condole with you upon this new acquaintance you have made? How the devil it found you out I cannot imagine – I suppose the father of mischief sent it to some richer neighbour at a greater house; but as Johnny *Osborne* was a character better known, and much more esteemed, the gout thought he might as well just take a peep at Farnham – liked the place, and the man of the place – and so, nestling into your shoe, quite forgot his real errand; – They guardian angel watched the whole procedure – Quoth he, 'I cannot wholly avert evils, but I can turn them into blessings – this transitory pain shall not only refine his blood, and cleanse him from other disorders – it shall also lengthen his life, and purify his heart, – the hour of affliction is the feed-time of reflection – the good shall greatly overbalance the evil.' – As I am unfortunately an adept in the gout, I ought to send you a cart-load of cautions and advice, talk nonsense about tight shoes, &c. with a farrago of stuff more teazing than the pain; – but I hear the ladies visit you – and, what's better, friendship in the shape of Messieurs *Spink* and *Brown* were seen to enter the palace of F——. I supped last night with Dr. *Rush*, where your health was drunk, and your gout pretty freely canvassed.

God orders all for the best.

Yours, &c.
I. SANCHO.

144

TO J'[OHN]' S'[PINK]', ESQ.

July 15, 1780.

DEAR SIR,

I received yours this morning from the hands of a gentleman, who would not stay to be thanked for the invaluable letter he brought me. – You truly say, that cold lowness of spirits engender melancholy thoughts – For my part, I should be a most ungrateful being to repine, for I have known good health, and even now, though not well, am far from being ill, and have the friendship of Mr. *Spink*, and one or two more who do honour to human nature. – But the purpose of this scrawl is to confirm to you a piece of good news this day arrived – which is, that both the Carolinas, and best part of Virginia, are all come into their allegiance.[1] The back settlers have rose, and mustered the reluctant. Thus the three richest and strongest provinces are now in the King's peace – for which God make us thankful.

Adieu, dear Sir. Mrs. Sancho (whose eyes kindle with pleasure while she speaks) begs to be joined with me in the most respectful manner to Mrs. *Spink* and yourself – hope Mrs. *Spink* is quite as well as you can wish her.

I am ever yours,
Dear Sir, to command,
I. SANCHO.

1. See Letter 138, n. 1.

145

TO J'[OHN]' S'[PINK]', ESQ.
Charles Street, August 18, 1780.

MY DEAR AND HON. SIR,

My long silence was the effect of a dearth of news – I could have wrote its true, but you would have ill relished a mass of thanks upon favours received – Minds like yours diffuse blessings around; and, like parent heaven, rest satisfied with the heart – Your goodness, dear Sir, is registered there – and death will not expunge it – No; it will travel to the throne of grace, and the Almighty will not wrong you. – I am just risen from table with my friend *Rush*, and we have toasted you most cordially in conjunction with the amiable partner of your heart, whom I hope in some happy time to see – I may say, hunger and thirst to see – its the wish of my heart – Providence has indulged me with many, and I will hope for the completion of this. – But to the point: – a gentleman in administration[1] (with whom I am upon good terms) about an hour since called upon me, to give me some fresh news just arrived from Admiral Geary's fleet – an engagement between a new French frigate, pierced for 44 guns, mounting 32, called the Nymphe, and the Flora English frigate, Captain Peer Williams*, of 36 guns. The Flora was peeping into Brest harbour, when the Nymphe was coming out full of men – they were both in the right mind for engagement – to it they went – The Frenchman began the affair at two cables length distance – Williams reserved his fire till they were within half-cable's length – It lasted, with the obstinacy of two enraged lions, for above two hours – A French cutter came up to teaze, but was sent off soon with a belly-full: – At last the French captain, at the head of his men, attempted boarding – when our English hero met him, ran him through the body – drove back his men – put them under hatches – struck the colours when she was on fire in four different places. – This affair happened the 10th ult. and he has gallantly brought his prize into Plymouth. – This is the greatest affair, take the number of guns, men, &c. altogether, that has happened this war. I am sorry to remark, that if the French fleets in general behave so well, it will be a service of danger to meddle with them.

---

*   Capt. Peer Williams is first cousin to Lady N——; and he will not fare the worse for that.

When Capt. Williams had conquered the crew, they found sixty dead upon deck; – the two ships exhibited a scene more like a slaughter-house than any thing imaginable – These, oh Christians! are the features of war – and thus Most Christian K*ings* and Defenders of Faith shew their zeal and love for the dying commands of their Divine Master. – Oh! friend, may every felicity be thine, and those beloved by thee! may the heart-felt sigh arise only at the tale of foreign woes! – May the sacred tear of pity bedew the cheek for misfortunes only such as humanity may soften! – Mrs. Sancho joins me in sincere and grateful respects to Mrs. *Spink* and self.

Yours truly,
I. SANCHO.

Sancho begs his respects to Mr. and Mrs. C——; love to Sir J*ohn* O*sborne*, and all who enquire after Blackamoors.

1. 'A gentleman in administration ... Peers Williams': I have been unable to trace a reference to Peers Williams or the *Flora* being active in the Channel or any other arena of war around the time of Sancho's letter; perhaps the 'gentleman in administration' was passing on gossip or trying to improve Britain's image in the wars with France and America.

146

TO MRS. C'[OCKSEDGE]'.

Charles Street, Sept. 7, 1780.

My greatly esteemed and honoured friend, if my pen doth justice in any sort to my feelings, this letter will not be a complimentary one – I look upon such letters as I do upon the ladies' winter nosegays, a choice display of vivid colouring, but no sweetness. – My friend Mr. R*ush* says, I stand condemned in the opinions of two ladies for an omittance in writing: believe me, my sorrow for incurring the censure is much more real than the crime; for when the heart is overcharged with worldly care, the mind bending also to the pressure of afflictive visitations – add to that the snow-tipt hairs announcing fifty odd – the fire of fancy is quite extinguished. – Alas! alas! such being the true state of the case, I dare abide by the

jury of your noble and equitable hearts, to be brought in not guilty.
– The shew of hands[1] was greatly in favour of Mr. Charles Fox and
Sir George Rodney; they will carry it all to nothing, is the opinion
of the knowing. – Lord *Lincoln* met with a coarse reception, at
which he was a little displeased. – Mr. B——g spoke like the pupil
of eloquence; – but the glorious Fox was the father and school of
oratory himself – the Friend! the Patron! the Example! – There now.
– I attended the hustings from ten to half past two – gave my free
vote to the Honorable Charles James Fox and to Sir George
Rodney; hobbled home full of pain and hunger – What followed
after you shall know in my next; at present I have only to declare
myself

> Yours and Miss *Crew*'s
> most obedient, faithful,
> humble servant,
> IGN. SANCHO.

1. 'The shew of hands ... I attended the hustings': the four-
   teenth Parliament, elected in 1774, was suddenly dissolved
   on 1 September 1780, more than a year short of its seven-
   year term. The election, 'I attended the hustings from ten to
   half past two', opened with a public meeting at which
   Charles James Fox, George Brydges Rodney and Lord
   Lincoln were nominated (for Fox, see Letter 149, n. 2; for
   Rodney, 142, n. 1). Fox's half-hour opening speech attacked
   Lincoln, perhaps prompting Sancho to remember Lord
   Lincoln's displeasure at his 'course reception'. One observer
   recalled, 'Charles Fox keeps us all alive here, with letters and
   paragraphs and a thousand clever things. I saw him today
   upon the hustings, bowing and sweltering and scratching his
   black ass.' Sheridan put the thought in other language: Fox
   'canvasses with great industry and treats his good Friends
   with a Speech every day besides' (*Letters of Richard Brinsley
   Sheridan*, (ed.) Cecil Price, Oxford, 1966, vol. I, pp. 135–6).
   Sancho's description is closer to that of Sheridan: 'Fox ...
   the father and school of oratory himself – the Friend! the
   Patron! the Example!' The high bailiff interpreted the result
   in favour of Rodney and Lincoln, but Fox's friends insisted
   that he had a majority of votes; after some altercation the
   poll was formally opened with all three listed. At the end of
   the first day the poll books show that Sancho supported the
   favourite candidates: Fox 296, Rodney 243 and Lincoln 160.
   In Letter 147 Sancho claims he received personal thanks for
   his vote from one of the candidates. Though Rodney was

absent in the West Indies (see letter 142, n. 1), he stood as administration candidate in Westminster and topped the poll.

147

TO J'[OHN]' S'[PINK]', ESQ.

Sept. 9, 1780.

DEAR SIR,

We are all election-bewitched[1] here – I hope Sir *Charles Bunbury* meets with no opposition – he is so worthy a character, that, should he be ill supported, it would impeach the good sense and honesty of his constituents. – Mrs. *Spink* and yourself, I pray God, may both enjoy health and every good. – I here inclose you this evening's paper, by which you will see how the Fox is like to lead Ad*ministratio*n. He and Sir George Rodney had my hearty vote, and I had the honour of his thanks personally. – And in writing also, I have to thank you for a thousand kind things, which I wish from my soul I could any way ever deserve. – May health and every blessing bestrew your paths, and those of all you love! – is the prayer and wish of

Your much obliged
humble servant,
I. SANCHO.

1. At the general election of 1761 Charles Bunbury became MP for Suffolk unopposed, though still a month under age. In the elections of 1774 and 1780 he was also returned unopposed, as Sancho hoped he would be. Bunbury retired in 1812, after representing the county for forty-five years.

148

TO MISS C'[REWE]'.

Saturday, Sept. 9. 1780.

DEAR MISS,

I have the honor to address you upon a very interesting, serious, critical subject. – Do not be alarmed! it is an affair which I have had at heart some days past – it has employed my meditations more than my prayers. – Now I protest I feel myself in the most aukward of situations – but it must out – and so let it. – But how does my good, my half-adored Mrs. *Cocksedge*? and how does Miss A——?[1] and when did you see my worthy Mrs. *Rush*? Are they all well, and happy as friendship could wish them? How is the Doctor and Beau S——,[2] all well? – Well, thank God – and you your dear self are well? Honey, and was not Lord N—— an Irish title? true, but the chield is Scotch born. – Pray give my best affections to Mrs. *Cocksedge*, and acquaint her with the state of the poll for the antient city and liberty of Westminster which I inclose. – I would not wish you to mention what I so boldly advanced in the beginning of this letter – No; let it die away like a miser's hope.

> Your most obedient,
> most humble servant,
> I remain, dear Miss *Crewe*,
> I. SANCHO.

The remainder in our next.

1. Miss A——: probably Sarah Adamson. See Letter 70, n. 2.
2. 'The Doctor and beau S——': Dr Norford and John Spink.

149

TO J'[OHN]' S'[PINK]', ESQ.

Sept. 23, 1780.

DEAR SIR,

I received this evening one of the kindest letters that ever friendship dictated – for which I rejoice that the time draws near when I shall have the delight to amend my health – and see the few true good friends – such as my soul delighteth to honour. – I inclose you an evening paper[1] – Thank God! although the people have been a little irritated, every thing appears quiet,[2] and I hope will remain so. – The week after next I hope to see the good Mrs. *Spink* and your worthy self, to whom Mrs. Sancho joins me in best wishes.

> I am, dear Sir,
> Your most obedient
> humble servant,
> I. SANCHO.

The principal business I had to write about had like to have escaped me, which is your kindness in offering your house for head-quarters;[3] which I would embrace, had not brother *Osborne* the right of priority.

1. The victory of Fox and Rodney (see n. 2 below) was re-corded in the newspapers of 23 September 1780. Fox took space in the prominent papers to advertise his thanks to the electorate. Rumours spread in *The London Evening Post*, claiming that Fox had been killed or dangerously wounded in a duel with Lincoln were dismissed as false in the *London Courant*: Fox was in perfect health.

2. 'Thank God ... every thing appears quiet': Sancho's choice of words suggests a lingering sense of apprehension about rowdy street crowds where the Gordon Riots had taken place just four months earlier (for the riots, see Letters 134–7). On 23 September the polls closed and the high bailiff declared Rodney and Fox duly elected: Rodney 5298, Fox 4878, Lincoln 4157. Jubilant voters celebrated in the streets, cheering, shouting, pulling down the hustings, carrying off the timbers and carrying Fox and Admiral Young, proxy for Rodney, through the streets of Westminster, Sancho's own neighbourhood. Fox's political career spanned thirty years; he was clearly identified with the Opposition by 1774, and became the acknowledged leader of the Opposition in the House of Commons. Fox became minister in the House of Commons and the first holder of the office of Secretary of State for Foreign Affairs, following his Westminster victory and the fall of the North administration.

3. Sancho must have been planning to visit friends at Bury and graciously refuses an offer of accommodation there from John Spink. The Sanchos visited Bury within a month of writing this letter; in Letter 151 Sancho writes to thank Spink: 'I never left a place with so much regret as you made me leave Bury with.'

150

TO DOCTOR NORFORD.[1]

Charles Street, Westm. Oct. 13, 1780.

HONORED SIR,

Were I to omit my thanks, poor as they are, for a single post, your honest, and more sensible dog, would be ashamed of me.

'A merciful man is good to his beasts.'[2]

The friendly hand which strokes and rewards his attentions, that same friendly hand has prescribed for my good – and under God has much benefited my health; – the eye of kindness, which animates the poor animal to deeds almost beyond instinct, hath beamed upon me also, and given me the pleasing assurance of new health. – I wish, dear Sir, for just as much credit in the point of gratitude, as you will allow to fall to the share of any poor honest dog. – For so much, and no more, prayeth, dear Sir,

Your most obedient
and grateful servant.
I. SANCHO.

1. Dr Norford: William Norford (1715–93) was a medical writer who began practising as a physician in 1761. He married a surgeon's daughter and eventually moved to Bury St Edmunds. See Letter 22, n. 6.
2. Proverbs 10: 12; the passage reads, 'A righteous man regardeth the life of his beast; but the tender mercies of the wicked are cruel.'

151

TO J'[OHN]' S'[PINK]', ESQ.

Friday, Oct. 13, 1780.

DEAR SIR,

I should esteem myself too happy were I at this moment certain that Mrs. *Spink* were as much better as I find myself; – but when I consider the professional skill, as well as the interest Dr. Norford has in the welfare of you and yours, I sit down satisfied in full hope that Mrs. *Spink* is at this moment better, much better; and as one spirit animates you both, you are better too. May health diffuse itself throughout thy house! and gladden all around it! I am better, my dear Sir. – Tell my good Mrs. *Spink*, I shall live to see her, and to thank her too mostly cordially in my child's name: for my part, your liberality in constant flow has tired me out with thank-ye's. Adieu, dear Sir. – I never left a place with so much regret as you made me leave Bury with[1] ——, nor ever met with the whole family of the Charities but at thy house. – Mrs. Sancho joins me in acknowledgements to self, good Mrs. *Spink*, and Dr. Norford.

We are, dear Sir,
Yours gratefully,
A. I. SANCHO.

1. See Letter 149, n. 3.

152

TO MR. S'[TEVENSON]'.
Friday, Oct. 18, 1780.

Pooh, no, thou simpleton! I tell thee I got no cold, neither is my breath one jot the worse. – I wish I knew that you suffered as little from break of rest, and raw air. – I am glad I have left you, for your sake as well as my own, my dear Stee.[1] – The corks flew out of thy bottles in such rapid succession, that prudence and pity held a council upon it. – Generosity stepped in, followed by a pert coxcomb, whom they called Spirit – and God knows how the affair is to end. – I intend to write a line to the worthies of your town, the good Mr. *Spink* and Dr. Norford. Oh, Stee! had I thy abilities, I would say what should credit my feelings, though it fell far short of the merits of such friends to mankind – and

Your IGN. SANCHO, in particular.

Love and respects to thy generous scholars[2] – the Greens – the Browns, &c. &c. to reverends Mess. Prettyman, and the other gentleman with pretty wife, whose name is deserted from the silly pate of thy true friend Sancho. – I have not seen Mr. J—— H——, but they are all well, as Mr. Anthony has just announced.

Say handsomely to the Greens – and much as you please to the Prettymans.

1. 'I am glad I have left you ... Stee': Mr Stevenson would have been among those friends Sancho visited at Bury.
2. 'Thy generous scholars': the names listed do not occur elsewhere in the letters, so perhaps they are new acquaintances among the spirited company at Bury where 'corks flew out of thy bottles in such rapid succession'.

153

October 25, 1780.

MY DEAR BOY,

This is to thank you kindly for the affectionate mark of your remembrance of your old friend. – After a long tedious voyage, you happily reached the haven of your repose[1] – found your friends well – and rejoiced their hearts by presenting, not a prodigal, but a duteous, worthy, and obedient child; – Theirs be the joy – but yours will be the gain – As sure as light follows the rising of the sun, and darkness the setting of it, so sure is goodness even in this life its own reward. – Of course you are in the militia – that will do you no harm; – spirit and true courage in defence of our country is naturally and nobly employed. – We are in the upper world playing the old foolish game, in the same foolish way, and with the same foolish set that trod the ministerial boards when you left us. Your friend D—— tries expedients, and gets nothing – he is very deep in my debt; but as he has nothing, I can expect nothing – for I never will consent to do that to others, I would not they should do unto me. – N—— does better, and grows proud – I wish him joy. – My dear youth, be proud of nothing but an honest heart – Let the sacred oracles be your morn and evening counsellors – so shall you truly enjoy life, and smile at the approach of death. – I have been exceedingly ill since you left us; – but thank God! I have got a fair fit of the gout, which will, I hope, cleanse me from my whole budget of complaints. – I shall live, I hope, till your good present arrives – and then I shall live indeed. – Send the girls some cherry nuts,[2] if easy to be procured. – Mrs. *Sancho* joins me in love, good will, and good wishes for thy peace, health, and prosperity.

Adieu. Yours affectionately,

I. SANCHO.

1. See the Introduction, n. 12, Letter 22 and Letter 90 and especially Letter 102, n. 2.
2. Cherry nuts: probably sweets or some other treat appreciated by children, though I have been unable to identify exactly what Sancho wants Mr Lincoln to send to the girls.

154

DEAR SIR,

I trust, in God's good providence, this will find Mrs. S*pink* in perfect health! and you so well, that it shall remain a doubt which is heartiest. – I am in the way of being well – the gout in both feet and legs – I go upon all fours – The conflict has been sharp, I hope the end is near – I never remember them to have swelled so much – I believe my preserver, Dr. Norford, would allow it to be a decent fit; – My grateful respects attend him: the issue is deferred till the gout subsides, and I find my breath somewhat better; but I can find no position easy. – I inclose you the topic of the day. – Mrs. Sancho joins me in every wish for the felicity of our much-loved friends, yourself, and better self.

IGN. SANCHO.

155

DEAR SISTER,

I pray thee accept the inclosed as a mite of thanks and gratitude for the tender care and true friendly obligingness, which a wife could only equal, and which I never expected to find from home.– I feel and acknowledge your kindness – *that*, and the *uncommon* goodness of some of the best of human nature, shall be cherished in my heart while it continues to beat. – Every body tells me I am better – and what every one says must be true; – for my part, I feel a very slow amendment; my cough is pretty stubborn; my breath very little better; body weak as water – add to this, a smart gout in both legs and feet. – Your sister joins me in love and repeated thanks for all favors shown to her poor, worn-out, old man.

I. SANCHO.

156¹

TO J'[OHN]' S'[PINK]', ESQ.
Charles Street, Nov. 18, 1780.

MY DEAR SIR,

It is a week this blessed day since that I ought, according to every rule of gratitude, love, and zeal, to have thanked my best friends for a plenty of some of the best wine, which came in the best time true kindness could have contrived it. – I should also have congratulated the many anxious hearts upon the happy recovery of yourself, and my thrice good Mrs. *Spink*. I waited from post to post to be enabled to send a tolerable account of myself – The gout has used me like a tyrant – and my asthma, if possible, worse. – I have swelled gradually all over. – What a fight! Dr. Jebb² will not suffer me to make an issue yet, as he would not wish to disturb the gout. – In truth, my best friend, I never truly knew illness till this bout. – Your goodness greatly lessened my anxiety – I find in it the continual flow of more than parental kindness; – as God gave the heart, he must and alone can give the reward! – Our joint best love, and most respectful thanks, attend you both, from

Yours gratefully,
I. A. SANCHO.

1. Misnumbered as 155 in the original text.
2. Dr. Jebb: Sir Richard Jebb (1729–87) was physician to Westminster Hospital from 1754–62 after which he was elected physician to St George's Hospital; he eventually resigned from hospital appointments and went into private practice. Jebb became a favourite of George III; by 1780 he was physician to the Prince of Wales and eventually to the King. His substantial private practice earned him fees of approximately 20,000 guineas between 1779–81, the period during which Jebb attended Sancho. Jebb's portrait by Zoffany hangs in the reading room of the College of Physicians of London. Jebb seems to have been a man whom Sancho would have taken to his heart, had he lived longer; Jebb's DNB entry tells us that he 'was fond of conviviality and music'.

157[1]

TO J'[OHN]' S'[PINK]', ESQ.
Charles Street, Nov. 27, 1780.

My friend, patron, preserver! were the mind alone sick, God never created, since the blessed Apostles' days a better physician than thyself – either singly, or in happy *partnership* with the best of women – Not only so, but your blessed zeal, like the Samaritan's, forgetful of self-wants, poureth the wine and oil, and bindeth up the wounds of worldly sickness – then leaving with reluctance the happy object of thy care to the mercy of an interested host – with money in hand you cry – 'Call help, spare no expense, and when I return, I will repay you.' Indulge me, my noble friend, I have seen the priest, and the Levite, *after many years' knowledge*, snatch a hasty look, then with averted face pursue their different routes: and yet these good folks pray, turn up their eyes to that Heaven they daily insult, and take more pains to preserve the appearances of virtue, than would suffice to make them good in earnest – You see, my good Sir, by the galloping of my pen, that I am much mended. – I have been intolerably plagued with a bilious colic, which, after three days excruciating torments, gave way to mutton-fat-broth clysters. – I am now (bating the swelling of my legs and ancles) much mended – air and exercise is all I want – but the fogs and damps are woefully against me. – Mrs. Sancho, who reads, weeps, and wonders, as the various passions impel, says, she is sure the merits of your house would save B——, were the rest of the inhabitants ever so bad. – She joins me in every grateful thought – In good truth, I have not language to express my feelings. Dr. *Rush* hurries me. Blessed couple, adieu!

Yours,

I. SANCHO.

---

1. Misnumbered 156 in the original text.

158[1]

TO J'[OHN]' S'[PINK]', ESQ.
Charles Street, Dec. 1, 1780.

Why joy in the extreme should end painfully, I cannot find out –
but that it does so, I will ever seriously maintain. When I read they
effussions of goodness, my head turned; – but when I came to
consider the extensive and expensive weight and scope of the
contents, my reason reeled, and idiotism took possession of me –
till the friendly tears, washing the mists of doubt, presented you to
me as beings of a purer, happier order – which God in his mercy
perhaps suffers to be scattered here and there – thinly – that the
lucky few who know them may, at the same time, know what man
in his original state was intended to be. – I gave your generous
request a fair hearing[2] – the two first proposed places would kill me,
except (and that is impossible) Mrs. Sancho was with me.

Inclination strongly points to the land of friendship – where
goodness ever blossoms – and where Norford heals.[3] At present
I take nothing, but am trying for a few days what honest nature
unperplexed by art will do for me. – I am pretty much swelled still,
but I take short airings in the near stages, such as Greenwich,
Clapham, Newington &c. &c. Walking kills me. – The mind – the
mind, my ever dear and honored friends – the mind requires her
lullaby; – she must have rest ere the body can be in a state of
comfort, – she must enjoy peace, and that must be found in still
repose of family and home. – Mrs. Sancho, who speaks by her tears,
says what I will not pretend to decypher; – I believe she most
fervently recommends you to that Being who best knows you – for
he gave you your talents. – My most grateful and affectionate
respects, joined with Mrs. Sancho's, attend the good Mrs. *Spink*,
thyself and all thy connexions. I cannot say how much we are
obliged to you; but certainly we were never so much nor so
undeservingly obliged to any before. God keep you in all your
doings – prays thine –

SANCHO.

1. Misnumbered 157 in the original text.
2. Sancho would seem to be responding to suggestions from
   Spink that Sancho should take another holiday, probably for
   the benefit of his failing health.
3. 'The land of friendship ... where Norford heals': Bury. See
   Letter 149, n. 3 for Sancho's recent visit.

159[1]

TO J'[OHN]' S'[PINK]', ESQ.

Dec. 7, 1780.

DEAR SIR,

I am doubly and trebly happy that I can in some measure remove the anxiety of the best couple in the universe. I set aside all thanks – for were I to enter into the feelings of my heart for the past and present, I should fill the sheet: but you would not be pleased. – In good truth, I have been exceeding ill – my breath grew worse – and the dropsy made large strides. – I left off medicine by consent for four or five days – swelled immoderately – the good Dr. Norford eighty miles distant – and Dr. Jebb heartily puzzled through the darkness of his patients – I began to feel alarm – when, looking into your letter, I found a Dr. S——th recommended by yourself. I enquired – his character is great – but for lungs and dropsy, Sir John E——t,[2] physician extraordinary and ordinary to his majesty, is reckoned the first. I applied to him on Sunday morning – he received me like Dr. Norford; – I have faith in him. – My poor belly is so distended, that I write with pain – I hope next week to write with more ease. My dutiful respects await Mrs. *Spink* and self, to which Mrs. Sancho begs to be joined by her loving husband, and

Your most grateful friend,
SANCHO.

*   Mr. Sancho died December 14.[3]

1. Misnumbered 158 in the original text.
2. Sir John E—— t: Sir John Elliot, MD (1736–86) was created a baronet 25 July 1778 and became physician to the Prince of Wales.
3. Sancho died after a long illness aggravated by gout and corpulence: 'In December 1780, a series of complicated disorders destroyed him' (see above, p. 24). He was buried at Westminster Broadway; see the Introduction, n. 5.

Appendices

I
Dating the Letters

The whereabouts of the manuscripts of most of Sancho's letters are not known, though fourteen are in the possession of Professor J. R. Willis of Princeton,[1] along with five written by Sancho's daughter Elizabeth, and a list identifying the names of Sancho's correspondents originally given in the text only as initial letters. Even without the manuscripts, however, errors either by the first editor, Miss Crewe,[2] or by the printer, can be identified by internal evidence. The most obvious example of wrong dating is that of the famous Letter 36 to Sterne, dated July 1776 by Crewe. Sterne's reply was written on 27 July 1766, so Crewe's date for Sancho's letter is exactly ten years out. Then Sancho's Letter 127 is given the date 5 January 1786, six years after his death, which looks like a printer's error and should clearly be dated 1780. Less obviously incorrect is Letter 1 to Mr Jack Wingrave in Madras, dated by Miss Crewe 14 February 1768. We know from Letter 68 that Wingrave went to India around 1775–6; furthermore, Letter 1 refers Wingrave to 'a little blacky … his name is S.' who has gone to settle at 'Madras or Bengal, to teach fencing or riding'. This was Julius Soubise,[3] who is said to have sailed in disgrace from Portsmouth for Madras on 15 July 1777, as we know from other sources, including Sancho's Letter 80 to Soubise, 'your noble, friendly benefactress, the good Duchess of Q[ueensberr]y … entered into bliss, July 17, 1777, just two days after you sailed from Portsmouth'. Further, the letter is addressed from Charles Street, into which house Sancho moved in 1773, which makes the letter at least later than this date. Thus, Letter 1 should be dated 1778, not 1768. Letter 2, dated 7 August 1768, also makes reference to Sancho's residence in Charles Street, so it must have been written later than 1773.

Yet another problem with Letter 1 is raised by Folarin Shyllon.[4] He quotes Miss Crewe's claim in her editorial note to the first edition that Sancho wrote his letters with no intention to publish, that all the letters were taken from originals, and that 'not a single letter is here printed from any duplicate preserved by himself'. Shyllon writes in a footnote to this, 'knowing that Soubise died in India, we are forced to ask the question: How did she obtain the original of the letter Sancho wrote to Soubise? Possibly, after Soubise's death in India, his personal effects were returned to England. Or, less plausibly Miss Crewe wrote to India, asking for Sancho's letters to Soubise.' Shyllon is clearly unhappy with both of his proposed explanations. The first suggestion, that Soubise's effects were returned to England after his death, would be unlikely to have provided Miss Crewe with the manuscript in time for the 1782 edition of the Letters, since Soubise went to India in 1777 and spent some years establishing his riding academy before his death. Henry Angelo records that Soubise 'obtained numerous pupils, and accepted an appointment, with a large salary, to break in horses for the government. Having departed from his former thoughtless habits, his talents and address had placed him in the way to fortune, when lucklessly engaging to subdue a fine Arabian ... he was thrown, and, pitching on his head, was killed on the spot.'[5] There was hardly time for all this to take place and subsequently for Soubise's papers to be rescued from oblivion in India by someone acting on Miss Crewe's behalf.

The most plausible explanation perhaps is that Miss Crewe's claim is as unreliable as some of her dating, or, more generously interpreted, that she is offering on Sancho's behalf a polite disclaimer of literary ambition typical of many an author of the day, supplied by herself now that he was unable to speak on his own behalf with such conventional modesty. Despite Miss Crewe's wish to preserve his reputation from any suggestion of vulgar literary aspirations, Sancho, like his friend Sterne, would probably have kept copies with a view to publication. The remark of George Cumberland about his meeting with Sancho quoted above, that 'nothing less than publishing will satisfy him', which is, in context, ambiguous, might well be taken as an expression of Sancho's own hopes. Certainly his reply to the request of Edmund Rack to publish some letters in his own collection, (Letter 83), displays only conventional modesty about his own literary claims and Sancho is clearly pleased with the idea of publication.

Patent errors of dating are to be found right through to the latter part of the collection. In Letter 77 of 15 October 1778, 'Kitty is no better'. Kitty is persistently ill throughout the letters, but Letter 77 also makes a jocular reference to Stevenson's exotic delicacy, 'Goose stuffed with grapes'. The same dish is being eaten by Stevenson in Letter 113 (14 November 1779) when 'Kitty is very poorly', yet Kitty's death is recorded in Letter 87 on 9 March 1789. Letter 113 should probably be dated closer to Letter 77.

Yet another problem of dating occurs with Letter 8 dated 1770 by Miss Crewe. In the letter Sancho refers to his 'six brats and a wife'. We can follow the birth of Sancho's children through the letters. In October 1769, Letter 6, he refers to his 'three girls', and by August 1770, Letter 10, Mrs Sancho is 'pretty round' presumably with a fourth daughter, since in November 1773, Letter 16, she has given birth to a 'fifth wench'. In Letter 29, a child is about to be born: 'I care not about its sex – God grant safety and health to the mother.' In Letter 32 to Miss L., dated by Miss Crewe in 1782 as October 1774, but corrected by William Sancho in the 1803 edition to 1775, a 'child' is born, said to be Miss L's godson. This must be William, the only surviving son,[6] since Letter 33 of December 1775 calls him 'the heir of the noble family'. Other letters confirm this, for instance 109, of October 1779, 'the girls – the boy – all well'; also Letter 112 of November 1779, 'Mrs. Sancho, and the girls, and Billy'. In Letter 56 of December 1777, Sancho calls himself with comic exaggeration, 'a poor starving Negroe, with six children' and as we look through the letters we learn their names: the five girls are Fanny, Mary, Betsy (Elizabeth), Lydia and Kitty, and the one surviving boy is William.

To return to Letter 8 dated 1770, with its 'six brats': it must have been written considerably later than Letter 6 of 1769 with 'three girls', and the 1770 date must certainly be a mistake, probably for either 1776 or 1779. A number of other peculiarities of dating will be discussed in the textual notes, for instance the undated Letter 22, and the preceding cluster, 19, 20 and 21, where letters dated July 1775 are followed by a letter dated June; and the 'St Swithin's Day' Letter 64, dated 17 May 1778, which is not only a month out in its prediction of rain based on the 'old saw', but refers to Sancho's receipt of a letter from New York dated 12 June 1778, nearly a month after the letter, according to Miss Crewe, was written.

Notes

1. For details of the article by Professor Willis, see the Introduction, n. 14, p. 19.

2. Miss Crewe: Stevenson's index has Crew. Her editorial note to the edition of 1782 is to be found in Appendix V.

3. There are accounts of Soubise in Paul Edwards and James Walvin (eds) *Black Personalities in the Era of the Slave Trade* (Macmillan, London, 1983) pp. 223–37.

4. Folarin Shyllon, *Black People in Britain, 1555–1833* (Oxford University Press, London, 1977) pp. 191, 202 n. 29.

5. Henry Angelo, *Reminiscences* (London, 1828) vol. I. p. 452. The passage is quoted in Edwards and Walvin, *Black Personalities*, p. 229.

6. See Letter 15, n. 1, Letter 29, n. 3, and Appendix VII for evidence of a son, Jonathan William, who was born and died before the birth of William (Billy).

II

The Portrait by Gainsborough

We do know something about the history of the painting, reproduced as a frontispiece to this volume. Gainsborough painted it
at Bath in November 1768, completing it in one hour and forty
minutes according to a note on the reverse of the canvas.[1] After
Sancho's death it was given by his daughter Elizabeth to his friend
William Stevenson, (see Introduction, n. 14) the addressee of several
letters, the 'dear Stee' of Letter 152, who himself was thanked by
Sancho, with 'the warm ebullitions of African sensibility', for presenting him with a portrait of Sterne, Letter 100. No doubt Elizabeth
remembered with gratitude Sancho's delight at Stevenson's gift,
when she presented her father's portrait to Stevenson, though
Stevenson was also deserving as her benefactor, since she received an
annuity from him, and after his death in 1821 from his son, until her
own death in 1837. Her letter reads:

> Feb 29 1820
>
> Worthy Sir it is with great pleasure I present my Dear fathers
> portrait to so great a friend of his Daughter If Sir you will be so
> Good to Let me know where to Send it Shall go Directly I hear
> from you and if my best Sir will be so Good To Advance me
> half a year of the income he so kindly allows me being about to
> move it will greatly add to my Comfort. I hope your Dear
> Lady is well and that you enjoy your health
>
>
>
> I remain Sir with
> all due respect most
> gratefully yours
> Elizabeth Sancho
>

The portrait was sold with Stevenson's books and curiosities on the
death of his son Henry in 1889, and found its way to the Canadian
National Gallery in Ottawa, its present location.

Another portrait that has been associated with Sancho is that
of the young black in Hogarth's 'Taste in High Life'.[2] Nichols

and Steevens in their early nineteenth-century edition of Hogarth[3] introduced a note of scandal: 'The young female was designed for a celebrated courtezan ... Her familiarity with the black boy alludes to a similar weakness in a noble Duchess, who educated two brats of the same colour. One of them afterwards robbed her, and the other was guilty of some offence equally unpardonable.' After these suggestive comments, the editors stir the dirty waters further by taking pains to indicate that this story had nothing to do with the Duchess of Montagu and Sancho. 'This miniature Othello has been said to be intended for the late Ignatius Sancho, whose talents and virtue were an honour to his colour.' Far more likely is that the story was a spark from the fiery and well-gossiped scandal concerning Sancho's friend Soubise, favourite of the Duchess of Queensberry (see Appendix I) who, according to Lady Mary Coke's journal for March 1767, was discovered in her boudoir 'half-dressed and half undressed ... talking to her black boy ... She told me she had taught him everything he had a mind to learn.' Soubise disgraced himself with one of the Duchess's personal maids and was shipped off to Madras in 1777.[4]

Notes

1. *Notes and Queries*, 7, vii. p. 325, and viii. p. 337; Willis, *Slavery and Abolition*, 1.3. 1980.
2. See R. B. Beckett, *Hogarth* (Routledge, London, 1949) pl. 140 for a reproduction of the painting. An engraving is reproduced in R. Paulson, *Hogarth's Graphic Works* (Yale University Press, New Haven, Conn., 1965) vol. I, p. 25.
3. John Nichols and George Steevens, *The Genuine Works of William Hogarth* (London, 1808).
4. For Soubise, see Letter 1, n. 4, and Appendix I, n. 3–5.

III

Manuscript Entries in Jekyll's Copy

Jekyll's own copy of the fifth edition bearing his bookplate, and apparently a gift from William Sancho, was formerly the property of Christopher Fyfe of the History Department and the Centre of African Studies at Edinburgh University, but owing to his generosity was given to Paul Edwards. It contains three handwritten items, two notes presumably by Jekyll himself, and a letter addressed to him by William Sancho. The details are as follows:

Jekyll's Note on the Flyleaf

This work was originally published in 1782, and a very liberal subscription exhausted the first Edition.

In 1803. This fifth Edition was printed by the Son of Ignatius Sancho.

Previous to the Publication in 1782 Dr. Johnson had promised to write the Life of Ignatius Sancho, which afterwards he neglected to do, and it was accordingly written by Mr. Jekyll in Imitation of Dr. Johnson's Style, but the name of Mr. Jekyll was not published till the present Edition.

The Engraving is by Bartolozzi,[1] and the Vignette in the Title Page from a Drawing by Mr. Bunbury.[2]

William Sancho's Letter

To Joseph Jekyll Esq M.P. From the Publisher As a most
    humble Testimony of
Gratitude for his great Liberality in Affording His Aid in so
    handsome a manner &
rendering the Life Still more interesting by his corrections. -
As a Tribute which by Reason of my Infancy I was unable to
    acknowledge when he

stood forth so very much the Friend of myself & Family. -
In very grateful Remembrance of these & other obligations
I beg leave to subscribe myself,

> Sir Your most Humble Srvt.
> Wm. Sancho.

Note by Jekyll Written on William's Letter

From the Son of Ignatius Sancho, who was many years in the
Library of Sr. Joseph Banks, and afterwards a Bookseller.

Notes

1. Francesco Bartolozzi, 1727–1815, was born in Florence,
   came to England in 1764 and spent the next forty years in
   London, highly respected for his skill as an engraver. He was
   a founder-member of the Royal Academy in 1769.
2. Henry William Bunbury, 1750–1811, produced a series of
   burlesque illustrations for *Tristram Shandy* and, as a friend
   of Garrick, was one of the circle of artists and literary men
   known to the Sancho family. His brother, Sir Charles
   Bunbury, bart., of Mildenhall, Suffolk, employed several of
   Sancho's regular correspondents, and also married Mrs
   Cocksedge, the beautiful widow to whom Sancho wrote
   many letters, and who presented Sancho with her portrait by
   Daniel Gardner, which Sancho hung over his mantlepiece.
   Sancho was a regular enthusiastic visitor to Bunbury House,
   the Bunbury family home. Henry William's wife, the former
   Catherine Horneck, also had her portrait painted by Daniel
   Gardner, see Letter 11, n. 1.

IV

Correspondence between Sancho and Sterne:
Variant Texts

Letter 1 below, from Sancho to his much admired literary friend, Laurence Sterne, was probably the most famous and influential of Sancho's letters because of its subject and style (a sentimental treatment of slavery) and because of the fame of the person to whom it was sent. It differs from the one included in the *Letters* (see Letter 36). Letter 1 is Sterne's copy of Sancho's letter, showing alterations presumably made by Sterne himself; Letter 2 is the text of Sterne's reply to Sancho; Letter 3 is Sterne's 'improved' copy of Letter 2. In each letter, alterations were made with an eye to publishing the correspondence.

1

IGNATIUS SANCHO TO LAURENCE STERNE

Reverend Sir –

It would be an insult (or perhaps look like one), on your Humanity, to apologise for the Liberty of this address – *unknowing* and *unknown*. I am one of those people whom the illiberal and vulgar call a Nee – gur – : the early part of my Life was rather unlucky; as I was placed in a family who judged that Ignorance was the best Security for obedience: a little Reading and writing, I got by unwearied application – the latter part of my life has been more fortunate; having spent it in the honourable service of one of the best families in the kingdome; my chief pleasure has been books; philanthropy I adore – how much do I owe you good Sir, for that soul pleasing Character of your amiable uncle Toby! I declare I would walk ten miles in the dog days, to shake hands with the honest Corporal – Your Sermons good Sir, are a cordial: but to the point, the reason of this address. In your 10th Discourse – p. 78 Vol. 2d.

is this truely affecting passage. 'Consider how great a part of our species in all ages down to this, have been trod under the feet of cruel and capricious Tyrants who would neither hear their cries, nor pity their distresses – Consider Slavery – what it is, – how bitter a draught! and how many millions have been made to drink of it'.

Of all my favourite writers, not one do I remember, that has had a tear to spar[e] for the distresses of my poor moorish brethren, Yourself, and the truely humane author of Sr George Ellison excepted: I think Sir, you will forgive, perhaps applaud me for zealously intreating you to give half an hours attention to slavery (as it is at this day undergone in the West Indies; that subject handled in your own manner, would ease the Yoke of many, perhaps occasion a reformation throughout our Islands – But should only *one* be the better for it – gracious God! what a feast! very sure I am, that Yorick is an Epicurean in Charity – universally read & universally admired – you could not fail. Dear Sir think in me, you behold the uplifted hands of Millions of my moorish brethren – Grief (you pathetically observe) is eloquent – figure to yourselves their attitudes – hear their supplicatory address – humanity must comply

in which humble hope permit me to subscribe myself Revd Sir, your most humble and Obedient Servant

IGNATIUS SANCHO.

July 21. 1766

Coxwould near York
July 27. 1766

There is a strange coincidence, Sancho,
in the little events (as well as in the great ones)
of this world: for I had been writing a tender tale
of the sorrows of a friendless poor 'negro-girl, and
my eyes had scarce done smarting, when your
Letter of recommendation in behalf of so many
of her brethren and sisters, came to me ——
—— but why *her brethren*? —— or yours, Sancho!
any more than mine? It is by the finest tints
and most insensible gradations, that nature descends
from the fairest face about St. James's, to the
sootiest complexion in africa: at which tint of these,
is it, that the ties of blood are to cease? and
how many shades must we descend lower still in
the scale, 'ere Mercy is to vanish with them? ——
but 'tis no uncommon thing, my good Sancho, for
one half of the world to use the other ;half of it like
brutes, & then endeavour to make 'em so. for
my own part, I never look *Westward* (when I am in
a pensive mood at least) but I think of the burdens
which our Brothers & Sisters are there carrying —&
could I ease their Shoulders from one ounce of 'em, I
declare I would set out this hour upon a pilgrimage
to Mecca for their sakes — wch by the by, Sancho, exceeds

your Walk of ten miles, in about the same proportion, that a Visit of Humanity, should one, of mere form — however if you mean ~~the Corporal~~ my Uncle Toby, more — he is y.ʳ Debtor,

If I can weave the Tale I have wrote into the Work I'm ab.ᵗ — tis at the service of the afflicted — and a much greater matter; for in serious ~~truth~~, it casts a ~~melancholy~~ sad shade upon the World, That so great a part of it, are and have been so long bound in chains of darkness & in Chains of Misery; & I cannot but both respect & felicitate You, that by so much laudable diligence you have broke the one — & that by falling into the hands of so good and merciful a family, Providence has rescued You from the other.

and so, good hearted Sancho! adieu! & believe me, ~~I~~ I will not forget y.ʳ Letter. Y.ʳˢ

L Sterne

2

Coxwould near York July 27. 1766

There is a strange coincidence, Sancho, in the little events (as well as in the great ones) of this world: for I had been writing a tender tale of the sorrows of a friendless poor negro-girl, and my eyes had scarse done smarting with it, when your Letter of recommendation in behalf of so many of her brethren and sisters, came to me – but why *her brethren*? – or your's, Sancho! any more than mine? It is by the finest tints, and most insensible gradations, that nature descends from the fairest face about St James's, to the sootiest complexion in Africa: at which tint of these, is it, that the ties of blood are to cease? and how many shades must we descend lower still in the scale, 'ere Mercy is to vanish with them? – but 'tis no uncommon thing, my good Sancho, for one half of the world to use the other half of it like brutes, & then endeavour to make 'em so. For my own part, I never look *Westward* (when I am in a pensive mood at least) but I think of the burdens which our Brothers & Sisters are *there* carrying – & could I ease their shoulders from one ounce of 'em, I declare I would set out this hour upon a pilgrimage to Mecca for their sakes – wch by the by, Sancho, exceeds your Walk of ten miles, in about the same proportion, that a Visit of Humanity, should one, of mere form – however if you meant my Uncle Toby, more – he is y^r Debter,

If I can weave the Tale I have wrote into the Work I'm ab^t – tis at the service of the afflicted – and a much greater matter; for in serious truth, it casts a sad Shade upon the World, That so great a part of it, are and have been so long bound in chains of darkness & in Chains of Misery; & I cannot but both respect & felicitate You, that by so much laudable diligence you have broke the one – & that by falling into the hands of so good and merciful a family, Providence has rescued You from the other.

And so, good hearted Sancho! adieu! & believe me, I will not forget y^r Letter. Y^{rs}

L. STERNE.

3

[A modified copy of the previous letter.]
L. STERNE TO IGNATIUS SANCHO

Coxwould July 27. 1766

There is a strange coincidence, Sancho, in the little events, as well as the great ones of this world; for I had been writing a tender tale of the sorrows of a friendless poor negro girl, and my eyes had scarse done smarting, When your Letter of recommendation in behalf of so many of her brethren and Sisters came to me – but why, *her brethren*? – or yours? Sancho, – any more than mine: it is by the finest tints and most insensible gradations that nature descends from the fairest face about St James's, to the sootyest complexion in Africa: at which tint of these, is it, Sancho, that the ties of blood & nature cease? and how many tones must we descend lower still in the scale, 'ere Mercy is to vanish with them? but tis no uncommon thing my good Sancho, for one half of the world to use the other half of it like brutes, and then endeavour to make 'em so.

For my own part, I never look westward, (when I am in a pensive mood at least) but I think of the burdens which our brethren are there carrying; and could I take one ounce from the Shoulders of a few of 'em who are the heaviest loaden'd, I would go a Pilgrimage to Mecca for their Sakes – which by the by, exceeds your Walk, Sancho, of ten miles to see the honest Corporal, in about the same proportion that a Visit of Humanity should one, of mere form – if you meant the Corporal more he is your Debtor.

If I can weave the Tale I have wrote, into what I am about, tis at the service of the afflicted; and a much greater matter: for in honest truth, it casts, a great Shade upon the world, that so great a part of it, are, and have been so long bound down in chains of darkness & in chains of misery; and I cannot but both honour and felicitate you, That by so much laudable diligence you have freed yourself from one – and that, by falling into the hands of so good & merciful a family, Providence has rescued you from the other – and so, good hearted Sancho, adieu! & be assured I will not forget yr Letter.

L. STERNE –

4

Coxwould, June 30 1767

I must acknowledge the courtesy of my good friend Sancho's letter, were I ten times busier than I am, and must thank him too for the many expressions of his good will, and good opinion – 'Tis all affectation to say a man is not gratified with being praised – we only want it to be sincere – and then it will be taken, Sancho, as kindly as yours. I left town very poorly – and with an idea I was taking leave of it for ever – but good air, a quiet retreat, and quiet reflections along with it, with an ass to milk, and another to ride out upon (if I chuse it) all together do wonders. – I shall live this year at least, I hope, be it but to give the world, before I quit it, as good impressions of me, as you have, Sancho. I would only covenant for just so much health and spirits, as are sufficient to carry my pen thro' the task I have set it this summer. – But I am a resign'd being, Sancho, and take health and sickness as I do light and darkness, or the vicissitudes of seasons – that is, just as it pleases God to send them – and accommodate myself to their periodical returns, as well as I can – only taking care, whatever befalls me in this silly world – not to lose my temper at it. – This I believe, friend Sancho, to be the truest philosophy – for this we must be indebted to ourselves, but not to our fortunes. – Farewel – I hope you will not forget your custom of giving me a call at my lodgings next winter – in the mean time I am very cordially,

My honest friend Sancho,
Yours,
L. STERNE.

5

Bond Street, Saturday. 16 May 1767.

I was very sorry, my good Sancho, that I was not at home to return my compliments by you for the great courtesy of the Duke of M[onta]g[u]'s family to me, in honouring my list of subscribers with their names – for which I bear them all thanks. – But you have something to add, Sancho, to what I owe your good will also on this account, and that is to send me the subscription money, which I find a necessity of duning my best friends for before I leave town – to avoid the perplexities of both keeping pecuniary accounts (for which I have very slender talents) and collecting them (for which I have neither strength of body or mind) and so, good Sancho dun the Duke of M[ontagu] the Duchess of M[ontagu] and Lord M[onthermer] for their subscriptions, and lay the sin, and money with it too, at my door – I wish so good a family every blessing they merit, along with my humblest compliments. You know, Sancho, that I am your friend and well-wisher,

L. STERNE.

P.S. I leave town on Friday morning – and should on Thursday, but that I stay to dine with Lord and Lady S[pencer].

V
Miss Crewe's Editorial Note
to the First Edition

The Editor of these Letters thinks proper to obviate an objection, which she finds has already been suggested, that they were originally written with a view to publication.[1] She declares, therefore, that no such idea was ever expressed by Mr Sancho; and that not a single letter is here printed from any duplicate preserved by himself, but all have been collected from the various friends to whom they were addressed. Her motives for laying them before the public were, the desire of shewing that an untutored African may possess abilities equal to an European; and the still superior motive, of wishing to serve his worthy family. And she is happy in thus publicly acknowledging she has not found the world inattentive to the voices of obscure merit.

1. See Appendix I, n. 4.

VI

Stevenson's Index of Sancho's Correspondents

William Stevenson's handwritten index is printed in facsimile in J. R. Willis, 'New light on the life of Ignatius Sancho: some unpublished letters', *Slavery and Abolition*, 1.3 (1980) pp. 345–58. Stevenson gives page references to the 5th edition, which have been changed here to the number of the letter. He provides the full name of some correspondents, but only the initials of others, as in the original text:

Browne, Steward to Sr. Chas. Bunbury Letters 13; 25; 62a; 119; 120.[1]
B——[e] D., Esq. Letters 118; 123.
Cocksedge, Mrs (now Lady Bunbury) Letters 19; 23; 26; 55; 62 ; 70; 99; 146.[2]
Crew, Miss (now Mrs Phillips) Letters 47; 62 ; 64; 73; 75; 148.[3]
F—— Mrs Letter 6.
F—— Mr Letter 58.[4]
G—— Mr Letter 86.
H——Mrs Letters 12; 16; 17; 60; 85; 93; 131; 133.
H——Mr Letter 66.
Ireland, Mr Maiden Lane Letters 65; 81; 96; 101; 107; 124.
Ireland Mrs——D——Letter 84.
Kisby, Mr Letters 5; 9; 38; 71.
L.——Miss Letters 10; 20; 21; 24; 27; 28; 29; 30; 32; 33; 106.[5]
Lincoln, Mr An African Letters 90; 153.[6]
Meheux, Mr John Meheux Esqr. 1st. Clerk in the Board of Control Letters 2; 3; 4; 8; 34; 37; 39; 40; 41; 42; 43; 44; 45; 46; 50; 51; 53; 67; 69; 74; 95; 97; 98; 103; 108; 109; 110.
Mrs Meheux Letter 121.
Osborne, Mr Brother to Mrs Sancho Letters 143, 155.[7]
Rush, Mr Valet to Sr. Chas. Bunbury Letters 22; 31; 35; 49; 52; 72; 78; 91; 105; 111; 112; 125.
Simon, Sr C Buny's Letter 11.[8]
Soubise Letters 14; 80.[9]

Spink, John, Esqr. Bury Letters 57; 82; 87; 92; 94; 95; 134; 135; 136;
    137; 138; 139; 140; 142; 144; 145; 147; 149; 151; 154; 155a; 156;
    157; 158.[10]
Stevenson, Wm. Painter Norwich. Letters 18; 54; 56; 74 ; 77; 79; 88;
    100; 102; 113; 114; 117; 126; 128; 129; 152.[11]
Stevenson, Rev Letter 116 (MA of Peterhouse, Cambridge, Rector
    of Truswell(?) Notts, my grandfather. S.W.S.).[12]
Wingrave, Mr Bookseller Letters 1.; 59; 61 and 68 ; 89; 104 ; 122;
    127; 130; 141.[13]

Notes

1. 'Charles (1733/4–1809), of Great Barton, steward to Sir
   Charles Bunbury', see Fiske, *Oakes Diaries*, Vol. II p. 331.
   Letter 62a, addressed to Mr Browne, was published in *The
   Public Advertiser* without Sancho's knowledge, see Letter
   62, n. 1.
2. Letter 62 is to both Miss Crewe and Mrs Cocksedge, but the
   concluding 'best wishes' makes it clear that the primary
   addressee is Miss Crewe.
3. Letter 62 is wrongly ascribed to Mrs Cocksedge, see n. 3
   above.
4. F—— Mr: can be confidently taken to be Jabez Fisher of
   Philadelphia, see Letter 83, n. 1.
5. Miss L——: can be confidently taken to be Lydia Leach, see
   Letter 20, n. 2 and Letter 10, n. 1.
6. He is also mentioned in Letter 1 as 'belonging to the
   Captain's Band, one Charles Lincoln', travelling to India on
   the same ship as Soubise.
7. Letter 155 is in fact addressed to Mrs Osborne, not her
   husband. Letter 83, from Edmund Rack to Sancho, which
   would be placed between 'Osborne' and 'Rush', is not
   included in Stevenson's list.
8. Stevenson must mean that Mr Simon was a servant of Sir
   Charles Bunbury, like Mr Rush and Mr Browne.
9. Stevenson spells Soubise oddly; his handwriting is hard to
   read, but it looks like 'Sobieske'. Soubise is also mentioned
   in Letter 1 as a 'little Blacky whom you must either have
   seen or heard of; his name is S——'; see also Appendix I,
   n. 3.
10. The pamphlet on the Gainsborough portrait printed in the
    article by R. W. Willis calls Spink, misspelled 'Spinks', 'an
    early friend and patron of Sancho's, and a Banker at Bury St.
    Edmund's.' Letter 95 is wrongly attributed by Stevenson;
    it is in fact addressed to Meheux. Stevenson has referenced
    'Letter 155a' because two letters are numbered 155.

11. An error; Letter 74 is addressed to Meheux.
12. Stevenson's parenthetical information refers to William Stevenson's son, S. W. Stevenson.
13. Letter 1 is wrongly dated, and written to Wingrave's son Jack, see Appendix I; Letter 104 is written to Mrs Wingrave; Letters 61, 68, 127 and 141 are written to Wingrave's son Jack.

VII
Roots of a Family Tree: The Sanchos' Children

Many of Sancho's letters provide a unique glimpse of the emotional bonds and domestic details of an African-Caribbean family in eighteenth-century London from a father's point of view. Research undertaken by John Gurnett, based largely on the parish registers of St Margaret's, Westminster, reveals the birth and/or death dates of Sancho's children, given below. This information helps clarify some problems of dating the letters and almost certainly verifies the full identity of Sancho's correspondent, Miss L—— (see Appendix I and Letter 10, n. 1). The parish records reveal a discrepancy concerning the birth date of the Sanchos' second daughter; her name is recorded as Ann Alice Sancho at St Margaret's, Westminster, but she is referred to as Marianne (Mary) in Letter 106 which gives 17 September 1779 as Marianne's birthday. Mr Gurnett has also identified a previously unknown 'Sanchonet', John William (see Letter 29, n. 3):

Frances Joanna (Fanny): born 13 January 1761; baptised 25 January 1761.

Ann Alice [possibly Marianne (Mary)]: born 2 August 1763.

Elizabeth Bruce (Betsy): born 10 March 1766; died 1837.

Jonathan William (? Jacky): born March 1768; died before December 1775.

Lydia: born 2 June 1771; died April 1776.

Katherine Margaret (Kitty): born c. November 1773; died March 1779.

William Leach Osborne (Billy): born 20 October 1775; died c. 1814.

Bibliography

Editions of Sancho's Letters

Letters of the Late Ignatius Sancho: an African, to which are Prefixed, Memoirs of his Life, 1st edn, 2 vols (J. Nichols, London, 1782).

Letters of the Late Ignatius Sancho: an African, to which are Prefixed, Memoirs of his Life, second edition, 1783 (two volumes in one).

Letters of the Late Ignatius Sancho: an African, to which are Prefixed, Memoirs of his Life, third edition, 2 vols, 1784.

Letters of the Late Ignatius Sancho: an African to which is Prefixed, Memoirs of his Life (Brett Smith for Richard Moncrieff, Dublin, 1784). [This edition is not named as a fourth edition, but was presumably taken as such by William Sancho, when he published his fifth edition.]

Letters of the Late Ignatius Sancho: An African to which are Prefixed Memoirs of His Life by Joseph Jekyll, Esq., M.P., fifth edition, (London: Printed for William Sancho, Charles-Street, Westminster, 1803). (Wilks and Tayor, Printers, Chancery-lane.) [This edition has an additional title page with the vignette by F. W. Bunbury dated 20 December 1802 (see Appendix III). It was also the first edition to name Jekyll as the author of the memoir.]

A facsimile reprint of the fifth edition, with a new introduction by Paul Edwards, (Dawsons of Pall Mall, The Colonial History Series, London, 1968).

A facsimile reprint of the fifth edition, in the Black Heritage Library Collection (Books for Libraries Press, Freeport, New York, 1971). [This edition gives the 1803 text only, without introduction or commentary.]

Annual Register, 1768–1780.

Sir Thomas William Bunbury (ed.), *The Correspondence of Sir Thomas Hanmer* (1838).

R. W. Chapman (ed.), *Boswell's Life of Johnson* (Oxford University Press, London and New York, 1970) (revised edition).

Charles T. Davis and Henry Louis Gates, Jr. (eds), *The Slave's Narrative: Texts and Contexts* (Oxford University Press, London and New York, 1985).

Dictionary of National Biography.

Paul Edwards, 'Unreconciled strivings and ironic strategies: three

Afro-British writers of the Georgian era – Ignatius Sancho, Olaudah Equiano, Robert Wedderburn', *Occasional Papers*, 34, Edinburgh University Centre of African Studies, 1992.

Paul Edwards and David Dabydeen (eds), *Black Writers in Britain, 1760–1890* (Edinburgh University Press, Edinburgh, 1991).

Paul Edwards and James Walvin (eds), *Black Personalities in the Era of the Slave Trade* (Macmillan, London, 1983).

Bernard Falk, *The Way of the Montagues: A Gallery of Family Portraits* (Hutchinson, London, n.d.) (1958?).

Jane Fiske (ed.), *The Oakes Diaries, Business, Politics and the Family in Bury St. Edmunds, 1778–1827*, Vol. 2 (Boydell Press, Suffolk Records Society, Vols. 32–3, 1991–2).

Percy Fitzgerald, *A Famous Forgery, being the Story of the Unfortunate Dr. Dodd* (London, 1865).

Peter Fryer, *Staying Power: The History of Black People in Britain* (Pluto Press, London, 1984).

Sir James Balfour Paul (ed.), *The Scots Peerage* (T. & A. Constable, Edinburgh, 1904).

Keith A. Sandiford, *Measuring the Moment: Strategies of Protest in Eighteenth-Century Afro-English Writing* (Associated University Presses, London and Toronto, 1988).

Folarin Shyllon, *Black People in Britain, 1555–1833* (Oxford University Press, London, 1977).

R. W. W[illis], 'New light on the life of Ignatius Sancho – some unpublished letters', *Slavery and Abolition*, 1. 3. (1980), pp. 345–58.

Josephine R. B. Wright, *Ignatius Sancho (1729–1780) An Early African Composer in England – The Collected Editions of his Music in Facsimile* (Garland, New York and London, 1981).

Index